About the Author

An ex-intelligence officer and career barrister, regularly presents on the parlous state of the justice system and the poor treatment of veterans; this is his homage to them.

Unknown Warrior

Keith Freeman

Unknown Warrior

Olympia Publishers
London

www.olympiapublishers.com
OLYMPIA PAPERBACK EDITION

Copyright © Keith Freeman 2024

The right of Keith Freeman to be identified as author of
this work has been asserted in accordance with sections 77 and 78 of
the Copyright, Designs and Patents Act 1988.

All Rights Reserved

No reproduction, copy or transmission of this publication
may be made without written permission.
No paragraph of this publication may be reproduced,
copied or transmitted save with the written permission of the publisher,
or in accordance with the provisions
of the Copyright Act 1956 (as amended).

Any person who commits any unauthorised act in relation to
this publication may be liable to criminal
prosecution and civil claims for damage.

A CIP catalogue record for this title is
available from the British Library.

ISBN: 978-1-80439-574-5

This is a work of fiction.
Names, characters, places and incidents originate from the writer's
imagination. Any resemblance to actual persons, living or dead, is
purely coincidental.

First Published in 2024

Olympia Publishers
Tallis House
2 Tallis Street
London
EC4Y 0AB

Printed in Great Britain

Dedication

I dedicate this to Nigel Neame, SBS, and all the others who had the misfortune to serve with us.

Acknowledgements

I thank my wife and children for their encouragement and for being willing listeners to each draft, and to my wife's sister Emma for her very helpful editing.

ONE

Harry hated hospitals. The chair by the bed was empty. He noted its dull reddish colour, burgundy perhaps you might say, if feeling generous. Slippery fake leather, no doubt for ease of cleaning. It was designed to deceive. It looked comfortable enough but as he sat down it confirmed his prejudice. There was simply no way of sitting on the damned thing without sliding off. Perhaps it was intentional. To make sure you didn't stay long. He shifted position but it didn't help. He glanced over at his friend who, notwithstanding the masks and tubes and other paraphernalia, seemed at rest. The bruising and contusions to his face were all too visible and yet as Harry knew masked the true extent of his injuries. His eyes were gently closed and the slow rise and fall of his chest was somewhat reassuring and mesmerising in its regularity and insistence.

Quite unintentionally, Harry found his own breathing tending to synchronise with that of his friend. Breath in breath out. Breath in breath out. It was as if his old comrade was ineffably saying 'I'm not dead yet, I'm not dead yet'. It was obvious he had taken quite a beating. Harry had listened in disbelief to the details. The area was not, as far as he knew, a war zone. Indeed, by surface appearance at least it looked like a place with a low level of violent crime. You might call it genteel. Surely such violent attacks were not the norm.

"You cannot stay long," the nurse said, in a strident voice. Bossy thought Harry but possibly well meaning. Her badge revealed her name as 'Steph'. Handwritten in blue permanent marker. Maybe by Steph herself thought Harry. Not a very elegant script. Not 'Stephanie', which Harry liked, but 'Steph' which he did not. His habit of picking up detail from observation was undiminished by age. Her shoes were none too clean. Her hands large and podgy. He could not help thinking she could do with losing weight. Frankly she was fat.

Harry decided to simply ignore her. Perhaps it was something she said to everyone. He had little inclination to argue and at the same time had no intention of leaving George alone. He avoided, as far as he could, any friction. Her message delivered, she left him alone. He dismissed her from his mind. Harry leaned over and opened the drawer in the cabinet by the bed and slipped the mobile phone he found lying there into his pocket. It was done surreptitiously and with certainty that he was not observed.

He sat still and quiet and waited as if on watch. He closed his eyes. What did they use to sanitise the place? There was the pervasive smell of what he assumed was some kind of disinfectant. It had assailed his nostrils at first but then he had quite rapidly become inured to it so it became merely part of the background.

He had been there for some time, maybe hours. Harry had learnt, and this was not easily acquired, the trick of simply being. He was not instantly aroused by surrounding stimuli, unless interesting or threatening. He had turned vigilance while at rest into an art form. He was rather like an old dog half asleep, perhaps with one eye ready to open, and yet who knew what was what. Ready to respond to any threat. No one showed any immediate sign of disturbing his watch. The steady rhythm of the heart monitor was reassuring but cold comfort indeed.

Harry glanced outside. It was quite dark though the remains of the day could still be discerned in the late evening gloom. His eyes were drawn to the last whisper of natural light curling under the horizon. The streetlights below began to crackle into life and the irregular traffic noise increased as people edged home. It was the rush hour. A stupid name for slowness and frustration. Harry observed all this quite dispassionately and with little real interest. He was not inclined these days and at his age, without serious cause, to rush about. If at all possible, he preferred to take his time and not waste energy.

He noted how some streetlights came on with a sort of red glow and some with greater rapidity into a yellow radiance, and yet others seemed not to want to come on at all. There were a couple of the very new bright white ones. "All part of saving the planet," Harry mused. Otherwise, there was just the noise of the intensive care unit to contend with and that smell which he now classified as a peculiar mix of sanitation and decay.

Harry sought to tune out these distractions, and as he sank into reverie his mind began to wander. He had made the decision to simply wait. He knew from long experience how to sit, patient, prayerful even, observing while not being observed. His eyelids began to close again. It was as if he were not quite there at all. Mind you he was not sure what he was waiting for apart from the obvious hope that his friend might wake up.

Aoife lay on the hotel bed, the bedding only a casually covering, her top half barely concealed, her shape defined by the pure white Irish cotton sheet. Her innocence was profound. Harry naturally lived in the moment, no time spent thinking of the past, or the future come to that, just the here and now. What other way was there to live? "Please let me stay here with you," he voiced silently in his mind. The memories were so vivid, visceral even. It felt as if he was there with her, right now. The smell of her, so sweet, her slight smile, as her chest lifted and fell away, so natural, so calm, so quiet in her sleep. He found he was holding his breath, as if to disturb the moment, to rouse her, would be a sacrilege.

He was determined not to waken her.

TWO

A woman in a different colour uniform, a rather fetching shade of lilac, was now standing at the end of the bed.

"I didn't like to disturb you. You seemed so peaceful."

And then, she asked, "Would you like a cup of tea?" She spoke in a warm and friendly manner and with a small smile.

Harry nodded. And murmured his thanks. He must have dropped off he reasoned, and it dawned on him that he had been dreaming. It took him a moment to assimilate this memory from so long ago into the reality of the hospital ward. He had returned to the land of the living if that is how George's condition or his could be reasonably so described.

Not a nurse he noted but as her badge revealed, a health care assistant. *Less pay more care,* thought Harry. He looked past her as his eye was drawn towards the movement. Newcomers in the corridor. Also, in uniform. Of the blue kind. A young policewoman and an even younger looking policeman, no doubt her partner, notebooks in hand. They seemed so very young to him and surely not realistically able to investigate the cause of his friend's admission to hospital. In general Harry was not keen on the police though admittedly he had known one or two he respected.

The nurse they were talking to approached and asked if he minded stepping into the corridor as the police wanted to ask him a few questions. Harry nodded and levered himself up with surprising grace for a man of his age. He went into the corridor and then followed the two police officers into a quiet anteroom. Harry did not sit down even though there was seating available. He stood with his back to the open doorway, slightly at an angle so no threat could approach without him being aware of it.

They introduced themselves. It seemed the woman was the marginally more senior or possibly simply chose to take the lead.

"I'm WPC Wingate and this is PC Phillips. Can I ask you a few questions?"

Harry nodded. *I have a few questions of my own,* he thought but said nothing.

"Do you know him well?"

"You could say that."

He tried to remember the last time he had seen George. Time seemed not to mean so much as it once had, and he often lost track of it these days. But then it seemed just like yesterday that they were both young men, young men with nothing to lose perhaps. There were just so many memories, which rather urgently and unbidden, converged into one abiding thought, his life must count for something.

"Can you help us with his identity?"

"His identity?"

"Yes, perhaps his name and address."

There was a barely noticeable pause.

"George, George Rogers." Harry was not sure why he gave the truthful Christian name. Perhaps he could not bring himself to bear false witness. He did not give the correct surname.

"I'm not sure of his address," he added.

"Can you tell me what happened to him?" He barely looked at them as he sought answers.

"We don't have many details, sir. We think he was the subject of assault. He was brought in last night, quite late, around midnight. There was no ID on him."

"Where exactly?"

"I'm afraid I can't give you that information."

Harry was tempted to ask them what bloody information they could give him. He contented himself with saying quietly,

"His condition seems serious."

"It is, sir," and added rather unnecessarily from Harry's point of view, "he is recorded as in a critical condition but stable."

Harry reflected for a moment on whether he was comfortable with his friend who was in a coma being described as stable. He decided he was not, but then merely shrugged. It was not worth debating and not with these two who were obviously in Harry's estimation at any rate, very junior and inexperienced. Just a mugging perhaps they thought. Nothing of any importance.

Harry had already established that George had been brought in after the attack, comatose and with major and life-threatening injuries including a serious concussion and possible bleed on the brain. He had several ribs broken and a punctured lung. His arm was broken. The list went on. His train of thought was interrupted again.

"Are you related to Mr Rogers, sir?"

"No."

"A friend then?"

Harry nodded.

"And your name is?"

"Pete Smith," said Harry without hesitation. This was amongst a list of names that Harry gave as not easy to exclude if an attempt was made to trace it.

'Peter Smith' noted the young policeman, dutifully without a trace of irony.

"We have your phone number."

"You do?"

"Yes. The nursing station provided it. If we need to speak to you again is this the best number?"

Harry already knew the hospital had the number. They had rung him on George's phone. He doubted the police had been told about the mobile. The nurse had used her initiative and was not hopeful of any response but was glad he had a friend 'who had turned up'. He wondered if anyone had told the police the casualty had a mobile phone. It seemed not, otherwise surely their interest in him would have been greater. They had not asked about the phone at all.

It should have at least sparked some curiosity, he thought, *but you can never assume anything with the police*. They might just feel they should carry out the task allocated to them, without much interest. Initiative was rarely rewarded. He did not detect that the police, or at least these youngsters, were emotionally invested or even particularly interested. Probably just going through the motions.

His telephone number was one of his few links with home. *Home is where the heart is*, his mother had once reminded him. The kind of woman who spoke innocently in clichés and meant them sincerely as insights. *Well, they were truths*, he supposed. *Where was his heart?* Harry did not dwell on this kind of thought very much and was certainly not inclined to do so right now. He wished to remain practical. He had found he could divert calls to his mobile automatically, which was handy. He hardly answered his phone anyway, and especially not from that redirected number. It was known to those who were not so friendly these days, as well as his old comrade.

They asked his address but did not ask him to prove his

identity. He gave them an address he knew to be false but plausible. The young policewoman had asked if they might contact him again if needed. She did not seem particularly interested and ditto her colleague. Harry ran this through in his mind. It reinforced his view that they were indeed just going through the motions.

The young policewoman repeated the question.

"This number, sir, is it the best one to contact you on?"

Harry nodded, and they seemed satisfied.

Harry was not sure what he expected exactly and had achieved his aim, namely, to minimise their interest in him, but he nevertheless felt that George deserved some greater attention and action. They did not even mention that he should remain reachable, beyond the mobile number, stay local or anything of that kind. He was not particularly surprised. The address he gave was in Leeds, and he had used it before many years ago. He was not even sure if it existed since there had been so many changes over the years. He was obviously not a suspect. He was aware of them leaving the ward and assumed they had left the hospital. His cynicism regarding their likely lack of interest in finding who had harmed George was not reduced by their apparent lack of enthusiasm to inquire further.

He looked back to George's bed. What did he expect? There was no change. Harry resumed his vigil, his mind wandering in and out of myriad memories. He found himself asking if these were reliable and deciding that it really didn't matter very much. His friend was in a coma, badly beaten, within an inch of his life very probably, for what? The contents of his wallet? Had he fought back? Knowing George, very likely. What had the attackers seen? an old man with a walking stick. No threat, beyond pathetic. They had not thought his mobile phone worth taking, but then who used an old-style Nokia these days. It was not a smart phone, only being able to send and receive texts and calls.

These hospital chairs, like a bad wife he thought, promise everything but delivering very little. Not even basic comfort. Had he deserved better? Probably not. He shifted his buttocks from one cheek to the other seeking purchase on the slippery seat surface. He took his coat off and stretched it over the seat. He tucked in the sides in a fastidious manner, with mini hospital corners, the irony of which did not escape him. His mind was not really engaged in the task. He sat down again. Harry was a practical man. Any fool could be uncomfortable. A bit better. Good enough. He settled in for the long haul.

It was perhaps surprising that no nurse or doctor disturbed him as he sat there quietly, with his eyes half shut, watching the chest of his friend lift and fall, lift and fall. He was less than happy that his friend looked so ill. He was a rather greyish colour, as if he had not seen the sun for a long time. He did not look well. On the other hand, as far as Harry could tell from the machines bleeping away, their luminescent numbers steady, all his vital signs seemed all right. If there was any change in his condition Harry wondered what he would do. He supposed alarms would go off and help would come running.

It dawned on Harry eventually that no change was likely. Still he lingered. How many hours passed? Harry himself was unsure. He was reluctant to leave George alone but he had the ward number safely memorised. He reasoned that he could call in again by telephone if not physically. His memory though sometimes patchy or perhaps more accurately characterised as partial, was very good still with numbers. Also, he wanted to avoid the police. Perhaps someone might come back who might think the case of greater importance, and start asking questions less easy to evade. Mind you the police interest seemed pretty perfunctory. All a matter of resources and priorities.

Finally, he concluded he was doing no good here. He took a deep breath in, levered himself upright and with a last glance at his friend's face, he slipped away.

He left via the emergency entrance. He kept an eye out for CCTV. There was none here. He hung about a bit till he sussed out where the paramedics and ambulance staff were to be found waiting for their next call, it now being quite quiet. There was a sort of common rom, or waiting room, where the emergency staff could rest. It struck Harry that like war, emergency medicine was feast or famine. It was either all action, or quite long periods of boredom. Rush to wait. He asked a friendly face if they had been on last night explaining about his friend.

"Hang on I'll ask."

A young paramedic appeared and Harry was pointed out to him. He was a bit unsure at first. After all Harry, though of indeterminate age, was obviously a bit old for the police or any job really. On the other hand, he appeared harmless enough.

"Are you from the police then?"

"No, not from the police."

"Newspaper?"

"No. Look it's just that George is my oldest friend."

He tried engaging with the young man's eyes, and adopted an unthreatening, open stance, hands lowered by his side, with a small slight smile, then added,

"I simply couldn't leave without knowing more about what had happened to him."

The young medic was still a bit unsure but looking into Harry's face and seeing the concern in what looked to him like a harmless old man, concluded that it was probably the right thing to provide any information he had.

Yes, he had been the one who had brought him in. He said where he had found him and Harry made a mental note of the place which was described as an alleyway leading to 'The Stray'. He said they had found him lying on the ground concussed, but breathing. Just about alive. The paramedic thought it looked like a mugging. He said he found a stick lying nearby broken in two. Harry noticed the young man seemed upset himself talking about it, which he reasoned was unusual. Paramedics, even young ones, had no doubt seen worse. He said he had been to the place before but usually to pick up a druggie who had overdosed.

"You get more than you might think of this sort of thing in Harrogate," he said.

He told Harry he was not surprised that there had been no police inquiries, well not of this kind of incident at any rate. Harry's prejudice was confirmed.

"Happens now and then, and doesn't usually generate much or frankly any police interest."

Harry turned to go.

The young man added,

"Take care."

Harry took this on board as more than a mere gesture and returned a small smile of thanks. "Kindness is its own reward," as his mother might well have said.

He passed to the rear of the hospital and with a brief check that there was no CCTV he removed the sim from George's phone and his own. He crushed the sims underfoot and chucked them in the nearest large waste disposal bin; the phones he would dispose of on his walk back to his billet, each in a separate public rubbish bin.

THREE

He found a pub nearby. It was of indifferent quality but Harry didn't care. He sat in a quiet corner nursing a pint. The seat was marginally more comfortable than the one the NHS had provided. He was barely aware of other customers though, as was his habit, he discreetly checked them out. There was the usual motley collection of hangers on and small groups. Typical for a Monday night. Maybe one or two worked at the hospital. There was one odd character, for example, sitting in a bobble hat though it was quite warm inside - LUFC. Harry surmised Leeds United. Harry recalled a random thought from his childhood, *Norman Hunter bites ya legs*. This thought provided some kind of comfort for Harry, increasing his sense of familiarity with the place.

The Leeds supporter, like Harry, sat alone at a table in the farthest corner from the bar. He didn't seem 'all there' but was happy enough, or so it seemed to Harry. There was a noisier pair by the bar. He ignored them and indeed was able to shut them out so that they drifted into the background. There were no immediate threats. They barely noticed him. Just as he liked it.

He found it difficult to shake off the image of George in the hospital ICU bed. He stared at his glass. Thoughts entered unbidden. Him and George Holland at Carlingford Lough, when was it, late 70s maybe 1978. That bastard McGuiness, like McCafferty's cat: never there. Harry had briefed George and the others on the mission – they were to apprehend the target as quietly as possible but if they met opposition, firearms were authorised and could be used to achieve the mission. Shoot to kill? Daft question in Harry's mind. What were the alternatives? Shoot to maim? Shoot to scare?

Harry could recall details of the briefing even now, even after all these years. IRA second in command at the time of Bloody Sunday. Armed with a Tommy gun on the day, a conduit for US funding, supplied bomb parts. Juries were routinely 'got at' or fixed. The solution was Diplock courts, who found him guilty but only six months in prison which simply increased his influence. Diplock on the other hand was never able to go anywhere without an armed guard even after retirement. All this Harry knew. In so many ways he was no fool. The problem was, as Harry liked to say but mostly to confused faces amongst even the more switched-on officers, military intelligence was an oxymoron.

"McGuiness?"

"That's right, General."

How could they know for sure? At least we think so. This thought was not voiced. *More like a possibility*, thought Phillips, the brigade major. No one told the GOC what they really thought, certainly not out loud. Major Phillips had not enjoyed being called 'wishy-washy' on early acquaintance with the general. Only facts were allowed. 'No bloody guesswork' as the general was apt to snap. Harry Case stood in the background observing Kitson without drawing any attention to himself. Nevertheless, Kitson caught his eye.

"And where are they now?"

"Carlingford Lough, sir." No 'we believe' or 'we think'. No qualification whatsoever.

General cleared his throat and in a clipped style which no doubt he assumed implied authority, clear mindedness and the implication that they should all know who was in charge, responded unnecessarily with, "Right. Keep me informed." With that he stepped smartly and briskly out of the ops room with that odious little sycophant Captain Brown his ADC trotting along behind him. 'Brown nose' the soldiers called him and that was when they were being polite.

Blinky's eye was twitching even more rapidly than usual. He breathed out a deep sigh of relief no doubt at the withdrawal of the general. Blinky stared at Harry who was smiling.

"What are you smirking at Lieutenant Case?"

Major Phillips did not like Harry Case, not least because he suspected him of being 'too clever by half' and of applying the sobriquet 'Blinky' to him. He was right. It had, of course, caught on. Everyone called him Blinky now, even to his face if they thought they could get away with it. The feeling was mutual. Harry did not care for passed over majors, aka poms, and Blinky as was common in his kind was still ambitious, clinging to the hope that his career could advance, climbing over others, notwithstanding his incompetence. Contemporaries had advanced with no more obvious superior qualities after all. Blinky was not a man who had much self-knowledge. He was a sort of paradigm pom.

Harry could recall the full Gaelic name of the target *Seamus Mairtin Pacelli Mag Aonghusa*. Aka Martin McGuiness. There was no evidence the man knew Gaelic at all. Ludicrous symbolism. Had they got him? Hard to believe. They had been chasing him for years from well before Harry's time but George could recall the early days. George was a good source of knowledge, going back to Bloody Sunday.

He was awoken abruptly from these reflections by the signaller.

"Sir, no comms."

"What?" barked Blinky.

"No comms, sir. From Bravo29," added the signaller and Blinky was predictably irritated.

"That's bloody obvious," he snapped.

There was a long pause. Blinky made a decision.

"Wait for next quarter."

He might be right, thought Harry. These bloody radios so unreliable. *I wouldn't wait*, thought Harry and became restless. He decided to challenge the decision.

"Are you sure, sir?" ventured Harry.

"I'm in command here Mr Case."

The problem was that the agreed signal simply two clicks on the radio followed by a five second pause and three clicks – which signalled all was well, had not been received.

Harry continued to stare quizzically at Major Phillips.

"I have made my decision," snapped Blinky, "it is probably interference. I am not reacting every time we lose a signal."

Blinky looked directly at Harry, but he could not hold his stare, and then looked round to see if anyone else was challenging his decision. There was silence, which was deafening.

Harry slipped out and told George to fetch Badger and meet him outside. They climbed in the Range Rover. It wouldn't start.

Badger kept pumping the accelerator and tried to coax the engine into starting. No luck.

"Christ Badger, now it's flooded."

George hopped out and made straight for the CO's Land Rover, hotwired it and the others joined him, all three in the front, and sped off.

"What about Blinky?" asked George eventually.

"Fuck Blinky," said Harry.

FOUR

They arrived at the rear of the hill which overlooked the farmhouse. They scrambled upwards as speedily as they could. Blundering around in the dark notwithstanding night vision kit meant this was hardly silent.

"For fuck's sake," hissed Harry. They approached the hide where they hoped to find the watching patrol, just two soldiers living well concealed, in the ground. Harry was a bit worried now as he didn't have the password. He did not want to be shot by a nervous soldier. Heavy whispered calls failed to rouse anyone. Then Harry found them. A strangely peaceful scene. The moonlight lit the ground briefly and vividly as the clouds flitted overhead, only obscured by the trees in partial leaf. It was unseasonably cold. The rustle of the branches in the light autumn breeze was oddly disarming.

Harry saw the smashed radio. It was not dug in. *Stupid little bastards*, Harry thought. What was the point of all that training, the emphasis on personal safety? They had been told. No need to take unnecessary risks. Remain hidden but alert. Dig your radio in so it is not damaged in stray gunfire or to prevent the equipment being easily disabled. The problem with these ops, was even if taken seriously in training, which was doubtful, on real ops typically nothing happened. It was bound to lead to boredom, and sloppiness and frequently did, with no ill effects. The two youngsters looked asleep and somehow at peace. In a way they were.

Close up their faces cast a deathly pall. No more than boys really. Never to wake up. They must have been taken completely by surprise as there was no sign of any alarm on their faces or even a flicker of anything that might have been untoward. They were each closed into their sleeping bags with the draw cord and head creating a strangely comical effect, like large bugs snug in their cocoons. Never to emerge as butterflies, that was for sure.

He posted Badger and George on the immediate perimeter to check no one was about. The last thing he wanted now was for his little team to be ambushed. He placed his hand over the mouth of the first soldier, young James McLean, a Scotsman from the Western Isles. He was only confirming the inevitable. Lovely lad who had sailed through SAS training. Harry had selected him personally, even though there had not been wholesale support for his unassuming ways.

Some thought he lacked aggression, but Harry knew better, or at least thought he did. He was tightly tucked into his sleeping bag, arms inside, his weapon nowhere to be seen. He then saw, in the half light, the stab wound to the lower neck, a very neat entry, and could feel the blood that had seeped into his sleeping bag already partially coagulated. He tried the other soldier who he hardly knew at all. Same thing. He called out quietly for George, told him the situation and George then retrieved Badger. They slipped away down the hillside, towards the vehicle and called it in.

They heard the helicopter before they saw it. Too soon to be a response to their signal. No doubt Blinky, finally reacting, all too late. The assassins would be long gone over the border. The Garda would be informed. Waste of time, but Blinky would want to follow protocol. Harry liked to think of the CO bursting in and asking, "Where's my bloody Land Rover?" Blinky briefing him, after all someone would have to tell Kitson. Blinky would want to avoid this. None of the higher command showed much consideration for dead youth, or any regard for those who might care for them. Harry could still feel viscerally his hands on the boys' wounds and in his mind's eye, could see the ghostly pallor of their faces.

He would like to ask George, right now, what he thought of the Good Friday Agreement, and those undoubtedly guilty of murder and terrorism who were now senior ministers in the Belfast government. He knew for certain they had blood on their hands, and so did George. But then who were the innocent in Northern Ireland?

He knew George had been exonerated, twice, for his role in Bloody Sunday but the inquiries were never ending. The Saville Inquiry. What a joke. Harry could imagine his replies, "It's all balls Harry." George could capture an idea succinctly, without surplusage. He ached to hear George say exactly this, "It's all balls."

FIVE

Harry thought it likely Harrogate would have a British Legion and a library. He spotted an older man wearing a military blazer and badge who predictably enough knew where they both were. He was keen to tell Harry that the British Legion was one of the oldest in the country set up by Earl Marshal Haig himself. And the library was a Grade 1 listed building, a Carnegie library no less. Harry respectfully listened. No time was actually wasted. The information was imparted in a few brief short sentences. One military man to another. The directions he gave were clear and concise. Harry was not surprised, indeed found this pleasing. He was not inclined, like some, to underestimate those with a military background.

Harry showered with his clothes on, he then used a bit of the liquid soap provided to wash them thoroughly, and then rinsed them and hung them over the shower tray. This was the kind of thing he had done in so many places around the world that it had become a routine.

The small bed and breakfast he had chosen was not the most obvious choice to anyone who might take an interest in him. To Harry this was not an excess of caution, simply good professional practice. There was a row of them and he had not simply walked into the first one with vacancies but rather was taken by one with a small front garden, which was tidy and looked well cared for with a nicely painted door. Harry surmised this might mean the proprietor would take care of their guests equally well. The garden still had colour from late flowering autumn plants.

He tended to favour a T-shirt and a fleece. With his trusty multi-pocketed coat he was warm enough. The fleece was washed only as required. His washable trousers were easy to launder in the habitual way with his T-shirt and socks. If his clothes were not completely dry in the morning, that did not bother Harry. If they were not completely dry in the morning, he put them on anyway and relied on his body heat to complete the task. He went commando as he saw no point in an unnecessary layer of clothing.

He still had a full head of hair which he kept short and preferred to trim his beard with a small pair of scissors. He had found that the beard tended to help him blend in these days. He was fastidious in keeping it tidy and looking sharp by shaving to shape it. He preferred using just the razor and soap but not even this if he was taking a shower. He had found running water provided sufficient lubricant in itself. In fact, his only other personal item was a small toothbrush. Both the razor and brush were cut short making them as compact as possible.

He found mobile phones in general a nuisance, but knew he had to have at least one. His needs had altered. He resolved to buy a couple of burners and a set of SIM cards the following morning. He had evaded the attention of his trackers at Heathrow, without difficulty. He felt relatively safe, though he was not sure really how sensible this was. He was realistic but preferred not to dwell on anything that might generate personal anxiety. It was all a balance, between being prepared and not worrying unduly.

He had slept in the surprisingly comfortable bed and slept soundly. This was one of his greatest assets. The fact was that he could direct himself to drop off and almost instantly fall into slumber. He could even direct for how long this sleep might be, and wake up ready for action, whatever the apparent stresses or whatever was on his mind. Indeed, sleep acted to finesse his thoughts, aid planning, and remove unnecessary detritus.

Once awake, he ate a full English breakfast in true military style, that is, as if he were not sure where his next meal was coming from. He had, after all, not eaten much the day before. He never ate to excess, and his uniform would have still fitted him now, though it was decades since he had last worn it. He had in many ways become increasingly less military as the years passed since active service. He did not even attend the Cenotaph, not that he had returned to the mother country that often, and not for many years past.

The local news was on the radio and was beamed into the breakfast room. This would normally have irritated Harry, but he listened intently for any news concerning the attack on George. Nothing.

He bought a newspaper and sat on a bench in the park the locals knew as 'The Stray', which wrapped round most of Harrogate. It was a delightful open expanse of grassland crisscrossed by paths and lined with trees. It was easy enough to find a quiet bench to sit on, unbothered by anyone. He flicked through the local rag seeking news of the attack. Nothing.

He called the hospital on a new pay-as-you-go phone which he had purchased from a backstreet mobile phone shop. He took the trouble to visit other such outlets to buy a couple of extra SIMs and a couple of burners. He adopted by training and habit a circuitous route. He used reflections in shop windows to check his rear. He would retrace his steps in a seemingly casual manner. He was not being followed.

No change in George's condition. He made one more call

setting up a rendez-vous. He texted '13:00' to confirm. He walked across The Stray towards the library. He wanted to learn something about the locality.

When he left he was not much the wiser, but slightly better informed. There were an inordinate number of churches of every conceivable variation of Anglican and nonconformist and Roman Catholic, and even more contemporary evangelic churches. No mosques though or temples, at least not as far as he could see. They were usually pretty obvious. By the call to prayer, which Harry liked. No minarets. Notable by their absence? It all depended perhaps on what you were used to and your expectations.

He paused to peer at a local display of art including the avenues of flowering cherries in spring. This small spa town with its handsome boulevards knew little crime or so it seemed, as the local rag tended to confirm. Harry wondered if local journalism amounted to much these days. The national news seemed very poor, there being little or no investigative work done. How could it be that in the world there was only the immediate news story on each and every channel?

He visited the local tourist office and picked up a map. It was a conference town, which seemed to be the mainstay of its economy, plus tourism as 'The Gateway to the Dales'. The great handsome villas, bounding The Stray, spoke of affluence. Harry knew the general area from training at York Barracks as a young soldier but not Harrogate. He had not taken much of it in then even locally to York, and so had little in his memory banks of any relevance to rely on. The map helped to orientate him.

It was not yet midday and Harry though he could be patient, very patient indeed, needed more information, more detailed pertinent intel, and as rapidly as possible. He had chosen the earliest time he could sensibly cross the threshold into the Legion, and here he was about to step inside. An excess of caution, perhaps, which had always served him well, especially entering a place of which he knew little or nothing, made him want to be sure he could enter without arousing any uncalled-for attention.

He was not naturally anxious, but careful and had a kind of sixth sense rather animalistic, prehuman even primordial or reptilian, for danger lurking apparently unseen. This was not like entering a pub where, seeking a pint almost anyone might enter. It was a special kind of place. A brief glance in the window confirmed the usual sort of suspects bent over their pints. He decided it safe enough to go in.

Hardly a head looked up as he entered, quietly and without fuss. He bought a pint at the bar. A quick scan and he confirmed the place did not present any obvious threats and he sat like most of the others quietly minding his own business. No one bothered him even though he was a stranger. Harry simply blended in, which was easy here. It was obvious enough he had a military background and his darkened skin testament to service overseas although it could have been cheap flights to the sun, now readily available. He noticed one old soldier who got up with difficulty, made towards the door wheezing as he went, pulling a packet of fags out of his pocket as he went.

In the old days, Harry thought, *there would have been a much warmer convivial atmosphere, even at this time of day.* Old soldiers smoking, bit of banter, few pints, a joke or two retold to general amusement or not, some stories retold embroidered, no doubt better each time till they formed a tapestry of half-truths and lies. Not for the first time he wondered how it could be justified that old men, in their own private club, some of whom at least had no doubt fought bravely for their country, done their best and so on, and now at the end of their lives, could be banned from smoking.

The local tendency to keep to yourself was confirmed. Harry knew the old sayings, which hardly rated as jokes, 'You can always tell a Yorkshireman, but you can't tell him much'; 'like Scots with all the generosity squeezed out of them'. He regarded these as jests at best and frankly not very funny. Some of the best soldiers he had known had been from Scotland and Yorkshire.

He was not inclined to nostalgia and anyway, regional politics and the tendency for government to limit the liberties of the elderly were not Harry's interest right now. He wanted to learn what he could about George, his life, his last movements, what had happened to him.

He glanced over towards the bar. The barman was paying him no attention but the door to the toilets opened and out came an unmistakable figure who took a seat by the bar, inhabiting the space with his huge legs sprawled out in front of him. Harry quietly approached the bar and the large man who sat there. Not an ounce of fat on him Harry observed, just like a lock forward, which indeed the man had been in his youth, joint services, almost international standard. He looked match-fit. Very weathered face, inhabited. Not perhaps as burnished by the sun as his own, but more lived in, like a North Sea or Scandinavian fisherman.

Yes, that was it, like a Viking. Indeterminate age but certainly beyond middle age. Harry welcomed the current medical thinking which encouraged the phrase 'active middle age'. It could be used to describe him and a select band of those older than him. It was not an unreasonable description though pension age had been reached and then some. There was no sign of frailty. In fact, the converse. There was a feeling of control, or let's admit it, controlled violence about both men.

This was even more obviously the case with the larger man. He lifted his pint of heavy, and strode over with surprisingly effortless speed, his pace being nearly twice the average. Harry knew this with precision from training, with a measured pace at night for accurate navigation. His had been 110 for one hundred metres, the big man more like 70. A straight line across more or less any terrain, guided only by compass and pre-luminated by torchlight. He seemed not to have shortened his pace with age. Glancing at the seat next to Harry, he sat down.

"Nutter."

"Hello Fergie."

Fergie's forearms moved outwards almost imperceptibly as if he were about to embrace the smaller man. The small gesture did not go unnoticed.

"All reet, laddie."

And then looking more intently at Harry, "Been in the sun have ye?"

Harry nodded.

There was a long pause as each man appeared to study his pint, lost in their respective thoughts.

It had been fifteen years or more thought Harry, but there they were as if not a day had gone by. Of course, Fergie was not about to ask him where he had been or any irritating nonsense of that kind. Equally, he did not expect to be asked.

Still neither man spoke.

Then Fergie looked up, and glaring into Harry's eyes, the blue of the big man's revealed from under his shaggy grey eyebrows. There was a kind of suppressed fury in his voice which gave it a razor edge and rendered it even deeper. He asked him straight out.

"What happened to him?"

"Not sure. I'm not sure at all," was all Harry could muster.

"He's in a coma."

"Yes. Extensive injuries, life-threatening they say, critical condition but stable."

"I canna visit, hate hospitals."

"Me too, Fergie, me too."

There was another long pause.

Each man took a sip of his pint, and then another.

"Who did it?"

"Wish I knew."

"The polis has no idea then?"

Harry could see the tightening in Fergie's face, the knuckles of his huge hands turning white. His breath was audible, as if he were preparing for some demanding physical sporting event. The kind of sound a lock might make before seeking to destroy the opposition's pack in a scrum.

He seemed to Harry, and not for the first time, like an old bear, or perhaps more a silverback gorilla, challenged by some unseen foe, seemingly relaxed, passive even, but far from it.

Harry was very glad his old comrade was on his side. You would not want him as an enemy.

"I am going to find who did this." Harry said this with conviction.

Suddenly Fergie fixed Harry with his brilliant green eyes.

Age has not wearied him, thought Harry.

"I'm in, laddie."

"Good," murmured Harry. "Got a mobile?"

"I had one once, lost it, never really felt I needed one, do ye ken?"

"Well, have this one, it's all set up ready to go. I'll ring you or more likely text you very soon. When I need you, OK?"

Fergie nodded and took the phone which almost disappeared into his great paw. As Harry got up to leave, he wondered if Fergie even knew how to use one.

SIX

They called it 'R and R'. Rest and Recuperation.

Harry was on high ground surveying the prairie in Alberta, the vast training area provided for military games for the British Army in Canada. British Army Training Unit Suffield. Harry rather perversely for a military man, avoided acronyms, or jargon come to that, preferring plain English. He had to admit that sometimes they became convenient and shortened communication which he was rather keen on. The fact was that everyone called it BATUS. This would have been an argument in his mind for choosing not to do so, but no one knew he felt this way, as he simply avoided using it.

It had been more fun than the usual nonsense that passed for training in the army. He only half listened to the briefing officer. "The area is 2,000 square miles available for armoured battle groups to fire their weapons, blah blah…"

Harry discovered that it did provide a more or less realistic setting. He found the calling in of air strikes as well as supporting massed artillery fire amusing, exhilarating even. This was all regarded as essential training, at least for units whose *raison d'être* was largely aimed at meeting the perceived Russian threat across the north European plans. This was the task of BAOR (British Army of the Rhine), to which Harry was attached as an intelligence officer. He never used this acronym either, except in official reports where he accepted it was simpler. Harry hardly ever wrote a report, as his way of working was by word of mouth, and then not more words than were needed. Harry preferred to work in smaller units in more clandestine roles. He was not, of course, always given a choice. So it was that he was drafted in as an ops officer.

He had enjoyed the Canadian BATUS experience as far as it went. Harry accepted these large-scale exercises had to take place if only to train up higher command and seek to improve multi nation armed cooperation. However, he was not best pleased to find himself appointed as an umpire in a very convoluted army exercise involving US and Canadian as well as British troops.

Harry, rather bored, found himself observing British troops defending a bridge, and US rangers who were tasked to take it. The US commander, who Harry later dubbed 'Colonel Redneck', stood up at the wrong moment and Harry determined that he had been shot and killed. Colonel Redneck then made a mistake. He did not accept that he had been hit at all.

Harry asked him politely twice to disengage, under the rules of the wargame, but still he refused, and became aggressive. He faced up to Harry and then made the error of underestimating him. Harry simply punched him without warning striking his jaw with a satisfying crunch, and down went the big American. The bigger they are the more satisfying the fall.

Harry knew from his boxing training that a quick punch delivered with sufficient force tends to knock out the recipient, leaving him unconscious. Harry had no intention of allowing the bigger man to be in any condition to continue the dispute.

Harry did not limit himself to the Queensberry rules, far from it. He was concentrating on his target and had not failed to notice he was being observed by a small gaggle of US soldiers. Even this did not deter him. He followed up his initial blow with a sharp kick to the head, which might have done serious damage.

And then another. If asked Harry might have expressed regret about kicking a man when he was down, but then when should you kick a man? Surely better when he is down, he would have reasoned.

A small war began between the British and American troops. Unfortunately for the Americans these part-time reserve TA soldiers from Britain were not what they seemed, as they were mostly drawn from Durham miners. To them, it was like a Friday night in their hometown. Needless to say, they had a great time.

To Harry's great surprise and relief, when there looked like there might be a major incident leading to who knew what, the American decided it was just too humiliating to him personally to admit what had happened, and especially that his Rangers had taken a beating from what he understood to be similar soldiers to the National Guard. An inquiry in the field was always possible, much to Harry's disadvantage. It had to be admitted that the American's only real complaint was that Harry had kicked him once he was down, but what settled it was that he would have had to admit that he went down rather easily, lacking what Rocky Balboa dubbed a granite jaw.

Of course, Harry's reputation was much enhanced, not least because the American had been much larger than Harry. Much to his surprise he was invited as soon as the exercise was over, to the US military club in the field, along with some of the other combatants. They had a great evening and Harry struck up a friendship with a younger US officer who didn't like Colonel Redneck much. The latter was notable by his absence. His new friend said something about him being recalled for an important duty elsewhere.

"Returned to unit?" asked Harry.

"That's about it," said the Yank. "Fort Bliss."

"Sounds not too bad."

"We call it Fort Piss," said the American with a broad smile. "Hot, isolated and frequent mean sandstorms."

"Couldn't happen to a nicer bloke," commented Harry.

After many many drinks – two being one too many but never enough, but then who was counting – it was his suggestion that Harry try exploring some of the less visited parts of Canada when the exercise was over.

He had adopted, it had to be admitted, an unusual method to improve relations between allied forces but had emerged without censure, and with some new friends, and at last he was now free to enjoy himself. He jumped at the chance after the training was over to explore a remoter part of Canada. This was a happy time, carefree, with the kind of friends really only military experience tends to create. Civilians may argue but what do they know.

Fergie had heard about Harry's run-in. He commented,

"Ye canna be trusted without me Harry."

Harry grinned. "That's true Fergie."

"Or with you," he added sotto voce.

It was Fergie who suggested canoes starting at Milk River. He did not think to mention to them that it was bear country. Perhaps he didn't know.

Four of them paired off in twos in their rented boats.

Snip and Pyro already knew each other. George was notable by his absence. Something to do with a local Canadian woman. "Best not to ask," had been Harry's comment.

They cut a strange pair of couplings, as Harry was not small but was with the huge Fergie, and Snip who was really very short was with Pyro who was below average height. From a distance the pairings looked similar provided that Harry and Fergie were in the long distance. It was all a matter of perspective.

The river was so very beautiful, and apparently perfect for the less experienced. Its sylvan setting enhanced by the early summer foliage, and the landscape although by no means flat tended not to rise above the trees. This created a strange dichotomy of enclosure yet freedom in the wilderness. The sun played on the surface ripples, just as you might see in your mind's eye. It was more than a simple cliched image. These young men rapidly shed their cares, and the sheer pleasure of being young, fit, strong and free took hold.

As anyone knows, one boat on more or less any stretch of water, can be a leisurely cruise with perhaps a picnic, but two is a race. As was typical sometimes with those of lesser stature Pyro and Snip made up for their size by technique. Unknown to Harry or Fergie both Pyro and Snip knew how to paddle a canoe. They had learnt as boys.

It took no time at all for Snip at the bow and Pyro in the stern to overtake the heavier weighted boat. Fergie of course tried to compensate by greater effort, succeeding only in thrashing the water and making Harry very wet. What could he do, there was no arguing with Fergie, or seeking to calm him down, especially as the derisory cries from the 'A team' flew across the water.

Harry made out one patronising cry with crystal clarity, 'You're doing very well'. Christ they were offering false encouragement now. The heavier laden boat fell further and further behind. In fact, they had to watch the little men disappear round a bend on the widening river and out of sight.

Once out of sight Fergie calmed down a little and began to pick up Harry's rhythm and they made much better progress. As they came round the bend in the river, they could see their comrades disappearing round the next bend but to Harry's relief this did not result in any silly stuff from Fergie. He had adapted to, or at least accepted, the situation.

The terrain had altered and now the rocks began to rise up as the water flowed deeper through the canyon. Glaciers had cut through the ancient rock, and as the river ran through it the landscape had adapted and changed. There was no doubting its majesty and the relative insignificance of the paddlers in the canoe. It naturally encouraged a sense of proportion.

As they paddled along, they became one with the boat, and the boat with the water and the water with everything. The sun cast its light magically upon the waters. There was a gentle breeze which provided a cooling effect. It was a commonplace, that Harry had often experienced, that rhythmic exercise produced a kind of hypnotic effect, and this was much enhanced by the flow of the river and its setting in the natural environment. He breathed in deeply and exhaled in a kind of mental and physical paradise.

Rather late, indeed too late as it turned out, Harry became aware of a new sound and then the reason for it. Rapids. He cursed Pyro and Snip. Why had they not warned them? Perhaps they were experienced enough to simply enjoy this challenge. It occurred to him that perhaps it had surprised them too, and who knew if they had survived. It seemed an existential threat to him, but it was too late to strike out for the bankside. There was no bankside. Only huge rocks washed by very angry water.

Harry and Fergie were not experienced. Fergie sitting in front of him half turned round. Harry could see his face and a sight not often seen on it. What he saw on the face of the big man was fear.

Shooting the rapids, they called it. It was a sport. Olympic medals had been won in it. It was one of the 'sitting down' sports the British excelled at. No medals were to be won this day. Harry kept his head. He always did in extreme crisis. Small things could bother him unduly, but the larger the crisis the cooler and more level-headed he became. His brain which was no different to any others in any obvious way, operated in a way as ancient as mankind. He was unaware that he was tapping into something prehistoric', yet there was nevertheless something primordial in his response, perhaps going back as far as to a world when all creatures lived in water.

Suddenly, just as necessity required, he found he was able to deflect the path of the canoe to turn it just enough this way and that, so it brushed smoothly across the face of the giant rocks and he was able to maintain momentum; just as Fergie doing his best swaying this way and that, sought to balance the boat. He gradually became more of a help than a hindrance which was typical of the man. *Not before time*, thought Harry.

Just ahead the ground fell away and the water with it. There was no time to panic. It fell away into a roaring maelstrom. There was an odd moment of calm when Harry believed they might have been able to stop the clock and escape. But no, of course not. Life had to go on and them with it. They came down the almost sheer drop and under the water, like a torpedo. Harry felt the water enter his mouth and nose and then he was under with the water, overwhelmed. Just when you thought it meant the end, the front emerged with surprising elegance, and with its human cargo still on board. Light rapids led to quiet water. It had all passed so quickly.

Harry could hear Fergie whooping, or a sort of Highland version of it. A kind of guttural explosion. He felt exhilarated himself. Young men do not tend to dwell on near-death experiences. It just goes into the memory bank as a great story to be told and retold, probably with greater distance from the truth with each exaggerated retelling.

After a couple of hours of quite hard paddling they came round another twist in the river and could see in the distance that the other canoe was now pulled up ashore, and two dots were moving about. Harry hoped they were setting up for lunch. As they drew nearer, they saw that there was a small cove, with its own natural landing stage formed probably by cattle crossing or drinking. This had worn down the banks and created an easy place to paddle the canoes and jump out without even getting their feet wet. There was the other canoe, and Pyro and Snip had set up a small campfire, and the coffee was on. The smell wafted over towards them.

"What kept you?"

"Just wait till I get my hands on you Pyro." This was said without any real venom or even vigour. Fergie was exhausted.

"You won't be wanting coffee and these rather nice brownies I brought with me then?"

Fergie was not really angry of course, and gratefully sat down, took the coffee and a big bag of brownies and tucked in.

"I might forgive ye," he said at length.

Harry just smiled. He rested his head on a natural rise in the ground, where some rough grass provided a pillow. He stared at the sky. The clouds, such as they were, hung in little wisps of indeterminate shape. Harry did not indulge in silly mind games given such phenomena. It dawned on him that he was happy.

They packed up after finding their own individual natural places for ablutions. That afternoon they went at a less competitive natural pace. Little was said. There was no need. The river proved its own value and worth.

They made camp after a wonderful day's paddling. They were tired but happy and cheerfully set a fire and pitched their small bivvy tents, rolled out their sleeping bags and attended to their personal hygiene on the principal that bears do indeed shit in the woods. Pyro was chef, and he soon produced a meal from mostly composite rations, which nevertheless was just the ticket, and they all fell on hungrily.

Fergie produced a bottle of malt from the small rucksack which was his constant companion, and it was clear they were set for a session. The fire began to die down, and Harry and Snip went off to forage for more firewood. Snip had not even noticed the animals further down the river, which was by this time rather beautifully lit by a full moon.

Harry saw them first. Two cubs, frolicking about playfighting at the water's edge. Where was the mother? No sooner had the thought entered Harry's head and before he could warn Snip, a large bear emerged from round the bend of the river. It rapidly became clear she was not keen, to say the least, to share the space with anyone, concerned as she was by the perceived threat to her cubs.

The sense of smell of a bear is many times better than a bloodhound, and over 2000 times that of a human. They can smell animal carcasses from 20 miles away. The black bear is not perhaps the most dangerous of bears. But this was a mother, protecting her babies, and obviously not happy. Even before Harry could call out, the bear started to make quite alarming noises. Snorting, slapping the ground, snapping her jaws, her body posture now low on all fours with her head down readying herself to attack. Snip at last saw the danger but was not sure what to do, and simply stood stock still. Then without further warning the bear charged.

Harry knew Snip's only chance was to behave big and noisy himself. Running was never going to work. The problem was Snip was not large, not even as big as Harry. Harry did his best, running towards the danger screaming as if in a bayonet charge first world war style. Snip got the message and copied Harry.

They were overtaken by a huge Scotsman, Fergie, who looked truly terrifying. He had without any apparent effort made himself huge and flailed his arms about like a banshee. Never had he looked more like an extremely aggressive silverback gorilla than in that moment. The bear thought so too, as it registered not two small threats, yes these, but also, one worth avoiding. The cubs had run off and she turned, sniffed the air, and followed them. Our three heroes watched the large bear disappear into the near distance.

Fergie said, "Now that wee bit of excitement is over, we need more wood. Didna come back empty handed," and he turned back towards the campsite.

"Why exactly do you want Sergeant Major Ferguson with you?"

"I can rely on him."

Seeing the dubious glance on hearing this, he added, "I know he is unlikely to be a calming influence, sir. I appreciate he will not be a quiet presence, so to speak."

Seeing the disbelief written all over the face of the staff officer he went on, "But he is good in a crisis, and I need him to watch our backs."

"Good in a crisis you say. Maybe. My feeling is that he is the man likely to have got you into the crisis in the first place. He is not known for his, shall we say," and here he looked up to the ceiling, and sought for the right word finally settling on, "subtlety."

"I will brief him, sir, and make sure he knows the boundaries."

"All right, Case it's your show."

Harry waited.

"Off you go then."

"Right, sir," said Harry, saluted and left the ops room.

Actually, Harry himself wondered why indeed he had insisted on having Fergie along.

Harry had liked him from first meeting. His six feet, five and a half inches – not to be described as nearly two metres, 'none of that metric nonsense laddie', was carried lightly with a kind of dancer's grace, which meant on the rugby field many a back bamboozled by his fleetness of foot, and gymnastic ability. Harry had played against him and knew him to be a formidable athlete. The Scot had represented the joint services in a 15 containing a number of internationals and other talent.

It was on the SAS selection course, where Harry was attached as part of the directing staff as an intelligence officer, and Ferguson was a junior sergeant in the regiment, that the strong relationship between them grew into one of mutual admiration. Harry was never in 'the regiment'. It was not that he thought the selection process or those selected were unexceptional, just that the process and the regiment were not for him. He was frankly not really a team player.

It was a surprise to all then that Acting Captain Case and Sergeant Ferguson struck up an instant and unlikely friendship from day one. The thing Harry liked beyond all other attributes, might be called an enthusiasm for the task in hand, especially when it was allied with an irrepressible good humour and optimism. These qualities you don't often find in a Scot, at least in Harry's experience. Moreover, which was more important, Harry felt he had a certain imponderable something which turned out to be fully confirmed over time, amounting to an absolute determination to complete the mission no matter what the obstacles.

It seemed like a pleasant enough day for it, albeit beyond the usual level of tension on these occasions, which went with the Orangemen and the marching, the bands, the bowler hats and other silly nonsense as Harry saw it. He knew about the different historical narratives, Cromwell, the potato famine, the Black and Tans. In fact, Harry had read up in detail all he could on the history leading up to the troubles. Harry saw his job in simple enough terms. Make no trouble. Keep the peace. Identify troublemakers. Deal with them. He was very keen to come away without harm to himself or his soldiers, or anyone else if avoidable.

What was this? Women and children disappearing hurriedly indoors. Always a sign of trouble. Gunmen? The problem is everyone gets so bloody excited, the adrenaline, testosterone, can build to a frenzy. Half bricks and stones being thrown, the noise, the shouting, the police sirens. Petrol bombs being thrown, tear gas fired, rubber bullets and there was Fergie charging in snatching a young lad a big silly grin all over his face. And here were the bloody cameras, BBC or ITV, whatever.

CS gas fired. The sound of the canisters being launched added to the general din. Harry could recall the training they had at Porton Down. They were shown all kinds of horrors, the nerve agents – some which just blister the skin, others which totally suffocate, insidiously entering the body silently and without any warning at all, no smell, and can just be picked up off any surface. Even Hitler had not used those, on the battlefield at any rate. Also, those that can be delivered by shell fire. HE was serious enough, but phosphorous was another story, the burning effect impossible to put out. These were not the biggies though, the nuclear weapons.

Nuclear destructive effect was emphasised, but the more terrifying somehow were the after-effects of gamma and fall out from alpha and beta particles. They could be fired from standard artillery weapons and if the wind was in the wrong direction you killed your own troops, who would die of radiation poisoning, seemingly well then gradually succumbing to a foul and miserable end perhaps over a week, the sickening inevitability of it, watching friends die in front of you. But it would be the only way to stop the Russians and their allies, crossing the great northern plain of Europe. Every war game showed that if not fired almost at the outset the friendly forces would be overrun. All this he learnt and much more. These were called tactical weapons, of greater destructive force than Hiroshima or Nagasaki, deliverable by steam gunnery.

The crowd control training was delivered on Salisbury plain in the deserted village, what was it called? He could not remember. The riot training where Harry himself became over excited and had to be withdrawn from the exercise for fear of causing damage to what were after all British troops playing the rioters. He could remember being in the CS gas training cabin, the gas fired inside, off with the gas mask, name rank and number shouted out 30 seconds in, and let out, eyes streaming, the panic generated by the seeming impossibility to catch a breath, the lungs filled with gas.

And yet here they were, the youth of Belfast seemingly immune, with just scarves over their faces throwing the canisters back.

Then the shots rang out. "Man down, man down," came the shouts. Who was it, who the hell was it? No not Kerry, surely not. He was Irish himself. Just a wee lad, eighteen – no more than that, a sort of regimental mascot. No face now. Ferguson seemed to go mad, leading a one-man charge, people falling back in panic before him. Impressive really. Had to get in there and get him out, protect him from himself.

Harry hurriedly formed a small squad. "Right on me lads, we're going to get him out," and with that he went in after Fergie, leading a small team of maybe six or seven young soldiers who gamely battled their way to rescue Fergie who had one arm round a small Irishman, and was using him as some kind of battering ram. He dropped the lad who scampered away not badly hurt.

Harry got in front of Fergie, hands either side of his face, drawing him gently down forehead to forehead. "You are being watched." Quiet words which seemed to quieten him. Then he was totally calm, the rage gone as soon as it had arrived. Eerie effect. He trotted off, and the rest followed, into a snatched Land Rover and away.

He had never imagined there would be an inquiry into it all, and then another and another. Every detail that could be misremembered and gone over and over would be, ad nauseam. In real time all was very different, and not amenable to judicial inquiry. There was no VAR, and think how unreliable that can be. Forensic examination could never capture the moment in context, as it really was to those involved.

What a failure of moral authority these inquiries represented, the misuse of intellect by the lawyers, the distortions and half-truths paraded as if justice could be had in the face of the vocative power of barristers, and judges, who simply had no understanding of what it was to be there. And how was it all reported, what was the public understanding? The problem was how to live with these memories, to live with honour. *Don't make me laugh*, said Harry to himself.

The truth like the past is another country.

SEVEN

He lay on his back and stared at the ceiling. He glanced leftward at the silky smooth almost porcelain skin of the woman who was his companion in lust that night. *She has a lovely back*, thought Harry. He had a bit of a thing about shoulder blades, the shape of them, the importance of them in the protection of the body, how they were fixed points in a sea of bodily change. He liked to cradle them in his hands. The light crept in through the triangular crack at the top of the curtains.

He listened to the woman breathing almost silently. It was a habit which came with wakefulness afterwards, and this woman was a bit special to Harry at least. She was lovely, and forbidden fruit. He noticed the downy hair on the back of her neck, which itself was impossibly slim and fragile looking. He found himself wondering how easy it would be to... and here he stopped himself. Why imagine snapping her neck? He spent little time on self-reflection but this mode of thinking alarmed him. He had, after all, already seen far more violence than it was reasonable for any young man to see.

Of course, he knew previous generations of war time soldiers had experienced far more. The thing about violence is that mostly it is experienced personally, and the context matters. The Falklands was apparently not a war, but a conflict, and Ireland was 'the Troubles'. Perhaps that was it? After all he had not expected as a so-called peace time soldier to experience such violence, and as he admitted to himself, to perpetrate so much of it.

He boxed these thoughts away and returned to his visual appreciation of the human being sleeping peacefully enough next to him. He knew that consorting with local women was bound to lead to trouble. He knew this yet he could not help himself.

Her name was Aoife – once he learnt to spell it correctly, but she had been introduced as Eefa. He had asked her what it meant, and was told in her mild manner, which was her way,

"It's just a name."

That voice, its soft sound. Her breath so sweet as she turned her head up towards him, with her mouth slightly open and her tongue just caressed her lips, no artifice, no sense of routine about this. He was barely aware of the gesture.

He could feel her lips on his with that first kiss which had taken him by surprise. After all, she had just turned to him and kissed him without warning. It was not a brush or caress of the lips either, but a full blown in his face, seeking of his lips with certainty and desire.

Why had he chosen that pub? After all it was in a Catholic area. But things had been quiet for some time now, and one or two of the lads regarded it as safe. "Like our local, sir," they told him. And this was the countryside. Not even border country.

He found he was holding his breath in his desire, her eyes were closed, and he eventually and reluctantly, closed his. He must have drifted off to sleep again.

He woke up as ever instantly alert, but somewhat confused no doubt a victim of wishful thinking. Where was the girl?

He became aware of the sound of the alarm which he surmised must have woken him up, and then another closer by George's bed. Something was very wrong as George started convulsing and then sat up and just as abruptly crashed back. Harry got up leaning over his friend, and looked round desperately for help but he need not have worried because there was the crash team hurrying to the bedside, shooing Harry out of the way. Harry heard the defib charging up, the call of 'clear', the call for more charge, the effort repeated, no pulse, no heartbeat, machine flatlining and whining. This went on for an interminable time and then all activity stopped. Harry stared in disbelief. His friend was gone.

He watched the consensus nods of heads. It was all almost matter of fact. Time of death announced. A change came over his face, like a kind of mask. Harry turned and with a determined step left the scene, without so much as a backward glance.

EIGHT

"Are there any identifying marks?" asked Detective Superintendent Ruth McIntyre.

"He had some pre-existing trauma to one eye, his right one."

"You can't tell what caused it can you? I mean apart from the beating, just on examination, can you?" This was said rather rapidly in a seemingly thoughtless manner.

Ruth looked at her young colleague with raised eyebrows. She intended to convey that she considered that it was a foolish thing to ask. Quite inappropriate, rude even. She decided right then and there that her young colleague had not gained sufficient experience of this sort of thing. She might give him the benefit of the doubt, and supposed she should have read his file, genned up as it were on the youngster foisted on her on the basis that what, he was local and keen?

The pathologist dealt pretty firmly with the question.

"I'm not an amateur. Mind you, we have no medical records to go on. There were abrasions to the eye caused by a serious trauma, some kind of heavy sharp blow to the eye. These were not recent. I estimate over twenty years or more."

Ruth repeated her question.

"No obvious ones."

"What do you mean?"

Ruth was not interrupted, and she gave a half smile to her subordinate. At least he had learnt something.

"Well, there is one," replied the pathologist.

The pathologist had seen a thing or two as he was fond of telling people, and especially in his nice little earner as an after-dinner speaker.

He was going to treasure this one.

Ruth was used to being treated as if she needed protecting, which on the whole she certainly did not. She and the pathologist were old hands really.

She knew Dr Richard Evans would tend to make her wait to tease out information. His Welshness was legendary in these parts. A sort of old school charm about him not to everyone's taste. But she liked him as he did not patronise her.

"You really shouldn't behave like some cliched old TV pathologist," she said with some irritation, but tempered by a smile. He wasn't going to change now. But then neither was she.

"Come on, please don't keep me in suspense," urged Ruth. She was pretty irritated being forced to ask him for information in this way. He always did this. Why could he not just tell her?

It ought to have been incongruous to him that this striking woman worked in such an environment. He had wanted to ask her out but never did. He had seen her rise through the police from local detective police constable, which was unusual in itself in his experience, to chief inspector in the murder squad and now superintendent. She had earned it even though this promotion came with the collapse of chief inspector rank. The latest reorganisation but not, to be sure, the last. They had this in common: they just got on with it.

"It's a tattoo."

Oh yes. This might be very helpful, she thought.

Her companion the young detective sergeant, Robbie, still had not learnt to be less noisome around her, and blurted out,

"But that's the end of his penis!"

"That's right," said Dr Evans. "You certainly know your anatomy."

Robbie blushed, which Ruth found heart-warming, even endearing, and her irritation subsided.

"Can you enlarge that?" asked Ruth.

Evans started to laugh, especially as Robbie corpsed beside her.

"Oh please, please be serious," said Ruth.

Both men were laughing out loud now.

"It's not that funny."

"Oh, but it is. You have just asked me to enlarge his penis."

He and Robbie gasped for breath.

"I suppose you want me to," and here he paused for effect, "blow up his penis."

This was too much for Robbie, who attempting to supress his laughter made it worse. Ruth decided to ignore him and press on. At least Evans was doing the practical thing and enlarging the image.

"Right, now, what do you make of that?"

Ruth seemed reluctant as she often was, to share her thoughts especially when not sure.

"They are a bit like wings?"

"Not just wings," said Evans triumphantly given her uncertainty, "they are wings of the winged horse." She looked quizzical. "You know, Pegasus the winged horse that sprang from the blood of the Gorgon Medusa as she was beheaded by Perseus." Here Evans paused as if this were a real event. "Quite how Poseidon managed to impregnate her is something of a mystery to me."

Ruth was beginning to become exasperated. Who knew how long he might go on in this vein? She asked, "Is it not the para emblem?"

"Yes, yes it is," Robbie agreed excitedly. "You are onto something there, ma'am. That's it, like the wings on a parachute regiment beret cap badge."

One glance from Ruth and Robbie stopped talking.

"Was it his injuries that killed him?"

There was no laughter now, and the mood darkened.

"It will all be in my report." Ruth looked at him with an expression that urged him to offer his opinion. He couldn't resist that, of course. "Yes I am sure it was one of the blows to the head, perhaps with a blunt instrument or a kick I cannot be sure. I understand the attack was in an alleyway?"

"That's right," confirmed Ruth.

"Could have hit his head when falling but I doubt that. Forensics may help you there, of course, but there are no obvious materials of interest found from a wall or ground. Perhaps need to check his clothing. There is no doubt that the skull fracture was caused by a severe blow to the head, which led to a cerebral haemorrhage. There are contusions and two lower rib fractures and one upper, which I think occurred before the head injury but I cannot be sure. He had a pneumothorax."

Robbie looked puzzled.

"That is to say, a punctured lung."

Robbie again spoke out. "There was no obvious reason for the attack. An old man walking through the town centre. It's Harrogate for crying out loud. Unheard of here really. He was practically beaten to death. It's a murder."

"Would you kindly shut up Robbie," said Ruth quietly but firmly. Why did he think they were there at all?

"Anything else?"

"Well, I think we can safely say he enjoyed a drink, which I can confirm on autopsy. You can't expect more now, my report will be with you within 48 hours."

"By the way Medusa was one of three sisters and she was a beautiful vulnerable woman, the snakes and the stare came later." Ruth told him with a smile. Steven Fry's book had turned out to be useful after all.

With that she turned to go with Robbie at her heels.

In the car, Robbie tried to apologise for talking too much and asking daft questions. Ruth simply waved her arm in a gesture intended to hush him up, and mercifully, from her perspective at least, he took the hint.

"So what do we have?" Ruth started quietly talking to herself. She did this almost without being conscious she was doing it. She knew it added to the general opinion that she was a loner, or at least preferred her own company and it was true that she would if she could work alone. Admittedly she cultivated the notion that she was formidable, and not to be messed around. But Robbie was here in the car driving her, so she might as well accept that he was there and could perhaps be some kind of sounding board.

"Caucasian male maybe age 70 to 75, medium height, good muscle tone for his age certainly. Somewhat gone to seed, slightly puffy face, red-faced, a drinker. I guess the tattoo meant he was either in the Paras or wanted to be, or maybe the territorials. It's a lead at any rate."

Robbie wanted to speak then but glancing over at her he thought better of it.

"He had two visitors then, but not more it seemed. One from a very large man, similar age to the victim or perhaps a little older. Scottish the nurse thought. Nothing she could recall further though he wore a long, big coat, and here he consulted his notebook, like a first world war soldier. A greatcoat I think they are called. We need to reinterview the staff at the hospital. And we need to get on with it."

Here Robbie felt emboldened to speak up.

"Ma'am. If he didn't have much money, maybe he bought the coat in a charity shop. We have lots of those in Harrogate. Those coats tend to be found in charity shops these days or handed out to rough sleepers maybe. I could have a go at checking this?"

"OK, Robbie, you do that. But first let's interview the staff at the hospital and any other staff." They set off for the ward.

The only other odd thing she remembered was his shoes which were highly polished. "And one other thing."

"Yes," said Ruth encouragingly.

"Well, he held himself very upright, and he moved with no sign of frailty which was at odds with his face, which was very you know 'lived in', even a little gaunt. If I had to guess his age I would have said over 70 maybe even 75. No fat on him though."

"And the other chap?"

"He stayed for most of my shift but I was very busy. I told the other police officers all I could remember."

"I know," said Ruth, "you were very helpful."

Ruth did not of course think she had been that helpful at all. Nevertheless, she tried to be encouraging.

"It's always difficult to remember what the main focus of the day was, and you really were very busy I'm sure. Sometimes we recall things better once they have settled in the mind."

This was not true, and Ruth knew it very well, but she had to try and recover from the abysmal failings in the first interviews. She knew if it wasn't fresh in their minds there was little reason for a witness to provide more reliable, better information later.

"Just try and think back and run through what you do recall once more."

Ruth tried to set the scene.

"It was late evening in your shift?"

The nurse warmed somewhat in response to Ruth's encouragement.

"He seemed a bit younger, and somehow more educated looking so to speak. His voice was low and no obvious accent, but I would say from the south somewhere. Yes, a southerner for sure. He hardly spoke though. Only to ask what had happened to his friend."

"How did he know to come?"

"Oh I rang and he answered."

"What?"

"Yes, on the casualty's mobile phone."

"Where is the phone now?"

"I'm not sure."

"Have his effects been collected and bagged by the police?"

"I don't think so."

Ruth nearly lost her temper at this.

She turned to Robbie, and he nodded. "I'll chase it up boss."

Ruth tried again.

"Can you describe him?"

"I'm not sure."

Ruth tried not to let her exasperation show. Witnesses were never sure. To be fair they were not used to describing those they had met in passing, so to speak. Even professional witnesses struggled sometimes. Again, she regretted that the first interviews had been conducted so poorly.

"Hair colour?"

"Brown, I think, dark, not balding. A good head of hair I would say, cut neatly, not short but tidy. Handsome looking for his age. Very suntanned, like he had been on holiday somewhere sunny for a good long time."

"Any obvious features, big eyes, nose – large, small?"

"Not that I can recall. No pronounced features, you know, average looking nose. I'm sorry it's hard to remember much about him."

Ruth should have been used to this. She knew people invariably found other people difficult to describe. This turned out to be quite frustrating not least as he had apparently sat there, twice, for a considerable period of many hours, but as was typical, it was clear the nurse remembered very little about him. She sent Robbie off to seek any other witnesses.

"His clothes?"

"Well, a sort of long coat, darkish trousers, perhaps they were jeans. T-shirt, well it could have had longer sleeves." She really was trying.

"I remember now he did take the coat off. And sat on it like."

"What, you mean on top of the seat?" asked Ruth. "I wonder why. Perhaps for more comfort. Perhaps he believed he was there for the long haul. This must have been someone who cared."

"He sort of tucked it in very carefully like, very neatly. Hospital corners."

Ruth looked at her with an open expression intended again to convey encouragement.

"Yes, short sleeves, and dark blue or maybe green, dark anyway." But the nurse said all this without conviction. She shrugged and then said she really was needed on the ward.

"I really can't remember anything else."

"Just one more question." The nurse had started to move away.

"What about his shoes?"

"What?"

"His shoes. Were they highly polished?"

She thought for a minute,

"Just clean, I think. I always notice if they aren't you see. Maybe brogues, yes brown brogues. He also had very clear, ice blue eyes. They sort of looked," and here she paused hunting for the words, "looked as if they were drilling into you." She said this with some embarrassment as if giving away a secret.

What a strange thing to highlight now, thought Ruth. This man was not trying to be conspicuous but had had greater impact than perhaps he intended.

"Was it just the one visit?"

"No, no," she thought for a moment. "I believe he came twice."

"How long did he stay?"

"I'm not sure but more than a short visit. Actually, now I think about it he was sat there, sort of most of the time. He was there when I went off shift and when I came back on. He was so quiet, no kind of nuisance, so we just let him be." Now she was thinking about it she remembered one other thing.

"He looked like he had spent quite a long time in the sun."

"Sunburnt you mean?"

"No, no, more like used to being in the sun like, a lot."

"Weather beaten?"

"Yes, well no, no. More than that."

"Not a person of colour?"

"I'm not sure. I don't think so."

Ruth wondered if this meant he was indeed a person of

colour or perhaps more likely, had lived abroad in a place where the sun was an unavoidable part of the way of life. She wondered if he too was a soldier, and perhaps one who had spent much of his time in hotter climes.

She thanked the nurse and asked her to give her sergeant her details.

"I think we may have to ask you to make a statement. Arrangements will be made as soon as convenient," she added, though more as a formality than anything. She handed over her card. The nurse rather reluctantly took it.

"Just in case anything else occurs to you, or perhaps one of your colleagues." She was not unaware that there would be gossip. 'Who doesn't know that nurses' stations are like this', she almost said out loud but of course she didn't. "Maybe something will pop up."

Robbie came back, and she asked him if anyone had anything to add.

"Really nothing. Except, he had been very nice to the care assistant who offered him a cup of tea."

"When you say 'nice'?"

"Very polite. Well mannered. She thought him a bit of a gent. Old style gentlemen, she said."

"An officer and a gentleman," murmured Ruth to herself.

"Anything else?"

Robbie shook his head. "I really did try."

What does he want she thought, reassurance?

"I'm sure you did sergeant." 'I really must try and be warmer with him' she told herself, though she knew there was little chance of this.

Robbie glanced at his notes and repeated what was written there, "The care assistant had said she noticed 'he just sat there rather like you might sit in prayer in church like'." He said this rather regretfully, as if it added nothing.

She was not surprised that Robbie had turned up so little from his questioning. She was somewhat annoyed that the young policewoman and her buddy had not recalled anything either, other than the clearly false name and address he had given. The only thing odd then she surmised was just how little was remembered of the man sitting by the bedside for so long. She turned over the comment 'prayerful' in her mind.

Although she had an idea or two which might prove useful, she did not think it much to go on. Still, it was better than nothing she told herself in an effort to stay positive.

NINE

Harry did not attend the Cenotaph any more and could not recall the last time he had. He did try to turn out somewhere where there was at least a memorial service. It all seemed so long ago and what really was his connection with these soldiers of the forgotten past. Nevertheless, he was drawn to the memorial square and sat down near the local cenotaph. Old habits die hard. He reflected on his current rootlessness and the sense of dislocation from his country but without any nostalgia or sentimentality.

He had been brought up mostly in the home counties and doubted anyone could sink roots there. His childhood had not been unhappy. His home was not far from Sandhurst where he recalled feeding the ducks with his father who had been a military man. The house he was brought up in was edged by a military training area principally used by the Royal Engineers, and was a happy place for Harry to adventure in. It was forested and had a lake where the army sailed. Quite an idyllic place for a small boy. He could walk to school through the woods, over the playing fields and past the memorial hall and the church.

His mother was Welsh. She was very old the last time he had been in Pentrefoelas where she was born shortly before the First World War. She had expressed a wish to see the small village once more, nestled in the foothills of Snowdonia on the old mail coach route, now the A5, just short of the very well-known tourist spot Betwys-y-Coed which boasts Swallow Falls and the old miners' bridge. Harry liked the place very much and it had special significance in his childhood memories.

Harry's mother Daisy was very superstitious but no more than any of her community. This was rural Welsh Snowdonia after all. He remembered her falling at Swallow Falls on a flat slippery rock. She broke her arm, and as Harry leaned over her, how old was he, perhaps fourteen, she said, "I told you it meant bad luck." The bad luck she was referring to was leaving new shoes on the kitchen table some six months earlier. Harry had thought his mother ludicrous for blaming him or believing such a thing. *But why not*, he now thought. *Who knows what causes apparent accidents to happen, mishaps and even tragedy to fall where it did?*

There are more things in heaven and earth than lie in thy philosophy. His mother often quoted bits of Shakespeare and poetry learnt off by heart in her schooldays.

To Harry myth and legend and superstition did not now seem so irrational. As he had grown into manhood he began to appreciate and tried to understand better his heritage, his Welshness. His own habits and routines were steeped in avoiding bad luck which he had imagined was just common sense but which he suspected now were part of some unavoidable historic ancestry.

It was inevitable that Harry would pass the small primary school where his mother had her first lessons. And on this day, pass it he did. Often he would retrace these steps or similar ones in his mind, with the smells of cut grass in his nostrils, from the rugby field opposite the school, and the powerful whiff of nostalgia, mixed admittedly with the smells of farming which were all around. Happy times. Harry spent long visits to his aunt's small hill farm. The joy of his personal memories was not qualified as perhaps it should have been by his mother's experience. They were not after all his experiences but hers.

She was beaten at school. His aunt had told him. He could scarcely believe it. She had to speak only in English. Welsh was forbidden. Beaten for speaking her mother tongue at school, or even if overheard on her way to school or in the village, by the vicar or schoolmistress, or another Anglo-Saxon conqueror or sycophant. It was with regret that Harry had never learnt Welsh as a boy. He was to be honest mostly brought up in Surrey, but the weeks spent in Wales on the farm, in winter lambing and in the spring shearing and the haymaking in summer, left an indelible impression. When he was young, he little thought it might matter that while his mother spoke only Welsh as a girl, her mother tongue but not his, that glorious language of poets and dreamers, he had only the English in all its dominant glory laced with hypocrisy. Perhaps this drove him to learn local languages as part of his soldiering.

The thing with Harry was that he was able to compartmentalise his conscience. This was yet another small corner of his mind that he locked up to avoid it troubling him. He did make some effort to learn Welsh later on but with limited success, mostly just the songs and some poetry learnt largely by rote.

All the family left the village to seek work or find their fortune elsewhere, except the baby, Gwen, his mother's little sister. She never left the village, though she married an Englishman. She had distanced herself further from her mother by choosing to go to 'chapel'. Harry's grandfather, carrying his memories of the First World War, chose to go with his younger daughter. Harry disliked the established church, but delighted in going with his Auntie Gwen to 'chapel'. The language was Old

Testament. Bishop Morgan's bible. He moved from singing treble with the women, and then alto, and finally when manhood drew closer slipping in with the men on the other side of the chapel aisle – a good singer either side so part singing, and the community of the choral, became a way of life, first as tenor and then as his voice settled, into a rich baritone. This proved possible even though his time there each year was limited. He was not aware at the time how generous the local community had been to this part time Welsh boy from the home counties who spoke no Welsh.

His mother's ancestry was enough for them, and it was 14 generations long at least, stretching back to time immemorial. His mother's claim to be descended from Owen Glendower was probably true but then ancestry tends to emphasise the roots one wishes to promote. We are all descended from some King Cnut or other.

He was walking back up the lane that led from the village to his Auntie Gwen's farmhouse, perhaps seven years old, when he learnt his mother's name which he had thought was Christina. A local was hanging out the washing and hailed him in Welsh, which he could appreciate but not really respond to. She spoke then in English when she saw his puzzled face.

"You're Daisy's boy aren't you?"

"No," he said tentatively. Then more firmly, "No." He was not sure though, as he stood there in his shorts and T-shirt and sandals with knee high grey socks. In his memory these trips to Wales were often warm and sunny, in August usually.

He remembered his visits to the farm during the lambing season, and even in winter. He recalled being there twice in the harsh snow-filled winters of his childhood. Pulling lambs out with his little arms and hands, 'very useful' his uncle called him. Harry was so proud of being granted this praise. He was perhaps only six or seven when he first performed this vital task. And the winters afterwards saw him there at lambing time and he knew he could attribute a certain confidence and toughness to these experiences.

He had been very young when he first went, it being part of his mother's life to return every year, and though he came back almost every year into adulthood, he was simply a visitor now. This was the difference. His mother was not visiting, it was fundamental to who she was. Visiting the place his mother was from and her mother and father, and so on and so on, each begetting a Welshness retained Harry hankered for an identity he really could not make his own.

Ironically his mother had tried to distance herself from the place. She had married shortly after the First World War, rather late in life, a sort of last chance. He was an English army officer, born in Malaya, who perhaps had a touch of the 'tar brush' as it was then called. A thought entered his mind. Why had she learnt so little from her reading which had been quite extensive? It was not a generous thought. His mother who loved poetry and it was part of her education to memorise much of it; she read 'great literature' in her youth but later sank to reading cheap thrillers, her thrills anesthetised in TV shows and popular fiction in the quiet boredom of Hampshire. Yet when she was very old and dying it was Keats, and Calon Lan and Welsh and the English poetry learnt off by heart and never forgotten that gave her comfort. Strange to think his mother's favourite poem was The Old Vicarage, Grantchester. Even in this very Welsh corner of Wales there was very little pure blood. *Good,* thought Harry. He was not interested in sentimental exile.

"She's called Christina," Harry managed.

"That's it," she said in triumph, "Daisy Christina."

She let him go on with a smile and a wave, and an offer of barra brith the next time he was passing. Harry turned over the new information in his mind and decided he was delighted with this secret. He skipped home happily the remaining mile or so. Not that he managed to keep the secret long, dancing into the farmhouse dairy where his mother was with Gwen, and singing, "Daisy, Daisy, Daisy, Daisy, Daisy."

It was not till much later that he fully grasped why his mother had tried to lose the name. She told him at the time it was because it was the name for a cow. She had, as she saw it, escaped poverty and a future as a dairy maid on the estate, with all the rural poverty that implied, by dint of hard sustained effort and the support of her mother and father. And she had escaped. There was truth in this. Her parents were determined she and all her brothers and sisters should have a secondary education at the grammar school and they all did. Each girl became a nurse, the boys schoolteachers. It meant an eight-mile journey across the Denbigh moors and staying in shared rooms during the week, which her parents could barely afford, the journey done on the early milk run cart, or on foot on the return journey. It also meant they left their parents behind.

Harry's mother associated Wales with poverty and cold and bitter wind and snow that killed livestock and sometimes people too, but her heart never really left it. If she had not escaped, it was probably true that she would have been a dairy maid on the estate where her father worked as a joiner. He made beautiful Welsh dressers when not fixing every problem in wood on the grand house occupied for a few weeks each year by the Wynn Finch family. What did their tenure produce? Disgraceful slums in the village and not much improved even in Harry's lifetime. A largely absent uncaring landlord.

He stood at the back of the churchyard in the village as his cousin played the cornet, The Last Post. Played so beautifully. Harry knew his mother's father had served right through the First World War in the Royal Welch. He was paid more in the army than he ever earned as an estate worker notwithstanding his superlative skills as a joiner and cabinet maker. Harry loved the Welsh dresser his mother had in her bedroom, its dovetailed joints a testament to his skills and craftmanship. Harry heard the haunting final notes of The Last Post float away. He listened intently, and if only for a fleeting few seconds felt perhaps something beyond the grave. The old soldiers now of his imagination, and much older ones, warriors of much more ancient times, in that equivocal relationship with the English. And as the last notes drifted away, his sense of ambivalence left him to be replaced by a profound sense of sadness and loss.

He had many comrades to remember and as he always did on these occasions, he tried to honour them. But he knew there were no glorious dead and amongst soldiers, hardly any glorious living. Dulce et decorum est pro patria mori.

And then there was his father to consider, the wartime soldier, the officer in the KRRs a very grand regiment indeed, though their officers tended to be of the self-effacing, understated sort only the English upper middle classes can really bring off. His father would declare to him, when Harry suggested he might join a less celebrated regiment, that this would be fine as 'there was no such thing as snobbery any more', which was clearly, in Harry's estimation at any rate, about the most snobbish remark you might possibly hear.

His father, a colonial civil servant, had adopted the child

which was almost certainly a product of the liaison with an Anglo Malay woman. Her good looks translated into a beautiful child. A public school education at home from the age of seven made sure he adopted the manners and mores of the English ruling classes. A kind of born-again Englishman. Fortunately, his colour was hardly noticeable.

From these schizophrenic beginnings his parents' marriage was quite a settled one, and Harry was grateful for this. He recalled going through his father's bureau after he died. These thoughts came unbidden at armistice day, not least because both father and son had been soldiers, all volunteers. What exactly had they been fighting for? His father's atheism puzzled him, and he adopted his mother's simple faith, a kind of Anglo Catholicism, reinforced by the King James Bible, the language of which Harry loved, and the Welsh chapel.

What did Harry believe? He was not sure but would not have described himself as agnostic. He simply could not believe there was not room in heaven for his father, who was unfailingly kind towards Harry and so many others. He tried to inhabit a quiet spiritual space with little success.

His father had written a poem that Harry had memorised which came unbidden to his mind. He had found it amongst his father's papers, a small brief case of items his father had kept, almost at random, placed semi-hidden under the bureau. Harry supposed they all meant something to the old man, perhaps some of it was of great importance. There was a photograph of his elder brother, the uncle he never knew, killed in the war. There was a letter to his father, expressing deep regret and expressing the sentiment that his brother was the finer man and an irreplaceable loss. And then Harry came across this poem penned but hidden,

I do not wish my memories to become hopes that came to

nothing,

I do not want to waste yet more time on useless ceremonies that pass for life,

The dead are dead and cannot be glorious however remembered and so I shall be dead too, maybe soon who knows?

Everything is temporary and must of necessity slip through my fingers like the sands of time.

It is useless to rage against the past and the dying light, Here is my tiny prayer: Let me find that still small voice of calm if only for a fleeting moment. I was once a soldier and am mercifully almost unknown. When I am dead let them say this of me, He loved his children, Each one equally.

Harry allowed himself on this one day for a few moments to think of the sister he never knew and this he used to displace the potentially more upsetting memory and loss of his comrades. He remembered also, and this unbidden, his mother's distress at the stillborn child. Her inability to love anyone after that was, he felt, understandable, and certainly not Harry or his father. It was an unspoken grief, and one barely acknowledged at all. This his silent prayer. *Shantih shantih shantih.*

But he dispatched all such memories into a box marked 'the past'. Harry spent no time on sentimentality as he would call it, and was able to package these thoughts like so many disagreeable memories, parcel them away, and press on almost as if he had no memory of them at all.

Where were these unknown warriors now, the ones condemned to live in Harry's memory? Harry's mind was not, when all was said and done, a very accommodating place. Harry himself was not given to feelings of guilt much less shame. He did sometimes ask himself why he did so little to see those he had known, that he would if pressed, have described as the 'warriors'.

Was it perhaps just laziness, or did he lack a developed sense of moral obligation or duty? Was he a good man? He did not ask himself these kinds of questions. Simply put, he preferred travelling light and alone.

He had not exactly run from his past so much as simply strolled away slowly and rather aimlessly and left it far behind.

TEN

Harry was awoken from his reverie by a cold chill which ran up his legs and spine. He shivered involuntarily, and levered himself upright and taking a deep breath or two strode off to find his new billet.

He checked into the Travelodge, which was conveniently not far from the centre of town and war memorial, and which he had spotted not too far from the bed and breakfast. He wanted to stay somewhere even more anonymous. This was driven not solely by habits developed over a lifetime aimed at not attracting attention or merely general caution. He had evaded, albeit with ease, the rather obvious attention of persons who he assumed did not have his interests at heart on arrival back in the UK, at Heathrow airport. Frankly the secret services or special branch or perhaps mercenary operatives, whoever they were, had not impressed him with their ability to conduct covert surveillance. He felt reasonably sure they did not have eyes on him. They obviously didn't train them as well as they once had, was Harry's judgment on them. He had hoped that his long period abroad had meant he was no longer of interest, but he knew that was unlikely. Best be cautious.

He was going to recce the place where George had met his nemesis which he already realised was probably just a mugging. With George's death some serious threshold had been crossed in Harry's mind. A tipping point. He was aware of it, albeit on a subliminal level, and found he felt tense, not yet hypervigilant but not relaxed, as if the mission was about to begin. Harry smiled. Let the action commence. But first rest.

He sat in the functional bedroom, with a view, from the surprisingly comfortable chair, of not much. Any chair might seem that way after the bloody hospital one. The bed began to look inviting.

He needed to sleep, and Harry notwithstanding his mood and a certain renewed state of arousal, was able to switch off. It was a knack he had. He kicked off his shoes. He began to tuck into the provisions he had secured, a Big Mac and fries, polished off with a large Coca-Cola. He toyed with the salad in the interests of a balanced diet, but frankly he was not that bothered. Fuel was needed, and of course, in its own way the fast food was ideal, and was enjoyable. He polished off most of it, wrapped up the rest neatly, and put it in the bin. His tidy habits were an asset tending to a clear mind.

He then took a shower allowing the hot water to wash away the angst in his mind and the tension in his body. He showered in his T-shirt and pants and then took them off and hung them in the shower to dry. He cleaned his teeth with the toothbrush and paste purchased from the vending machine as he came into the place.

It was not a bad choice he reflected. It had all that Harry needed. The main thing was how inconspicuous he felt there, which was always the aim. He snapped the shaft of the toothbrush in half so that it might more easily be carried. He shaved while the water was running with a cheap double-bladed BIC razor. He snapped the shaft of that too, as with the toothbrush. The habit of travelling light once learnt had never left him. He was able to secrete the basics about his person. Never was travelling light met with greater minimalism.

He got in between the sheets and set his mental body clock

to wake at eight the next morning, and promptly fell asleep. The dreaming seemed so real.

"Nutter."

Then again more urgently and with greater emphasis, "Nutter," the voice hissed.

"Here George."

"Right there you are then. Bollocks." George allowed this to escape his lips in a kind of rasp, as he nearly fell over Harry. "All this blundering around in the f'ing dark is not f'ing easy."

Harry knew this was rubbish as no one was better at fieldcraft than George.

"They are just over that ridge, about 200 yards, do you see?"

"How many do you reckon?"

"Practically fell over their forward trench, maybe a battalion. They are on the reverse slope. No sentries or if there are, they are not very alert."

Lucky for them, thought Harry.

"Miserable I reckon. It's this unrelenting rain and it's not exactly warm, is it. Must be getting them down," said George with a grin. Harry could see him pretty clearly, his night vision properly established.

"Must be, George. It's getting me down." He returned George's big grin with a smile of his own.

"Got any response on that radio yet?" asked George.

"Not a dicky bird."

Harry thought through his options.

"OK, George get yourself down there" he said, inclining his head to where friendly forces were to be found "and bring up some support, a gunner FOO with a signaller would be ideal, or mortar platoon commander. We need to shift those Argies."

"Okey dokey," murmured George and he slipped, or more

accurately slithered, off into the gloom. Apart from a slight squelching from his boots George made little or no sound as he made his way down the slope and out of sight. It was bitterly cold notwithstanding that the night sky was covered in cloud. It began to rain once more.

Harry sat quietly in his little nest, under the large rock overhang. He was really quite comfortable, except for the piercing cold, and even had a soft head rest made of lichen covered rock with a mars bar and hip flask of brandy for company. Harry rested quietly and waited. There was no sign of any movement and he was glad of it. He shut his eyes and rested them. The rain continued to fall.

His plan was to shift those Argies with a bit of artillery or mortar fire. At the very least he wanted to make their life very unpleasant. He hoped they would simply run away. It was likely they were not really battle-hardened troops but conscripts probably sent with little training and inadequate equipment. The conditions were appalling even for professional troops.

Harry assumed nothing, as you never could tell how they might react until push came to shove. British Army standard issue equipment was not much better, but the training was another matter, and GORE-TEX boots bought personally from the Dutch Naafi helped. Harry also favoured aircrew undershirts, insulating, not bulky and comfortable. He was dry and relatively warm. It was still perishingly cold. He was very glad of his charcoal handwarmers.

The Dutch Naafi was a great place to find kit the British Army simply did not supply to its soldiers. It was not of course the real Naafi but frankly much better. The Dutch conscripts were much better catered for, and it was a great source of really modern basic items, and the first Sony Walkman. Harry knew it wasn't appropriate but he liked to carry his even here in the Falklands.

He had first used one to listen to music while training in the mountains of Austria and Germany for the ski championships. It allowed him to listen to Grieg's piano concerto while putting in the miles on cross country skis. It came in very useful while whiling away those very boring times the army required you just to stay put and do next to nothing. In the Falklands as no doubt in many wars before and since, it was all 'rush to wait', a mantra Harry would often hear repeated by British soldiers who seemed willing to put up with almost any amount of bullshit. They would man even utter seditious statements. 'See me, I'm just heading for the coast if the Ruskis come', was typical enough.

Harry was asked by George what he was listening to once. Harry passed over the Walkman with Grieg playing and George who had never listened to such music before, was very taken with it. "Beethoven is it?" he asked.

"Pretty much," answered Harry.

Harry reflected on what the army had given him. Mostly the camaraderie, he already knew that. Also, a love of the mountains and the outdoors, which his background already encompassed, but enhanced by the opportunities in the Alps, the climbing, the skiing, the langlauf, the laughs. Would he have skied at all without it. He doubted it. And the sailing. Little or no chance. And the physical manliness of it. The testing himself.

"Fuck me Harry, who is that then, f'ing Beethoven again is it?" George expressed his considered musical criticism in concise language. "Can I get one Harry?" he asked. Harry promised to buy him one. Another broken promise, which seemed at the time a small matter, though now lying deep in Harry's memory, as the order to move from home base to the Falklands had come with insufficient notice. Harry never bought George a Walkman. That seemed to matter now.

He reminded himself that the enemy at Goose Green had not been such a pushover so you never could tell. In Harry's view, and he was not alone, there was no need for that battle to have taken place there at all, as here they were approaching Port Stanley bypassing any superfluous nonsense elsewhere. The attack at Goose Green was of no strategic significance whatsoever. And then that Colonel H, some bloody hero, charging the enemy head on.

He was shot dead but frankly what was he doing there. True a platoon was pinned down. True no one fancied chancing their arm in the face of determined enemy fire. True the attack had stalled. What was the point though - as a little patience, the use of say the battalion's mortar platoon and calling for other serious fire support from artillery and air would have won that battle albeit with some delay? The HQ company commander had even asked to come forward with reinforcements. As it turned out, the failure to delegate and command from a more suitable position meant the battle was nevertheless won and with it a posthumous VC. How glorious was that. But frankly it had not been his job to lead such a charge.

His musings were interrupted as George reappeared with a very young looking forward observation officer from the gunners, and a slightly out of breath signaller. Young he may have been but he was very enthusiastic and efficient. You had to admire it.

"Hello Zero, this is One Nine." The grid number was delivered and confirmed back.

"Fire one for effect."

At the gun position, some 10k back, a round was loaded, the

correct direction and elevation given. Much as it might have been two generations before. Steam gunnery, but effective.

And within a few seconds they heard the shell whistling over their heads and land just short of the ridge.

"Add one hundred," came the order.

That's it, thought Harry, and he was right.

"All guns six rounds HE fire for effect," came the order.

And all hell let loose. The effect on the troops over the ridge was not hard to imagine.

"Repeat," came the order.

Nutter sent George off to see what the outcome was, as more and more rounds were brought down on the Argentinian heads. Very sensibly, to avoid friendly fire, George set off in a wide arc but moved rapidly. Harry called for a lull in firing.

"Check firing," ordered the gunner.

George reappeared. "They've buggered off I think," reported George. "Saw them running down the hill. Seemed to have abandoned their weapons and everything."

"Right, what's your name, Lieutenant?"

"Crean, sir."

"Just Harry," murmured Harry. The error was understandable as Harry was clearly in command and wore his father's Mao Tse-tung jacket without insignia. It was very warm with its high collar. Far better than anything issued in the British Army.

"OK, Crean." Harry spoke as he did to most officers – especially young ones – with a barely detectable irony in his voice. Mind you the difference in their ages was not great.

"Who are you supporting?"

"2 Para."

"Good," said Harry, "let's get some troops up here then. Can you manage that do you think?"

The rhetorical question was met with a grin, and Crean got on the radio himself and within a few minutes Harry could see a sizeable force rapidly moving up the slope. It was the Paras, in company strength at least.

"Right let's get over that ridge and secure that vital ground."

With that up they went and over the ridgeline. Harry saw one silly sod sky-lined on the top, his arms outstretched as if in a gesture of triumph. There was a single shot from a rifle, and down he went. Sniper!

"Bugger this is going to be more difficult than I thought."

"Stay put," he said firmly to the company commander who had appeared at his side. He went forward and met George edging round the side of the ridge, a big grin on his face.

"Got the bastard," he said with satisfaction, wiping his commando knife clean on his combat trousers.

ELEVEN

Aoife sang to him perhaps or to herself. He could hear her. Her sweet voice. He had pretended to be asleep.
    Softly, *"Harry is my darling, my darling, my darling,*
Harry is my darling,
No one else can touch me, touch me, touch me"
Her voice drifted away sotto voce, al niente.
    The early morning light was showing itself.
    They had only partly drawn the curtains. That typical consequence of the curtains not closing easily without leaving a gap at the top and a slighter gap all the way down. They had not considered this important the night before as they had other things on their mind.
    She slipped out of bed careless of her nakedness, innocent yet knowing, like Pandora perhaps, and peeped out to sea, the vastness of the Atlantic Ocean lay before her, nothing between her and eternity. She then did an odd thing climbing onto a chair perhaps to see further. Harry did not interfere, simply not wishing to spoil the moment.
    You could see the Giant's Causeway from there. Harry caught a glimpse of the sea and sky framed by the triangular gap between her thighs and her buttocks. It was a singular image. She stayed like that for a while. Whatever she gazed at had her complete attention. She had his attention that was sure.
    Last night it had been him she focused on entirely. He found that in making love to her he grasped something tangible which

sadly was never to be his again. This was real and going to last, yet even as he felt it, it began to slip away. The autumn sun was not warm at that time of day, and she shivered a little. She turned her head towards him looking over her shoulder. Harry had never seen anything so beautiful as that look. She loved him that was certain. She slipped gracefully off the chair, and with a small laugh she slipped into bed beside him. Her cold thighs and arms enveloped him in their grasp, and she pulled his warm body towards her as all graceful feelings left her and they made love somewhat slower and more sensual than the night before, but with a fierceness that surprised Harry.

Did he love her? He did not answer the question only asked it silently to himself then, and she did not ask him. There was no doubting the passion, the lust, in that their first night together. Was she a virgin? He was not sure, as she gave herself to him with such confidence and trust and a broad-mindedness that almost shocked him and certainly surprised him. They were compatible physically and emotionally. She took him to places he was not at all sure he wanted to visit. He did not like the loss of control and was somewhat confused by how willing he was to give himself to the moment. He doubted he had taken her innocence. She had knowledge that was instinctual, and till now unpractised. The craving for her never left him.

She had released some of his supressed violence and had enjoyed it, taken it into her, absorbed it.

He had driven with her to this, in her eyes, amazing place. She had no idea such places existed. As a Belfast girl it was beyond her ken. A small inn in a smugglers' cove, which looked nothing from the front but the bothy at the back had a large window that provided the astounding views, obviously opened up for the purpose.

Its thick walls were a testament to wise building practice of a long-gone era. It was a surprise, for the place was snug, yet astounding. It was a haven, a place of peace in a far from peaceful land. Lovely fresh food taken from the sea, cooked simply and to perfection, eaten in front of an open fire.

Harry knew the risks he was running, but simply didn't care. This young woman simply meant so much to him, though he did not yet know it consciously. If asked he might have admitted desire, lustful and healthy enough, but it was more than this. She had taken an age to choose her food, unaccustomed as she was to such a place. It was obvious she wanted to enjoy the experience, and perhaps was a little afraid of getting it wrong. Harry was in no rush and simply enjoyed watching her. She read and reread the menu. He was delighted by the simple pleasure she took in it, this breaking of bread together.

Finally, she said, "I think I would like to have something I've never had before. What are scallops?"

Harry said, "Why not try them."

"I shall." She said this with conviction. She trusted him.

He ordered what she asked for and joined her in having the same plus the inevitable pint of Guinness, and a small glass of the black stuff for her. The landlord took their order and then had left them to it, and no one else bothered them. The inn was too remote for much custom, even during the early autumn, and there were no more than three or four in that evening. They were not unfriendly but simple common sense dictated that this couple of young love birds should be left to their own company.

She asked him so little about himself. She eventually plucked up courage to ask, quite possibly simply to make sure the talk was not all one sided. She was truth be told, quite happy to sit and listen to him.

"Do you have a place that really matters to you?"

She asked this without artifice. He described his love for Wales, and the mountains, and the little village near Pentrefoelas, Ysbyty Ifan. She had not thought about it at all but now she absorbed that he was not simply English. He was a British soldier. The complexities were not really interesting to her, but she did not accept the nonsense her father and brothers came out with. She didn't want anything to come between her and this man. She simply ignored any other voices.

She repeated the name 'Ysbyty Ifan', and she had a good ear for she had no difficulty getting her tongue around the sounds, and in her Irish-Belfast-Catholic accent it sounded so very much like the way his mother might have spoken it. He found himself telling her the story of Knights of St Johns, the crusaders, and the hospital founded on the banks of the Conwy in Snowdonia where the clean cool waters allowed wounds to be cleaned, and a chance of recovery. She liked to hear of the religious women, some very young, who tended to the wounded. She could see herself in them.

There was so much more to this man certainly than any of the boyfriends she had had. To her he seemed truly exotic, and though she might not have the words for it, oriental even. She lacked experience of everything really, place and travel and men. She knew about Jerusalem, at least as taught in her school and church. It was, she had been taught, the centre of the universe. She was very keen to start life, and to her this was a very good place to begin. For her the centre of her universe was right here with him. She resolved to remember, and treasure it, forever.

Afterwards she was fascinated by the scars she traced over his body with her featherlight touch. She desired him but she did not feel confident she had the right to him. She did not know the hold she had, the power over him she had already established. She did not wish to have power over anyone. She simply lived in the present and left the rest to the devil. So, unknown to him, was his daughter conceived.

TWELVE

Harry heard on the jungle telegraph that the girl had ended up in hospital.

He was not sure what to do. His immediate instinct was to rush to her bedside. But this was Belfast. It might get them both killed, and he was aware rationally that he had to proceed cautiously. When Aoife slipped into his consciousness or in his dreams the question was always there: Why had he not gone? He knew there was no answer that he could muster that would have any moral impact whatsoever.

He simply learnt not to spend time looking over his shoulder. To him it was not a matter of reconciling himself to the past, but simply accepting it had happened and there was nothing he could do about it. He was essentially a practical man.

Harry did not exactly regret losing touch with his former comrades either. It was simply that life happened, and this meant time simply passed, even many years, and reunions, if they took place, were apparently random or attended if convenient. In the early days they were military and more to do with certain skills in short supply that made what looked coincidental more or less inevitable. Harry had so much he wished to forget. He had learnt to spend little time looking over his shoulder. Life had to be lived forwards.

Eventually Harry found himself embedded with some very unlikely company with little connection to his earlier military career, yet he still now and then heard of the exploits of George, the one-man fighting machine with the very odd stare. The tribesmen took Harry to meet the new clan chief. Harry, who had been entrusted with large bags of US dollars, was always more or less welcome, his US minders, less so. Harry's great advantage was patience. He also reckoned there was no need to rush. Time would take care of itself.

He had once watched Lawrence of Arabia as a boy though approaching manhood, and it made a great impression on him. He watched it again and again. He learnt later that Lawrence himself had lost his manuscript *Seven Pillars of Wisdom* on a train at Reading station, just left on a seat, never to be recovered, and so had to set to and rewrite it from scratch. 250,000 words. Was it a better version, a different version? Were all the tales true? So much of it was unverifiable, but some of the more bizarre undoubtedly true and then again, some not. But those arguably contained greater truths.

Harry lodged all this in the back of his mind. It influenced his life greatly and it formed part of his rich hinterland, to be drawn on as each new experience confronted him. Now was one of those times.

Harry rapidly adapted his dress to suit the outer reaches of Afghanistan as it bordered Pakistan. He tried to blend in and this ability was a source of professional pride, but here it was harder. His skin colour helped, and it deepened in the sun and sand and wind of the desert regions. He did not, however, kid himself that he could pass for a native.

Harry sat with the tribal elders. At first a little apart. It was a matter of courtesy as he saw it, and if he were to be accepted at all, it could not be rushed. He could not help but think of it at first rather like 'circle time' in primary school, or 'show and tell'. It was sitting on the low three-legged stools that did it. And the rather silly looking hats they wore. But eventually he began to see it as inherently valuable, and essential to the local community. They retained their childlike appearance and approach, but there was no childishness.

He was older than some of them. He stayed quiet. He listened. He learnt. One advantage in not speaking the language well was that he tended not to speak. This meant he was treated as a man who kept his own counsel. The talk was of al-Qaeda, the Taliban and the other western names, which had no content in reality for these peoples. All that counted here, and had always counted, were ties of blood and adopted blood, forged in the white heat of warfare. It was all a matter of trust, and who you wanted at your right hand when facing your enemy. Harry knew this by experience, just as they knew this, by a way of life that seemed to stretch back to pre-history. It was rumoured that they were descended from Alexander the Great's army which had passed through this way. This was a myth but a story that the tribe were happy to tell themselves. In fact, recent genetic research has tended to support the myth that the Vikings settled here and intermingled with the locals.

Nothing had persuaded these people to fight as one, until the westerner came. This meant in recent times the Russians then the US but also meant the British. The stories were often about the British. History was made by tales told around the campfire here and passed from generation to generation. Harry realised they were talking of conflict over a century ago or more, that meant the first and second Afghan wars. And folk memory went back so very much further. He was told of their lands south of the Amu Darya and west of the Indus River in Pakistan. These people were not Pashtun, as was commonly supposed, very much not Pashtun, and especially not Pathans who speak Pashto, which was a language much disliked locally. The Hindu is and was the ancient enemy but locally, tribal enmity Harry learnt as he had suspected, is a complex matter. He found most people did not travel very far. But what were their origins, Macedonian, Greek, Viking? Did it make any sense to think in these terms?

Harry learnt that the Pashtun may owe their origin to the lost tribes of Israel and were reputed to be descended from Saul and King David. Of course, they were now Sunni Muslims. Perhaps the myths were stories these peoples told themselves without reference to so-called facts, but belief is often stronger than historical truths even if the latter were discoverable. Harry did not underestimate the complexity of the region which had a population, after all, of about 210 million. Harry's enquires revealed that no one knows the true population figures as there has been no reliable census.

Locally, the elders recalled some attempt perhaps fifty years earlier. The old tribal chief told Harry, "When I was a boy, they come."

Harry listened quietly.

But they did not return to Kabul, Harry thought, *perishing no doubt at the hands of those they sought to count.*

The next time they tried there was a similar result. It was rumoured that the appointed emissary and his team decided not to try and carry out their task, and simply made up the figures to satisfy their masters and hopefully live longer. There was no incentive to accuracy. The results were hardly reliable.

National borders meant little and local borders could shift. Most disputes locally were settled without violence, but there was no guarantee. There was little established process beyond the clan meetings. There was not even a set of principles akin to

Sharia law. What represented a border was of course much more to do with established rivers and mountain ranges, a matter of geography.

Harry rapidly understood the official border was merely a useful retreat for any anti-western force. Western forces, as had the Russians before them, discovered that hostiles found haven in what was nominally Pakistan. The response was typical and not really effective. Trying to hunt them down was nigh on useless.

Bombing was attempted but mercifully not locally. Harry found the elders very unimpressed with the bunker-busting bombs that sought to take out the hiding places in the border region. In a way it had nothing to do with them. So long as they were not attacked. Frankly the military planners must have known that the region was simply far to extensive and porous, fed and supported by the more than tacit approval of the Pakistan army. It was obvious, to Harry and the local chiefs, that little of strategic significance could be achieved. Still the carnival of treachery and deceit played on.

It seemed to make little or no difference to the fighting forces, and hardened the attitude of survivors and created new recruits from the next generations, just as the napalm and carpet bombing by the US in Vietnam and Cambodia had created the same useless outcome. Crossing borders provided no refuge. What were borders anyway to the tribes of the Hindu Kush? What impressed Harry was how much the elders of the tribe appreciated all this. They did not care so long as their own peoples were not harmed. The Nuristani were simply hardly understood at all. They were happy to try and stay as neutral as possible and accept any 'compensation' coming their way especially in US dollars.

News had reached the locals of the MOAB, the mother of all bombs. The sheer power of it did make an impression. The Nuristani saw it at best as simply killing hostile forces who might threaten them, but were keen to stay out of it. The tribal elders were resistant to ISIS, and this was reported in simple minded terms by US 'intelligence' as the local Taliban fighting Isis, which was simply not to understand how fragmented these entities were, and how little could be said to unite them.

Gradually Harry was adopted by the Nuristani. These people owed their allegiance such as it was, in theory to the two ancient tribes, who had split many generations earlier over some Lilliputian dispute not now understood by either. Harry reached a kind of status he never would have achieved in his homeland, and he was not at all sure he wanted it here. There was no specific rite of passage or ceremony. He found gradually he was invited to sit nearer the senior elder, and his advice was sought, and not merely on an abstract level.

He was able to tell of what he had read and learnt. They listened. He seemed to offer them some protection from western hostiles. Harry had little or no inclination to inform the 'masters of the carnival' what he had seen and learnt here. He knew it would make no difference and only bring misfortune onto these people.

Harry recognised the harsh magnificent landscapes, and the peoples were similar to those that formed, in his imagination, the poetic backdrop to Lawrence's memoir. The passages where the very troubled young adventurer found peace and a kind of inner calm, accompanied by moments of sudden and extreme violence, resonated deeply with Case, and he really didn't care if some of the very detailed accounts were complete fabrication or not.

He was not a literary critic or a historian, and critical theory left him cold. He was concerned with living his own life, as well as he could. He found no hint in the very lengthy narrative of what the seven pillars might have been. It did lead him back to the Bible and the Book of James. He plucked up the courage one evening to tell the elders of his understanding concerning the seven qualities of pure wisdom.

As usual they sat round on the little stools, and the chatter hushed as Harry spoke falteringly in their own tongue. The evening sky had a purple hue to it as the sun fell, which was not unusual for those parts, but at its edges barely detectable were other colours.

Harry spoke:

"They are nothing more or less than the seven colours of the one ray of heavenly truth which has been revealed and has appeared in Christ himself."

The elders waited and it was more than mere politeness. Their interest was piqued by the holy words. They listened attentively.

Peaceable, gentle, easy to entreat, full of mercy, good fruits without partiality without hypocrisy.

Harry was essentially a modest man. Over time he was emboldened to speak again. It was clear that he already had their respect. His was a new voice but had not come at them hastily or with conceit. This they all saw and duly recognised. Gradually they began to see him as a wise counsel and then more than this, as a kind of shaman, not that he himself ever presumed he had such status or position.

The point of view that most attracted Harry, as it had Lawrence, was the wisdom spoken in the desert by the tribal elders, in particular one Aouda whose words Harry committed to memory.

"Why are the Westerners always wanting all? Behind our few stars we can see God, who is not behind your millions. If the end of wisdom is to add star to star our foolishness is pleasing."

The Nuristani were not simply using the westerner to learn how to combat and survive the intrusion of western forces. They treated him as a human being. They began to accept him into their hearts. The old man, the clan chief, was as a matter of fact, younger than him, though they were almost contemporaries, and the chieftain began over time to rely on him. He delighted in telling Harry his name was Haji, which he thought was Harry to all intents and purposes. Harry asked him about the Taliban, and the old man looked about him as if to check even here that he was not being overheard. He then said something that Harry found very interesting.

"The young know very little and choose violence to have their way. This is the path of ignorance."

It did not occur to Harry, who was a man of few words anyway, that his desire to speak only in their native tongue was going to be so effective. It was unique in their experience that the westerner tried to do this, to relate to them, to live with them to speak to them and listen to them without a translator. It was an easy position for Harry to adopt. He was not there, he reckoned, to teach them anything, but to learn. He had direct conversations almost before he could speak in their language at all. So much of communication he knew is in gesture and attitude, and something much deeper, beyond words.

Of course, at first, he could understand more than he could speak. This was one of the reasons that encouraged him to listen more and with greater intensity. This flattered the speakers, very much to Harry's advantage. They warmed to him and might have done for this reason alone. Many of them knew how hard it was to communicate in a foreign tongue. He had to work hard to find the words he needed, and this made them very carefully crafted. They liked his thoughtfulness and taciturnity.

Harry had with him his own treasured copy of the King James Bible which had been his mother's. It had very thin pages, and was gold embossed. It was written in a beautiful script. When he produced it and read from it to himself, he was observed doing it, and it gave him the appearance of a holy man. He would read from it, whispering the words, committing them to memory. Harry whispered to himself from Proverbs, *He that hath knowledge spareth his words: and a man of understanding is of an excellent spirit.* These were words that had greater impact now on him.

Harry took to going off into the foothills of the mountains, to meditate. Haji would never let him travel alone. He effectively gave him his eldest son, Yusef, as a bodyguard and minder. From the young man, little more than a boy when they first met, he learnt more than he taught. He made good progress with the local dialect and encouraged the boy's interest in learning English and more of western ways.

THIRTEEN

"Hari?"

"Yes."

"Why did you come?"

"I was sent."

"But you stayed."

Harry asked a question back.

"Why do you stay?" Harry asked this knowing the answer.

"What do you mean? This is my home. I have no other."

Harry looked directly at him and said, "Perhaps it can be my home?"

The boy smiled a broad smile.

"You are very welcome Hari."

They sat side by side, the boy who would be a man, and the man who wished to be a child.

"I should like to benefit from your counsel."

This was said with such humility, Harry was rather taken aback.

The boy went on.

"The way of a fool is right in his own eyes: but he that hearkeneth unto counsel is wise. That is from your holy book I believe."

Harry, taken by surprise, but all that time as a boy spent in chapel had not been entirely wasted. He knew it was from the Psalms.

He replied, *"If any of you lack wisdom, let him ask of God, that giveth to all men liberally, and upbraideth not; and it shall be given him."*

And then added, *"But the wisdom that is from above is first pure, then peaceable, gentle, and easy to be intreated, full of mercy and good fruits, without partiality, and without hypocrisy,* and, *Happy is the man that findeth wisdom, and the man that getteth understanding."*

The boy was not unimpressed, and later told everyone of the wise sayings. Perhaps this is where his reputation as a kind of guru found its origins.

As he picked up more of the local dialect, he began to enjoy the elders' meetings. Some of these would be very quiet affairs. Some louder and more argumentative, some truly wild. Some were short and some long, there seemed to be no rules governing these. One redeeming feature was that no rancour was generated, and consensus guided by the senior elders seemed to be the most sought after and desirable outcome.

He was called to one meeting, and with great quiet good grace, was asked to stand by a simple gesture from Haji. In his hand was one of the caps, finely embroidered with colours of gold and red and blue. He asked Harry to lower his head and placed it upon his crown. Harry was to wear it as a mark of his acceptance amongst the elders. Harry thought you didn't need the brains of an archbishop to know this was a very great honour indeed, and noted that the ceremony lasted less than a minute. He doubted the Church back in the home country could manage such a ceremony with such grace and dispatch.

As it was placed on his head the hairs on the back of his neck stood out, and it was if a warm hand ran down his spine. The feeling flowed through his body and to his feet and into the earth under his feet. Harry felt grounded in a way he found hard to capture in words or thoughts.

He overheard the elders one evening talking quietly, and realised he was the subject of the conversation.

"Do you trust him?"

"There have been no attacks on us here since his arrival."

"But do you trust him?"

There was a long pause.

The fire around which they sat flickered and burned. Harry held his breath.

Finally Haji spoke, "I do. He speaks rarely but when he does, he speaks from the soul."

There were general noises of assent and no dissent.

Thus Harry learnt of the regard he was held in and the responsibility that implied.

He determined not to let them down.

FOURTEEN

One day a man was dragged into the encampment. He stood in the circle and then fell onto his knees. He clearly thought his number was up. His face was a bit of a mess – that is his nose was at a very odd angle to one side clearly broken. There was blood on his face perhaps from the nose or perhaps blows to the head. He had taken quite a beating. One arm hung uselessly to his side. He held his head down, as if in supplication. He probably believed his end had come and he had accepted his fate. What else could he do?

He was Pashtun, from Kabul, and he had been found with one of the villagers. Her name was unpronounceable to Harry but sounded a bit like 'Eila'. She was undoubtedly attractive by almost any aesthetic, even given the local 'standards' which were very high. These after all were the very people chosen by the Nazis as a kind of urtext Aryan folk. Harry had read somewhere that twenty of them were brought back to Germany as breeding stock. The westerner again showing moral bankruptcy.

Harry knew immediately that her life was in danger for this act of adultery. He stood up from his stool, which was quite a journey since they all sat on those low stools. Harry was glad they didn't tend to sit cross legged on the ground, as rising may have been even more undignified and as near as impossible. Haji nodded. This was the first time Harry had done this.

"You wish to speak, brother?"

Harry had learnt that to the tribe payment could alleviate the trespass or sin. This had its origins in the difficulty in establishing any property ownership in such hostile environs. This had been the case since time immemorial or certainly as long as anyone could remember. Thus, compensation was preferred in moveable property, and in modern terms, in dollars. This could seem mercenary and sometimes this did indeed create a problem as it tended to encourage trumped up allegations, no doubt seeking to extract payment. The payment used, not so long ago, was typically in cattle. Harry offered to pay the compensation in dollars. When the woman realised what Harry intended, she threw herself at his feet.

Haji asked the woman, "Do you wish to stay or leave?"

"Stay, stay, oh please, please, let me stay."

"You cannot stay with this man." Haji pointed to the Pashtun.

The woman begged for him to be spared.

Harry spoke up.

"I will take him back to Kabul." He knew that otherwise there was a good chance he would simply be executed. Even to think he might be escorted back by tribesmen was rather fanciful.

Haji, after a brief pause, nodded his assent.

"You, what is your name?"

She looked up and stared directly at Harry.

"Eiela."

"You must serve this man. It is a great honour for you. Hari is without woman."

And so, it was settled.

There was so much to Harry's life in the village that he found easier than anywhere else, but there was much more to it than this. It was of course the mutual respect and more than that, love from all the tribe that was nourishing him. The place itself was only part of the story.

He especially liked the slow pulse of day which led without any hurry into the evening, and sunset, and then eventually the wonder of the night sky. The night sky, without light or any other kind of pollution. The night sky as revealed to man when he first walked the earth and is only known to people who live simply in remote places or to seafarers who leave the sight of land. It was no accident that three of the world's great religions were born in places such as this.

Harry could give one reason beyond all others that confirmed he was in the right place for him. He found he could breathe here.

Harry loved mountains. He remembered his mother's home and the farm with Snowden in the distance, and he had learnt to climb at Capel Curig. He was also used to the Alps, climbing some seriously challenging peaks, but the mountains here were something else again. The high snow-capped peaks some over 25,000 feet to the east and to the north, and the land seemed to buttress the Pamir mountains where the borders of China, Pakistan, and Afghanistan meet.

On this evening Harry sought to capture in the moment and in his memory, those hills their shape uncertain in the dusky light yet now so very familiar unchanging yet yielding nothing to stasis. They have a colour in the darkening that is not of this world, or at least any other place Harry had experienced, a kind of lilac hue as if a great artist with an immense pallet but a simple mind, had chosen just this shade of purple, constant yet ephemeral. Harry did not tend to romanticise. He was a realist. Nevertheless, he felt the mind in a moment seeking to capture the eternal but doomed to failure.

And yet it was here Harry found peace and acceptance of

what was beyond human understanding.

Shantih shantih shantih.

"And peace be with you, my friend." Harry heard a quiet voice, Haji was sitting close by, unheard by Harry. But this voice came from he knew not where precisely. The Sanskrit greeting found its response.

The thing was, Harry was certain he had not in fact spoken the words out loud at all but simply brought them into his mind.

As they sat together waiting for the sun to fall looking out across the valley, the light turning from gold to lilac, the air moved, and did so invisibly and a kind of caressing breeze touched Harry's face. He became aware of a small plant in flower, tiny white petals by his feet, and he plucked it up and held it before his eyes and then folded it into his palm and handed it to Haji, childlike as if he were offering his greatest treasure to his friend.

Harry had found that every time there was a visit from a US military or diplomatic person, trouble followed. He began to find reasons to avoid these for himself and the local people. He was difficult to contact, always on a fact-gathering mission and certainly was 'not there' even when he obviously was. He became unavailable for any liaison with US or UK forces.

His father would be asked when gardening at home in 'gawd blimey' trousers as Harry's mother called them, if the major was home. He always answered 'No', even though he was standing before them, unseen so to speak. Harry was not 'at home' for his minders.

He was not embedded now so much as forgotten by his paymasters, the 'masters of the carnival'. He suspected he was not even regarded as a sleeper. Harry had no idea if he was even being paid any more. He did not check in. The satellite phone had been left by Harry unanswered now for many months or was it years. It was kept charged up by the solar panel. It was still there, dug in next to Harry's tent.

Back in Kabul he was reported missing, and then assumed dead. No one asked for him from England or anywhere else. He eventually slipped off the radar. Eventually it was assumed he had been killed and this is what was reported back to British secret services, who were no doubt relieved. It was felt, if he went rogue, which was always possible in his masters' eyes, he would become a one-man walking liability given all he knew. No news of Harry Case was good news. Even better would be news of his death.

FIFTEEN

There was a buzz of excitement in the village. The young men were gathering, and some kind of selection process was taking place. A raid had been proposed. The old man asked Harry to go along. It was obvious why he wanted this. The raid was to be led by his son.

Haji's second son was an Adonis with unusually blond hair. This was very rare and believed to be a gift from Allah. He had liked Harry from the first day he had arrived. The boy was only a youngster then, perhaps fifteen years old. His name was Muhammed.

Harry felt himself too old for this kind of thing. He surveyed the hills in front of him with his bino's. The little band of marauding Nuristani could have been part of Alexander's troops, but for the modern weaponry. Harry had made sure they had seriously up to date rifles, lightweight and effective. He also took along the two-man team he had trained to use the GPMG. Otherwise, they were armed to the teeth with traditional weaponry, daggers and knives. It was no accident that almost all fighting forces over the centuries had avoided fighting the Nuristani. Even the Russians, the British, Attila, Genghis.

Their plan was two of their number to herd some goats brought from the village, and simply walk into the enemy encampment. Who was there, no one was sure but probably a very hated figure from the Nuristani perspective. The Nuristanis disliked almost everyone including Pashtun Afghans but even more they disliked Arabs. There were very complicated reasons for this and Harry was only beginning to scratch the surface of the nuances. Any pretext seemed enough so it was not always clear if it was simply the desire for the fight, any fight, that brought it about.

al-Qaeda leaders were said to be in the rather more built-up village meeting local Taliban leaders. Harry ought to have called this in but simply decided it would cause more trouble than it would prevent. Why not let this low-key assault do its work?

Afterwards of course he wished he had not tried to act alone. Professor Hindsight, that great teacher, that bloody know-it-all. He also knew they were going in 'on a wing and a prayer' as they had not done any reconnaissance and had no up-to-date intelligence, just rumour and local knowledge. Harry had serious misgivings. To their advantage they knew the settlement pretty well, and had traded with the local people. It seemed small compensation to Harry for the foolishness being displayed.

What these people enjoyed more than anything was traditional hand to hand fighting. In modern warfare it is difficult to get close enough. Their fieldcraft learnt from birth meant they could, like the Gurkha as Harry had learnt, arrive right on top of their enemy without being spotted if the terrain allowed it.

They got in all right. The plan seemed to be working at first but it did not survive contact with the enemy. The forces were so much greater than had been anticipated, confirming that this indeed was an important gathering.

The herding of goats into the village was not unusual, but rapidly the extra security provided for the meeting or conference or whatever it might have been called, meant they were challenged before they could do any damage.

He first heard the gunfire, then like so many retreating ants, through his bino's he observed his young men scurrying out as fast as they could.

Across the terrain where Harry could observe the situation, no vehicle could follow. This was very fortunate as the Toyotas were in full pursuit, three of them. Taliban? al-Qaeda? Certainly hostile. They sped down the track sending up clouds of dust. Each was packed with fighting men. Harry through his bino's reckoned each had at least six in maybe more, no doubt angry warriors, who were not seeking to take prisoners, or if they were it would be the last thing you would want, better death than that. Harry knew that little had changed. In the Afghan wars British soldiers were taught to keep one bullet for themselves to evade capture and the horrors that would inevitably follow, before death.

Harry had his machine gun set up, and hoped the training he had done with the two young men next to him would prove good enough. It was the first time they had fired it in anger. Ammunition was short so Harry controlled it.

Harry's demonstration of the weapon had started with a short lecture,

"The L7A2 General Purpose Machine Gun (GPMG) is a 7.62mm x 51mm belt-fed general purpose machine gun which can be used as a light weapon and in a sustained fire (SF) role. In the SF role, mounted on a tripod and fitted with the C2 optical sight, it is fired by a two-man team. In SF mode, the GPMG can lay down 750 rounds-per-minute at ranges up to 1800 metres.

The GPMG can be carried by foot soldiers and employed as a light machine gun (LMG). A fold-out bipod is used to support the GPMG in the LMG role."

And here he paused and looked at the two young men who had volunteered to be instructed, and whose excited faces indicated that their interest went far beyond the average recruit Harry had instructed in the British Army.

"Normally you would be grouped in a specialist machine gun platoon to provide battalion-level fire support.

But here we have only one. You will learn to know it intimately, to love it, to take care of it as your best friend. To guard it with your life. To take it apart and put it back together in the dark, when cold or in the heat of the day."

Harry knew how to train men and had done his work well. He had willing students and they practised and practised without the need for any prompting at all until they had reached the standard Harry demanded and he felt they really could be trusted, in terms of handling the weapon at least.

He had his own rifle equipped with an underslung grenade launcher, and again he waited till there were clear targets.

As the pursuing vehicles came to rest in a swirl of dust and sand, and the enemy began to leap out, he indicated they should fire. So far so good. They had not fired till ordered. They had shown good discipline. They might still come out of this well if they were efficient and especially only fired when it was effective. This meant drawing the enemy towards the killing field.

The position of Harry's little section was near perfect, and his relatively inexperienced compatriots did not let him down. The enemy were in the open, and seemed unaware of how vulnerable they were, more or less milling about in open ground in range of the well-trained defenders. They killed or injured perhaps more than half of the enemy in seconds. The bursts of machine gun very rapidly did their job.

The attackers were now not so sure, and simply lacked clear leadership. They should have dispersed, set up sectional attacks, with firepower being met with fire and attempt to suppress the enemy or win the firefight. All this lot did was start to move about more or less at random in a panicky manner. Obviously they needed to decide whether to continue the attack, or to withdraw, which was something they would not usually contemplate. The fact was they had no clear idea of what they were facing. They had reason to fear determined defence supported by western forces.

The withdrawing section had retired in good order and taken up a firing position over a small ridge and began themselves to engage the attackers. Unwisely the Taliban or whoever they were threw caution to the winds and tried a frontal assault up the hill towards the ridge where hostile fire was now taking its toll of victims.

The thing about high velocity bullets meeting their target that is not commonly understood by the civilian is that they easily can go through double brick thick walls. Meeting soft tissue sinew and bone, the effect is far from comical. Bits of body are simply blown off the target, blood and muscle splattered everywhere without discrimination, bones are shattered, creating an artistic effect as fountains of blood spurt from the dead and the dying. Skulls are smashed, brain mass and fluid sprays in all direction, and sometimes bullets enter more cleanly but burst out from the rear leaving holes which a fist would not fill.

The grenade when it explodes is not a matter of a high explosive going off nearby as is commonly believed, lethal though this could be. It sends shards of steel spinning into the enemy cutting them to pieces.

It is literally death by a thousand cuts.

The foolish but admirably brave charge up the hill had presented Harry's machine gun section with the perfect opportunity. They waited till the hostiles were halfway up the rise, and presented themselves in enfilade to the machine gun and Harry's rifle. Harry began to launch grenades at those who had thrown themselves to the ground seeking cover, scrabbling along the rough ground, twisting and turning in panic. It was not a good look especially after they met the lethal response of Harry's little army. Those who survived saw the slicing and dicing effect of the grenades, close to and graphic and the bullets continued the remorseless slaughter. Still the enemy presented a threat as the more experienced enemy found enough cover to begin firing at close quarters.

Haji's son, Muhammed, then made a brave decision. He saw his moment. He charged down the hill with his band of brothers, and this was enough to make the enemy – at least the few who were still able – decide to run.

Then Harry spotted an ominous danger. As if in slow motion, the driver of one of the Toyotas, who had stayed with the vehicles, appeared from the blind side, raised his rifle and took aim and fired. The bullet hit its target and Muhammed went down. Harry leapt up without thinking ran down the hill, picked him up in a fireman's lift and carried him over the rise.

He lay panting on his back having gently laid his load down.

"I knew I was too old for this sort of thing," he muttered to himself.

He peered over the rise. The cries of the wounded were not pleasant. To his great relief the Toyotas had driven off.

The boy's leg was keening blood. He was being very brave and made no sound. Harry tied a tourniquet and injected a phial of morphine. He rigged a stretcher, and arranged the lads into teams, much as he had done at Sandhurst in training all those years before. And they ran their casualty back to the village.

Harry carried the boy off the stretcher, for that is all he was, into his own tent and dressed his wounds himself. He used his personal morphine to bring him relief.

A little later, the boy's mother, for he was not yet really a man, appeared outside Harry's tent. She looked wretched, her face contorted and her mouth a grimace.

She waited permission to enter. Harry beckoned her in. The only nursing she could offer was traditional and not terribly sanitary. Harry tried to explain that her son needed antibiotics and not just the pain relief that the local poppy could provide. The objection was the use of needles but Haji intervened, and encouraged by Yousef, told her that she could trust Hari. Muhammed's pain was so very great that his pride fell away and he simply began to howl. At that his mother relented, Harry injected more morphine and the boy calmed somewhat, and Harry administered the antibiotics.

He taught them how to keep his wounds clean and to bandage them effectively.

Muhammed's life hung in the balance. He had lost a lot of blood. Three days and nights the internal battle raged. The mother never left his side, wetting his lips and comforting him as best she could. But then the fever fell and Muhammed was past the worst of it.

The boy did not die. As with all young men his recovery would prove almost miraculous. A wound to be proud of – and show it off he did – and slight limp were the only long-term consequences.

Later the old woman came to him.

"You will allow me to wash your feet."

It was not a question.

Haji approached Harry and stood next to him and then took both Harry's hands in his own, and bowed and kissed them, each of them in turn, and then he looked into Harry's eyes, and uttered a prayer for the living. His son had been saved, by an act of God, and by Hari.

After his feet were washed and dried, Harry stood up and walked barefoot out of his tent.

No other youngster from the village had been hurt.

It was clear that the whole village wanted to honour Hari. They had formed a kind of guard of honour, a pathway through which he passed, each one gently touching his hands as he passed. Harry carried on walking. They made no attempt to follow him. They readily understood his need to be alone.

As he walked away from the village on the oft travelled path, he began to feel the warm sand beneath his feet, and his feet were untroubled by the rough earth. He had grown the kind of thick skin that all the villagers had acquired. He wandered towards the ridge towards the same spot he had sat and meditated so very often on the human condition. He looked out towards the mountains that he now felt were his own, like old friends. They bounded the valley to the east, and the river which founded the possibility of a more settled existence, including now perhaps his own.

He sat for some indeterminate time on the same spot looking out into the valley until night fell. He felt the warmth of the earth disappearing and the still surprising rapid fall in temperature. He eased himself upright and returned to the village.

When he reached his tent he found a vision of beauty standing at its entrance, lit by the fire the tribe had built for him.

She had been sent by Haji.

She was rather wraith-like, and of a lighter coloured skin

than the generality found locally. Long hair tied in a complex pattern behind her back. It reached her waist. Not young not old. Harry found he was being stared at, and her stare was itself a sight to behold, her eyes were huge and a deep, deep brown, with jet black pupils like inkwells. This was Haji's daughter.

She lay with him.

They spoke very little.

After it was over, when she had served his needs, she left almost as if she had not been there at all. Harry realised, perhaps a little late, that he now had two wives.

He lay on his back. Staring at the sky and then closed his eyes to rest them. He was at peace. He fell into a deep sleep. He dreamed of Aoife in another time and another place though the distinctions in his mind between this dream and the present reality, were lost.

Suddenly he was awake. The satellite phone was ringing. A call diverted from the UK. It was a call from George's phone.

After the call, Harry made rapid arrangements to leave, saying only that his brother was in trouble and needed him. This explanation was all that Haji and his people needed.

He set off with two armed men from the village, Haji's best, and so he began his journey back to England.

The phone on the desk rang. It was one of those old-fashioned black phones, which you might find these days in a bric-a-brac store. The desk was not in an office officially sanctioned by the government. It was in a shabby part of Vauxhall. Outside the offices were signs giving hardly any information about the activities inside. An Inland Revenue tax office which never saw any tax officers. Now and then an innocuous looking civil servant type would come in or leave. It housed as a matter of fact a lesser-known section of the security services.

The senior man was behind his desk, not in uniform. A rather vulgar pinstripe, Thieves and Sharks no doubt, and a guard's tie.

"Colonel?"

"Yes."

"Harry Case."

There was a slight pause. The colonel shifted his buttocks slightly and emitted a small fart. His club chef was to blame, not that he really cared.

"Yes?"

"He has just boarded a flight from Kabul to Heathrow."

"Have we eyes on him?"

"We will have."

"See that you do. Keep me informed."

SIXTEEN

Harry woke unusually for him rather earlier than he had intended. It was not the fault of the bed in the Travelodge. He had slept in far more uncomfortable billets. He could have simply turned over and commanded himself to go back to sleep. He allowed himself a small indulgence, and opened his mind to the dream world of the night just passed. He recalled the night sky, the Milky Way as ancient man must have seen it, pristine in unpolluted dark, the sky as he had found it in the far-off place which he had made his home. He considered the need for more sleep, decided it was unnecessary and stretched his arms. He went through his morning routine the most interesting feature of which perhaps was, given his age, how intense it was.

The stretching from top to toe was over in less than two minutes, the push ups were rapid and strongly conducted. Harry never counted how many, simply going till he could do no more than adding an extra five. More flex exercises and abdominals followed. The whole performance was over in twenty minutes. He had refined this into the three-minute burn every day and the longer one, which this was, every second day, and a day of rest. He had designed these exercises from pre-military days through everything the army PTIs had insisted on, the specialist training, the serious sporting endeavours where every kind of coach had their own regimes and advice. He knew what worked for him. He was very fortunate. Recent research showed that only a limited proportion of people could stay fit on such a meagre exercise routine, but some like him needed no more.

Harry always felt his time was too valuable to waste on gyms and extended exercise regimes. His body was a testament to his opinion, as even though there was arthritis and some pain, he was very fit. Fit for what is the real test. Fit to fight. In some ways on that test, he was fitter than ever. He had physical and mental fitness, and experience, and skills adapted to age. He never rushed for its own sake. Efficiency was his watch word.

Text from Fergie. It read, **Rv cenotaph Harrogate 11:00 hrs.**

Time for breakfast. And a think.

Fergie's text was admirably correct and concise. Apart perhaps from the 'Rv' rather than 'RV'. *Quick learner,* thought Harry.

He did not need to have seen Fergie to imagine him, squinting at the tiny screen, stabbing with his fingers and swearing, under his breath, the mobile miniscule in his enormous hand.

Rv not Tv, and then capital R capital V, not Rv.

For fuck's sake! Harry imagined Fergie responding vocally to the difficulties of the older man trying to text, especially on an unfamiliar phone.

Harry surmised that he finally managed to produce something usable and sent it on the basis that it would have to do. The phone was probably lucky to survive as there could be little doubt Fergie would have been tempted to beat it into submission.

Harry made the rendezvous with a good ten minutes to spare, and there was Fergie striding towards him. Clearly, he had obeyed the military ten-minute rule himself. They sat on a bench nearby, quite inconspicuous amongst the many generally rather elderly population of the town. Harry seemed to recall reading somewhere that it had come out on top in some Sunday newspaper profile as 'the best place to retire in Britain'.

"Why are we here then Fergie?"

"Seemed right enough. I reckon I ken where he was attacked. And it's on the route from where he lives to the Legion through town."

"Right, Macduff, lead on."

Harry was well aware of the true quotation and its import. It was, of course, an invitation to join battle. "Let slip the dogs of war," Harry added somewhat needlessly. He wondered if they were about to retrace George's last steps.

"Ye can drop the f'ing Shakespeare, laddie. I'm no' in the mood."

He strode off in the direction of town, and then dipped down past the back of Marks and Spencer's, where there were some bins to be found and no obvious way through.

"You can get through at the end," indicated Fergie with a huge extended finger.

It was an odd snicket narrowing to a path that led towards The Stray. It was no more than two man's width although over the wall at the end were some flats and other domestic buildings and then it opened out onto the sward. The unwary might not have sensed any danger at all. There was some graffiti, '*abandan hope*' misspelt. '*Welcome to Hell*'. Harry was unimpressed muttering 'comedian' under his breath. He began to look more carefully as he could see one or two syringes on the ground, and the paraphernalia that was easily associated with smoking skunk, and then some used condoms on the ground at the back of the bins. An old, abandoned sleeping bag was lying on the ground behind one of the larger ones. No one resident.

Harry could see the wall was scuffed, and it even became

obvious where someone had fallen. George? On closer examination some spattered blood on the wall already grown faint, and at the base of the wall, more blood which had taken on an oddly greyish hue. Further scuff marks which Harry was quick to read. At least one heavy foot and the other being used to kick out. And then again and again, in Harry's imagination at least, he could see George's head being kicked in, his now weakening attempts to fight back. Growing futile. Too many of them. Not as strong as he once was, far from it. Put up more of a fight than they had expected perhaps. Infuriated them. Definitely more than one of them. His friend being beaten down, his arms now limp by his side, not even protecting his head. There had been little damage to George's hands.

The snicket was not particularly alarming looking, especially in daylight, and as if to prove it here came a mother with a pram making her way through which meant Harry and Fergie had to turn sideways out of the way. She thanked them cheerfully enough.

Fergie had moved on further up the path and made a find of his own. Here was George's walking stick or rather one broken end of it. He gestured to Harry who came over and stared at the broken piece of wood in Fergie's hand.

"Maybees he went down fighting doont you think?"

Harry's thoughts were similarly speculative, but he could not avoid them. Perhaps the stick had been broken over his friend's back as this feeble attempt to use it as a weapon was wrested from his grasp and turned back on him, perhaps for not taking his medicine or protesting or daring to fight back. He did not share these thoughts with Fergie, seeking to protect him. He knew really that this was useless as Fergie was no fool and would form his own conclusions. Harry could feel his friend's usual calm unruffled demeanour, very much disturbed, as his own heart rate rose.

He was a bit surprised to see coming towards them a perfectly innocent looking little old lady with a west highland terrier who was using the snicket as a short cut. No doubt many did who knew the area. It annoyed Harry somehow that everyday life simply went on and no one even knew that this was where his friend had been attacked. She hurried past as Fergie made himself as small as he could. He still presented a substantial obstacle notwithstanding his best efforts, with barely enough room to pass. The attack was certainly not deterring anyone from using this pathway, and during daylight perhaps it was not what it might turn into once darkness fell.

Of course, George had used it that night, but then he had used it no doubt many times before without mishap. It was on his way home. He had nothing to fear.

Fergie murmured, almost as if sharing a guilty secret, "I never went with him you ken."

"What do you mean?"

There was quite a pause, and then Fergie drew in a longer breath as if in preparing to speak, he really needed one.

"He never wanted me to walk home with him, I'm not sure why. I never thought there was any real danger to him. I never thought," and here Fergie's voice took on a strained pitch, "I just never thought…"

And here his voice faltered.

"I know," Harry murmured, "I know," trying to reassure him.

Harry was keen to give Fergie a practical task which might serve to distract their minds from this train of thought.

"Can you see over that wall there?"

"Aye," and then he spotted it. It was George's wallet lying on the other side of the wall in a small car parking area.

Fergie said, "I know it's his even though I hardly saw it of an evening, ye ken?"

This poor joke fell flat. But the attempt at humour indicated that Fergie was back on task. Harry was impressed as he heaved himself effortlessly onto the top of the wall, held out a hand for Harry and pulled him up beside him, as if he weighed nothing at all, and they each lowered themselves gently down.

Harry picked up the wallet with Fergie leaning over his shoulder, and he revealed it was empty except for an old receipt from a supermarket, a dry-cleaning ticket and in an inner pocket a Yale key. Nothing else at all. Harry put the wallet and the receipt and ticket and the key into his pocket, and the two of them after a last scan of the immediate area, simply walked away.

"Harry?"

He looked at Fergie and waited for his question.

"Why didna the polis question the paramedic and others who might have found him?"

"I don't know Fergie. I don't know."

"I'll bet they didna interview anyone or ask any question locally, in these flats for instance or whether anyone had heard or seen anything.

"He just didn't rate Harry. He just didna matter at all," Fergie said bitterly.

There was no evidence of any police attention. No indication, for instance, that the police were treating the area as a crime scene. Harry felt that Fergie had this completely right and that it was unacceptable. It seemed likely no attempt had been made to find witnesses, or to gather evidence. No doubt it fell into the kind of case marked 'don't try too hard and resources need not be employed', by some desk-bound apparatchik.

"Well good," said Harry to himself. So be it. His face had that hard and determined look that indicated he was now in mission mode. And where Harry went Fergie was sure to be nearby.

Harry and Fergie parted at the end of the alleyway. Harry told Fergie he would be in touch with a plan. Fergie was sensitive enough to know when Harry needed time alone, and that he preferred to plan on his own.

"Alreet, laddie, you be sure to run it past me first now wont ye. Don't be tempted to go it alone."

Harry looked up at Fergie and nodded.

"I mean it, laddie."

"George's address would be handy."

"Right ye are. I'll be working on tha'."

Harry watched him lope off and disappear in no time at all round the corner, in the direction of the Legion.

SEVENTEEN

Harry walked through to the end of the alleyway where it opened out onto a patch of open ground that the developers had forgotten and perhaps the town planners had decided belatedly to protect. Here were the typically impressive mature broad leaf trees common to the wider Stray, and stone walls demarcating the houses built at various periods. It was all so bloody pleasing, so pleasant, so smug.

There was a rather incongruous higher rise block of flats which looked like it had been built in the sixties. Not on the scale of developments in major cities as part of slum clearance and a better life in a land 'fit for heroes', but rather more expensively built. Harry reckoned from the view he had, which was admittedly only of the upper floors beyond the immediate houses backing onto this small parkland area, that it would not have many socially deprived residents. On one side was a fence to rather older houses, and a very odd-looking bungalow at one end, on slightly raised land. Maybe someone had seen something from the very large window that looked out onto the area immediately before the alleyway.

He was keen not to draw attention to himself. But he had to gather intel if he could. He decided to take the chance. He made his way to the front door. He pushed the button marked 'press'. No sound. It probably wasn't working. He rapped gently on the door which had opaque glass allowing light into the hallway. He could make out a figure approaching from inside.

A face appeared. A very elderly face. Piercing blue eyes. No doubt that all the 'lights' were on. She opened the door somewhat wider.

She looked Harry up and down. Harry made himself as unthreatening as he could and proffered a smile. She must have liked what she saw because she offered a curl of the upper lip, which might have passed for a smile, though it was difficult to be sure, in return.

Harry in dulcet tones, "Sorry to disturb you."

"You're not."

Harry got straight to it. He surmised this might work best. It did.

"My friend was hurt, beaten up just there." Harry pointed.

She looked at him quizzically.

"Last week," he added.

"I know. I saw it all."

"From here?" asked Harry.

He knew full well she had only a limited view from where they were standing.

"No, of course not. From my living room window," and she pointed down the hallway.

"Through there," she told him.

Harry nodded in what he hoped was an encouraging manner.

"Do you want to see?" You might think she was offering something improper, and Harry surmised she was very happy to have his attention.

"Yes please," said Harry.

"In you come then. Wipe your feet." She could have been addressing a small child.

Harry complied.

He was rewarded by the expansive view from the window

especially as the bungalow was on raised ground.

She gestured with a sweep of her hand presenting the whole vista that lay in clear view before them.

"I heard them too." She pointed to the upper window which was open. "I like fresh air.

He fought the little fuckers. Got more than they bargained for didn't they."

Harry was impressed by the entirely appropriate use of the Anglo Saxon.

"Swung his stick like a sword. This kept them off for a bit but he tired you see. They got him down in the end, and started kicking him. One lad in particular seemed to go berserk. The others tried to pull him off. Then ran leaving the one larger lad behind.

He kept saying, 'It's your own fault. It's your own fault. Stupid old bastard, stupid old bastard."

"Was he still kicking him?"

"Yes. Each word. If he wasn't wearing those silly white shoes they all wear I think he would not have survived at all."

"Silly white shoes?"

"You know, trainers. What do they call them?"

"Designer?" offered Harry.

"That's it, with the big tick on 'em." And then she managed to demonstrate with altogether surprising athleticism, kicking out, 'Stupid', and again, 'Old', and finally 'Bastard'. She said this last expletive with a kind of rasping snarl.

"I heard one of them call

'Come on Bosey or Boosey' or some stupid nickname. I mean no one is called that are they? Then he walked away."

"Walked you say?"

"Yes almost running, with his head down. You know like it

was stuffed into his hoodie."

"I called the police."

"What did they do?"

"What do you think? Nothing. Of course."

"Why do you say of course?"

"I have reported the druggies over and over again. They just ignore me."

Harry thanked her and took his leave. He felt slightly sick. She offered him a cup of tea, but Harry could see it was not really what she wanted to do, and he certainly didn't want one. She was already edging towards the door. She let him out. He stood outside for a moment and breathed in and out trying to regularise his heartbeat which was racing. His vitals settled and he was able to walk away.

EIGHTEEN

The pathway led from another route into town, with a small sign for the railway station, which Harry knew was only a short walk away. Harry sat on a convenient park bench where he could see the alleyway, and felt it was far enough away not to arouse suspicion or even interest. He was just one bloke past middle age certainly, and therefore largely invisible especially to the young. He was able to stake out the locus in quo hiding in plain view, which was something of a talent Harry had used all his life.

Anyone who cared to look at his face might have noticed a look of grim determination. If anyone took the trouble to scrutinise him they might not have assumed that he was a harmless old man past his sell by date.

He let his mind wander which was he had found the best way to pass the time when all that might happen was nothing at all. He wanted to allow his mind to absorb what he had just heard. Could have done with the Walkman, as he had not adjusted to using a mobile phone as a source of music listening.

He watched people go by. He was amazed how many people especially youngsters had ear plugs stuffed in their ears. He had seen it on his recent flight home and at the airport. Of course, even in the remote regions Harry was used to operating in, there was some modern technology including satellite phones and so on but not technology ubiquitous as a source of entertainment. Really, he had no idea of how modern life, in the old country at any rate, functioned.

Harry walked through the alleyway again and onto the small patch of parkland. He noted the mature trees, the new planting, the well-tended grassland, the quality of the housing, not perhaps of the first rank but owner occupied, not much rental, expensive cars. Harry wondered how they afforded it all. He sat down on a park bench, where he could again observe the alleyway, and settled in to observe and wait. He was not conspicuous. He had already noted that Harrogate had its share of older male residents, no doubt lonely old buggers with no woman in their lives, or friends, and he looked just like another of those hunkered down into his coat and collar, an old man with nothing to do and not valued very much either. Certainly, as Harry knew, such people were invisible to the young and to most people, or certainly not very interesting. He sat slightly hunched over and allowed his mind to settle and then allowed it to wander again like an old dog who was half asleep yet still alert.

Harry had had a dog which he had called George in honour of his comrade, a jack russell who went with him everywhere. It amused him to tell George to sit and he sat. George the old soldier hardly ever did as he was told. Truth be known neither did the terrier. The dog had some similar characteristics to his old mate. Provided no one bothered him, or presented aggressively, all would be well. Any hound or human who failed to approach George in a friendly manner or at least without aggression got a lot more than they bargained for. For their age neither dog nor owner was in their prime, but their virility was still very much in evidence. This and a surprising capacity for violence, sometimes got both of them in trouble.

That alsatian who had attacked them, was it the man or the dog who first displayed aggression, it was hard to tell but George took evasive action and then decided the best form of defence was attack. It was not funny really watching a very large undoubtedly vicious dog running around with the much smaller terrier attached to the underside of its neck. It was not clear who the victim was, as the alsatian shook its head furiously. The small white terrier swung to-and-fro and eventually the big dog tried to dislodge him by rolling onto the ground.

George wisely did not let go, and if anything increased his grip. The owner of the alsatian was shouting something incoherent and lurched in an ungainly manner towards the combatants. Harry sensibly hung back, and rather half-heartedly commanded George to leave, but then with increasing urgency shouted 'leave', as it became clear that the alsatian was more than merely losing the battle but might not survive. Objectively judged the smaller dog had taken defensive action. George was never going to let go, as he was not stupid, and he was after all only doing what came naturally to him and his breed.

The dog's owner was a bull-headed, no-neck pit bull type, who looked like he would not approve, to say the least, of the likely outcome, so when eventually George did let go as the alsatian sank to its knees bleeding copiously from its neck, Harry could not help taking pleasure in his dog dancing around taking a few more bites out of the larger animal's hind quarters. As Harry and George then beat a hasty withdrawal he could not resist saying to his brave little companion, "Well done, Georgie, well done."

Harry wished he had the little dog with him now but of course even though he lived to a good age they cannot live for ever. Harry was not given to existential gloom but he could not shake off an uneasy feeling, a sort of foreboding, that on this mission things were perhaps not going to end well. His mood reflected a kind of fatalism that became his abiding emotion.

His mind wandered further, and he saw in his mind's eye the girl, Aoife. He murmured her name, and it was as if she was with him, her smell so sweet, her red hair, those lips, the shape of her thighs, the tight waist, the womanly breasts under the tight-fitting dress both demur and revealing. As ever he was taken by surprise specially by how vivid the memory was and even more by how he tended to welcome these thoughts. *What were they? Hallucinations?*

There was not much more to be seen and he called it a day and went back to his billet. He went straight to his bed following his usual routine, and found as usual which given the detail he now possessed of the vicious attack on his friend, might have been somewhat surprising that sleep did not evade him.

In the half light, between the night and dawn, with his mind in freefall, the morning after the night before at the Smuggler's Inn came into his mind unbidden. He welcomed the memory.

The first morning light had been enough to awaken them. She had responded once again to his attentions, willingly and with abandon. Afterwards, they must have dropped off into a deep slumber. He remembered going down to breakfast without her and the radio being on, which he would not normally pay much attention to but the music programme, probably Radio 2 as it was playing innocuous popular music was interrupted by a news flash.

He was shocked by what he heard on the radio. Who wasn't? Only the criminally insane. The real world entered *sans merci*. It was on the news. A small fishing boat had been blown up, killing Mountbatten and other innocent lives, including Mountbatten, one of his twin grandsons, Nicholas, aged just fourteen and Paul

Maxwell, just fifteen who was a local employed as a boat boy.

Later Harry learnt that the bomb had been planted by the IRA. Who else? No warning was issued. An elderly passenger also injured, Baroness Brabourne 82, died the day after the attack.

Harry rushed up the stairs, woke Aoife, and told her what he had learnt in a few words. She accepted he had to leave her behind. She reassured him that she would be fine, that she understood.

"Go, go," she urged.

He left her all his cash, to be sure it was enough for a taxi to the nearest station.

It was a long wait for her, for the bus. She never wasted money. It was a bit of a comedown after the glamour of her trip with Harry. But she didn't mind. She kept Harry inside her from that night on, and he never left her, at least in her imagination.

Harry drove as fast as he reasonably could back to Stormont. He was ushered into the general without further ceremony or briefing.

"Where the hell have you been Harry?"

"On leave," said Harry not unreasonably.

"Well, you need to get out to Sligo. The place is called Mullaghmore. You are my liaison with the local police. You can use my staff car and my driver. He should be there now, ready and waiting. You can go in mufti."

Harry waited. He sensed there was more.

"What has been done is simply beyond the pale, unacceptable. There must be a response."

Harry nodded.

"Off you go then."

Harry said nothing, and simply left closing the large door behind him. He loped outside and found the staff car waiting. His driver was not the chatty sort or having the general to drive about meant he had learnt to keep his mouth shut. This was a relief to his passenger.

He was aware that he was returning back along the road he had just come from. He was unable to switch into rest mode, and not because of the terrorist attack but more because his mind was totally absorbed by the young woman and their blossoming love affair. Perhaps it was the unreality of the night before, which had created a distance between himself and what he was now confronting.

They arrived at the harbour, to be greeted by more shocking intel which had just been delivered on the police radio. The massacre of British soldiers near Warren Point close to the border. Harry looked around him. There was a sort of collective shock and resultant torpor. This was the kind of atmosphere in which Harry came into his own.

He walked across purposefully to the senior police officer, and his unhurried tread produced a kind of rhythmic pulse, allied to his calm authoritative but unthreatening manner which all contributed to an immediate response from the senior man. He turned towards him, and stopped his handwringing gestures and his face became less contorted. It was as if a young strong oak had suddenly planted itself next to him and offered himself up, as support for his back. To lean up against perhaps so there was no longer any feeling of falling.

"I need to leave," said the senior man, "I need to be at Warren Point."

Harry simply asked him, "Who will you leave in charge

here?"

He pointed to an older police detective.

Harry simply said, "Right, leave this to us then. Off you go. It's in safe hands," he added by way of further reassurance.

Later Harry learnt that the bomb had been planted by the IRA. No warning was issued. An elderly passenger also injured, Baroness Brabourne, eighty-two, who died the day after the attack.

And of the massacre of eighteen young soldiers at Warren Point. The majority from 2 Para.

On the park bench, Harry's mind returned to the here and now. He began to feel the cold. He shifted his buttocks one to the other and back again. How much time had he spent he mused simply sitting and waiting, his arse taking the punishment, and his mind the boredom.

Harry decided reluctantly to leave his watching post and to return in the evening to see what might take place. He went back to his room and allowed himself three hours' kip.

When he returned later that evening, he took up his watch over the alley on the park bench once more. Nothing to observe of any significant interest immediately. Harry allowed his mind to settle and then to wander. He rested there rather like a sleeping dog, whose eyes are closed but who can be relied on as soon as anything of interest arises to awake, alert and ready, willing and able to do his duty.

Again, Harry's mind wandered and he let it. He recalled the park bench just like this one in the small sleepy town not far from Belfast. The girl was already sitting on the bench waiting for him. Her red hair, her smell so sweet, that pale skin, those lips, the shape of her thighs, her slim waist. Her breasts held tightly and just the hint of cleavage revealed without artifice or intention. He was shocked by how vivid the memory was after all these years, her scent especially hung in heavy evening air.

"Harry, Harry," she spoke softly and the words drifted over him like a caress, "What would you have me do Harry?"

Even now he willed himself to answer, but as then no words not a single one. She was Catholic, an abortion was out of the question, not here in Ireland at any rate. She knew that and he knew she knew he knew it.

"I can give you the money," he finally managed to say.

It was as if he had struck her forcefully and viscerally. He immediately regretted it. Such words lie on the ground like a cowpat, irretrievable. He sat there staring straight ahead and wished, to put it mildly, he could unsay it. Now even more than then, if that were possible, sitting on this bench, he wished it. It was equally impossible now as then. What was said was said, and what was done was done. Some things cannot be parcelled away even in a mind as tidy and organised as Harry's.

The destiny of their child was not his to decide.

His memories of her were again so vivid. The virgin white sheets barely providing any barrier to Harry's lustful urge. He felt the desire grow very strongly within him. Her chest barely lifted as she slept, lifted and fell away. He found he was holding his breath, as if any movement or sound might awaken her, and he would lose the moment.

She turned her head in her sleep. Anger rose in him, rising to an almost uncontrollable rage. He saw again the bruises on her face. She would not tell him anything, and he had not insisted. He knew he was the cause of the beating she had suffered, and he felt this as he had inflicted it himself. And yet here was this immediate need, driven by desire. It was not as if she had sought refuge with him. No, this was the confirmation of life, and the denial of any power her father, her brothers, believed that had over her. It was a denial of the bloody ignorant Irish Catholic patrician nonsense that would seek to justify inflicting such punishment upon her.

She stirred in her sleep, and reached out for him, and he took her in his arms and embraced her. He sank his face into her full head of russet coloured hair, a reminder of her conquistador roots.

He had decided to return to this misleadingly idyllic spot to see what might emerge, and he felt that the evening might be the best time for that. He reasoned unless it was simply a random attack, George must have disturbed some activity, the most obvious candidate being drug related. George could have been in the wrong place at the wrong time, and it was just bad luck, but Harry's instincts had told him otherwise. And the old woman in the bungalow had confirmed his judgement.

NINETEEN

Harry had a lot on his mind.

He noticed just how upset Fergie had been, and he perhaps underestimated the extent to which a line had been crossed. The irony of it all had not slipped past unnoticed.

Here in this sleepy spa town, George had met his nemesis. Fergie was unlikely to be satisfied until he had punished those responsible in the severest possible manner. Harry understood that Fergie had assumed guilt for not protecting his friend, for not being there when he had been attacked. Harry's sense of guilt was just as intense, if not greater. After all he had not been there for any of his old friends and comrades, or family or anyone. He had just gone away. Run away if you like except that description implied speedy action. Harry tried not to reflect on his own feelings on the matter. But they kept nagging at him. He was not sure how he felt, but it was unignorable, something like an abscess in a difficult to get at back tooth, a tooth so rotten that it simply had to be exorcised.

He knew what Fergie was capable of, and his simply enormous strength and courage, the former might have diminished somewhat with age but the latter never.

Fergie sent a text.

'15b Bilton Rd'.

Harry surmised that this was George's home address.

It was a rather nondescript yet incongruous modern block of low-level flats, purpose built in the seventies, planted at the end of a Victorian terrace. There was a 7/11 corner shop where Harry imagined George perhaps buying a newspaper and necessaries and a barber where he might have had his hair trimmed. Across the road were couple of charity shops.

Harry went up to the flats and saw there was an outer door arrangement and an inner one with post boxes for the residents. It was hardly homes fit for heroes, but not too bad at all.

He slipped in as someone came out. 15b on the first floor.

Harry worked out, four flats to each floor, lettered. He walked onto the relevant landing. He did not want to break in as this was rarely as easy to engineer as it is portrayed in films, with a sort of simple wiggle with a credit card or other nonsense. Of course, people did sometimes leave an easy enough way in, a skylight not secured perhaps, or a window not closed properly on its inner catch. Harry hoped George would not have deadlocked the door and he was right. He produced the standard looking Yale key from an inner pocket of his coat and sought to slip it into the door lock. He thought at first perhaps his optimism that this was indeed George's key allowing easy access, was not going to be correct. As was typical it needed some encouraging, but with a bit of wiggling, in it went and turned easily enough, and Harry crossed the threshold into George's home.

He closed the door quietly behind him. The little flat was clean and tidy and well decorated, though it looked like this was done some time ago. Harry was impressed. He was not sure what he expected but had assumed that the drinking and age implied a less ordered domestic life. Old habits die hard. George had always been spick and span in his habits and military training had entrenched this. No artwork. Three photographs. In one was George and Fergie. In another George and Snip. Then one of them all. No family. A larger one of some training course or other. One on manoeuvrers or was it an op, with soldiers Harry did not recognise. No holiday snaps. He removed the photos of him, Fergie and Snip. No frippery. A telly. Comfortable furniture. A well-used sofa. An ashtray made out of an old artillery shell. Small kitchen. Two chairs. Everything washed up and tidied away. One mug on the draining board.

Harry moved through into the bedroom. A small double bed. He sat on it and thought for a minute. Where might he hide it. Perhaps in plain view. He got up and tried the top of the small wardrobe. Inside was a neat rack of civilian clothes and a dress uniform. Shoes in the rack at the bottom. He ran his hand over the top of the wardrobe. Nothing.

He opened the drawer of the bedside table and pulled it out. There was a package taped with black duct tape. Harry extracted it and pulled open the drawstring of the velvet bag. Inside was the gun and box of Taylors tea. No tea inside it but two packs of ammunition. The gun was immaculate. Harry cocked it and found the action well-oiled, the gun had been cleaned probably regularly and was ready for use. George had been as good as his word. He had promised Harry he would look after it and he had. Into his coat it went with the teabag box.

Harry was amused by Fergie's next text. He must have had predictive text on, and using the speller it came out as,

'RV. 1600 hrs Meat me bus stop near club, going Now you toaster. Toaster'.

'Meat' was easy enough to understand but 'toaster'? It took Harry a moment to realise what Fergie had meant to write. He was used to Fergie calling him a tosser. Harry murmured, "For fuck's sake," mirroring no doubt what his friend had said when trying to formulate the text. Oh well Fergie was just trying to be endearing. Perhaps though the misspelling of 'meet' was all

Fergie's own work. Harry had never seen him read anything, not even a newspaper or write anything come to that.

So here they were. Two old men apparently waiting for a bus, sheltering from the rain. The shelter offered little in the way of protection, and nothing from the wind at all. Harry could recall proper bus shelters that actually offered shelter, and a haven for youth for exploratory juvenile activity, known as petting and if you were lucky quite a bit more, with girls. He could not help himself but remembered one girl with very nice breasts that he dubbed Pinky and Perky.

"Right Harry." Fergie interrupted him from his private thoughts.

"I have hung around that alleyway."

So he had the same idea as Harry. Never mind, except Harry felt they should coordinate their actions in future.

"I can tell you, it's a place where the local toerags hang out, and there is a very strong smell of skunk hanging about the area. It looks like local drugs deals go on there. Anyways, I hung around a bit more and saw a more interesting looking blokie, thicker set, older, he arrived at the end of the alley in a boy racer car, black, Peugeot maybe, nothing special but not something you'd pick up for nowt.

"Later I saw a black Range Rover, it pulled up next to the Peugeot, and there was something passed between them. Hard to tell what. Supplies maybe?"

"Roger. Thanks, I'll call you if I need you."

"You do that, laddie," Fergie breathed out and repeated under his breath, "see to it that you do that reet?"

Harry nodded. He did not tell Fergie of the conversation he had had with the old lady in the bungalow. He reckoned Fergie was fired up enough without more details.

Fergie levered himself up with no apparent difficulty and strode off with the same lengthy stride that Harry knew so well, firm and strong. *Not a whiff of old age about him*, thought Harry, watching his broad back disappear round the corner and out of sight. Harry felt his heart rate rise, and even to feel a new emotion not known to him, a kind of rising panic. For some strange reason, Harry nearly went after him and even was tempted to call him back. He could do with close support right now. There was no doubt that George's death had really got to them both, and in ways Harry at least, was not ready to admit even to himself. He took a deep breath and exhaled slowly. Now was not the time for self-doubt.

Harry got up and started walking with deliberately regular strides, which had the effect of restoring his equilibrium. He made his way steadily to the alleyway and parked himself again on the bench near the small wooded clearing now bounded by newish houses and fencing aimed at achieving privacy. *A small part of Thatcher's Britain*, thought Harry a matter which he felt entirely neutral about. The property-owning democracy. Harry though did not care that much about the haves and the have nots, the whys and the wherefores, social navel gazing was not his style. He simply cared about his old friend, his comrade, who had been attacked, and he was going to make sure whoever did it, whoever was responsible, paid for it.

TWENTY

Ruth was reading from the autopsy report, injury to spleen, two breaks to the arm, one a compound fracture, likely deliberately broken, at least three broken ribs, punctured lung. It was a savage beating there was no doubt about that. Not your average mugging. Hard to be sure which blow killed him, but probably the blows to the head. They literally kicked his head in. She was sure that it was more than one, while he was unconscious maybe, and on the ground. She hoped actually that by then he was unconscious.

Why had no one treated the locus in quo as a crime scene? Here they were three days later and only now was she being asked to look at this. She suspected some desk-bound operative had decided it fell into the 'let's not try too hard here, and we can write this one off'. Well, she supposed an attack was nothing that special, a mugging commonplace even in Harrogate. Was it his age? Was he somehow unimportant? Thought of as a 'down and out'? But he was more smartly dressed than that. He was drunk, and had signs of alcoholism, perhaps that was a partial explanation but no excuse in her mind. Perhaps this was why it hadn't rated. She was not sentimental about her work, or delusional. She knew the police often failed to prioritise correctly. But this was murder, even if it were a mugging that went wrong because the old boy had had the temerity to fight back.

Harry felt the balaclava in his pocket and sought out with his fingers the gunmetal wrapped carefully inside it, keeping something precious protected and warm. The Glock 18 is a selective fire variant of the Glock 17. It had been developed by commission at the bequest of the Austrian counter terrorist unit know as Cobra. Its commander simply said such a weapon was a necessity and as every schoolboy knows, necessity is the mother of invention. It was rumoured that some of its training by Cobra derived from Nazi times. Harry had met one or two of their operatives, once in Cold War days when Austria was supposedly neutral, and later on a NATO exchange. From this exchange came Harry's love of mountains, climbing and skiing.

As a young man he could not believe his luck. There he was at taxpayers' expense, quite well paid, and had an overseas allowance, and really he was mucking about in the snow.

He had claimed greater skiing ability than he actually had. Not much can really be learned on a weekend adventure training trip to the Cairngorms. This was an entirely different proposition. Piers, he learnt, was the German senior world cup champion and he had agreed to train him following quite an interesting session in a *stüblie* on the German-Austrian border.

Harry got the kit on with some difficulty but by copying Piers managed to give an impression of a man who knew what he was doing. Carrying his skis rather awkwardly perhaps gave the game away, and they were rather large skis, certainly too long for the average beginner.

Then on the individual chair lift. That lift he learnt later had been there as one of the first to be fitted pre-war. The mountain had been used to train the Alpine Korps. It had no safety bar, and Harry sat back and did what he always did in these circumstances. He pretended he was not frightened, which was near enough to not in fact feeling the fear. The chair would swing to-and-fro, but anyway of course it reached the top, and there was a helpful hand to help him slip off and pull the chair behind him and up and away on its circular journey. He arrived just after Piers at the top of what seemed a very steep slope to him, and Piers helped him into his skis. Piers by now had his suspicions confirmed that his companion was not very much more than a beginner, perhaps a complete novice.

He asked Harry if he was a Christian. Harry was not sure why but he nodded. Piers pointed with his arm lengthened by his right ski stick, and there on the skyline was a huge crucifix.

"Keep eyes on the crucifix Harry, and follow me. *Hab Vertrauen.*"

With that Piers set off down the slope and Harry said a little prayer, and did as he was told. It was a matter of faith.

They went down the steep slope gathering speed in a straight line, Piers leading and Harry in his tracks. Faster and faster and then up the other side, and Piers fetched up with an elegant turn at the base of the crucifix. Harry crashed out just below him, in soft snow, no harm done. Harry emerged from the snow with an enormous smile on his face. Harry was hooked. His love affair with skiing in the mountains began right there. It never ended.

Piers simply stepped down and helped him up. *Jetzt noch einmal*. Yes again, right now. They traversed this slope up and down many times till Harry was exhausted, and still it went on. He began to learn to put in a turn or two, no concession to snow plough, his skis were largely parallel copying Piers.

Then as the sun fell schnapps up the mountain. *Prost*. Piers wanted to know the English for this invitation to down a drink. "It's *bollocks,*" Harry lied, and was gratified by the sight of the way this greeting spread, raised glasses, clink '*Bollocks*' all the

Germans and Austrians cried. "*Noch einmal,*" he said, and sang a little song "Let's have another one just like the other one, let's have another do," which the Germans tried to copy. Their own songs and then yodelling, and Lili Marlene, the log fire, the happy men making merry, made for an unforgettable atmosphere.

It was completely dark outside when he finally emerged from the mountain *stüblie* and there was the welcome sight of Piers's children who were there to fetch their father home, and proved willing to guide *der Engländer* down. Many tumbles later, all soft landings in powder snow, a very drunk Harry found his way to his bunk.

The next day, *noch einmal.* It took Harry less than six days to reach quite a decent standard, according to Piers for *ein Engländer*. This was good news as Harry's extravagant claims of skiing ability was taken at its face value and he was appointed to help run Special Forces mountain training. He asked if he could appoint Piers to the role of chief skiing instructor and mountain guide, and if there was funding to pay him. There was. The British Army always found money for skiing. It was after all a military skill, especially if there was climbing and surviving in the mountains, cross country combined with shooting. There was even some actual survival training of a limited kind, building an igloo for instance. Downhill skiing was somehow just included in this and formed the majority of it, without question.

Harry had learnt much and had much to impart. They were certainly efficient, the Austrian Special Forces, and demanded an efficient weapon – and one was produced as a result, and he met some interesting people.

He liked to take a coffee and perhaps a brandy and a cigar in a little café with pretty alpine curtains, and friendly waitresses dressed in Tyrolean dresses and what his mother would have called 'a pinny'. It was well off the beaten track reachable only on langlauf skis or with snow shoes. It was made of timber and looked a little bit like a witch's hut from Grimm's fairy tales.

He noticed a man quite a bit older than him perhaps the age of his father, who was often in there at the same time of day, always in the same seat, perhaps like Harry, taking time after an energetic day's exercise.

Today the man deliberately headed for Harry's small table. He was quite short and yet held himself well, no sign of bending towards the grim reaper, age not yet a factor, and introduced himself with some formality but with a genial smile as Graf Wilhelm von Oberstaufen. In good English, with a mild accent only, he asked if he could buy Harry a drink.

Harry was happy to accept, and said, "By all means," and gestured with an open palm to the seat opposite.

"If you please to call me Willy with a V Harry."

Willy turned out to be a junior staff officer with Rommel in the desert campaign, and this prompted Harry to say,

"I believe my father was on Montgomery's staff."

This greatly interested Willy, who asked if he could perhaps write to him as he was writing a book on Rommel and the desert war.

Harry learnt later that he had in fact been greeted by the founder of the German Alpine Corps. He took Harry up to the alpine corps memorial looking out towards the Austrian mountains and told Harry the tale of Karle der Grosste and his beard, and that one day he would return to save the German race. Harry took all this in good part. It reminded him of Welsh tales of myth and legend. Prince Brutus descended from the Trojans and other nonsense. Hitler's mountain retreat at Berchtesgaden could be seen clearly. Willy later told him how much he loathed

Hitler and his henchmen, how he had escaped arrest at the time of the attempt on the corporal's life. Rommel had not been so fortunate.

He invited Harry to meet some younger German officers. They were delightful, happy, intelligent young men. They took Harry to a shooting range and introduced him to their favoured weapons, including the Glock handguns. Immediately one was placed in his hand he liked it. He was astounded when at the end of many shooting sessions accompanied afterwards by schnapps and singing, the officers presented him with one. What a gift.

It was superlative. A 1986 Glock 18C then brand new. It was a kind of machine pistol, with a lever type fire control selector switch, installed on the serrated portion of the rear left side of the slide. Harry found comfort, even now, from running his trigger finger over this regular patina, his touch reassuring him that his training and experience were not forgotten. With the selector lever in the bottom position, the pistol fired fully automatically, thus allowing rapid neutralising of a room or enclosed space such as a bunker. In the top position the pistol fired semi-automatically, allowing single shots if used expertly and with restraint. A very effective weapon indeed. It had a 33-round capacity, and early models were ported to reduce muzzle rise during automatic fire. It became Harry's personal weapon of choice.

Harry was more interested in subtle use, and the compensated variant was both effective and exquisite. It had a keyhole opening cut into the forward portion of the slide, similar to long slide models, but had a standard-length slide, allowing comfortable pocketing or holstering of the weapon. The keyhole opening provides an area to allow four, progressively larger from back to front compensator cuts machined into the barrel to vent gases upwards, affording more control over the weapon especially if rapid firing. Harry liked control. Especially in his firearm. It reduced the chances of something going wrong, of unintended outcomes. When it came to shooting Harry liked good engineering, precision, and certainty. This was a gift worth keeping. He was glad he had kept it.

TWENTY-ONE

"Hey Harry."

"What is it?" Harry was busy with his own thoughts but like all of them was in fact very bored.

"Fergie's built something."

"What do you mean, built something?"

"Come and see."

"Oh OK, anything is better than just sitting here guarding these wankers. I simply don't care if they spread shit all over their cells, why would I?"

Privately Harry had been reading into the background to the hunger strikes and their refusal to accept criminal sanction. They claimed they were political prisoners, and Harry, rather typically of him, wanted to see whether the claim might stack up. He had reread what he knew of Cromwell, the potato famine, Palmerston, and the 1916 uprising what a joke and the first Bloody Sunday. The more recent history he knew quite well from those who had been involved.

"Oh, didn't you know Harry, they're political prisoners."

"Political prisoners my arse," was Fergie's contribution.

"You'll need your shotgun."

"What?"

"You'll need—"

"I heard you."

"Look at what Fergie's built."

"Come and see."

Harry was more than merely intrigued. He followed George out into one of the quadrangles of H block. And there it was, a fully functioning clay pigeon trap.

"It's not exactly a work of art is it."

"Does it work?"

"Too right it does. Watch this."

Fergie and George crouched over the trap.

"Ready!"

Then George shouted, "Pull!" And a clay shot over narrowly missing Harry's head. He didn't even have time to duck.

"Needs a bit of adjustment Fergie," commented George.

"Didna ye worry about that, laddie."

A tightening of a screw fitting and Fergie set off another one, a quite decent trajectory.

"You going to give it go then?"

Harry thought, *Why not?*

He took up position on the far edge of the quad, loaded both barrels and on 'ready' raised the shotgun.

And then yelled, "Pull!"

The clay arched over his head, he tracked it, *blam*, first shot missed.

Then, *blam* again, and he took out the clay which splintered in a most satisfactory manner.

"You always were a rubbish shot."

The sounds ricocheting off the walls created quite a din. A head appeared round the corner of the quad, took a quick look and disappeared just as quickly.

The boys from Special Forces, and Captain Case, who seemed to be attached to them in a role not really understood by any of them, were notorious, and no one interfered with Fergie when he was enjoying himself.

"Your turn George."

Blam. Blam.

Then it was George on the trap, and Fergie yelling, "Pull!"

No clay appeared over his head, and there was a sudden cry, almost one of outrage but certainly serious. The makeshift trap had no guard, and the flying arm had swung round and had struck George in the eye.

"Bloody hell Fergie, he's hurt!" shouted Harry, and ran over to where George lay out cold with blood copiously gushing from the wound on his head. Harry took his jacket off and wrapped it round his scalp and pressed hard.

"Get help Fergie, get a medic. Go! Now!"

Fergie ran off to fetch help. Harry was wrestling with his shirt to add to the compress. George began to moan which Harry took as a good sign, still alive, still alive.

"You're OK George. It's all going to be all right."

"Stay with me George stay with me," Harry pleaded. George's one good eye began to close, and his breathing became shallow. He turned a very odd shade of grey.

"Don't leave me George, don't leave me."

He could hear a siren in the distance faint at first but growing rapidly louder, and here was a medic with Fergie, who pushed Harry out of the way and took over wrapping a battlefield compress over the wound.

"Harry?"

"Yes."

George's head was wrapped in a bandage over his eye. They were in the hospital.

"The army won't want me now."

This was said as a statement not a question. Harry didn't know what to say. He thought it quite likely they would invalid George out. He returned to HQ.

"Sands."

"Yes, sir."

"He's roughly your age. Almost exactly."

"You're Welsh?"

"On my mother's side." He voiced silently, fourteen generations all lined up in the same graveyard. Harry could see them now. Where he played amongst them as a small boy, the wildflowers allowed to grow amongst the less than well-tended graves.

"Church of Wales, not chapel I see. Small village Pentrefoelas. Wynn Finch estate. Very fine family Welch Guards."

Harry nodded.

"Do you know him?"

"Who, sir?"

"Wynn Finch."

"Not well but yes," said Harry noncommittedly. He recalled the estate in Wales, the slum houses in the village, the subsistence wages, the tenant farmers grubbing a living on the hill farms, and his mother taught to touch their forelocks.

"Your grandfather was in the Royal Welch?"

"That's right, sir. He survived the Great War."

"Your father was KRRs."

Harry nodded. He clearly knew this already. This was quite a file they had on him. The staff officer was flicking through it more it less at random Harry felt. The suit next to him said nothing and was not introduced. He had an unopened file of his own in front of him.

Harry thought about it and decided he must be some politico or perhaps and this was more likely military intelligence.

"Well, Harry, this gentleman has a proposal for you. The GOC has made it clear we are not to force you to do this, it must be a choice as it will change your security status."

Harry wondered what that meant.

"Sign here."

And a copy of the Official Secrets Act passed over the desk.

"Of course, you are bound by this statute whether you sign or not."

"Just easier to prove I knew what I was getting into, as if that were true," mused Harry to himself.

"What is it you want me to do?" asked Harry.

"We want you to talk to Sands."

"When you say 'talk to'. Harry stared at them both.

"Yes, win his confidence if you can. Perhaps use your support for Welsh rugby as a lever."

"What do you mean?"

"Let it drop how much you enjoy seeing the English beaten."

"Maybe I could persuade him I am descended from Owain Glendower," murmured Harry.

"Are you being bloody facetious?" the staff officer demanded.

"No, no," intervened the suit. "It's the right idea, along the right lines so to speak."

This Celtic myth stuff might just entice some empathy.

Harry had expected serious repercussions from the clay pigeon trap debacle and yet here he was being asked to, well what exactly? Surely he was not expected to befriend Sands.

As George once put it: "Nutter is the kind of man who can be dragged through a hedge backwards and still come out looking as if he has just been for a stroll in his mother's garden. You know smelling of roses."

His adaptability was certainly being tested.

"Take time to consider this if you like. Of course, if you accept, we could ignore the incident in the maze quadrangle," said the Colonel." It's a bloody fortunate thing that George Palmer was not seriously hurt."

"Will you look for something for George to do? Will the eye mean he's out?"

"Don't worry I'm not losing him. His eye is not seriously damaged and I'll not lose him."

"Right. I'm in." He said this without conviction, but that didn't seem to matter.

A file was passed over the desk. It was sizeable, difficult to heft. "Bedtime reading for you, Case. You meet Sands the day after tomorrow."

"That's Good Friday."

"Yes."

"Symbolic."

"Not particularly. Any questions?"

"Just one."

His would-be masters both looked up.

"What have you told him?"

"Nothing, you will simply introduce yourself and take it from there."

Sands was the number one prisoner in the Maze. The powers that be obviously wanted to know if he would in fact starve himself to death as he had threatened.

Sands had threatened this more than once before and not carried through. This was cold comfort indeed and the problem remained. It was alleged the government had agreed to his demands, and then for various reasons not kept their word. It was considered important not to create a martyr. His death was otherwise unimportant.

Harry knew this was a serious decision and recognised that from this day forward he would be a marked man, one of those who had to check over his shoulder, peer under his car, worry for his friends and family.

Well, good then that he had neither. Perhaps it would all come to nothing. After all, why would the now-legendary IRA commander talk to him at all?

The handshake which was not a warm grasp on either side, neither firm nor limp, lasted for the minimum time possible. The welcome to the intelligence services had almost past him by. Surely there was more to it than that?

TWENTY-TWO

Sands sat opposite him in the interview room. Harry introduced himself. Not much conversation was likely it seemed to him, as Sands had not spoken to his captors. 'How you getting on', didn't seem appropriate. Harry asked him directly, "Are you going to go through with it?"

"With what?"

An answer. Progress.

"This, this futile gesture?"

"We'll see if it's futile."

"I know the English," said Harry, "they will never quit."

"You are English, so I suppose you do know the English."

Harry asserted, "But I'm not English."

"What are you then?"

"Welsh."

Sands looked up and a smile broke over his face, and Harry could see he was finding it difficult not to laugh out loud.

"I hope you are not laughing at my being Welsh."

"Why would I? But you quit the struggle centuries ago."

"Maybe. Maybe and you don't need to trust me on this, but I think I might understand you better than that lot."

"Really? Why?"

"Take Cromwell."

"You want to talk about Cromwell?" Sands was incredulous.

"Yep. The Lord Protector of England, Scotland, and Ireland, but note no mention of Wales."

"So what?"

"We didn't even have a lord protector."

"Lucky you, he killed a quarter of the Irish. Soldiers and civilian women and children without discrimination. The British never really understand the history."

"The English."

"What?"

"Not the British the English, certainly not the Welsh."

"You think it matters? Why?"

"It's the numen of place."

"The numen?"

This word clearly interested Sands who, though had left school at fifteen, was a self-didact of some considerable well-earned repute.

Harry had read thoroughly his brief and the file. He had decided on the line he would try.

"It's the spirit or divine power presiding over it all. O bydded i'r heniaith barhau."

"What does that mean?" Sands was interested, that much was obvious.

"Long live the old language."

Sands, who like his captors, was in general very bored, and not a little frustrated, as he had so few levers to pull militarily, and politically. He had been focusing on what he considered the inevitable end game. Harry thought that Sands did not actually believe the British government would crack. But nevertheless, Sands perked up here and began to show some interest.

"Go on then, if being Welsh matters, what is Welshness?"

Now this was a difficult nut to crack.

Harry tried his best. He had decided to speak from the heart.

"It's the power of an old language learnt at your

grandmother's knee. It's pre-Roman, pre-Christian, and not just language but a matter of landscape. These things cannot be separated. It is the call of legend, the Trojans and Tintagel, the allure of ancient friendships and kith and kin, the sounds of your ancestors, speaking from the very ground you walk on, and the collective desire to resist. Welshness is Dylan Thomas, poets and wizards, witches and soothsayers, and ancient medicine, and saints and footballers, and the rugby, goats and miners and singers and fairies and magic, and angels. And Boyce. It's a grand old country, tough and beautiful."

He was breathless now as there had not been room in his mind to take in air. He paused as he must, and let these thoughts resonate round the largely unfurnished room. Harry wondered if the pathos was lost in the purple prose. Oh well, bathos it was then.

"Full of humour too."

Sands voiced under his breath, "It's Ireland."

"It's a common heritage."

"The Celts."

"The old land of my fathers is very dear to me."

Harry broke into song, humming at first then louder with clearer words in the old language.

It was *Yma o Hyd,* which he hoped would resonate, and it did.

Sands turned his face towards him and said simply, "Teach it to me." And Harry began to do just that.

"Er gwaetha pawb a phopeth, ry'n ni yma o hyd."

"In spite of everyone and everything, we are still here."

The senior officer called to the door reported back.

"They are singing, sir."

"What's that?"

"Singing."

"Singing what?"

"Some gibberish, difficult to make out, no hang on maybe in Welsh, or Gaelic." He tailed off, "I'm not sure."

Harry visited George in his room and was startled to see his comrade sitting in his chair with a bottle of whisky in his hand.

"You look a mess."

"The eye is damaged Harry, but I can still see out of it."

"Good thing you've got two then."

"I don't want them to chuck me out Harry."

"The regiment is not going to do that George."

Harry had his fingers metaphorically crossed that the staff colonel would keep his word.

TWENTY-THREE

"Harry is my darling, my darling, my darling…"

And then again her voice asking, "What are we to do?"

Even now he knew again the only answer, and that an abortion was out of the question, for her at least.

Come with me, he willed himself to say, *back to England*, except he never said it.

Why not? He surely loved her. But Harry did not speak the words, and that moment was gone.

She stared at him, a long stare seemingly without end.

He tried to read her face. What was the message behind that stare? Disbelief, anger, despair. He simply couldn't read that look, she who was usually an open book, a child of nature even though hers was an entirely urban experience. And nowhere does urban quite like Belfast.

So, he said nothing, as he said nothing now. He believed nothing came of nothing and he was, logically, correct. And she was gone.

His attention was pricked, and he turned slightly towards the alleyway. There was a boy on a bike, too small for him by some margin, or was it a stunt bike of some kind. The lad riding it had a hoody pulled well down over his head. Nothing remarkable about that, yet there was something about the way the boy loitered as if waiting for something or someone that made Harry focus fully on the here and now and what was being played out in front of him.

His effort was rewarded because sure enough here was another bike perhaps more of a standard type ridden by another youngster in a hoody. It was quite cold, so perhaps the hoody which was after all endemic amongst the young and not so young come to that, was not really any kind of signal. No lights which may or may not indicate something. How many youngsters on bikes have lights? Harry thought perhaps it depends on how well parented they are.

The evening gloom began to settle over them. A third arrived, and they circled about a bit aimlessly, without much chat, but Harry could hear pings on their mobile phones. *Someone loves them,* thought Harry euphemistically.

At the end of the road, a large black SUV drew up. Likely the one Fergie had already noted. Harry paid it his full attention. It was such a cliché he thought to himself. Blacked out window, the passenger side gradually lowered, to reveal apart from the driver a thick set man. It was hard in the light to make out his features, but parking under a streetlight meant he was not entirely concealed either. He was Caucasian, and not more than twenty-five, Harry reckoned. One of the boys cycled over, handing over something and received a small package perhaps, then the second, then the third. The first two cycled off rapidly. The third boy stopped by the window and what happened next was not at all like the first two.

The door to the driver side opened rapidly and the kid found himself pinned to the side of the car. The passenger side opened and his partner joined him. Harry could hear the boy now pleading, "Don't hit me, please don't hit me."

The thicker set of the two men slapped the by hard across the side of his face.

He heard an accent, was it local, hard to tell.

"Shut up!"

"I'll have it all next time."

"You will have it all next time." Each word was accompanied by a slap, first to one side of the head then the other. Then, one more slap heavier than the others.

The boy was released and ran off to get his bike and cycle off.

Not too badly hurt then.

Harry was used to drugs in so many places he had served. He even had more than a passing familiarity with where drugs might come from. Their point of origin.

The whole thing seemed so banal to Harry's eyes and ears at any rate. But he did not know that this was England now as he had been away for so long. It was obviously some kind of drugs ring, and this youngster had not played his part to the full as required by those controlling him. He immediately understood that Harrogate as an affluent place would be targeted. He was a bit surprised by how young the boys were.

After observing all he could of this and taking a mental note of the number plate, which stupidly was some kind of personal plate, Harry left to make his next rendezvous with Fergie. He had told Harry to expect company, and was coy or something like that about who it might be that would be joining them. He would provide them with a summary of what he had observed.

Harry decided to take the bus to the pub where Fergie had said they should meet. Anyone who watched him would have seen an older bloke, past retirement perhaps, but maybe a bit more upright than the average, and certainly no fat on him but not skinny either. He went unnoticed, to the bus station, climbed on the bus more or less without fuss, except he did not have the change for the bus driver who complained about being given a five pound note, and then asked him if he had a bus pass and did he know he could get one. Harry did not think he was in need of a bus pass.

The bus took him across town, and out across the countryside towards north Leeds. Harry looked out at the cityscape which contained as the city approached high rise flats in abundance. The general terrain was not really visible as night was beginning to fall.

He settled into a seat not too far from the front so he would be able to exit easily.

The pub was not far from the barracks where Harry knew some of his former comrades had trained, and he knew as soon as he saw the main barbed wire walls that as Fergie had texted, he should get off. Fergie said he would meet him, and sure enough here was the man himself.

TWENTY-FOUR

Harry caught the return bus.

Harry's mates were delighted to see him after all this time. He had some serious catching up to do. He was greeted as if he had just been away for a week or two at most. Fifteen years is a long time and it is no time at all. Pyro and Snip greeted him as if he had just returned from a short but difficult mission. With little demonstrable backslapping.

"Surprised they let you back in," said Snip.

"Proof of the lack of immigration control," added Pyro.

Harry was not fazed by this style of greeting. It was what he expected and he found it comforting.

He was not surprised that his old comrades especially Snip had very strong memories of George. They had connections that he did not know about. Fergie had leaned over Snip when he was collapsed on his back like a dying beetle trapped by the weight of his pack. "We'll just have to leave you, laddie." It was George who pulled him to his feet and explained the buddy system.

Of course there were a few loners but basically everyone needed a buddy to watch their back, make a brick or two in urban operations, and haul their buddy up when unable to climb to his feet because of the sheer weight of the pack, plus ammo, plus rations, plus water.

It was George who ensured he passed P company and won his red beret. It was George who arranged for him to try Hereford and into the regiment. It was George who had noticed Snip had talent with a rifle and sent him on the marksman course. It was George who spotted the essential problem caused by Snip being rather short in leg and arm. It was George who intervened when a not very calm Snip would suddenly show terrier-like furiousness when the piss was taken out of him for his lack of height, or practically anything else. George harnessed Snip and gave him direction. The regiment did the rest.

Snip had been in care and came up through the Army Apprentices College in Harrogate. It was George who invited him home, essentially on leave, to the little Durham miners' village where he met George's old man, who had fought in the Durham Light Infantry. He was a master craftsman cabinet maker and joiner, who crafted a bespoke wooden stock for Snip for his sniper rifle.

Harry did once remember driving with Snip who had a new fast car and wanted to show it off. Driving down the A303 looking for the turning off to Bulford, Snip stopped the car on the edge of the road, got out and ran up to the large directional sign. When he got back in Harry asked him what he was doing. Snip said "Why do they have to make those signs so indistinct." Harry pointed out they were to his eyes as clear as clear could be. Snip wouldn't have that. Harry asked him how he passed his test. Did he not have to demonstrate he could read the number plate? Snip claimed those were often difficult to read, but anyway when the man was measuring out the required distance to test his eyes Snip stealthily crept forward enough so he could memorise the plate and then stepped back into line all without the examiner noticing. Harry mused he must have done the same in his army medical.

Snip explained to him that his eyesight was actually an advantage when it came to shooting. Snip explained about the mistake people make quite apart from not settling their breathing, lying still, having a rifle stock that fitted correctly, and the myriad of problems or snags identified routinely by weapons instructors.

"No look," he said, "the main problem was they attempt to line up near sight with the one on the stock with the target. What you had to do, was have a sense of the target and make the weapon, its barrel and mechanism part of you, so it moved with you, so there was no intervening possibility for error, to allow the brain to perform its miracle."

Harry understood then that in effect what a marksman did was to sense the trajectory of the bullet, and execute its flight path, without hindrance or error. Snip had no need of sympathy with laser guided firing. He needed to feel and sense what the conditions were and his sheer genius for hitting the target was uncanny. Harry felt even Snip only knew part of the explanation and that it was beyond words to articulate anyway.

Harry was aware that Fergie knew Snip better than he did. He resolved to ask him about Snip. He should take more of an interest in his old comrades. Before it was too late.

Harry found it impossible to tell his comrades how he really felt. For him his country, that frankly he had always found a difficult mistress, had changed and not as far as he could see for the better. He could not tell them he was not really glad to be back. His mood was not good which they each picked up on, but they of course interpreted this as a consequence of the attack on George, and George proved the main topic of conversation.

Harry told them what he had observed and found out. They had quite a bit of useful background to offer him. He had learned quite a bit. 'County lines' it was called. The boys were drafted in from places like Bradford, and even Liverpool. Sometimes their families were threatened. They were told their mothers or sisters would be raped. They even took over homes. Harry listened to the details of this and it reinforced his prejudice. His country had gone even further to pot than he had thought. It tended to confirm his view that he was glad he had left it. Seeing his old comrades was a reminder of what had been worth something. It did not make him think well of his country and not for the first time, he questioned whether his country was worth fighting for.

He was tired and had had too much to drink. A general fatigue passed over him. He was not best pleased to find that two women chose to sit right behind him, as the bus was almost empty of passengers. They were two old biddies in head scarves and they began to converse more loudly especially as the bus laboured up the hill out of Leeds, and though Harry tried to zone them out it proved impossible.

"She lost over three stone."

"Never."

"Yeah she did true as I'm standing here."

"But you're not standing Doris."

"You're right I'm not," and she giggled, "I'm sitting ain't I?"

and then they both started laughing.

They're my age, thought Harry. *Probably attractive once. Might have fancied them.*

"Wired up her jaw."

What did you say? Harry almost asked them, his mind between worlds.

"Wired up her jaw, had to. She had a broken arm, what do yer call it, you know when it sticks out?"

"What sticks out?"

"The bone."

"Mmm, is it com, whatsit, compound maybe?"

"Yeah compound."

"Or maybe it was both her arms."

"She said she fell off her kitchen stool, you know one of them tall ones."

"She had a kitchen island fitted."

"Did she really fall off?"

"Of course not, he was always punchy."

There was silence for a bit as the bus trundled along.

"Still, she lost three stones, in three months."

Not a bad idea that, thought Harry. Wire the fat fuckers up, why not. Nothing else seems to work. Will they never shut up? But he found they had perhaps exhausted their chatter for a bit at least. He found his eyelids dropping and he fell asleep.

She lay there, on the hotel bed, her striking red hair casting a splash of colour on the white sheets. The bedding only casually covering her. Her top half unconcealed, her shape defined by what was seen and what was unseen, by the pure white of the sheet.

In those days Harry spent no time thinking of the past or the future, but just lived in the moment, in the here and now. And now his memories of her were so vivid, her scent, the smell of her, the slight smile on her face as she slept, her beautiful eyes so large when open. He was tempted to wake her just so he could look into them. But he let her sleep on, her chest rising and falling, the slight smile on her lips unchanging. She was so calm when awake but when asleep too.

He found he was holding his breath, as if he could hold onto this moment. If he stopped breathing. Perhaps he simply didn't wish to disturb her and even his breathing might do that. He felt desire grow again within himself, for which he felt some self-loathing. What could be less called-for right then. The anger returned, as she turned over and the bruises on her face were apparent as they had been when she fled to him the night before. That phone call, the timing of it, so inconvenient, but Harry dropped everything and waited at the bus stop, and as she got off, he rushed to her. She was limping badly and clearly in pain. She pulled the hood down from her coat, that coat that he had bought for her, to keep her warm, had framed her face so sweetly, and the bruises were revealed. Later as he eased her into the bath, the full extent of the beating became apparent, the bruised thighs, were they trying to kick her in the crotch, probably. He imagined her foetal-like on the ground as they all took it in turns to kick her and insult her. Nothing she could say would ever replace the wildest imaginings of Harry's mind as he held her and tried to sooth her.

He thought of hospital and doctors, but she said no, and he found them this little place, where he could at least try and nurse her. At least there was no obvious permanent damage, and though he worried that she might have a concussion or some equally damaging internal injury, he trusted her when she said she was fine and just needed to sleep.

Essentially he had done very little, and now it had all passed beyond regret.

He wiped the window clear of condensation caused by his breath as the bus pulled into Harrogate and Harry ever the gentlemen let the two women off first, and then sloped off to his temporary billet.

TWENTY-FIVE

Harry had a problem. He needed to renew his medication. He wanted serious painkillers to compensate for the absence of the poppy. He made as few visits to the doctors as possible, but there was no avoiding it. He drew out the NI card in the name of Peter Freeman. He always chose names as his handler had advised, which any glance at an old-style phone book would have told you were difficult to tie down. Ubiquitous but straightforward names were his preference.

The driver's licence confirming his identity was not perfect as it had not in fact been through the proper procedures. It was a forgery but a very good one. In fact, there was no one better in the art of drawing up false papers than Harry's former colleague at the old firm. Harry wondered how old he must be now, maybe eighty or more. His skills as a graphic artist were not to be underestimated and he had been used by the state for these purposes since the second world war. Harry had abandoned the false IDs provided formally by the state, since he trusted them not at all.

Harry was seen as an emergency patient, he filled in all the forms and the endless patient history questionnaire. His birth date was to be 7th July 1951. No point in raising suspicion by choosing an age far off his own, though he was tempted to shave off a year or two. All in vanity. His address was simply picked from a local block of flats. The utility bill was barely glanced at.

He took a seat. He waited. He drifted off. Harry had a high

regard for medics, but his experience had been mixed. In the waiting room which was overly warm he found himself sinking into a deep sleep and there he was surrounded by chaos, mayhem and death. It was ironic that Harry who had escaped more or less unscathed from so many conflicts was here in this river in peacetime on a post-Northern Ireland exercise intended as R & R, to be faced with possibly the most serious challenge he had yet faced. Death and the dying lay all around him.

The 4-tonne wagon was leaving the training area in Belgium when fully loaded with soldiers and was, as was typical for the time, in fact technically overloaded with twenty-eight soldiers in the back and four including the driver in the front.

The hill was steep and stretched down for over quarter of a mile to a junction to a wider road which led out of the military area. On either side of the road were concrete bollards over a metre in width and no doubt solidly planted in the earth to some considerable depth. No vehicle except perhaps a tank could cross them.

As the transport edged its way down the hill the driver noticed his brakes were very spongy then they failed altogether. It was a steep hill perhaps over one quarter of a mile to the T-junction at the lowest point. *Never mind,* he thought, *I'll apply the dead man's anchor.* This failed also and the hydraulics in the steering and the handbrake when applied made things worse because as the lorry still picked up speed and approached the junction beyond which there was a steep drop, some 100 metres to the river below, the attempt by the sergeant in the front to edge them round by pulling on the wheel, turned the lorry over and it rolled beyond the precipice and turned over at least twice before coming to rest in the river on its side.

Bodies were being shed on the way down. They were

perhaps the lucky ones. Others ended up in the river and some were left in the lorry, or what was left of it as it rolled over on its way down the steep precipice. Human bodies do not easily resist damage from such collisions with tonnes of metal in free fall and colliding with road and rock and it is hard to do justice to the harm done.

Harry arrived on the scene in his Land Rover only because he was somewhat surprised by the delay in the arrival of the main transport and ordered his driver to return along the way they had come. He had expected the lorry to arrive at the temporary base a few minutes earlier and could not raise them on the radio.

It was as if a bomb had gone off. Or worse. The irony of this thought did not escape Harry's mind. After all they had just returned from duty in Northern Ireland. The hillside leading steeply to the precipice was marked by bodies thrown from the lorry. The lorry itself lay on its side in the river, its top frame and tarpaulin torn off. In the river were multiple bodies, and the cries of the injured reached him even before he took in the visuals.

Harry told his driver to get on the radio and seek help. He descended as rapidly as he could and a major and his driver arrived after him and stood as white as a sheet at the top of the parapet. No use at all. A medic arrived driving himself, with the regimental medical officer. He rapidly began to try and attend to the worst cases. He was manifestly overwhelmed.

Harry in his efforts to get to a young soldier who was convulsing on the opposite bank of the river, trod on the shattered legs of another soldier, who cried out over and over, "My legs, my legs." With good reason as they looked as if they had been sliced open by some kind of angry butcher.

His eyes lifted upwards, and he saw one young man on the upper slope with a shaft of metal stuck through his back and protruding at what seemed an impossible angle but holding his body off the ground who was crying out, it being possible Harry learnt to still be alive even after such violence "Help, help me." The boy for he seemed so young cried out again and again. Would it ever end?

Real help then arrived. US paramedics from the nearest base. Helicoptered in like a scene from Apocalypse Now, which Harry could not help seeing it like in his mind's eye, even as he tried to sort out who needed help first and immediately. If only it was merely a film set.

Eight soldiers died at the scene. Harry later was surprised it was so few. Twenty were CASEVACed to the nearest US airbase hospital. Four of those died later. Only four walked away from the accident. One was Snip and the one of the others was Pyro. They had been thrown from the front lorry through the smashed windscreen and fortunately, miraculously, had landed softly enough onto the bank at the top of the ridge. Pyro said later he was rather surprised to find he landed right next to his friend and though knocked out came round to find Snip's arm around his shoulders cradling him.

One of the soldiers whose life hung by a thread quite literally as his spinal cord was almost severed at the neck, was placed on life support. He was barely nineteen years old. Harry had to meet the parents. His name was Snow, he was a leading member of the ski team. Harry told his parents as he had been told that he would never walk again. He did in fact recover and skied to a medal in the next winter's ski races. Youth can sometimes recover from almost anything.

Harry did not go in for casual racism. His own background tended to militate against it. He did not actively seek to reprimand those who sounded-off using unfortunate language. It was all so much part of the culture. He did not get angry about it. Any residual racist attitudes Harry may have latently held were lost that day for when the lorry turned over it did not discriminate.

As Harry scrambled back up the hill, he saw the soldier tangled beneath the tarpaulin partially hiding the body. He knelt beside the young black soldier, little more than a boy, who looked up at him, and mouthed the word 'sorry'. Harry was holding the back of his head, as blood pumped out into the palms of his hands he tried to push it back into his skull. He was a bit surprised by the rather strange milky liquid that flowed out between his fingers, even as he attempted to push it all back into the busted skull. It took Harry a moment to realise that he died in his arms. Harry closed the boy's eyes with a small gesture of his own, gently passing his hand over his eyelids. The boy looked strangely beautiful in that moment as if nothing bad had happened to him at all.

This soldier had been a thorn in Harry's side with his dreadlocks and Rastafarianism, which objectively judged had little place in the military. Harry wondered what had motivated him to join up.

He took it upon himself to visit the boy's mother. He was vaguely aware that Tottenham had been the scene of quite a few accusations of racism especially against the police. Here he was in Broadwater Farm. What an ironic name, as there was nothing rural about it. It represented perhaps the hopes of post-war planners, but surely it was doomed from the start. If not it certainly looked beyond redemption now. No one approached them as they walked across what had no doubt been designed as a communal area. There were the remnants of a children's play area. He noticed the graffiti of course but also the remnants of serious drug activity, including needles. They walked across towards the entrance indicated by the address Harry had memorised, and into the block of flats. Of course, the lift didn't work. There were twelve flights of stairs to climb. Harry could perhaps have treated climbing them as penance, except he naturally avoided sanctimonious hypocrisy. He and the padre had to pass a couple of youths on the stairwell to the floor they needed. Interestingly they cast their eyes down, as even they understood the meaning of this visit.

The knock on the door. Harry in uniform with the padre. The sister no more than a primary school age, maybe ten, came to the door, in dreadlocks similar to her brother's. She was stunningly beautiful. She called for her mum.

The uniforms did nothing to protect them, though it made any formal announcement unnecessary. The poor woman did not imagine her son had won a medal. Her husband was notable by his absence, but not for the reason Harry initially thought. He was still on his shift on the underground. Here they were the Windrush generation and their descendants.

"My husband will be back soon." She even smiled at them. She was in nurse's uniform. St Thomas's Nightingale nurse. "He is on his shift." Harry looked at her with a quizzical face. "London transport innit. Sorry," she added as if it were her fault that they were keeping Harry waiting.

After the none too short wait, he was roused by the sound of the tannoy calling his name. He then found himself sitting opposite a very pleasant-looking female GP, who Harry could not help appreciating. Old habits die hard.

"Let me see your hands."

She took his hands in hers and gently turned them this way and then that. The evidence of arthritis in his fingers especially the index knuckle joints was easy enough to see.

She invited him to make a clenched fist with first the right which he did with difficulty and then the left, slightly easier.

"You are right-handed, can you write well enough, I mean hold a pen?"

"Yes."

"Without difficulty?"

"Yes."

"Or effort?"

"Well, it's stiff and I can't pretend it doesn't hurt."

"Pain elsewhere. Neck?"

"Yes and lower back."

"I suppose you are retired." She asked, "From what exactly?"

"Civil servant," said Harry.

She looked a bit quizzically at him, as there was nothing about Harry that implied this, and his hands did not either.

She asked him what he did for exercise. Harry was somewhat noncommittal. She asked him his weight, which at 90 kilos was a bit high she felt for his height at five feet eleven inches. But frankly when you looked at him closely you could see there was not an ounce of fat on him. He simply had a larger than average skeleton, and better muscle tone than his numerical age implied.

Harry was concerned that his grip did not seem what it was, and the pain in his index finger particularly troubled him. He could not help reaching over his shoulder to the old wound where the knife had cut deep. She had already asked him about any other problems, aches and pains and so on. He did not bother her with his Achilles tendon injuries caused by the parachuting, and that maybe that was the cause of his back pain which constantly troubled him, or perhaps it was the extreme loads carried in training and in conflict. He did not mention these, and the doctor did not enquire further. He did mention his left hip, when she asked him as he was aware he was limping slightly. She had noticed this as he came into her surgery. *Very observant,* thought Harry.

She said he should perhaps have the hip x-rayed, but Harry shook his head. She asked him about sleep. He told her he never had difficulty sleeping. He did not think his tendency to dream, and sometimes his inability to distinguish between dreams of the daytime and the night were worth mentioning.

He left with a prescription for some serious painkillers. She also suggested Ibuprofen as an anti-inflammatory.

His main concern was his trigger finger, and whether his ability with a firearm might be affected. He had not mentioned the occasional tremors he felt but which mercifully did not manifest themselves very often.

TWENTY-SIX

He put in a call to Fergie who said he knew just the place.

The old gravel pit was used by a clay pigeon club that Fergie belonged to and the farmer who collected them from the nearest train station asked few questions. Fergie said that he could be trusted. He left them there for a couple of hours as agreed and promised to collect them for the return journey and indeed offered to drop them back in Harrogate. Harry accepted as he preferred to be as little exposed in company as reasonably possible and Fergie was memorable even if he was not.

Fergie set up the targets and Harry produced his weapon and the ammunition. Fergie did not ask where it came from, and Harry did not volunteer any information on this. Harry knew that if more weaponry was required Fergie probably could produce them. And they had Snip and Pyro to rely on too if needed.

"Call that a grouping ye useless sassenach."

Fergie was scathing about Harry's accuracy, but truth be told it was good and his firearm technique was little changed from active-duty days. And the grouping though not as tight as the very best was still six rounds in half an inch and this from 25 metres with a small arm would perhaps not win prizes at Bisley but was damned good.

Fergie himself produced a sawn-off shot gun, which he blasted at a few targets, to amusing effect. He offered Harry a go, who simply smiled and declined.

On the journey back to Harrogate in the old Mark 1 Land Rover the farmer introduced as Mark by Fergie, revealed he was as Harry already suspected, a former soldier who had been trained by Fergie. He explained that he was meeting his wife for dinner, who was driving into a nearby village in her car. Harry knew not to ask questions about what training Mark might have had from Fergie but supposed it would have been not simple infantry stuff. Mark parked up and then got out leaving the keys in the ignition. "Try to look after her won't you."

"Dinna ye worry," said Fergie who climbed into the driver's seat and drove off towards Harrogate.

As they trundled along, Harry drifted off to sleep.

In his mind he could hear the gillie speaking, the old hunter in charge of the deer cull. What was his name? Harry loved going with Fergie on this more or less annual jaunt. He remembered Snip coming along. Was George there? He couldn't remember. Maybe not that year.

Angus that was it. Angus the gillie was there to greet them.

"That is a very interesting rifle you have there, laddie."

Snip was used to this. After all, the stock was bespoke to fit his shorter arms but the barrel was quite long, which should mean it was rather unbalanced.

Snip handed it over to the gillie for inspection.

The old hunter and poacher turned gamekeeper turned the rifle over in his hands. He set the weapon on its side seeking the centre of gravity with his finger beside the trigger. It was perfectly balanced.

"I don't suppose you want to reveal its secrets?"

Snip glanced at Fergie. "It's up to youse, laddie."

"I trust this man with my life if that helps" added Fergie. "He is my clan ye ken."

Harry looked at the two of them, Snip and the gillie.

And whether it was true or not, he saw a similarity. What was it? Something in the way each stood, a sort of relaxed awareness. It was subtle but it was there.

"It'll not be steel alloy, that barrel," the old man passed the rifle back to him.

Asked like this, by a connoisseur, so to speak, Snip told him.

"Well, no it's not, it's an alloy of tungsten and rhenium. This accommodates more pressure allowing in the final analysis for more explosive behind the bullet and greater muzzle velocity."

"I see. I like the trigger mechanism, so quiet yet so efficient."

It was no good wondering how he had sussed this out. He had seemed to be ignoring them, but this seeming casualness hid a very highly detailed degree of examination carried out deliberately, yet without disturbing the one being evaluated and judged.

Harry listening in heard Snip unstoppable now, sharing his knowledge, right back to his apprentice days with the REME, and so much more. He shared this technical talk with the gillie. How long would this have gone on for?

Fergie gently intruded. "How about we exercise and improve our stalking skills."

It was obvious that this experience was going to be worthwhile. Snip told him later that it was the most valuable he had ever had, notwithstanding the exposure to Gurkha training and Special Forces and so on.

Fergie had been brought up with this. The big man was surprisingly mobile and despite his size could move without fuss and remain hidden from view. There was more to it than this of course. Snip was already used to Fergie's abilities.

So much depended on smell and staying downwind of the

target, man or beast. In the Highlands there were proposals to reintroduce predators, but the instincts and developmental advantages that might have protected deer from them had not completely disappeared. Without predators, culling was necessary. Snip took full advantage of the opportunity.

A minute or two later they were scrambling up a hill-face aiming to gain height fast.

The old man was so efficient and quick that the younger men found it hard to keep pace. Harry was not unused to small mountain men and their abilities but this was something else. The heather and tussocks of grasses, which to him seemed such a nuisance, always in the way and random, were inhibiting Fergie, yet seemed to provide a springboard with each step to their tutor, as he raced up goat-like over the ridgeline and out of sight. Snip proved more than able to keep up.

When they reached the first ridge, they could see the old goat, rampaging ahead, with Snip closely on his heels.

Towards the next ridge and again out of sight.

The wind was blowing away from them and provided some assistance as it began to pick up speed, and they arrived at a boulder strewn hilltop. Angus had apparently disappeared.

Soundlessly he stepped out from the shoulder of a large rock and urged them with a clear gesture, to adopt a prone position. He approached them and told them they would be keeping as low as possible and using the terrain to the hunter's advantage.

Harry and Fergie were more or less on their knees at this point and sank lower into the long dead grass using it as a pillow to rest for a moment or two.

Angus was slithering towards the ridge top between two boulders and his little patrol followed him. Again he was moving rapidly like a large grass snake.

He was lying motionless as they each caught up with him first Snip and Harry and then the rather slower Fergie, which gave the quicker men some satisfaction. They each copied Angus and peered over the ridgeline. There in the slightly lower ground not 200 yards away was a young stag, the target a 14 pointer?

Snip was given the shot, and it took him only a few seconds to set up, but something alerted the animal and it took off down the valley towards the river and some trees.

Snip felt he had failed, but Angus, murmured "That was not a fair chance lad."

"Yon deer can smell a sassanach from 500 yards."

He set off skirting the hillside hardly visible except if you knew he was there, Harry, Fergie and Snip copying him for all they were worth.

Eventually they fetched up on a small hillock overlooking the river, and there on its banks was the young stag, maybe 800 yards away.

"Do ye want to try from here?" whispered Angus.

Snip nodded. His problem was that he was somewhat out of breath, and this he knew would affect his ability to shoot.

He set his rifle after rapidly checking for firm ground with his body in a fully prone position. His breathing was settling now. The stag had not moved. Then it raised its head, and looked directly at them as if it sensed what was coming.

The crack of the rifle seemed coincidental with the fall to its knees as the bullet entered its heart. A perfect shot that killed without unnecessary suffering, cleanly and mercifully.

Angus who knew he had witnessed something a bit special, gave a small nod of his head in respect. He had sometimes had to track a stag for many miles before delivering the coup de grace after a poor shot from one of the silly people they allowed to shoot for sport.

They rose as one and walked smartly down to the dead animal.

The ritual that followed, which was preparatory to the butchering seemed like something ancient and unquestionably right. Angus asked them to stand vigil while he fetched the Landy to bring the animal back.

Hauled up on a rope over the rafter of the bothy, Angus invited them to attend to the butchering post mortem. Fergie was the only one to show enthusiasm for this.

"We'll need a wee dram," and took his hip flask out. "No need to share with the sassanachs."

The animal now seemed merely an object, as Angus treated them to a lecture on the need for culling, Lymes disease, over population, the lack of decent alternatives to stalking. The content mattered so much less than how freely he talked directly engaging Snip in particular, who he had clearly taken a liking to. Snip had passed some kind of test. He was a bone fide member of the clan.

When called upon Snip would not miss the target. His reverie was interrupted by Fergie.

"Almost there, laddie."

Harry pretended he hadn't been asleep at all. "Just resting my eyes, Ferg."

Harry was not normally interested in material possessions, but he could not help but admire the Landy, its condition was the stuff of collectors and would not be out of place he imagined in those vehicle rallies where owners vied to show off their prize restorations.

"Your friend has looked after this Landy."

"Aye, well, it's not his."

"What do you mean?"

Fergie let out a long sighing breath.

"It's Badger's."

"Badger's?" said Harry, surprised by this news. "Where is Badger?"

Fergie took his time answering.

"Dead."

"What?"

"Dead," and not wasting time on softening the news, "suicide. Harry I went up to his hoose, it's in Argyll. The Sutherlands welcomed me. Another regiment gone." Fergie seemed distracted. Then he came out with it, or at least part of it.

"His son was killed ICD, Iraq."

"I didn't know," was all Harry could muster.

"I ken ye didna." This was said without accusation, though it was yet more evidence of Harry not being there when needed.

"I was his son's godfather, God help him," Fergie added.

"Anyways, I went to his funeral. His wife gave me the keys to his lockup. What I didna ken was that he had done the deed, in this very vehicle.

"She told me he had purloined it from the REME when he left the army. He had laid out every part and cleaned it and renewed what needed renewing. She never saw him, he was always in the lockup. This was after the wee laddie had lost his life.

"He drank. Well, we all knew that. He stored up the sleepers prescription drugs. Took the lot, enough to kill an elephant. Got in the Landy and piped the exhaust into it. He had been meticulous. Every crack was carefully sealed. I left it with Mark, to look after. Didna have the stomach to use it."

Harry asked no questions. He stayed quiet. He glanced over

at his old friend, and saw tears, his face awash with tears. "It's as if he is with us now, laddie, on the mission ye ken?"

"I do, Fergie. I do."

"We have wheels now. Then, Fergie."

Harry kept his next thought to himself, which was that the vehicle though unusual was probably untraceable.

"That's right, laddie. We have wheels, and tools and back up."

"We do, Fergie, wheels, tools, and backup."

TWENTY-SEVEN

Harry went back to his billet. He waved gently as Fergie took his leave.

"See soon, laddie," were Fergie's parting words.

Harry was glad of his painkillers. He took a good dose and settled in for the night. He did not attempt to set his body clock. He slept for once without dreams, or at least none that he recalled. He woke ready enough for whatever the day might bring. He was surprised to discover that it was past eleven. No wonder he felt less alert than usual he reasoned. Time's winged chariot. His exercise routine helped bring him to match fitness.

He found a place that served all day breakfasts and tucked into a hefty brunch. He had decided to stake out the locus in quo again but thought there was little point till later in the day. He doubted the suppliers were early risers. He went for a longish walk along the River Nidd which he found more or less by accident as he roamed the outskirts of Harrogate. It was unseasonably warm, and he sat by the riverside amongst the trees and rested. He was able to identify the trees accurately relying on his mother who had often told the interested little Harry their names on their walks in Minley Woods. At length he returned to the town. Again, Harry took up his watch on the bench. This time he did not have to wait long.

He was rewarded by the kids on bicycles spinning about rather aimlessly. There were four of them. Time for action. Harry walked towards them and realised that one of them was rather older and larger than the others.

"What do you want grandad?" This impertinence was from one of the tiddlers.

Harry walked on till he was within touching distance of the larger lad who tried to simply cycle round him. Harry moved deftly to one side to prevent this.

"You don't want to do that. Get out of the way."

Harry of course was not going to get out of the way and simply stood his ground.

"I have a couple of questions for you." He said this without menace but in a tone of voice which anyone would register as one of authority.

"We don't have to answer your questions."

"You can't tell us what to do."

"Tell him to fuck off Frog."

There was something about Harry's manner or posture or some unidentifiable menace that commanded attention.

"Do you know a Boosy or Bosey?"

"What's it to you?"

No denial then, noted Harry.

"Where can I find him?"

"Fuck off granddad." This from another of the tiddlers. Bravery in numbers. Out of range.

"Yeah, why not fuck off grandad?"

Mistake.

Harry simply stood to one side as if to let the larger lad past, but then leaned into him and sent him crashing to the ground, and then placed his foot on the bike holding the youngster down. The other three looked on not sure what to do.

"Tell them to go home," suggested Harry.

"We'll get the police onto you," protested one of them.

"Right, you do that," said Harry. "Off you go now."

Harry increased the pressure on the pinioned lad.

"Mister it really hurts."

"Tell them to bugger off," ordered Harry and pressed down again with his foot.

"Just fuck off" Frog shouted.

The kids decided to scarper. So much for loyalty.

"You're on your own now Froggie boy," said Harry.

Harry released the pressure just enough so that he could drag the lad from out under his bicycle. Frog tried to get up. Mistake.

Harry simply knocked his legs from under him and knelt on his neck.

"Mister please I can't breathe."

"Silence" said Harry. And there was silence. Harry's eyes bored into the lad's own, increasing the level of fear as intended.

"You and I are going for a little chat. If you are a very good boy you will come to no harm." Harry pressed down harder until he felt the boy go limp, and then released the pressure. Frog gasping for breath came round and looked up at Harry with very scared eyes.

"You nearly killed me," he whimpered. He had wet himself.

"What I want is an address for Bozo."

Harry had so established ascendancy over the youth that when allowed up, he even accepted Harry's hand to help lift him. He meekly walked in front of Harry as ordered and led him back to where he lived. It was not far but was quite a change from the Harrogate the tourists and gentile residents knew. Past the rugby ground they went, and Harry saw allotments on one side and beyond an industrial estate. They turned into a road part of older council housing. Here few doors and windows revealed owner occupation. At the end of the road was a footpath, and here Frog tried to run off. Harry was alert to this possibility and with a turn of reactive speed clipped Frog's heels and down he went.

Frog then simply gave up. After all he did not want to feel the pressure of Harry's knee on his neck again or worse. As he sat there Harry ordered him to apologise. Frog looked up at him and mouthed 'Sorry'.

"Right let's get on with it."

And with that he meekly led Harry to the house without further incident.

The dwelling had seen better days. Once someone had cared for it, as it had replacement windows and the signs of a well-kept garden now overgrown and gone to seed.

"Do you live alone?"

"It was me grandad's."

"I didn't ask you that."

"Yeah I live alone."

Harry imagined the old man's dismay that he who took pride in his house had now left it to this scum. Harry was taking a calculated risk. Yet he was pleased by the response. He detected the lad had decided to simply answer truthfully.

He waited patiently while the boy fiddled with his Yale, and finally getting it to yield, in they went.

He led Harry into the hallway and towards the open door that led to the kitchen.

"Sit down," commanded Harry quietly.

His measured quiet steady tones were not at all comforting to Frog.

Harry sat down opposite his victim.

It may be supposed that Frog imagined his submissive attitude and quiet obedience might make this all go away. After all, here they were sitting down together at his own kitchen table. Of course, the kitchen was a mess. He regretted that somehow as he felt it was wrong not to have tidied up. If he imagined he was in for an easy ride he was very much mistaken.

"Why Frog?"

"What yer mean?"

"Your silly name."

"Good at high jump, me, at school, and long jump."

"Right."

Frog was lulled into a false sense of security by the 'softly, softly, catchee monkey' style of questioning.

Harry had the serious question ready and launched it.

"Were you there when my friend George Palmer was attacked?"

"Who is George Palmer?"

Wrong answer. Harry produced the Glock.

Frog felt a sudden extreme tightness in his chest, and heard his own breath stop. Nothing is more noisome than unexpected silence. Frog had seen this sort of thing often but only in the virtual world of first-person shooter games he was so keen on. Looking down the barrel of a gun held by someone who Frog instinctively realised knew how to use it, was a quite different level of experience.

"Stay still."

Frog needed no prompting.

"I am going to tell you about George Palmer. When I have finished, I am going to ask you a couple of questions. If you answer honestly, I will leave and you need never see me again. Got it?"

Frog nodded.

Harry told him about George, and what he had done for his

country and his regiment, and his comrades, in some of the most dangerous war-torn places. Harry told him he owed his own life to George.

"So, you see it is very important that I track down who was responsible for his death. Do you understand?"

"Yes. Yes I do," stammered Frog, who did indeed understand, certainly enough to realise that this might not end well for him.

"Where is your phone?"

"Here. Here it is." He stuck his hand in his pocket and shoved the phone in its wallet towards Harry.

Harry examined the contents carefully. He set the phone to one side.

There were several bankers' cards, with different names on them, and a driving licence. The licence photo was clearly Frog. Phillip Morse. And there it was. The banker's card in the name of George Palmer.

"By the way why Bozo?"

"It's just a name me and me friends use for him."

"Yes but why?"

"My product. You can get it online innit. Buy or sell online."

"I see. BOZO."

"I want you to think back to that night now Phillip."

The use of his Christian name was no comfort.

"You talk like a polis."

"But I'm not a policeman Phillip.

Remember George did what he did to keep little boys like you safe."

Harry's voice was becoming darker and more menacing.

Frog started talking and found he couldn't stop. It all came gushing out like a first confession. Which in a way it was.

"He fought back mister, we didn't expect that, he was an old man. Why did he fight back? If I had known he was an old soldier."

"You attacked him. You hit him. You kicked him too, didn't you?"

Frog nodded, resigned now, surprising himself by preferring the truth.

"But I tried to stop him. I didn't want him to keep kicking him. He went mad."

Harry laid the card in front of Frog. He had not taken his eyes off the gun barrel. Harry told him to look at the card.

"Read the name on it Phillip. Read it out loud."

Now the gun was much closer, almost touching his forehead.

"Read it."

"George Palmer."

"Where does Bozo live?"

He gave the address. It was obvious he was telling the truth. No need to check.

Harry picked up the phone again.

Frog started saying in a panicky voice, "It's not my phone. It's not mine. It's not mine."

"Really, but it had your driver's licence in it. Unlock it."

"It's not mine."

Harry glanced again at the driving licence. He entered the date of birth as a six-figure number. The phone opened up.

Harry went to the photo library, and there it was. A video, of George, on the ground. And a voice recording. And laughter.

"Kick him again, Bozo."

Frog had gone very quiet.

Each of the next kicks was accompanied by the words "You stupid bastard," just as the old lady had told Harry.

"Who supplies Bozo?"

No answer.

"It's an easy question."

Still no answer.

"Look I can make this easy or very much harder for you. I imagine you couldn't really tolerate the sort of pain I could inflict."

Frog was beginning to really panic now. His breath came in short panting gasps.

"The only chance you have is to tell me what I want to know. Who supplies you?"

Frog had reached a tipping point.

"I only know his name as Ali. I really don't know anything else. Bozo does it all. It was all Bozo."

"Got any cash on you?"

"Yes, yes." Frog said this with relief as he thought perhaps payment would relieve him of punishment. He scrabbled to get into his side pocket. He produced two neat rolls of cash. No doubt gained from his punters.

Harry without pause raised the gun and shot Frog right between his eyes. It left a very neat hole to the front, to the back a gaping hole and quite a bit of splatter.

Harry lent over and lifted the cash. He had solved the immediate problem of lack of funds. He did not want to use a banker's card which might be traceable.

He hunted round a bit to find the casing for the bullet and slipped it into his pocket, the bullet he found embedded in the rough plaster of the wall. He took this as well for later disposal. The bins of Harrogate were filling up with his detritus.

He let himself out.

TWENTY-EIGHT

Bozo lived in Bradford. In a larger house than might have been anticipated, in a road tacked on almost as an afterthought to what had been the council housing, at end of a cul-de-sac.

Harry was pleased to see Fergie waiting for him, leaning on a telegraph pole set back from the road with a small area of grass verge between him and the footpath, not particularly inconspicuous, Fergie could never be that, but he just looked like an old man enjoying a ciggie outside, and nothing more.

The two of them had a little conflab: "We have funds, comms, intel, wheels, tools, and backup." Fergie thought this a more than adequate sitrep and he was now ready for action. He had picked up a bit of 4x2 which in an average hand would have been a clumsy weapon and perhaps overly long, but it lay neatly inside Fergie's greatcoat, and frankly he could have held two of them in one hand if he so chose. Fergie opened his coat enough so Harry could see the sawn-off shot gun neatly held within the large low inside pocket. Harry was a not in the mood to reason with his comrade much. These lowlives had earned what was coming to them, Fergie wanted to punish these creeps that much was obvious. Harry simply pointed out that quick in and quick out might be best.

"Reet ye are Harry."

"I prefer no gunfire."

"Reet Harry, no gunfire."

Fergie led Harry round the back of the house via a small

pathway, used for bin collections and the like. He had already carried out a recce that much was obvious. The rear of the house had a wooden fence and a gate, which Fergie shoved open without much resistance. It might have been bolted or it might not, but a shove with Fergie's shoulder was easily greater than any security provided by the gate.

They slipped into the back yard.

From then on it did not go quite so easily or cleanly, as a very tough looking pit bull of uncertain parentage greeted their arrival. Fergie was not in the mood to argue and anyway they needed to keep the element of surprise if they could. The silly dog launched itself at Harry, and nearly succeeded in sinking its teeth into his leg but for the very deft swing of the piece of 4x2, which knocked the dog seemingly senseless with one blow. They walked past the dog and peered into what seemed to be the kitchen, though not one you would want to cook in if you wanted to avoid food poisoning at any rate.

There were three of them sitting round the kitchen table, boxes of half-eaten food of the more dubious pizza and kebab type of takeaway. Plates seemed to be either an unheard-of luxury, or maybe they were simply piled in the sink awaiting a volunteer to wash them up.

As they were peering in, the dog tried for revenge and jumped up and tried to sink its teeth into Fergie's arse. Big mistake. Fergie hit it with his fist, and laid it out cold this time, for sure.

Unfortunately, even the drug addled idiots inside wondered what the commotion was all about. One of them levered himself up shouting, "Shut up you stupid cunt, Milly."

Milly didn't answer. Unconscious dogs don't bark.

"Go on out and check."

"Do I have to Bozo."

"I won't ask you again."

Harry decided they might turn this to their advantage if any of the occupants decided to investigate. The yard was not overlooked and so provided the perfect killing ground so to speak. Out came Milly's owner. To meet a blow from the 4x2, fully in the face, which stunned him and he sank to his knees with a surprisingly quiet and rather feminine sounding moan, and then keeled over and lay still.

Bozo piped up again, "What the fuck is going on, go and see."

The second victim stuck his head out and if he had had his wits about him might have noticed the man and dog lying rather neatly beside each other on the grass like some kind of artistic installation beloved by Tracey Emin and friends.

"What the fuck," was all he managed, as he too went down.

Fergie was really enjoying himself now, and growled,

"Bozo, Bozo, coom on out, Bozo, or I'll hauff and I'll puff and I blow ye hoose doon."

Harry decided to simply watch the entertainment.

Bozo came out. He obviously thought he could handle more or less any threat. He was quite big, rather fat though. His arrogance went before him. He presented a sizeable target.

Big mistake.

Fergie was not going to treat him lightly.

The piece of 4x2 was made of quite good stock considering it was just a piece of pine. Fergie hit him low to one leg and then to the other as if swinging a highland battle axe. Fergie's hand came over his mouth, and he pulled his victim towards him.

"Not a sound now," he said through gritted teeth.

"What do you want?"

"I told ye not a squeak out of ye," and he twisted his neck to emphasise his words.

"Let's talk inside shall we?"

Bozo was in no position to argue.

Harry kept a low profile and Fergie simply half lifted him and half pushed him inside and sat him down. Fergie swept the mess off the table. Looking over his shoulder he commented, "Thanks for ye help."

"You were doing fine on your own."

"You know why we are here don't you?"

Bozo shook his head.

"Do you remember mugging an old man in an alleyway recently?"

Bozo shook his head again.

Harry placed Frog's phone on the table in front of Bozo and played the film.

Bozo to his credit hung his head. Was it in shame, or was it simply fear? Harry was not inclined to give him the benefit of the doubt.

Harry then produced his gun which he also laid on the table. Bozo stared at it.

"Bozo, what is your real name?"

"Robert."

"Robert what?"

"Booth."

"Booth, Bozo right. Buy or sell online."

Bozo nodded. There seemed to be conversation here, maybe things were not as bad as he thought.

"Well, Robert is there, anything you want to say."

"Sorry. Sorry. Sorry."

"Who supplies you?"

"If I tell you I'm dead."

"You're dead if you don't. This is Judgment Day and it has

come to you right here. How convenient is that?"

Bozo was having difficulty breathing. Harry recognised the signs. There was no fight in Bozo. The interrogation was successful.

"Ali innit."

"Address?"

He gave an address. It was also in Bradford.

"How do you know him?"

"He found me. I was already doing a bit. He's a dangerous man. You don't want to mess with him."

Harry nodded. The interview was over.

Fergie who had after all not seen the film on the phone before, leaned over Bozo, looked down briefly at his feet. He pulled his head back and in one swift movement wrenched his head to one side and snapped his neck.

"He's wearing the silly white plimsoles did ye see, said Fergie as if this alone justified retribution on the scale meted out.

"Right let's get those bodies back in here."

That done Fergie legged it back to the Landy and reappeared within five minutes with a can of petrol. He doused the pit bull in the fuel, set it alight and chucked it through the window.

There was a gratifying noise as the gas which Harry had left on ignited and there was a satisfying explosion. "That should cover our tracks a bit," Fergie said.

"I certainly hope so Fergie."

Harry and Fergie drove off. They passed coming the other way a fire engine and a police car, blue lights and sirens.

"Hey Harry."

"What?"

"It's a good thing we didna use the guns. Might have been noisy and attracted attention like." Fergie could be quite eloquent when he chose to be.

TWENTY-NINE

Ruth did not need to be told that two murders in Harrogate within a week of each other was highly unusual. She could do with a name for the old soldier, 'George' was not enough to go on, but his age meant a search of military records and she hoped her contact in special branch might help her.

There was no fingerprint or DNA evidence of the deceased which was disappointing as many former soldiers were on the database somewhere as they frequently ended up with some kind of criminal record either in service or out of it.

Where was his bloody phone? His effects had simply been lost. Or perhaps he didn't have any. After all he was an old man with no obvious identity. "I tried boss," Robbie had said reporting the bad news, hoping she wouldn't shoot the messenger. He was in luck. Ruth simply nodded. She knew she had to accept it.

His age was all they had otherwise, though she felt she might get a surname by talking to service organisations, and charities, and maybe the British Legion was a good place to start. She could reply on the Para connection of this she felt sure.

Phillip Morse was easy to connect with Bozo. Had they both been involved in the attack on George Palmer? But this killing had strange features. He was known to the local police for being involved in relatively low-level drug supplying about which of course little or nothing had been done. Was this connected with county lines? The bullet between the eyes was efficient and meant the killer had delivered the coup de grace, eyeball to eyeball. Why? Not even the average professional hit which usually involved a second back up bullet. One was enough for this killer. He knew what he was doing. Police, military, who else. She could not imagine why the security services might be involved.

She supposed the drugs squad would become involved, though she doubted they would be much help. She wanted to find George's killer, but perhaps someone had got there first. She felt the other deaths were connected notwithstanding that this might just be a natural bias created by the unusual happenings close in time and place. In common with most detectives, she did not believe in coincidence.

She carried on speaking her thoughts aloud. "These killings seem more personal than simply the result, say, of keeping more than his share of money derived from supplying drugs. But perhaps it was intended as a message to anyone else tempted to stray. And what about the dog." Ruth understood that it might well have been a serious obstacle, so the killer or killers had to deal with it. Using it as a means to set fire to the house seemed relatively inefficient, but nevertheless interesting. It implied a certain level of brutality. This person or persons were not messing about. She could not help wondering if the dog was dead as it was hurled through the window but did not think she could really raise this with the SOCO or forensics. One of the victim's lower limbs had been broken and not by a fist but more like a weapon of some kind, not the gun, but maybe a baseball bat or something similar.

The explosion had made the crime scene almost impenetrable and certainly reduced the likelihood of anything useful from forensic examination. Booth's neck had been broken.

This was an extreme level of violence. She would have to wait for forensics on the potential murder weapon, but she doubted it would at this stage narrow it down much as to who the killer or killers might have been. She felt that it was not a lone wolf but possibly two or maybe more. She hoped door to door would turn up something, perhaps a description of the intruders or maybe a vehicle? Would she even get the resources she needed?

Ruth had asked for all serious crime reports from Harrogate. Apart from the shooting there really wasn't anything much to report. The connection with a known associate of the victim had led to Bradford and the burnt out house, and the dog used as a weapon. She had to reread this section, but it was clear the dog had been used as an incendiary device. She read it again. There were three bodies. Legs had been broken in one case, a face hit hard in another. The brutality was the most significant feature and that no one had seen anyone or reported anything untoward, apart from the loud explosion, initially thought to be caused by an accidental gas leak. This was, she felt sure, an execution not merely a killing. Who behaved with this level of violence? The silly phrase 'shock and awe' came to mind, she really must try not to allow her mind to speculate in this way. Concentrate on the facts.

Five killings: first the old man in the hospital. Then the young man, now these three. Was it military, or drugs or something to do with both? Did these drugs people use military force? She felt sure, whatever the uncertainties, this was not the end of it.

There was a quiet knock. Robbie put his head round her office door.

"Can I come and see you, ma'am?"

"The coat, ma'am. I went round the charity shops, there's quite a lot of them, ma'am."

"Robbie have you anything to tell me?"

"Right, well yes, big Scotsman, and I mean very big, bought one."

"I also went to the British Legion. I got short shrift, but I had the feeling that they were not willing to talk to me."

"Yes, well, I'll visit, and we'll see."

"No, ma'am." Robbie had already anticipated this and knew that the boys, old or young, in the Legion were not going to respond well to a female police officer and not a senior one or anyone really.

"What?" She was not used to Robbie asserting himself in this way.

"What I mean is I already sent someone."

"We have a sergeant here, he's the custody sergeant actually, Phillips."

"Oh do get on with it Robbie."

"He's ex-military you see."

"Oh right." Ruth saw the advantage of this. It was beginning to dawn on her that Robbie was indeed an asset. She must try to treat him better.

"Anyways, he went and reported back. He said there is a huge Scotsman. He's called Ferguson, an ex-sergeant major. Getting on a bit now."

"An address would be nice Robbie."

"No address. They sort of clammed up when asked. Sergeant Phillips added that he felt no more information would be given. He did ask them who he had drunk with regularly and so on. He said this actually, 'There's no point, once they knew I was police they clammed up, practically sent me to Coventry. I had never been, now I am not sure I would be welcome back.'"

"Well, I am sorry we spoilt his social life, but I suppose we might have to accept that we won't get much more out of them. Leave it with me, Robbie."

Robbie went to leave, and at the last moment, almost before he was out of the door, Ruth added, "Well done, Robbie."

He positively beamed.

"There," said Ruth to herself, "that wasn't too hard was it."

THIRTY

The two men reconvened in the Landy. Harry spoke, Fergie waited for the plan to emerge.

"I want to take Ali Baba out of his comfort zone. I don't think he is the type to go anywhere on foot. I doubt he walks those dogs. They are there as a deterrent to intruders, and might be loyal to him, but I doubt it. There are the usual signs up concerning security and who might be guarding the premises and so on, largely sale puff as no serious intruder would be deterred by silly signage, but no sign of onsite security. Once he gets in the Range Rover we could tail him and look for an opportunity, but I reckon he travels with muscle, and not often alone, which could make taking him down messy. In any event I want to interrogate him, and find out how he fits in, what his place is in the great scheme of things. Perhaps he does sometimes set off alone."

Harry was talking it through aloud. Fergie was used to this.

"I haven't seen any obvious signs of surveillance from, say, the drugs squad. Somewhat surprising."

"Probably cuts mean no money for round the clock stuff," contributed Fergie.

Harry went on, "There are cameras attached to the house and the driveway, but nothing leading out to the railway track, and behind the garages. Very poor CCTV layout, and I doubt there is any link to the police, so perhaps there is some internal security.

"I think he is quite an arrogant son of a bitch, so likely to think he is safe in his own house, probably armed. I am pretty sure I know which is his bedroom and so we could take him from inside. If we then snatch him and take him away in the Landy we would have to deal with the dogs, if they are roaming the grounds, but I came to the perimeter of the woods, and they showed no interest. Nothing a bit of steak won't deal with.

"If we do enter the house we would have to rapidly assess the layout, and if not questioning him in situ, we would have to have a clear pathway out and through the woods say over the railway track and away. He is quite a weight so really he would have to be made to walk under his own steam.

"OK so here's what we are going to do," and Harry laid out his plan to Fergie, who smiled and nodded.

"Let's get to it then, laddie."

Of course, all plans are only as good as their execution. It was now quite dark. They allowed their eyes to become accustomed to it and took time for nature to deliver their night vision. They crossed to the rear of the garages easily enough, the roofs of which connected to the main part of the vast house via a covered walkway. You might have expected Kevin McCloud to appear and wax lyrical about the house, except even for him this example was beyond vulgar.

There was an enormous velux-style skylight in the roof, but this was at a steep angle. Harry left Fergie on the roof of the walkway, where glancing back he saw his old comrade making himself really quite comfortable, wedged up to the corner of the garage roof out of sight, one of his huge legs stretched out and the other bent at the knee in a casual manner, as if he were contemplating a bit of sunbathing somewhere sunny.

Harry eased the velux open and peered into the upper storey of the main house and could not believe his luck. He had identified from external examination in daylight the arrangement of drainpipes which indicated a bathroom was under this window, but there was Ali in the sunken spa bath, like the poor man's Nero, bubbles rising, water swirling about. Rather disappointingly no naked maidens or asses' milk.

Harry dropped through the window. Ali was somewhat surprised to say the least to be confronted by a man dressed from top to toe in dark clothes face masked by a balaclava with barely a slit for the eyes. He did not, however, fail to notice the weapon Harry held in his hand and then the finger pressed to his lips.

Ali was at a serious disadvantage, and he knew it. For a moment, and as a first reaction, he was tempted to cry out. Help would surely come, but he was looking down the barrel of a gun and this tended to reinforce the desire if it were lacking to do exactly as he was told. He supressed the cry which disappeared as soon as it left his throat in a kind of pathetic croak.

The much more difficult part of the plan was about to be tested, and Harry knew it was very risky. He felt a frisson of excitement but did not allow the adrenaline to divert him from the task in hand. He had his escape route worked out if all went wrong and he hoped he could once out of the house, disappear behind the garages with Fergie, and over the short open expanse into the trees over the railway track and away. Fergie could deal with any pursuers or at least Harry imagined he would. Who would doubt it?

THIRTY-ONE

Harry spoke in Urdu to Ali who was somewhat taken aback, but understood well enough Harry's words. "We have your daughters. Stay quiet and do as you are told, and all will be well. Nod your head if you have understood." Harry wished to be clear but not to indicate anything about who he might be and what he wanted at this early stage.

Ali nodded. In fact, Noddy had nothing on Ali. He was far from reassured, and in fact understandably really quite scared. His security men were in the annex and sometimes wandered into the kitchen. He had only to press the alarm and they would come running. But what if this man was telling the truth and harm might result to his daughters. Ali was not really as brave as he sometimes wanted people to believe. The idea of tackling this man alone did not appeal to him at all.

"We are leaving by the back door. You will walk towards the garages. I will be right behind you. You will be met there and you will simply follow that man. Do you understand?"

Nodding some more Ali reached for his dressing gown. Harry watched him attempting to put on slippers. His feet couldn't easily do it. His legs wouldn't obey him. He was terrified, Harry noted with satisfaction.

Finally, after several attempts he got them on. Harry noted how grotesque they were, monogrammed as if Ali were some kind of aristo, like Churchill maybe. They walked outside. There was no challenge. Ali regretted not employing more muscle, or perhaps more intelligent muscle. Largely he relied on reputation. Those he threatened and used were in no position to challenge him.

The dogs started barking but by then Fergie was down off the roof and had left the hounds happily chomping on the large steaks he had brought with him in his handy shooting knapsack, and he led Ali towards the woods, and away. Then it was a simple procedure. Hood over his head, plastic ties round his thumbs and ankles and into the back of the Landy on the rear floor.

Ali did not have much experience of men even nastier than he was himself, but it dawned on him that these men were no amateurs. He knew he had better take them seriously.

They drove him to where, he did not know.

The track leading down to the bunker was no challenge to the old Landy, but to the man trussed up in the back it was an uncomfortable ride to say the least. Fergie and Harry were unconcerned about his comfort. They wanted him softened up and ready to answer questions.

They hid the vehicle off track. And spent a bit of time brushing tyre marks away, laying a few branches ahead of the Land Rover to help achieve this. Once driven into the forest and the branches had been picked up and dragged from nearby as camouflage and their tracks disguised, even if you knew the location of the bunker, you would not have easily found the means of transport.

THIRTY-TWO

Ali was pulled out of the Land Rover from the flattened tailgate and stood up. He was truly beyond fear now, in a sort of comatose state generated by terror, and his bladder gave way.

"Mucky boy," growled Fergie. Harry made a mental note to try and ensure Fergie gave no sign of their identities. No speaking. Especially for those with Glaswegian accents. Ali showed no sign of having heard Fergie speak.

Harry and Fergie took an arm each and manhandled him towards the bunker. Ali could just about shuffle along even though his ankles were tied. He realised he would be dragged if he didn't. His thumbs were beyond hurting now. His hands and upper arms suffering under the angle they were forced to adopt behind his back.

Ali tripped on a branch and nearly fell but was surprised to find he was almost lifted up bodily especially on the side where the larger man was supporting him. Fergie increased his grip on his upper arm and was tempted to reinforce his grip by issuing instructions but refrained from doing so. Words were not needed.

Fergie wrenched open the large steel door to the bunker, and in they went.

It was more difficult now to manoeuvre their captive as there were steps to negotiate, down into the inner recess of the bunker. Its thick walls intended to provide some kind of sanctuary in the event of nuclear war. Built in the 1950s, Harry wondered when it was last used. How the hell did Fergie know about it? He would find out later perhaps. For now, they concentrated on manhandling their captive down the stairs, where there was another door.

Fergie pulled it open, and they went in like some kind of bizarre three-headed creature.

Ali was encouraged to sit. He obeyed.

Harry spoke quietly in Urdu.

"If we take the hood off, you are not to make a sound. If you do, I'm afraid it will be the hood back on." Harry spoke calmy and politely.

This Ali found not comforting at all. The good manners were of course deliberately more undermining to the prisoner than simple thuggery might have been.

The hood was removed to reveal two chairs, either side of a table and one candle, unlit. The only other light was provided by the head torches worn by the men in balaclavas.

Harry sat on the seat opposite Ali.

Fergie stood behind Harry, a very menacing figure indeed all the more because he did not seem inclined to speak.

His brooding presence was enough. His silence alarming.

"Now before we start, I want to remind you that your daughters are still at risk." Harry left a pause for this to sink in.

"No speaking unless it is to answer my questions." There was a frantic nodding from the Ali.

The lights from the headtorches were very bright, not least because they had been turned to maximum strength. LEDs provide a powerful light for little power wastage.

Ali blinked and blinked and tried to turn his head to take in his surroundings while at the same time looking at his gaolers.

"Try to stay calm." Harry liked saying this as it tended to produce the opposite effect.

"The only light you will be allowed is this small candle. If you do not cooperate, we will leave, the door will be closed and in quite short time the candle will go out."

Ali started hyperventilating at this, he was obviously having some kind of panic attack, his breath turning to a rasping sound, and he struggled against his bindings. To no avail.

"Calm down," insisted Harry, which of course had the opposite effect. Ali struggled and tried to get up. Big mistake. A cuff from Fergie's paw was enough to bring him to his senses.

He accepted in that moment the uselessness of his position as he stopped struggling and his breathing returned to a more normal sound though still quite rapid.

Harry indicated that the hood should be put back on. Ali's eyes pleaded.

Harry placed something on the table in front of Ali.

The hood was in his hand.

"This is your phone."

There was silence.

"We need the access code."

Ali showed a little more spirit. Perhaps it had dawned on him they were not going to kill him right away. They wanted something. He did not of course want more punishment. He understood violence but usually handing it out. He had been protected. He had been born in England, in Bradford, and simply didn't have the hinterland. All that money his innocent parents had spent on him, the private education, the expensive vacations, the latest phones and gadgets and no expense spared. He did not trade in fear to his own person. He had few resources hidden or otherwise in the courage department. If only his grandfather was there. He would know how to handle these two.

His grandfather, who Ali only knew by reputation was a

tribesman, from the Pakistan side of the Afghan border. His son had found refuge in the UK. Ali's father had been successful in his 'import export' business, evading the taxman was all part of it, and employing near slave labour. Ali had been sent to an expensive school.

Harry was somewhat surprised that Ali was so resistant to giving up his phone access code. Probably because there were revealing things on there, Harry concluded without taxing his deductive powers very much, if at all.

"Where's your wife Ali?"

Ali was surprised that the questioning seemed more friendly than he had expected.

"She left."

"And took the kids with her?"

Harry asked this quietly with apparent empathy.

Harry asking him in Urdu disturbed Ali especially since he hardly ever used it these days. His grandmother only had spoken it to him, but she was long gone. His wife never. She called her father-in-law 'that bandit from the mountains'. He had enough to understand Harry clearly enough. He couldn't quite place the dialect though. Ali plucked up the courage to ask.

"Where you learn to speak like that?"

Harry had achieved his aim. There was now a conversation, which was his preferred interrogation technique even when time was of the essence. It was not a conversation between equals.

"I've spent time amongst the believers and the righteous," explained Harry.

"I'm not an infidel. I'm not, I'm a believer."

"But you are not a good man," said Harry stating no more than the simple truth. "You have dishonoured your wife and family."

Ali knew enough of a more ancient culture to know this was serious.

"No, it was her, it was her," shouted Ali, who thought he had understood why he was here now.

Harry took a wild guess.

"But you beat her. You hit her."

There was deafening silence.

"Do you repent?"

"I do, I do, I do," whimpered Ali. "I really do man," pleaded Ali sinking into the vernacular.

"Let me out of here man," said Ali in English, turning his head slightly to look over Harry's shoulder, attempting to appeal perhaps to Fergie. Fergie made no sign he had understood anything at all.

It dawned on him that these two men may not allow him to leave, ever. They were going to kill him for the way he treated his wife. Was it her family that had employed these thugs?

As if reading his mind, Harry continued in Urdu, "You may be permitted to leave, but only after you answer my questions."

"You ain't English are you?" said Ali. "Are you Afghan maybe?" If this was a wild guess it impressed Harry as it was closer to the truth than was comfortable.

Harry simply put his finger to his lips. Ali fell silent. Afghan was not good.

He was becoming more and more confused.

There had been no violence beyond the rough handling in his arrest. But his situation did not look good, and that was because it wasn't.

He had no idea where he was. The two head torches more or less blinded him but he was aware that the only other light appeared to come from one small candle.

"PIN number for your phone."

Ali was confused. "PIN?"

"Give it up now."

Ali did not answer.

"Last chance," said Harry.

Still silence.

"Right. Off we go then." And Harry got up to leave. Fergie followed him.

"No, no don't leave. Please. Please." He began to beg.

"Don't worry. When you feel the need for company just knock quietly on the door. Maybe someone will come… but then again maybe they won't."

This all delivered sotto voce, in a language Ali barely recognised.

As Harry rose he picked up the phone, and they turned away. Ali was left with very little to comfort him. The little candle provided very little light.

It was all too obvious that it would only do so long as it burned. The terrifying thought entered his head unbidden and unwanted. This might the last light he would see. He was absurdly grateful they had not replaced the hood.

As the door closed firmly and he was left alone, it could be assumed, not surprisingly, he began to panic. Listening at the door not a sound could be heard inside. The soundproofing effect provided by the nuclear bunker was too great.

Balaclavas now off the two men stood outside for a minute or two. Outside the bunker in the woods was a fallen tree trunk. Harry gestured to Fergie to sit with him. He wanted to have a short debrief before taking any further action.

"Twenty minutes tops and he will be in darkness."

"Let's give him an hour."

"Or two."

Fergie volunteered to extract any information Ali had but Harry was keen to try and ease information out of him and wanted to maintain discretion, and the weight of the interrogation in Urdu. He knew this approach might reveal better results providing intel that could be relied on.

"The thing is, at present he has no idea who we are."

"That lingo, what is it Harry?"

"Urdu of a kind."

"Where did you pick that up then Harry?"

"Now is not the time Fergie, but the Hindu Kush if you must know."

"The Hindu what?"

Harry provided no more information. Fergie had no more questions as he wanted time to process. It didn't matter very much to him. It was like old times.

In his experience some old comrades simply became too tired and old to bother with getting in touch. When younger the feeling was why not live in the moment, and then there was always time, and then there wasn't. Fergie had not spent much of the last twenty years out of Harrogate, except for one or two visits to the auld country.

He had watched the twin towers crash and burn. Who hadn't? Part of him regretted he was not still in the military. The army seemed to offer once again interesting opportunities, but he had taken retirement, and no one asked him to become involved. He was not much interested in the politics and was not inclined to confront the absurd 'axis of evil' promoted by Bush and his cronies. What was it to do with him? He had largely allowed world events to pass him by and cared only for those close to him. As it panned out, as yet another military disaster, he was on balance glad to have kept out of it, though of course several soldiers he knew died or were injured in the obviously pointless conflict. He realised now that Harry had been involved. It mattered nothing to him that Harry had not kept in touch. He had not either. It was part of the way their relationship had always operated. They were clandestine by inclination. He was glad he was by his side again. It was where he felt he should be.

"Youse are not thinking of him coming out of this alive?"

"Actually, it is possible. The balance of advantage may lie with seeing who he runs to."

"Or who comes for him," contributed Fergie with some satisfaction.

"Or who comes for him," agreed Harry.

THIRTY-THREE

"Harry have we really got time for this?"

"I want him to give up as much information as possible. If we go in too early when we question him again and leave him he may think we are going to come back again."

"OK, Harry. It's your call."

Harry suggested they got some sleep.

Harry was impressed when Fergie told him the water system and boiler all still functioned. There was an underground blockhouse arrangement with kitchenette and showers. They showered. There was hot water.

"I didna think I want to sleep down here."

"Me neither Fergie, me neither."

So, they returned to the Land Rover, and made themselves more or less comfortable. They were after all, old soldiers and a Landy was a home from home. They each closed their eyes and fell rapidly asleep.

Harry woke first and thought to rouse Fergie. This was always a risky business, as he could easily mistake the person who woke him up for an assailant.

Harry had had the common sense to approach this tricky operation from outside the Land Rover. He opened Fergie's door carefully, and with the door between him and Fergie only opened enough to gently awaken him, he gently pushed Fergie's upper arm.

Fergie's great hand suddenly launched forward towards Harry's throat. Harry rapidly withdrew his arm and pushed the door between him and the great hand, while saying quite loudly,

"No Fergie, it's all right, it's me, Harry."

Fergie seemed not to realise what was going on at first. He stared at Harry wild eyed, a fearsome sight, but then with a shake of his head, came to his senses.

Of course, he neither apologised nor offered an explanation. He simply carried on as if nothing untoward had taken place. He clambered out of the Land Rover and led Harry back to the bunker.

Fergie eased the door open and listened hard. There was no sound at first. And then a small whimpering, like a lost animal, a small dog perhaps, no words.

They had the powerful headtorches on again. And the double beam picked out the creature who held his arm up to his eyes with his back to the wall and his knees drawn up. There was a very unpleasant smell.

As the lights zeroed in on his face, a slightly more coherent sound passed his lips.

"Cha cha na cha cha na."

And again, and again.

Fergie mumbled under his breath for Harry's ears only, "Is he mad? He canna want to dance."

"Dance?"

"Cha cha chachacha."

Harry shook his head. Harry produced the phone and tapped in the numbers. They were Urdu for 669669. The phone opened. Harry nodded and gestured towards the chair. Fergie lifted the man up and levered him across the bunker. Harry took one arm and provided some assistance. They sat Ali down on the chair, released his bindings, gave him a glass of water.

They left Ali once more despite his pleading and found a dry spot to examine his phone. The number did indeed open it up. So far so good.

Then Harry saw the photos. He was not happy.

"What is so interesting on his phone Harry?"

Harry just handed the phone over. It looked small in Fergie's massive palm. Fergie began to emit a noise from his throat not unlike a growl.

"Some of the wee lassies are na more than fourteen, if tha'."

"I suppose we shouldn't be surprised he was not just into drugs."

"Wha' we talking aboot here, Harry, trafficking?"

"Maybe. Maybe more local. Hard to tell from the photographs, but I would say they are local."

"Not just porn then. Virtual stuff?"

"I don't think so," said Harry. "I think this maybe some kind of gallery of what's on offer."

"OK, Harry but it's nothing ta do wi' George reet?"

"What's this number with a name? Nautilus? Some kind of ship maybe?"

"And he rings this number the most," Harry pointed out. "Time for more focused questioning, I think."

They knew it was better to wait for a time to soften Ali up further.

On the other hand, Harry wanted to get on with it, and Fergie was not a patient man.

They need not have worried, because Ali had now lost all courage. He had after all given up his phone and must have known the game was up.

He had one more card to play but he was not sure really what he was dealing with and how it would play out. Might this not hasten his end?

Harry observed, "I doubt he has the moral fibre to hold out any more and what really can he add?"

Fergie had manhandled him back onto his seat.

Harry once more sat opposite him.

He simply blurted it out, his trump card.

"I'm with the police, they are bound to be looking. I know virtually nothing about you. You can just let me go."

Harry shook his head slightly.

"Even the police don't do deals with child pornographers and people traffickers."

"They don't know about any of that man," said Ali desperately.

"I'm not, I'm not. He was struggling now to find the right words.

"I'm not involved in that stuff. Not directly," he added. He then decided to sail a bit closer to the truth.

Harry reckoned if he were 'with the police' he could only be some kind of snout, not undercover.

"Who is this Nautilus?"

"Dunno."

"He deals in the shipments doesn't he?"

"I don't know."

But Harry detected he was now onto something. He was trafficking in people, in children, young girls, families, but separating the girls. He could not help speculating in his mind, seeking for the possibilities. And drugs. Or were the drugs separate?

"Who is your contact for the drugs, the supplier? If you want to see the light of day just tell me."

Ali told him.

"Right," said Harry. "We will check it out and be back."

"No no, don't leave me here. Please man, please."

"Will it check out?"

"Yes yes it will."

Harry produced two small candles and lit one.

"Let there be light," were his parting words.

Ali's eyes reflected in the candlelight, a looming sense of panic, but there was no fight left in him. They left him sitting there.

"How are we going to check it out?"

"We are not going to do it immediately."

"We could text on Ali's phone and say that he has to see any contact in person."

"There is text traffic which shows how it goes on still on his phone."

"Not very security conscious. Bit of a chancer, I reckon."

"Thought he was safe enough."

"If he is a snout won't the police be monitoring his phone?"

"Probably," said Harry.

"How you going to deal with that?"

"We will have to be careful won't we," murmured Harry.

"You are serious about letting him go?"

"So we can see where he goes and who he meets."

"Alreet, laddie, it's your decision. What if he simply runs off to his minder and tells all?"

"I don't think they will gain much intel from that."

THIRTY-FOUR

Ali was pathetically pleased to find his captors had returned.

"Would you like a chance to wash?" asked Harry.

"Yes please. Yes. Yes please."

"OK I'm going to go through the phone, your contacts, and you tell me who they are."

Ali resisted not at all. Harry made pencil notes in a little notebook of the kind issued to army officers in a bygone time.

"Right off we go."

Ali looked at Harry in disbelief. He was bewildered.

"You have been a good boy, so we are going to set you free. Shower first I think."

Ali began to believe, after all why otherwise would they allow him to clean himself up? He was too ignorant to know the irony that a shower being offered to a Jew might have generated.

Just an old T-shirt, pullover, and a pair of draw-cord trousers. A clean pair of socks.

Ali enjoyed putting those on. It surprised him how much comfort they brought.

His shoes were clean and left by the shower door.

It was all quite surreal.

Ali looked alarmed by the prospect of the hood being produced again. Nevertheless, he meekly accepted it back on. What choice did he have? He didn't believe that they were going to set him free, but he simply wanted the ordeal over. A quick end.

They got Ali to his feet, up the steps, out into the open. He was bundled into the back of the Landy.

Half an hour later they stopped and pulled him out.

"Please don't kill me, please, please," he whined.

"Stay quiet now," insisted Harry. They shuffled him off the road and into the woods.

They left him sat in amongst the trees a few yards from the side of the road. He sat there with the hood on. Who knew for how long? He grew cold. He found his voice. "Anyone there?" he whined. No answer. He tried again. Silence, only the sound of the breeze brushing the trees.

Eventually, he plucked up the courage to lift the hood enough to sneak a look about him. He fully expected to be severely reprimanded or worse for daring to do this. It was quite dark.

He became aware that in his pocket was a phone. He was not tempted to call the police. Looking at the phone, which was fully charged, he saw there was no signal. It was a long walk into the nearest settlement, and he couldn't rid himself of the sensation that he was being watched, or that they might come back for him. Any vehicle he saw, and there were mercifully few, meant he reacted by stepping off the road and into the tree line unsure if it were his captors returning.

Eventually, he recognised the village as only some ten miles from Bradford. It felt truly bizarre. Eventually the phone indicated one bar, and he was able to call for an Uber.

From Ali's perspective these dangerous men had the details of his contacts, and he was not at all sure this would end well for him. He knew those contacts included people who were unlikely to thank him for passing on their details. He was a worried man.

Harry and Fergie drove off comfortable that Ali couldn't identify them, or even the type of vehicle very easily as they doubted he would know the old Land Rover's tell-tale sound and smell. Every old soldier knows it. Ali was not an old soldier or any kind of soldier at all except in the virtual world of gaming or in his imagination. His experience had proved that that was nothing like the real world. They were pretty sure Ali would not want to involve the police. If he chose to warn those higher up the food chain, so be it. Harry and Fergie had factored this possibility in. Bring it on.

Harry thought it now important to brief the whole team. They would for instance need the full team to track and trace Ali's visitor, and the friendly access to reg number identification.

This was clearly not going to be a simple two-man operation.

THIRTY-FIVE

Ruth levered herself out of the bath. She liked it hot, but she had lingered and allowed it to go cold. Lost in her thoughts.

The house was small, but big enough for two with perhaps a child. One large bedroom and one small. A quiet cul-de-sac and a place to sit outside albeit back-to-back to the next little street, allowing only a small front garden. Ruth had bought it because she liked it, and without much concern then for the future. It was the first and last house she viewed. It was built of stone, which implied in her mind at least, some degree of permanence. She grew cornflowers and nasturtiums from seed in the small front beds. She liked to sit quietly often solitary in the sun in her own domain. It had the same bathroom suite as when she had bought it, an unfashionable avocado, and a whole wall as a mirror. It had come with the house, and she had liked it at first. She was after all single, young, and she had the body of a dancer which she had loved in her teenage years and before. The mirror allowed her to enjoy her reflection, and to take in the whole, her warm complexion. She was if she thought about it at all proud of her body. Now though the reflection reminded her of so many unwise and failed attempts at love, the easy giving of herself. Brief lustful disappointments, fumbles and even where successful, what was the outcome, bloody men who couldn't be trusted.

She was only forty-eight for God's sake. She still had a good body. As if to prove this she ran her hands down her sides and along her thighs. She was tempted by her own hands to provide some semblance of sensuality. A good body 'for her age' she supposed the young men who she now dated would say. Dated. Fucked more like. Each and every one a petit mort. No kids. *Thank God*, she said to herself, with a kind of wistfulness that revealed a high degree of self-deception. They might think her barren or perhaps didn't even care to know. They certainly didn't ask her.

She would never forget the night she decided to rid herself of the beginnings of new life, that she had suspected and then confirmed lay within her. Just a dot easily rubbed out, like a smudge of ink perhaps. The stain remained. The memory had grown if the child had not. What seemed the right choice, a 'no brainer' all those years ago, emerged as her number one regret.

Those years as her career took off, and she was still young, and even though she had decided she would not make a good mother, it was not anyway the right time, all the usual banal justifications any woman uses to justify delay, now all seemed built on sand.

The child would be all grown up now. She imagined him, for it was always a him in her mind. How beautiful he would have been. She greeted news from others, now and then a female colleague, complaining of the stress their children caused, the conflict, the disappointments, with very mixed feelings. Their pride in every small success was not enjoyed by her. Of course, she made the right noises. Her self-justifications unspoken, grew louder as time passed. How would she have supported the child? How could she hope for success in a man's world, especially as a policewoman?

And she was a success.

She had experimented without makeup. Men didn't wear it, at least on duty and on the whole not off duty either, so why shouldn't she do without? She was very attractive with or without, but she found with distaste and not without some self-recrimination, that putting on her 'face', helped her confidence.

She resumed drying herself. She abandoned her masturbatory impulses, on the grounds of lack of time, and the inclination soon passed. She started applying, skilfully, her war paint. As she did this she found, as ever, she was able to push all sentimental thoughts out of her mind. As she applied eye liner and peered closer into the mirror, a thought entered unbidden. What would she do when the day came that she lost her prepossession and self-control? She pulled a face and stuck out her tongue and the childish gesture made her laugh at herself.

The job in hand must come first. She had what she believed to be a dangerous killer to track down. She looked at the notebook left by her bed. What had she written. Soldier? Tattoo. Pegasus=Para? Special Forces? Security services, the visitor? The big man, also soldier? Easier to find. She wondered if their footprint would be heavy or light. No names. 'Pete Smith' she dismissed and then thought again, better check. Hiding in plain view might stretch to a name. She felt instinctively it would not be easy. She had been brought in late, only after the old boy died. She was already preparing excuses, justifications for failure. She did not have a good feeling about this inquiry.

She would contact Tim. She thought about doing this as she drove towards the station. What sort of team would she get, if any? Would there be much local support? She had Robbie of course. Maybe he had turned up something already. She resolved to be more encouraging. His keenness was an asset even if she found it irritating to say the least of it. He was not to know how little she wanted to hear of his young children, his lovely wife, the photos in his wallet. Why had she asked to see them? There was one of the undeniably pretty wife and two boys, blonde hair, maybe four and three, happy smiling faces, and a matching one of the grandparents doting on their grandchildren. Christ. How fucking smug they all looked. No, that would never do. She must try and be more tolerant. How often had she said this to herself?

Tim. Oh Tim. The young officer of her memory swam before her mind's eye, and even if she was reluctant to admit it, he had never left her thoughts really. Unwelcome memories would strike her unbidden, uncalled for, and yet not banished, treasured even.

She had followed his career from afar. He was now Colonel Tim Falks OBE. He had looked after her at Brize Norton, when her need was very great. She had seen him on the telly, standing next to Paddy Ashdown in Kosovo. She recalled his Para red beret. She wondered idly why they called it red when it was, to her eye at least clearly not red but maroon. The RMP beret was red. She might ask him. No, surely she could do better than that.

On the telly he had that small self-assured look with a trace of a smile. He might help her. She found herself helplessly drawn back, her mind wandering and then focusing on a memory that could hit her anytime. The offloading of the coffins. The Union Flags draped over them, the escort guard. The band playing. The bugler, inevitably the Last Post. How cold it seemed though the sun was shining. Was there wind, she couldn't remember. This bothered her, as if she should remember every detail. Then the officer that led her to the reception area, really just part of the hanger.

She had not cried then, and still had not shed a tear. The last tear had fallen when her father died suddenly in front of her mother. One moment there he was sitting on the sofa, and the next he leant forward and sort of slithered onto the floor. Hardly a groan or a murmur.

There was a kind of anger deep inside her, and it still simmered away. She sometimes felt the loss inside her grow as if the life she had killed had survived and grown in spite of her decision to rid herself of it. Too bloody right she had. The whole thing was a fucking abortion. This stupid ceremony. The comforting words, meant sincerely and kindly. How can words help?

Suddenly she was aware of a truck, a large one, coming towards her, straight towards her, head on. She was on the wrong side of the road. She could see the panic in the truck driver's face. She swerved violently to avoid collision, and nearly rammed a bollard on the near side of the road. The truck mercifully passed by without striking her and she came to an abrupt halt. The truck did not stop. She sat stock still for a moment and was aware of the cold clammy sweat on her forehead which she attempted to wipe away with the back of her hand. She looked about her and was relieved. No one was taking any interest in her near-death experience. She restarted the car, backed up a bit and made her way forward towards the station carefully and deliberately, without haste.

THIRTY-SIX

"Tim."

"Tim." This time more insistently. Tim looked up from his Telegraph.

"There's a call for you, some woman. She seemed to think it important, said she knew you from Brize Norton."

Tim Falks looked at the name hastily scrawled on the scrap of paper his wife thrust into his hand, as she headed towards the hallway.

"Going to Waitrose darling, back soon."

Falks stared at the name on the paper. Why now, wondered Falks. He was not keen on voices from the past, especially if they might be relatives, unable to move on or otherwise crying foul. He did recall the name Ruth, of course he did, but the surname was indecipherable so perhaps it was another.

"Hold on a mo'," he called out, but his wife was already on her way, and he heard the front door falling shut behind her.

Could it really be Ruth? Did he want to speak to her again? This was frankly a ghost from the past he could do without. "Right," he said to himself, "I had better deal with this straight away." Best dealt with while his wife was out. In any event, procrastination was not in Falks' nature.

He left a message on his wife's phone. In his work she was not unused to this. The discovery that Ruth was now a senior policewoman, and investigating a murder prompted a quick response. She had been very circumspect on the telephone, but it was enough to pique his personal and professional interest.

Anyway, his curiosity got the better of him. So here they were meeting informally in the very pleasant surroundings of Betty's Tea Rooms on the edge of the Stray, in Harrogate. She looked out of the window onto the floral gardens, green sward, and mature trees of the Stray. She gave him the bare facts. He listened carefully. She waited for him to speak.

"You realise I am retired now?"

She nodded. He must have been nearly sixty she supposed. God he looked so much younger than that and yet she couldn't help comparing him unfavourably with the officer she knew so many years before.

"Early retirement was it?"

He nodded noncommittedly.

They were interrupted by the waitress who took their order, just coffee.

Ruth was not going to introduce anything from the past. She could not help but recall their last meeting. So cliched, grief producing desire. Even then it could have meant the end of his career. Now it would presumably be just embarrassing. Certainly to her.

Falks was relieved when she clearly did not want to reminisce, and she got straight to it.

Ruth told him the bare facts, and why she was sure he was a serviceman. She also told him about the other two bedside visitors.

"Not much to go on I'm afraid," she half-smiled and looked at him apologetically.

She told him why she thought the dead man might have been an ex-Para.

"Lots of those about."

Ruth thought she detected a bit more interest than that but said nothing.

Then she asked, "Am I wasting your time then?"

"No, no, not at all. I might be able to make some enquiries."

He tried to sound as if he was only doing this as a favour, but Ruth was beginning to think there might be more to it than that.

Falks' mind was racing now. These were people he did not expect to appear on the radar again. Long gone, and best forgotten. "Least said soonest mended," as Nanny would have said, he thought. He was not sure about George, or the other man the police knew as Pete Smith. He had his suspicions but the big Scotsman, he had to be Ferguson. Of course, he could not be sure, but he was already certain. Who else could it be by that description?

Falks told her nothing more. He needed time.

He tried to distract with pleasantries. How lovely it was to see her after all this time. Looking so well. He asked her about her career, but she sensed he already knew about it all.

He drank up his coffee, and he offered to pay, which Ruth accepted with good grace, and he took his leave. Ruth had decided to stay seated, not that she wanted any more coffee. She simply didn't want an embarrassing and insincere farewell, or frankly to spend any more time in his company. It was nice enough in the café, with its view of the gardens. She wanted a bit of time to herself. Watching his back as he left she could not help remembering, his lithe strength as he picked her up and grasped her in his arms, the ease with which he slipped her panties to one side or was it her who slipped them to one side. She recalled now how she had been, open and ready, wet and willing. She would never tell anyone this, but she understood well the phrase 'gasping for it' and how grateful she was for his enthusiastic thrusting into her against the wall of the ladies' lavatory compartment.

The interesting thing was how little it meant now. Just a memory. Neither good nor bad. She hadn't felt much then at least on the surface, and as is sometimes thought usual, there was no remorse afterwards. There was none. No, the conscience came later as she realised she was already pregnant, and the repeated intrusion into her mind of the life she simply destroyed. It was hard not to hate him, and herself.

THIRTY-SEVEN

Harry was somewhat surprised by the quality of people going in and out, or more properly by their lack of quality. He supposed it was inevitable that some of the contacts in Ali's phone would be lowlives and had already decided that this one was not worth diddly squat. He really wanted to tackle those higher up in the food chain and this was a distraction. He turned to walk away from the bus shelter he had been using as a temporary shelter to observe those going in and out of the big run-down Victorian house. It looked imposing but had had little or no maintenance probably for at least a decade or even two in Harry's estimation. It was a testament to the mixed areas of affluence cheek by jowl with deprivation on the outskirts of Bradford.

A hoodie started walking along the path towards him. Harry sought to avoid trouble unless it came to him, and simply turned to walk away. It was unfortunate that this silly youngster decided to try it on despite Harry's best efforts. Harry was keeping to his policy of not seeking confrontation and anyway wished to remain as anonymous as possible.

Perhaps the idiot thought Harry would be an easy target for a bit of cash or cards or his phone or whatever.

"Where you goin' grandad?"

Harry did not turn round and did not reply and kept walking.

The young goon was bigger than average and Harry could hear him breaking into a ponderous run behind him. Probably his best effort.

Suddenly Harry turned and ran towards his assailant, that is straight at him, head down, without the slightest hesitation, accelerating rapidly. Attack is the best form of defence. This caused uncertainty in the mind of his attacker. Harry had decided simply to take him down. He had already assessed that it was relatively safe from observation as he now had the bus shelter between himself and the road and the high unkempt privet hedge on the other side of the path. No one was coming down the path in either direction. All this Harry had taken in, assessed and response decided, and to be fair so had his assailant. Of course, neither could legislate for passing cars.

Quite who was attacking whom was now less clear, as the woman who drove past reported later to the police. Not that she saw much as she deliberately put her foot down and accelerated past the incident. The result was a desk examination some weeks later and no action. Filed away for insufficient evidence but then none had been gathered. The police were nothing if not consistent in their lack of interest as they had been in the case of the attack on George Palmer.

The distance between them reduced rapidly. The hoodie's foot went out in a kind of pathetic attempt at a kung fu style kick. Perhaps the puffy youth played video games or liked the Karate Kid films. He was living in a fool's paradise, a phrase which he would not have understood, but an idiot is still a fool even if he can't understand the Queen's English and had not paid attention at school. It ended very badly for the fool. Harry simply maintained his momentum and unleashed his upper body, crashing his forearm into the neck of his target. It was the kind of blow that earned you a red card in rugby these days, actually, probably a sending off at any time in the history of rugby and for good reason. There was not even time for the loser to show surprise.

Harry followed up the first blow with a Zidane head butt which smashed into his attacker's chest, and down he went, and he followed it up with a hard kick to the side of his temple, obeying the mantra taught by his army instructor, never kick a man until he is down. Harry knew that the temple is the weak spot on the skull which offered little or no protection. Maybe because he was going soft in his old age or some semblance of something like reason intervened, but Harry had not used full force in the kick, and the lad was still breathing. He rang for an ambulance.

Harry dragged the inert body into the bus shelter and arranged it somewhat as if asleep or drunk and comatose, but in the recovery position so that his airways were free, and with apparent casualness walked away with his swift yet unhurried regular stride.

He felt the need for some rest after all this excitement, but he was not for lingering in Bradford, as this was no longer where the trail was leading and might become too hot to stay, inviting discovery.

What they needed, Harry surmised, was to find the importer and the port of entry or perhaps there was more than one, and eventually the money men.

THIRTY-EIGHT

"Do we have a solution?"

The question was directed at Pyro Pete, the combat engineer. They were now a fully operational unit of four. Fergie, Snip, Pyro, and Harry. There was no feeling of hierarchy about the group though they naturally treated Harry as their leader.

Harry had mixed feelings about Pyro. He was undoubtedly gifted with explosives, electronics and IT. But he was a loose cannon.

He had shown this to Harry even when just a schoolboy. He happened to live just across the way from Harry's home. They had both been army cadets at school, and while there, tended to do the ordinary run of shooting, camps, and so on. Pyro, armed with his chemistry from school and simple materials gathered in his dad's garden shed was much more dangerous than the average boy. The turning on of the tap to allow the petrol to flow and then lighting it was not good as it burnt his dad's garage down, only not spreading to the main house because the wind was blowing in the other direction. Harry, who was a couple of years older than Pete, was drawn to the flames as he could see his neighbour's garden from his own, which stood on higher ground. Harry learnt later that there was some fuss with the insurance company and allegations of the fire having been set deliberately though never proven. Pete stayed shtum about it and got away with it. They were not exactly friends because of the age gap which to schoolboys was almost impossible to bridge, but Pyro's invitation to blow up some stuff was irresistible.

They both lived near Minley where the Sappers amongst others trained, and Pyro's house backed onto Ministry of Defence land. In a way given this background it was no surprise that youngsters living nearby, for whom the woodland and open space was a playground, were drawn towards the army and indeed played war games at every opportunity. There was even a lake where sail training and fun was to be had though there were silly signs largely ignored which read things like 'Danger! Poisoned' to deter mucking about in the water. Of course, to a certain kind of youngster, it read as an invitation if not as an imperative.

There were quiet corners to these military training areas, which were largely broadleaf woodland, large pathways, and smaller ones across heathland, and amazingly up onto higher ground where there was a small airstrip built by the engineers as a training exercise, and still used for helicopters to land troops and practise other military manoeuvres. From this vantage point the Royal Aircraft Establishment at Farnborough could be viewed, and a free ticket to watch the famous air show. Harry saw Concorde on its first test flight, was surprised by jump jets which would land nearby, hiding amongst the trees, and watched all kind of military manoeuvres especially from engineers practising river crossings and building bridges.

Harry was known to Pyro as the boy who lived in the big white house on the hill. It could be reached through a bucolic indeed idyllic stretch of woodland, but only two minutes on foot from Pyro's home assuming you knew the short cut through the woods.

Pyro arrived with his small rucksack. Inside was some copper tubing cut to maybe twelve-inch lengths, a neat hole drilled in each to allow a magnesium fuse to be inserted into the bottom of the tubes. Hammered shut, Pyro then poured in his explosive mix which was sugar as a catalyst but sodium chlorate principally – aka weedkiller – from his dad's garden shed. All this he explained to Harry. The dangerous bit was the gaiety and abandon with which Pyro used a small hammer to close the other end of the tube once loaded with the explosive. He led Harry to a sort of lightly excavated sand gravel pit, where large trees on its edge were exposed by falls of terrain, exposing their roots.

Pyro crawled into the tunnels which had formed naturally no doubt by the action of the weather, and scrabbled about churning out more sand as he ventured under the overhanging tree roots. Harry was not keen to climb into these tunnels as it seemed obvious to him that falling earth and sand presented an avoidable hazard, and a fall could lead to being buried alive. He did want to see what the effect of the bombs might be, so he stood and waited nearby.

In a minute or two a breathless Pyro was at his side and the first one went off with a sort of muffled crump, and the satisfaction of a tree falling neatly into the pit. The second one was louder and more sand and gravel were blown out of the tunnel.

Success.

"Timber!" yelled Harry and Pyro joyously.

Pyro was keen to set another. Harry was not so sure but was caught up in the excitement.

This third one did not go so well. Pyro had miscalculated, or let's face it as Harry told it later, it was all pretty roughly calculated. The thing blew early before Pyro could get out of the tunnel, and he was submerged under the sand and gravel that fell upon him, and the tree above swayed about as if trying to find its feet, its stability undermined but perhaps not completely lost.

Harry had no time to consider the danger, and in he went scrabbling with his bare hands for all he was worth. It is sometimes said that there is no better baler at sea than a drowning man in a boat armed with a bucket. Ditto, Harry with his bare hands who showed the same level of desperation, as if he were rescuing a miner from an underground collapse, which in a way was exactly his situation.

After what seemed like endless scrabbling, he was rewarded by the sight of part of Pyro, just his left foot though, and tugging it did not release the bits that mattered. Harry knew he had to get him out. He was truly alarmed now and redoubled his efforts. Adrenaline can have a remarkable effect. He removed enough sand and gravel to take some weight off both legs and tried again. He was not the strong man yet, that was to come with maturity and training, but he was strong that day, for he managed to pull Pyro out even though he felt the strong suction of the sand seeking to prevent him as he inched Pyro out.

Harry had had a very primitive form of resuscitation on the battlefield taught to him in the cadets, and he cleared Pyro's airways and reached into his mouth and pulled his tongue forward. Without a further thought he began what was the recommended method of breath followed by chest compressions. At first he was not rewarded but he was very proud of himself as he did not panic but just kept going, even though the casualty was turning a very odd shade of blue. Then suddenly, there was a choking sound, and Pyro sat bolt upright. "Get off me you fucking poofter," he managed to blurt out.

It was a good thing that Pyro recovered so quickly as their manoeuvres had attracted attention. A dog walker appeared at the edge of the new lip to the sand pit. And as they scarpered, they could just about hear the adult call, "Oy what you two scallywags up to? Come back here." The boys heard no more as they were long gone. Harry did wonder, as he lay in his bed that night reviewing what after all had been a very interesting and indeed exciting day, if anyone ever did 'come back' when so called.

Pyro tried for the army and was successful. 'Full of vim and vigour' as his selection report commented, without it necessarily being a compliment. They liked him in the combat engineers. He had natural talent for the work.

"It's just a question of remote firing of explosives and knowing the target." At least this was how Pyro described it. Harry preferred not to use military speak and wanted to know that only the target would be hurt. He was determined not to have unnecessary harm done, and especially did not like such harm to be called 'collateral damage'. Harry preferred not to use such language as camouflage for serious unnecessary injury especially to the completely or even the relatively innocent.

Pyro reassured him.

"We will know everything about who goes in who goes out, what they say, even what they dream."

"What?" Harry raised his eyebrows.

"Yes well OK, that's a slight exaggeration. We will have the intelligence we need for a successful op. Come on, Harry, you can trust me."

"Right," said Harry, who felt far from wholly reassured.

"How'd we get in?"

"Snip and I have already worked that out," and laid out his plan to Harry.

He had seen what Pyro could do and had good reason to respect his work. He also had reasons to worry about collateral damage. To be fair, Pyro was not a one-trick pony. His surveillance techniques using electronics were, as Harry had good reason to recall, second to none. He had not been best pleased to discover his liaison with Captain Mandy at Woolwich had been filmed and recorded.

Captain Mandy had been in the habit of visiting other officers stationed or laying their heads at the Woolwich officer mess, in the early hours of the morning. She would ask if they could 'fill up her drinking glass with water as her taps did not seem to be functioning'. Once in the room she came on pretty strongly, often just letting her dressing gown fall open to reveal her naked body. This plus a smile was usually enough. Mandy was a very fit young officer. Harry had fortunately used a condom. Not everyone had. One officer consulted the station GP and was found to have gonorrhoea. What made it a potential scandal was that when Mandy was called in to trace her contacts, she made a list of over one hundred officers, some were generals and married.

They could not just blunder into this house and kidnap the owner. He was after all a government minister. He would have close protection and anti-surveillance techniques would be used. Harry wondered how up to date Pyro was. It was after all nearly two decades since he had been on operations with him.

He need not have worried.

Pyro was very, very good at what he did. As he sat opposite Pyro, with Snip next to him, he was transported to the dirt-floored hut in the compound. Harry was there to support the Foreign Office led mission. The elders had received them. The money was in the large holdalls. Stuffed with dollars. Everything was dressed up as tribal honour and justice done and recompense for denying the poppy crop and so on. But actually, it was just big bags of money and serious danger. There were some who thought principle more important than cash in dollars but they were usually the ones who were not being offered the bribe to behave as the western alliance wished them to.

This was a particularly controversial meeting of tribal elders and war lords. Harry recognised one of the Taliban as someone who had tried to shoot him just the day before. "Nothing personal," the man had said with a smile when he spotted Harry.

The internal threat was to some degree covered by the Special Forces and gooks who were everywhere, and at least some level of vetting had gone on. Of course, a suicide mission is just that, but no one had got in with any weapons, of that he was reasonably sure. The snag was especially as time went on, and these meetings were often lengthy as everyone felt the need to have their say, and no doubt to make sure they got their share. All did seem to be going well as the talks dragged on into the night.

Gradually the talks petered out as the elders rose one by one in a strange protocol of seniority not really understood by anyone but especially not the western forces present. As they drifted off into the night it was decided very much against Harry's advice to stay put till morning. Harry wanted to consult with someone he could trust and looked around for support and for better or worse, there was Pyro.

Pyro had decided to act independently as usual. He had disappeared an hour or so earlier. When he reappeared, he briefed Harry on his efforts, saying there was now only one route in, or out, of the compound. Harry was not entirely surprised and let Pyro show him how to identify the very narrow path in and out, identified by small sticks that glowed in the dark through night vision goggles. What were they these twigs? Harry looked closely and could have sworn they were lollypop sticks. The dab of fluorescent paint was a neat trick, as a quick shine with a torch and they showed up clearly enough if you knew they were there. Otherwise, they were near invisible. Harry went back to brief the close protection teams and suppressed argument stating there was no time to change this defensive plan now.

Harry decided he must rest. As usual he was able to sleep in a moment. He was just drifting into a very pleasant dreamland when he was awoken, but by what? Instantly awake and alert, he heard loud bangs and then saw flares lighting up the night sky. Harry went to the inner compound where he expected to see the bags of money well guarded. They were gone. Harry never learnt who it was. A local or perhaps a US renegade, or opportunist? In his view you really cannot hope to secure anything much in terms of trust and good outcomes by simply handing over large bags of dollars.

He ran to the nearest vantage point, a small slit in the upper wall allowing a view. The battle, which was quite extensive, did not go well for the Taliban, or whichever of the local warlord and tribal fighters had decided to attack the compound. Pyro's incendiaries were having a decided effect, providing a ring of steel of a seriously lethal quality. Nevertheless, the attackers were very well organised and were determined, and Harry knew they would not quit easily. After all at least some of them believed dying trying to kill the infidel meant paradise awaited them, and failure could result in very unpleasant consequences inflicted by their own leaders. Harry wondered to what extent these young men believed in the cause for which they were fighting, or perhaps it was just they had not much to lose, and something to gain from showing extreme levels of bravery. Mind you these fighters were not all mad, and tough though some of them might be, they did not tend to fight on if the outcome was obvious. Harry did feel it was their land and not his. He found it difficult to reconcile being there and handing out death, with serving Queen and country. There was no time in the thick of it for such moralising.

Ammunition was not a problem because Harry had anticipated trouble and made personal efforts to ensure plentiful supplies. Relying on the US forces was often a good idea, as they went in for overkill, routinely. The British were parsimonious and sometimes this led to serious shortfalls in acute situations as reports would sometimes relay. In other words, soldiers ran out of ammunition and had to try and get out of the area with little or no means to defend themselves.

As the battle wore on, all participants knew that daylight would mean air support. For the attackers this meant they would inevitably have to withdraw. For the defenders, it meant their chance to get out of there alive. Harry went back to the inner compound to begin planning the evacuation. He found a small figure in the corner whimpering. It was the Foreign Office representative. Harry attempted to calm him down.

"Please don't let them kill me, please, I'm a married man, I've got children." Harry was unsympathetic but wanted to stop him whimpering. He promised him no harm would come to him. He kept that promise. As the first signs of dawn broke Harry was able to reassure the poor little man.

Harry was never to meet him again but in passing noticed twenty years later that he became an MP and then a minister.

Not for the first time, Harry questioned the quality of those who rose to the top and proposed to govern the little people.

Pyro's ring of steel extended further out than anyone had anticipated. As the attackers withdrew, there were explosions and cries much further from the compound, so far indeed that Harry began to wonder if there was some kind of counterattacking force. But no, it was simply more evidence of Pyro's efforts. *Bloody hell Pyro*, thought Harry admiringly. He had obviously been further out laying mines and ICDs, no doubt of his own making, and ingenious traps. The explosions went on and on and the cries of the wounded rang out into the night. Harry realised that Pyro had singlehandedly prevented the enemy from succeeding in their attack and further, from regrouping and launching any kind of second or counterattack once beaten off. It was all very useful as he could now concentrate on the evacuation.

He found Pyro in the compound remotely firing off his remaining bombs. The look on Pyro Pete's face was as close to sublime as you will ever see on this Earth, at least that was how it struck Harry. It was as if he was some kind of ancient warrior transported into modern times and using modern methods.

In terms of the current operations Harry upon reflection decided he need not be worried at all concerning how contemporary Pyro's skills and knowledge were. He had found his vocation and reacted as a man obsessed. As a matter of fact, Pyro was the kind of man who all his life had followed the 'cutting edge' as he called it and was interested in what was new. He had landed a job at the weapons testing station at Larkhill near Salisbury plain, run by boffins. His job was to take what they developed and see how it might be used in practice on combat operations. What was conceived there was testament to the ingenuity of UK academic research into ideas that might have a military application, but their practical improvement owed much to men like Pyro. The youngster who would enjoy blowing up anything he could, had found his mecca. His desire to try new technology was undimmed. He seemed to know unerringly when tried and tested old ways were best, and when to try something new.

"So what do you think of the plan Harry?"

"The plan?" Harry asked. He had been several thousand miles away and two decades past in Afghanistan and simply said, "It sounds like a great plan."

And then as if it was an afterthought, "Just run it past Fergie when he arrives."

At least, thought Harry, *I will only have to hear the plan expounded once.*

Fergie had decided they should have a little base of their own, and it might as well be his house. He made sure Harry knew how to find it, and Harry decided to walk. Snip would drive Pyro in. They parked on a nondescript street on the edge of The Stray with free parking.

Fergie's house was a good choice as it had odd vehicles in the driveway and an extra set of garages or outbuildings at the back reached down a track. All rather surprising in an urban environment. It was quite central too and had a little used area of open ground at the back which belonged to the nearest neighbour, an old woman who was rude to everyone but tolerated Fergie.

"I can't stand Scotch people," she once said to him, "but you will scare off the burglars all right.

She was a person who made a fetish out of minding her own business. Even the postman avoided her, and Fergie come to that.

They each had a box put up by Fergie at the end of the track leading to the rear of their respective houses.

THIRTY-NINE

"Where has Harry gone?"

"To track a shipment coming in via a port in Wales."

"Ali's phone and movements?"

"Blimey how far is this going to go?"

"Are ye not having a good time?"

"Oh no it's fine."

"But he also said we had to track a shipment into Hull."

"And Liverpool."

"And once he has done all that?"

"We are going after the big boys."

"Bloody Norah."

None of them expressed any doubts or any sign they wanted out. Far from it. This was like the old days. Live for today. Life was never dull with Harry.

"Carpe diem," said Pyro.

"What's that mean?" said Fergie.

"God knows," said Pyro.

Pyro set up his laptops and there was a slight whirring sound as they came alive.

They now had eyes and ears inside the building albeit electronic.

Harry didn't ask how he had got in or how he had set it up. Frankly why would he care?

Fergie was impressed.

"Right so we need to observe for twenty-four hours and see

what the pattern is, who goes in, who comes out, what the security is and so on."

Pyro said, "I know already who is providing security and it's the security services."

"How do you know that?"

"I recognised one of them."

"This is not good news, surely sooner or later they will detect the electronics we have installed."

Pyro looked crestfallen. "I thought you might have more faith in me than that."

"Listen, I have doubled up with Russian stuff. They will find that but not the real stuff I have employed. They will think they have done their job. They do not think this guy is very high level. They only seem to deploy a three-man team, though it is a twenty-four hours operation, plus of course the alarm to the local bobbies. I doubt Special Branch. It's usually one or the other. But not both."

They had photographs from Google Earth of the house and gardens. This would be a different proposition to Ali's 'grab and run'.

"I have something else for you," said Pyro.

And the other screen revealed Pyro had hacked into the server linked to the laptops being used in the house. One was of no interest, being used to play Minecraft and virtual games, TikTok type apps implying a teenager or overgrown child perhaps. The second was his wife's, which was very interesting and the third had a firewall to the Ministry of Defence, and another very odd link to a curious security firm that Pyro could only guess at.

After Pyro made a few more enquiries he found a hint of a link to what he thought was some kind of heavyweight wealth fund that seemed legitimate but not to have any proper accounting attached to it.

Harry asked Pyro, "Have you done any obvious checks to find who might live there, like voting records and that kind of thing?"

"Yep," said Pyro, and brought up another screen and copied it into Harry's phone.

What interested Pyro about the wife was her attachment to certain dating sites similar to Tinder but rather more discreet. Perhaps this could be used.

In summary Harry established that there was the minister who had been a soldier briefly in some cavalry regiment after university, the man had become a merchant wanker, and then politics. No highflyer, but junior minister in the Foreign Office and then Defence, caught Harry's eye. He looked familiar. His mind returned to the compound in Afghanistan: the snivelling little tosser, now grown fat. He supposed he would have security 24 hours a day.

Why then would this man's phone number be in Ali's phone. Was it just for a supply of party drugs for occasional use recreationally? Maybe.

Didn't really matter to Harry or any of them. Was it enough to justify an untimely end?

Fergie was simply on the mission. Snip and Pyro would do whatever he asked. It was down to him then to decide.

Harry was deep in thought.

Fergie decided to prompt Harry. "Reet, what the plan then?"

Harry looked up and said, "I think we should take down his assets."

This idea swam about the room a bit.

"What do you mean exactly?"

"Well, we have established this man has a ski chalet in Switzerland, Verbier isn't it?"

"That's right," confirmed Pyro.

"And a yacht in Antigua?"

"Yeah, English Harbour."

"Anything else?"

"A flat in Belgravia."

"Right let's concentrate on the first two.

And the Hull and Liverpool offices and large amounts coming in via container ports."

"Principally from Afghanistan, we think."

Likely from the very place Harry reflected that he had made his home.

The realisation began to fill his mind. He knew that this thing was bigger than all of them and that actually it was probably futile to try and stop it. Nevertheless, there had to be retribution.

The minister had to suffer. He was a main player, linked to the money men.

He began to consider what might be the motivation of such a man. Greed? Lack of real power? Envy of those who had been promoted where he had not been? His actions had serious effects. In a sense no one would miss him.

FORTY

"Right. Ali is now out and about."

"Won't he just run to the police?" Fergie was worried.

"He can't afford to do that even if he is a snout."

"What if he is undercover, laddie?"

"Same deal he wouldn't want to blow it now."

Harry did not think Ali was an undercover operative. If he were to be an asset of that kind he was a strange combination of the very convincing and the not very good. Harry noted that might work as cover, but it seemed unlikely.

No, it didn't add up.

"I think either he will run to his supplier for protection or his supplier will come to him, wanting to know why he hasn't shown up."

"Let's get Pyro on the job. He can put trackers on his phone and any vehicle," suggested Fergie.

He drove with Harry to the motorway service station, promising to pick him up in an hour or two at most. Fergie ordered a double Big Mac meal deal and took off alone in the Landy to brief Pyro. He had Ali's phone safely in his inside pocket. The service station had an outside seating area and an area to walk dogs. Not a sylvan setting but good enough to enjoy a meal such as the place had to offer. Harry chose the healthy option which included a salad, which was not too bad at all.

Harry felt his eyes close and was glad they had soft seating. He dropped off and was awakened by a waitress cleaning his table and saying, "You can't sleep here dearie." Harry was not cross as he supposed from her point of view he might look like he was some kind of down-and-out.

He levered himself up and realised he fortunately did not need to find any other refuge or place to wait, as here was Fergie and Pyro.

"Right, we have been to his place. His car has a tracker on it. And I've done better than that," said Pyro. He had a very pleased with himself expression on his face. "We can listen into any conversations in the car and on his phone, and any texts or emails he sends."

He will probably get rid of the phone, thought Harry, but it was worth trying for you never knew, and he smiled at Pyro encouragingly. Harry's style of leadership was all about morale.

Harry's plan was to simply see what Ali did next. First the bad news.

"No signal from his phone."

"Oh well he must have got rid of it."

Now the good news.

"He has been talking on a new phone in his car. He was rowing with his wife about not being there as agreed for his daughters. Well actually he hardly got a word in, I almost felt sorry for him," admitted Pyro, who was divorced and had a son, now well into adulthood, who sadly had not kept in touch with his dad. Pyro didn't talk about it much but the view was as Fergie told it, that his ex-wife had turned him against his father. It had to be admitted that Pyro was probably not a dutiful parent, but still. It was a rather commonplace story felt Harry.

Ali was on the move, and there was no evidence of any police contact.

Harry did not assume the police were not interested in Ali,

but maybe they did not know of the extent of his criminal activities.

The tracking of Ali had led to this address. A large house in Bradford in a poor area. There were older Asian men, of Pakistani origin most probably was Harry's guess, who went in and later came out – some in twos or threes but most singly. Fergie was convinced this was connected to the gallery pictures found on Ali's phone.

"Fergie, I don't want to get distracted."

"I am not goin' to stand by and allow these wee lassies to be treated like that."

"OK, Fergie but we can't clean it all up, we really can't."

"I ken that, but I'm going to clean this one up."

Harry knew he couldn't stop Fergie so simply didn't try. He wondered what good would come of it, as the young girls involved came from where, locally, eastern Europe, maybe both. Would anyone care?

He speculated as to whether it would be better to alert the police and social services even the press. Maybe these agencies would get involved after Fergie had been in and taken action. It was not in his hands after Fergie had seen what was on Ali's phone and connected it with a rundown pair of houses in Bradford. They formed the last two in a terrace of four houses, the other two seemingly unoccupied. Harry accepted the inevitable. What would be would be.

Snip had set himself up in the Landy with a short-barrelled rifle. Harry was with him. "There will be no shooting, Snip."

"Sure Harry," came the reply. "No shooting."

Harry went to meet Fergie at the back of the houses. Pyro had found his way to the rear which had the typical cobbled service road full of bins and rubbish. He had collected a few dead rats and was busy stuffing them with Semtex. Harry did wonder if this was strictly necessary but decided not to interfere. Pyro was enjoying himself.

From the rear and looking over the ramshackle fencing, the back room was lit up and two older men could be seen sitting down. A young girl came in and one of the men got up and went out with her. Another girl came in and she looked no more than ten years old or eleven at most, though she could even have been younger.

Fergie posted himself by the back door. He shouldered the door in, stepped back and to one side, taking cover, and Pyro launched his rats. The rodents sat there, three of them in the hallway.

A young Asian man who stepped into the hallway armed with a gun was taken by surprise to see the rats, which though dead seemed to him to be looking at him. They were each also fizzing slightly as the fuses made their way towards the Semtex. It was reasonable therefore for him to ask and he did, shouting in alarm.

"What the fuck!"

What he did not expect was for them to each explode, one after the other, with loud bangs, covering him in dead rat. The ensuing mayhem was a sight to be seen. An older man came running down the stairs, without his trousers, and then stopped mid step. He was undecided whether to retrace his steps or what but was pushed down by the panic behind him. As he tried to escape from the rear door, Fergie's great paw swiped him down. Behind him was another younger man, armed, and this is when things got tricky as the young girls appeared at the top of the stairs. Fergie was now halfway up and urged them into an upper bedroom. They did not argue and did exactly as he urged them to do.

Harry against his better judgement had followed in by the rear door and was just in time to take out the gunman who was levelling his pistol at Fergie, with a sharp blow to the neck. Harry relieved him of his gun and used the handle to knock him out.

Snip arrived at the front door just as a rather fat Asian tried to leave, and he was very fortunate that Snip obeyed orders and simply laid him out with the stock of his gun.

What a shambles, thought Harry.

Fergie upstairs was confronted by a large Asian man who thought he had what it took to challenge him. He put his fists up as if the Marquess of Queensberry was watching.

Big mistake. Fergie simply took hold of his right arm, spun him round, arm up his back and half ran him half pushed him to the top of the stairs and then with a good hard shove let gravity do the rest. The fat man rolled awkwardly down the stairs, arse over tit, and then broke something important, maybe an arm maybe a leg, maybe both, and then mercifully his fall ended. He was jammed between the lowest step and the balustrade. Harry stepped over him, his shoe sinking into the man's midriff as if into a peat bog. Harry half expected there to be a squelching sound as he pulled his feet out of the man's belly and onto the step above the semi prone body.

Harry started to talk to a girl a little older than the others. He asked her name. She gave him one, 'Rosie'. He thought she might want some reassurance that this raid did not just mean they would be taken to another place to be used and abused. She was not even visibly shaken. He wanted them out of danger. He hoped he could do enough to set them free.

She led him to the attic where there was quite a sight. He could see figures lying on mattresses, and the signs of serious drug taking, the needles, the silver foil, the mini heaters, lighters and other paraphernalia, tabs of this or that prescription drug lying about the place, Temazepam, Zopiclone, Dihydrocodeine, what else, all the usual suspects and some he had never seen or heard of before.

He asked 'Rosie' if they were all English. "English?"

"We are all from Bradford."

They were all young white girls. White trash. Somebody's kids. Nobody's children. A problem he could not solve.

Harry looked up the number for the local social services and rang it. He got an answering machine. He left a brief description of the premises, and the address, and the salient fact that there were at least six underage girls in what amounted to little more than a brothel. He then rang the local newspaper and asked for the news desk. He knew he could not do more. He could not afford to wait for the police and was not tempted to ring them.

As they drove away no one spoke.

FORTY-ONE

"Ma'am? I've sent you a report. It's attached to an email. I can't be sure but I think it may be connected."

"Right, Robbie."

She settled down to read what Robbie had gathered. She found it difficult to remain impartial. The girls had been exploited for sure. Two of them were very young. They seemed to have no history at all. They didn't have a digital or paper record for their lives. No birth certificate, no NI number, no health record, no school record, nothing. Their countries of origin were uncertain. They were white Caucasian, and that was all that could be established.

Who was behind this network of exploitation? Who was behind the attack on them? The attackers had shown military skills. This is what Robbie was rightly highlighting.

She felt tired, and her eyes began to close. She roused herself enough to drive to her own little house, and once there prepared a simple meal, and tried to simply let her mind rest. She decided to await events.

Surprisingly she slept well.

FORTY-TWO

"Harry wake up. We need to move."

Harry was instantly awake. His head ached.

"Good news."

"What is it Pyro?" Harry's voice reflected his fatigue.

"Ali is on the move, and I'm pretty sure it's for a RV with his supplier."

Pyro played the recording back. It certainly sounded promising.

"Can we know where?"

"He's on the M1."

"Better get after him then."

"Fergie has already fired up the Landy. Snip is on it already. He will report back." Pyro was reticent about raising the issue over the Land Rover. "It's just not fast enough," was his justifiable opinion.

In its military incarnation circa 1950 it was a terrific military vehicle derived from the Second World War, the Willys MB Jeep. In many respects it had all the virtues of that vehicle, but road speed was not one of them. Snip on the other hand in his BMW M would be well able to pursue Ali provided he did not invite attention from the boys in blue.

Pyro's phone rang. It was Snip.

"I've got him in my sights. He's either in a hurry or maybe he always chances his arm and always drives fast.

"He has turned off to the services. Sending location."

The satnav on Harry's phone estimated an hour to reach the target RV.

"I've got eyeball on him.

"The other vehicle is a Mercedes. Reg to follow by text."

"He is meeting a suit, quite well cut I would say," volunteered Snip.

"Not young. Maybe fifty, maybe younger, good haircut.

"Mercman is alone and does not seem best pleased to see Ali.

"Ooh what's this then? He has opened the passenger door and shoved Ali inside.

"Ali now in the passenger seat.

"Ali now out again and back in his vehicle.

"Mercman is driving off."

Harry intervened. "We are still forty-five minutes away, tail him."

"I'm on it," said Snip. "What if they split up?"

Harry thought for a moment. "Just follow the Merc."

A few minutes later Snip reported. "No need to worry. They are in convoy."

An hour later the convoy was on the A58 heading towards the Menai Bridge. It was a place Harry knew well.

"Mercman turning off, followed by Ali, signposted Dinorwic, the marina. It's a cul-de-sac."

Snip sent his location which was perfect for an RV out of sight but on a reverse slope, at the top of which a wide view of the marina was revealed. About 400 yards away the Merc and Ali's 4x4 were parked up.

It was, even in the close season, when little or no sailing went on hereabouts, an idyllic scene with a view of the Menai Bridge and Anglesey, and the backdrop of Snowdonia. The developers had tried to create a sort of Mediterranean feel with Spanish-looking terraced houses round the marina. Sadly, it was not popular, 'maybe overpriced' reckoned Harry, as it had a kind of run-down feel, and plenty of empty looking houses although perhaps most were second homes and therefore not much occupied out of season.

There was a kind of separate dock which used to be for working boats now more or less deserted and mostly out of sight of the main marina, separated by a boat yard typical of such a place, mostly providing opportunities for ripping off yachties. It too looked fairly rundown, with one large shed and boats scattered about on the yard. There was no one about.

All this Harry took in, as he massaged his legs, aching from sitting in the Landy.

Fergie proffered his bino's and pointed out to sea where a small dot presented itself as a sailing vessel of some kind. As it drew closer the yacht turned into wind, and dropped its sails. Harry estimated it as a 40-footer, not large but seaworthy, and it could have come from anywhere.

Snip had already chosen a spot with a view of the working yard, its dock and the wider marina. He was setting up the tools of his trade. Pyro opened his flask and poured a coffee and went over and shared it with Snip. He then gave one to Harry and Fergie.

"Biccie?"

"What you got, Hobnobs?"

"Better than that, chocolate Hobnobs."

"Outstanding."

"This is nice" said Snip as he leaned back on the small bank which hid his rifle now on its tripod from view.

"So what's the plan Harry?"

"I'm just going to have a look."

"You're joking, not without us you are not? Mercman might be armed. They might be armed. Ali might be armed. Bloody hell Harry. Ali might recognise you."

"He might. But I doubt it."

"I'm coming with ye, laddie."

"Fergie you can't. You do tend to create a memory even if he never saw your face. I'm no threat am I. Not an obvious one anyway. I'll just be a local who is out and about taking the air looking at the boats and what-not. Snip will keep me covered."

"Why do it Harry?"

Harry explained. "I want intel before we mount an operation. It's too exposed here for us all to pile in, without knowing what we are facing. I don't want gunfire and casualties, especially amongst you lot."

Harry, the local walker, casually made his way down to the road leading into the marina, on his one-man patrol. The others reluctantly accepted his reasoning. Snip was there ready, willing and able. They reckoned they could help, if needed, pretty rapidly. Pyro and Fergie went back to the Landy to bring up supplies, and more weaponry.

FORTY-THREE

Mercman and Ali stood by their vehicles. They were as Harry suspected taking a close interest in the yacht as it came in.

Harry could see three men on board. He did not assume all the crew were on deck, but it seemed pretty likely because they were busying themselves docking in the inner pen dockside to the boatyard.

He felt the Glock in his jacket pocket. He had already made sure it was loaded. Last night he had found time to disassemble, oil and reassemble it, and had taken his time. There was a time when this might have taken less than a minute, but Harry had been realistic. It was surprising how well he remembered how to do it, and if a little more time was needed, so what?

Harry saw an opportunity in that the crew were messing around with the mooring ropes and did not seem very efficient in prepping for docking. He stood on the dockside and offered to take a rope.

Mercman seemed undecided as to what to do and Ali of course took his lead from him. His indecision meant that Harry was now making an obvious gesture, readying himself to take the bowline of the boat. Harry planned to lead the boat into the corner of the yard, some two boat lengths, which would make it less easy for the yacht to escape.

The skipper of the yacht was shouting now as a wharf came flying over from the stern of the yacht, thrown by a thick-set ugly man in his forties, and landed in the gap between the yacht and the dockside. The man forward, who was also a bit of a gorilla, tried to throw a rope to Harry, but it fell into the water. Another man came up from below. Harry could hear their names now, not that he cared. He assessed their ability as poor.

The skipper agreed with Harry's assessment it seemed. He heard him shout to his companion down below. "These wankers can't even step ashore and moor up. Get up here Sam and let's get the boat moored up." Sam was a small guy but he seemed to know what he was doing as he took the rope out of the hands of the buffoon on the foredeck, tied a bowline loop in it and coiled it with rapid efficiency. He threw the knotted end neatly into Harry's waiting outstretched hands.

In all the commotion it was easy enough for Harry to ignore the skipper and lead the boat to a tight corner. He also had a pretty clear idea of the respective abilities of the enemy. Harry left them to finish off their docking for themselves.

Mercman and Ali had stayed where they were. Harry wandered off casually away from the boat and followed the path round the back of the boatyard sheds. He scrambled unseen back up the slope.

He accepted the cup of tea and the biscuit and settled down with his mates to brief them on what he had seen and learnt. He already had his plan ready. Harry did not need more time than the short scramble up the hill to formulate it.

He wanted to keep Mercman alive as he might have useful intelligence, ditto the skipper. The others were expendable. Snip proposed simply taking them out from range. Harry's plan of course would take advantage of Snip's skills but everything depended on timing.

They took it in turns to watch what went on below. Harry wanted to know if anyone else was about. He hadn't seen anyone but you never knew. He was keen to be able to get out of there rapidly so he spent time on the exit plan, and emphasised the need to not seek unnecessary interest. Of course, once Snip or anyone else started firing it was likely to mean unwanted even innocent attention. Snip was far enough away and actually his gunfire might simply cause confusion. He was not to fire too early and only if necessary, defined as mortal threat to any of his comrades.

Once all were fed and watered and the plan understood, there was no rush.

Harry reckoned he could re-emerge from the boatyard, and they might all just see what they expected to see, an old guy out on a circular walk who had after all been helpful to the docking of the yacht. He supposed Mercman would be armed, and he was not sure about Ali.

He assumed the two bigger men on the yacht were not there simply to make up the numbers, and they were not competent crew so unlikely to be there for their sailing skills. They were muscle, lifters and dogsbodies.

The muscle were sitting on a large abandoned rusty steel beam, each smoking a rollup which might well have been a spliff of some kind. The onshore breeze took the unmistakable stench of skunk up the hill to the nostrils of the well-trained noses of Harry and his men. They were hidden from the yacht by another larger sailboat on its winter cradle. Mercman and Ali were still waiting by their vehicle.

Harry approached the yacht, and the operation became more active.

"Hello Sam," said Harry.

"What hey, how do you know my name? Do I know you from somewhere?"

Harry hit him in the face. It was a powerful blow that to some extent Harry regretted as it was undoubtedly going to trouble his arthritic fingers for some time to come. It knocked Sam straight into the water with a very satisfying splosh.

Fergie popped up behind the girder. One gorilla was pulled backwards and down he went. Fergie knocked him out cold with one tremendous short punch with his great clenched right paw. His mate who was by now fully under the influence of the skunky spliff he had almost finished, looked across and began to urge himself to his feet. But even before he could show the required level of surprise that might have produced an adequate response if you were an optimist, he too was hauled backwards, his head was lifted by Fergie and rammed against the girder, which though rusty had lost none of its integrity. Three down.

Snip on the hill was now totally focused on Mercman and Ali, who were moving towards the yacht, without stealth but kind of cautiously crabwise, crouching down a bit as if in some silly TV crime drama. Snip would have smiled for all the difference it made to him. He did not smile though, as he never allowed emotions to spoil a clean shot.

The journey from Mercman's car and the yacht took them past the boat in its cradle and the temporary spliff seat used by the monkeys Fergie had removed from the game. Unfortunately for Fergie, Ali, glancing nervously about, saw something that made him even more uneasy. Two large men on the ground, apparently asleep.

"Mr Parker, Mr Parker," Ali anxiously hailed Mercman.

Mercman turned and saw what Ali was pointing out. Both Ali and Mercman drew their guns. Ali then saw the unmistakable figure of Fergie emerge between the girder and the boatyard sheds. He raised his pistol, and Mercman yelled out, "Shoot!" and a shot was fired. But not from nearby. This confused

Mercman, who spun round looking for where the shot came from. The sound ricocheted around what was effectively a sound chamber created by the marina, its neat little houses, and the nearby terrain. Ali lay on the ground. Mercman was unsure what to do. Of course he didn't care about Ali, but man is by nature curious, he is made that way, and he wanted to know if indeed Ali had been shot and perhaps killed. Was he on his own in this very worrying situation? Mercman was heavily into self-preservation. It did not take long for him to process what he had experienced as extremely dangerous, and he decided to run.

Pyro should not have done it. It was not in the plan. He just couldn't help himself.

Harry remembered being shown by Pyro how little a quantity of Semtex, if contained by a cucumber was needed to blow a big hole in anything. Under the Merc's wheel arches the small explosions did just that. Both the rear corners of the car crumpled and then after a few seconds up went the fuel tank. Even diesel will explode under the right conditions. Pyro had used two small explosions to make a much bigger one.

Mercman stood stock still and stared. Understandably, even though he was not usually a pushover, it was all just too much for him. Pyro emerged, relieved him of his weapon and marched him up the hill and down the track to the Landy, trussed him up and left him there.

Spectacular. Snip was very impressed. Harry later had cause to regret all this commotion, fireworks and drama, but it was effective in the short term.

Fergie was now by the yacht and saw Harry pointing his Glock right into the face of the skipper who, stammering, gave his name as "S-S-S-Simon." He was carrying a holdall. Quite a big one.

"Right, S-S-S-Simon. I see you have your luggage. Let's go."

"Where?"

"You'll find out. Now move it," barked Harry.

As they left the marina road, they passed the blue lights going down towards it, police cars and then a fire engine and an ambulance.

Harry's heart sank in inverse proportion to his comrades' jubilation. The mission had become very very much more hazardous.

Simon's debrief started in the back of the Landy. It was clear enough he knew very little. He just picked up the cargo in Holland and was paid with a bag of money left in a lockup with a security code.

Harry made a command decision and simply ditched him by the side of the road.

Mercman was not so lucky.

FORTY-FOUR

Ruth felt a little pang of conscience. After all Robbie had proved his worth. The drive was quite a long one and it might have been more sensible to let him drive her. But frankly she simply could not stand his incessant chatter and would rather be alone. She didn't even want the bother of having him there and no doubt eventually becoming cross. She preferred to avoid the stress.

"Robbie, I need you here as my eyes and ears."

He looked crestfallen, like a dog who desperately wanted to come on the walk but being told he had to stay at home.

"Look how little resources we have been granted anyway. Without you how could I hope to have learnt about the movements of Ali? You did superlatively well tying him in with the attack house in Bradford."

Robbie wagged his tail, or at least if he had one, he would have done.

"The drugs' squad had been watching him," he volunteered modestly, "and I managed to find out through them. I have a good contact there, we were at Hendon together."

Ruth didn't wish to discourage him. In her mind, the words loomed, *Oh, do get on with it, Robbie.* She held her tongue though and even managed to smile encouragingly at him.

He told her what he could about the incident in north Wales. The name of the place was unknown to her, Dinorwic. It had made the main news. There was a photograph of a Mercedes or the remains of it, where the fuel tank had been blown up. Robbie had contacted the local force who revealed that it had been almost certainly deliberately done, and that there was one man shot, who they had already identified as Ali Haji. Unknown thugs with serious injuries and one man pulled out of the water, drowned. No one was talking from those who weren't dead.

The skipper of the yacht, Simon Le Bonnet, was as daft as a brush, and offered nothing reliable. His description of the attack convinced Ruth that it was connected with her case. His description of the man who had taken the ropes so to speak, was so lacking in detail as to be almost useless, except to Ruth. A not too tall but not short man maybe in his fifties or forties or sixties. No hair colour, but he did recall him as a man who he felt had a deep suntan. This was surely the man she was looking for. And the attack had all the hallmarks of a military operation, well planned and well executed, if a bit over the top.

She decided to go to the locus in quo. In some ways, in many ways, she was an old-fashioned copper who needed to see the crime scene for herself.

Maybe forensics could still establish more from the car itself, but Robbie had its plates assuming it was legitimate, and it was registered to a company. The company Robbie told her was a shell with no trading activity. She asked him to try and track the sale and purchase of the car.

He came back almost immediately and told her it had already been checked. It had been sold at auction and purchased in the name of this shell company.

This did not look like a fruitful lead. She had thought of sending Robbie to interview the auction house, but was it likely they would recall who physically had bought it? She doubted there would be a money trail, especially since it was probably paid in cash.

She thought she should question the skipper herself but knew she would not be allowed to do that. After all she was not supposed to be operational at all.

FORTY-FIVE

Pyro handed out the new phones. He advised driving two each of the old ones and dumping them far apart. No need to smash them up. They could be useful decoys. He had cleaned them up. The contacts only as many as needed were now in the memory of the new phones.

They divided now into two parties. Snip would drive into Liverpool with Pyro and find a suitable base for them to RV later.

It had not taken long to break Mercman, who turned out to be called John Parker. This amused Fergie who kept saying, "I hope ye will not think me nosey Mr Parker."

Harry had directed Fergie onto the Denbigh Road and across the moors past the 'Highest pub in Wales' sign.

Here Harry pointed out a track off-road to Fergie. They passed an old shepherd or farmer on the track. Harry hopped out and the old man who Fergie heard Harry greet as Pentrevellyn, was heard to say, "See no evil, hear no evil, speak no evil."

Harry had no need to tell Fergie that this man was no quisling. He would not let on anyone had passed that way that day or at all.

The old hunting lodge loomed out of the mist like some ghostly apparition. It was a trick of the lie of the land and the topography that from the road it seemed to be on top of a hill. But once there only the frontage could be seen and no one could approach without warning.

Fergie pulled up as directed round the back of the building, which was now more obviously a ruin.

Fergie asked Harry about it. Some local bigwig after the First World War wanted to set up a grouse estate on the moors. This had been only partially successful and had fallen away with the depression and never roused again. The building itself fell into disrepair and as the sign all but reinforced, was hazardous.

"Please don't hurt me," begged Mercman. He had after all seen Ali shot, his car blown up, had been held at gunpoint, suffered a very uncomfortable hour or more in the back of the Land Rover on the floor. He had not been able to control his bowels and had pissed himself, and then shat his pants.

He was squatting as directed by Fergie in a very awkward position with his back to one of the ruined walls.

"Name."

"John."

"John who?"

"Parker, John Parker."

Fergie burst out laughing. This did not increase Mercman's sense of security one bit.

"Reet, Nosey. Ye'll not mind me callin' ye Nosey?" It was not really a question, rhetorical or not.

Parker nodded. And kept nodding.

He did have a rather large nose and from which snot was bubbling out. He cut a very sorry figure.

Harry was a remote figure now standing outside the hunting lodge, lost in memory. Bala Lake lay before him in the distance.

He remembered coming up here as a boy with his mother for a picnic, while the men drank themselves silly in the pub. She told him how as a girl she used to pass the hunting lodge on her way to school in Denbigh. She had been a clever girl and won a scholarship to the grammar school and had her mother and father's support and encouragement. It meant taking the milk cart to Denbigh and staying four nights there and only coming home on the Friday. Sometimes she missed the cart home and had to walk the eight miles across the moor. She hated the wind allied with driving rain for the rest of her life, and the unrelenting cold generated by weather systems falling upon her as if with personal malicious intent. "I will never come back here to live," she said prophetically.

Harry loved it whatever the weather, perhaps even because of it.

Harry went to find the shovel from the Land Rover. They were going to need it.

Mercman had found, as he must have realised, his final resting place.

Fergie had the whole sorry story now, including names and addresses. It was not a difficult operation. Every few weeks he was given a location by text, and he simply turned up at the allotted time and paid over the rolls of cash, and was given the supply, usually of cocaine but sometimes other goodies. He was pretty sure there was nothing more to learn.

He had made Parker open his phone. Fergie was distracted for a moment as there were photographs of underage girls, with unspeakable things being done to them. Fergie forced himself to look and though he tried to avoid it, the conclusion he came to was that they were not all being forced to participate. Some were. He was not sure which was worse.

Parker said they were supplied by Ali. He rather gave the impression this was a conveyor belt. He even tried to justify the photographs as 'just photographs'.

Perhaps of more immediate interest was the name Parker

was more reluctant to reveal. This was his supplier in Liverpool.

Then Fergie struck gold: Nosey claimed to know where he came from.

"What do youse mean?"

"I followed him once, from a safe distance. He went into an office building, a smart one in Liverpool. I took a photo of the nameplate."

"Where is the photo?"

"I deleted it."

"Do you remember it?"

"I'm not sure."

Fergie glared at him.

"Maybe I can help your memory."

"Can we rely on it?" Harry invited Fergie's opinion.

"He is not as stupid as he looks. Perhaps he thinks playing this card might at least earn him a reprieve.

"I think we could get it out of him. It is possible he has forgotten but will know where it is. But the best way to find out is to take him with us. He thinks he will remember more details once there."

Parker was not a big player, but it was clear enough that he may be the link to something bigger, much bigger.

Harry reluctantly returned the trenching tool to the Landy. Nosey Parker would survive for a few hours yet.

FORTY-SIX

There was an enormous noise and Harry saw the RAF fighter jets, a pair of them, disappear over the lake as the sonic boom followed them. It was deafening. As his ears returned to near normal he could hear Fergie continuing to question Parker.

"I canna get anything more useful oot of him."

Parker was a snivelling mess but was not badly hurt as he kept whining.

"Please let me go. I won't tell anyone. I can't even remember what you look like."

Harry had returned with a mechanics overall, a bit oily and very capacious which indicated it was probably one of Fergie's.

He stepped into the space and gestured to Fergie. When he came out Harry presented his plan.

"Fergie let's get him cleaned up. There's a burn just beyond the rear wall where he can wash himself off. He can put this on. We can secure him in the back again but so he can see out, and we can check out his story."

"What are we going to do with him afterwards?"

"I don't think he is a threat but let me deal with that."

Fergie looked doubtful but didn't argue, "OK, Harry, youse the boss."

It never occurred to Harry to wonder if Fergie was being facetious.

Harry briefed the prisoner and told him if he was a good boy this might yet end well for him.

They led him down to the burn.

He took off his clothes as indicated and stepped into the icy water. He washed himself rapidly and used his fleece to dry himself. He was not an outdoors kind of person, but he turned out to be quite fastidious about cleanliness. It was obvious he was glad to wash his own faeces away.

He then did a mad thing. He had noticed that Harry and Fergie were no longer paying him any attention and he took off across the moor, absolutely starkers. His short, fat, out-of-condition body did not allow for speed. He looked bulky and strong with his clothes on, but without he looked what he was, an unfit fat little man. Too many pies, beer, fast food, and no exercise. But he was very scared which meant for a short time adrenaline carried him forward.

In fact he was going so fast the distance between him and Fergie looked like it was lengthening. What he had not allowed for was the boggy moorland, which was full of hazards for the unwary and untrained. In his mind Parker might have fancied himself as a tough cookie, the kind of man who could waltz through say the marine commando course with ease, who would look good wearing a green beret. Sadly, he then tripped and fell.

Fergie was after him and one slap from his great paw was enough.

He quit struggling and just lay looking up at the sky like a dog who knows its number is up.

"Now I'm annoyed, ye wee twat."

Harry caught up with them and rested his hand on Fergie's shoulder. It was intended as a calming gesture.

"Can you walk?"

Nosey could, though his ears were ringing from the tap Fergie had delivered.

"Go up there and put your T-shirt back on and then the overalls."

"Ye going commando Nosey," remarked Fergie. Even he thought this was a poor joke for he did not smile much less laugh.

"Youse coming with us."

FORTY-SEVEN

Pyro was driving. Snip had let his old friend give it go, and although he was anxious about it, he liked basking in the compliments that flowed from Pyro.

"What a car this is Snip. How fast can it go?"

"You are not finding out now."

"Over 150 mph," admitted Snip with obvious pride. 0-60 in less than five seconds." So it went on, all the way to Liverpool. Pyro was quite sorry it was a relatively short journey. He drove it in a surprisingly sedate manner, showing respect to his friend. Pyro could be quite careful and had understood they needed not to draw attention to themselves. More than they had already.

"So where are we staying Snip?"

"You'll like it," said Snip.

He directed Pyro to the dockside, and into a private car park. Snip had the barrier code.

It was very smart indeed in a glitzy sort of way. In through a glass foyer, and all codes, not keys needed.

"It belongs to a friend of mine. I don't think you know him."

Pyro didn't press him for a name. Professional courtesy and discretion are important.

"Works overseas. Security consultant, Middle East. Dubai right now and away for at least three weeks. He lets me stay here now and then. We have done some interesting work together."

Snip let Pyro in and took him out onto the spacious balcony with an extensive view of the marina and the wider harbour.

"My mate was born over there, and I think it give him a kick looking down on it from here," remarked Snip pointing to a rather run down area of back-to-back terraced houses.

"Mind you they have all been cleaned up. The survivors, what were slums and typically in the past destroyed for tower blocks are now all poshed up."

Snip showed off the gaff.

"There are three bedrooms, so I hope you won't mind using the sofa bed in here."

Pyro nodded.

He accepted that Harry and Fergie would have a room each.

It was all very comfortable.

Snip said, "Look why not have a shower? I'm going to. We can then go to the Tesco and provision up, and maybe get some basic clothes."

"Bet you Fergie and Harry have got nothing with them."

Snip made them a coffee with no milk as there was nothing in the fridge.

"How long do you think we will be here?"

"Who knows? It's all up to Harry. Why, you got somewhere better to go?"

"No, no it's fine." Frankly Pyro was impressed.

Snip had even thought of where to park the Landy.

He was going to show something very special to Pyro. He was going to break a personal rule and reveal his personal logistics store. This had been put together over time with his comrade in arms, whose apartment this was.

FORTY-EIGHT

They packed away the provisions and put on their new clothes, black T-shirt and fleece and jeans plus underwear.

Pyro wanted to try out the shower again. It had jets that you could direct to any part of your body. New clothes provided the excuse.

Snip sent a short text with the postcode. He got one back. 'ETA 2 hours'.

Interesting. Longer than he had thought. He wondered what Harry and Fergie had been up to. Well, he would soon find out.

They went down to the RV. There was the Landy with Parker now in the back.

Snip wandered over to the Landy. "Wait here, I'll open up."

In the back street where there was not any obvious activity, Snip opened up the shutters and upon a signal from Snip, Harry drove in.

It had obviously been a car mechanic's workshop, with serious-looking drills, and lifting gear, and with a vehicle pit. But what Harry noticed most was that around the walls and generally Snip had left the place very untidy.

This was not like him at all.

Fergie brought Parker in and sat him down in the small inner office. He looked onto a cursory view strangely in keeping with his surroundings in Fergie's oily overalls.

Harry briefed Pyro and Snip on what they had learnt and the identification of the swanky offices which Parker had asserted were his contact's business premises.

The company was listed as an import-export company with a seemingly excellent reputation.

Pyro cleared a space on a workbench, plugged his laptop in, was pleased to find fast broadband, and set to work to check it out.

Snip was keen to show Harry and Fergie something.

He opened up the vehicle pit and led them down some steps and then to what looked like a seamless blank wall. He pushed on the wall at one side, and an inner sanctum was revealed.

There was quite a cavernous space through the narrow door which folded out to allow two men through at any one time. It was tardis-like in that it was a much bigger space than one might expect. There was even enough space for Fergie not to feel cramped.

Along the walls were laid out the tools of Snip's trade. A redneck American ex-marine psycho who feared imminent meltdown in society would have been impressed by what was to be found in this armoury.

Apart from the perhaps to be expected rifles and rapid firing machine guns, there were even 2x anti-aircraft missile launchers and an antitank Karl Gustav. One machine gun was of the heavier type, perhaps typically to be seen on the back of a Toyota in Iraq.

Snip began an oral inventory.

"OK Snip," remarked Fergie, "we'll tak' it as read. It's a very fine armoury. Well done," he added so as not to undermine Snip's enthusiasm.

There were ammo boxes, no doubt Harry thought, full of ammunition. Snip lifted one lid and murmured, "Hand grenades."

Frankly there was enough weaponry to start a small war, which was not at all what Harry had in mind. He was not reassured to see the extent of the hardware Snip had available.

There was a small freezer in the corner, which Snip gestured towards, and said, "Semtex."

"Does Pyro know about all this?"

"Not yet," said Snip.

"Well, you can show him can't you a bit later once he has done his research."

He too wanted to encourage Snip but was frankly not keen to learn any more detail. He was not, like Snip, a munitions nerd or any kind of nerd come to that.

"We need to decide what to do with Nosey up there," observed Fergie.

"I think we will use him to set up a meeting. I don't completely trust his identification of the company offices, all seems a bit too slick and open."

Pyro confirmed that at least on the public record and a brief internet search, the company was legal, kosher so to speak.

He might learn more once he could interrogate a PC or server within the building.

"Did he need access for that?"

"Ideally," he said.

"Tell Parker the good news then. He is working with us for now."

FORTY-NINE

"I think we can keep him here for a bit. Is he fed and watered?

No? Well see to it Pyro will you."

"Do we have to guard him?"

"No, I don't think so. I don't think he has any fight left in him."

"We'll just lock him in here then."

"There is a loo through here, with a wash basin."

"Great we don't want him dirtying himself again. Let's try and make him a bit more comfortable, get him a toothbrush and so on. Make him feel loved." Harry smiled.

"How about you show us our new digs Snip."

Snip couldn't wait.

After a quick dinner pizza delivery style, Harry enjoyed the en suite facilities and made the right noises about how wonderful the place was. Snip's morale was important to him.

He stuck his head round Fergie's door. Fergie was already safely tucked up in bed. He looked surprisingly unthreatening when asleep, a feature he shared with quite a few large predatory members of the animal kingdom.

Harry had decided that once the contact with Parker's supplier had been made, he wanted a plan which would take them into the premises so Pyro could do his work on the data which might be kept on enemies' computers or the servers.

The details of the plan would emerge and he knew he could trust himself on this.

He took two ibuprofen and levered his very tired body into bed. He promised himself seven hours and set his body clock to achieve that. This invariably worked especially when in a mission, and this night was no exception.

FIFTY

"Set up a meeting with your supplier. We will be listening in. Any funny business, even a whiff of it, and I won't be responsible for what my friend here might do."

Harry had briefed the others on his plan.

"Pyro. You go in with him once the place seems more or less empty in the evening. Timings to be fixed.

"Snip. You will provide cover from the opposite rooftop or suitable other vantage point to be recced today.

"Fergie held in reserve. He will be on the lookout for any trouble or disturbance."

Pyro reassured Harry he could get them in. He might need to do a little recce of his own which he scheduled for the late morning.

Harry set the next orders group for 15:00 hours. He was going to spend the morning with Parker and see what might be revealed by the RV with his supplier.

This meant driving out to a supermarket carpark on the edge of town and parking up, out of sight of CCTV. He assumed there would be a discreet corner of the site.

Parker was dressed in the new T-shirt and fleece and underwear and trainers that Harry had kindly provided. He had shaved with the single BIC and soap Harry gave him. Harry enquired after his health. He had not had a good night he said. Both of them knew why. His future was uncertain to say the least of it. Harry understood full well that such uncertainty could be even more disturbing than the prospect of certain death. It is not despair that a man cannot stand but hope. The prospect of a swift end once accepted often produced a bizarre sense of calm.

FIFTY-ONE

Harry deposited Parker back in the lockup. He secured him in the inner office. He told him to try and get some sleep and he would be back for him later.

He texted Snip to drop in some suitable food for Parker.

He then went to sit by the dockside marina, to give himself a chance to think.

The trouble was that with all the less than discreet activity especially in Dinorwic, Harry did not think that he should involve his old comrades further in what had really been a personal mission of his own making.

It could not end well for any of them. There was surely a chance that if he could persuade them to drop it, he might simply go it alone and they might escape the attentions of the police. He had already accepted his own future was very much in doubt, and he needed only to make a small shift in his mindset to accept the inevitable and he could perhaps find again his well-earned peace of mind. He knew he was not yet ready to drop the mission. He was even more determined to make those who had created the conditions under which his friend had died, pay. Part of his difficulty was that he realised he was not wholly rational about this. The proximate cause of George's death was now quite some distance past, and the chain of causation far from clear.

There was nothing Harry could do to prevent emotion from guiding his decisions. Like any other kind of addict, he was now on a path from which deviation seemed impossible.

Thus, he began the 'O group'.

"I have good news and bad news."

"What's the good news?" Pyro and Snip chorused together.

"Ay laddie," joined in Fergie "What's the good news?"

"We will be finishing the mission tonight."

"Really?" contributed Snip.

"Och aye, that'll be reet!" Fergie shook his head. "When I said I'm in, I meant it."

There was no menace or malice in his voice. It was said as a matter of fact, but he did not imply any argument was feasible.

Harry could be stubborn though and he fully intended this to be an end to their involvement. He put it this way,

"You caused this," looking at each of them in turn. "I asked you to do things discreetly. How was it discreet to blow up Parker's car," he looked at Pyro, "shoot Ali and take out the two heavies?" He looked at Fergie, who put his great hands out in a gesture implying he had meant no harm.

Harry added, "and that's just the recent history."

"Who left the gas on?" murmured Fergie.

"That was to hide evidence," countered Harry.

Snip defensively added his two pennies' worth into the debate. "You set the terms of engagement. Ali was going to shoot Parker."

"I doubt Ali could hit anything from more than five yards."

This was descending into argument even into farce, as they each started defending themselves.

Harry called a halt to it, by simply saying, firmly and with quiet clarity, "I want to work alone."

The looks on their faces. You could have heard a feather fall.

Then slightly more encouragingly he asked, "Will you help with this last mission?"

He looked at each of them in turn and each nodded their assent. Fergie was not the only one with his fingers crossed behind his back.

Pyro opened his laptop, and the cameras he had installed in the offices came on. He had plugged his computer into the huge telly that hung above the faux fire. He rapidly went through the rooms he had eyes on and those he had bugged.

"Even better," he said and waited for Harry to look suitably expectant.

"I have tapped into their server."

"Do we need to go in?"

"Not really," said Pyro.

"OK" said Harry. "All we do need to do is deposit Parker in their offices. We can post a note on their server to come up on their laptops can we Pyro?"

"Well not exactly like that but yes," said Pyro.

"Can you do it selectively?"

"Of course."

"OK. So, once we have identified the guiding hands, we can leave the following message or something like it. I may need time to refine the message.

"Just post a photograph of Parker and state that this man has told us everything."

"What will they do to him?"

Fergie told Snip, "It's none of our business is it, laddie."

"Right, this is the plan for tonight at the offices of the importer."

Harry talked through how it was going to work. Parker was invited along. He was not too keen to go in, but Harry was quite gentle with him now and he did what he was asked without protest.

FIFTY-TWO

In the offices, the 'two fuckers who matter' were identified by Pyro and confirmed by Harry. He was somewhat taken aback to discover one was a female, but then he thought, *So what?*

A message was flagged as urgent on her laptop. There was the photograph. There was the six-word message. There in her office was Parker, bound by plastic ties to his chair. And gagged.

What to do?

It might have been easier if Parker had not seen her. She had remained hidden till now, at least as far as she knew. She went to great efforts not to be noticed, not to be found, not to be identified.

She did not do any dirty work herself. She did not like the grubby side of the business she was in. And what was that business? Essentially the drugs were a sideline. She accepted that. A kind of necessary evil. She liked technology. She knew immediately that the server had been hacked. This concerned her even more than the inconvenient fact that there was a large male sitting tied to her office chair.

Harry read the materials Pyro had revealed by hacking into the server. He made mental notes on the targets, for that is what they had become. He surmised that she found the most money was to be made in simply using people, beautiful young people in particular. Certainly, this was the business she was in. Desperate people, people who would otherwise starve and would do anything to protect their family members, their elderly mothers, their sisters, their young brothers.

The drugs were another financial stream that was all, though the two streams were clearly connected. The name of the company was SPD, Speedy Prompt Delivery.

Harry wondered how she had achieved this wonderful state of mind, where apparently her conscience was never troubled. Harry found this window into her soul that the hacked files revealed, deeply troubling. He simply could not fathom her motivation. It is not as if, as far as he could tell from the hacked evidence, she found pleasure in her actions or any obvious pleasure in her money making. He speculated. Surely it was not simply the avoidance of boredom? She did not glory in it either. There was no hint of any grandiose ideas of self-worth, narcissism or other labels beloved of therapists. There was no sign of extravagant living or excess expenditure.

She was not even obviously cruel. Perhaps she had scruples. He surmised that she left all that kind of thing to others. Those lower down the pecking order. The female of the species.

He wanted to know more. Harry's interest in human nature had no bounds. A good intelligence officer will always want to try and understand the target. Harry had met all kinds, even women willing to die for a cause. They were not all duped. Some were willing to kill for the cause. In the Middle East some welcomed being sewn into suicide vests. There was something about this woman though that represented something new to him. It was that there seemed to be a sort of callous disregard for human life, shared he knew by certain politicos and the money men. Perhaps women were his blind spot. He too easily forgot what they were capable of.

He turned his attention to the other target.

This was the money man. A quick Google check revealed he was behind some kind of investment fund. There was something about him that triggered a memory in the deep recess of his memory. The memory lacked detail or focus. Harry would work on that later. He had direct links to the politico, who a quick Google check revealed was the junior minister of defence.

They would fear exposure, but no doubt imagined they were untouchable. In his own small way Harry was going to disabuse them of that notion.

"Hot Lips is leaving the room," announced Snip who was on duty, watching the surveillance cameras.

Her name at least as far as the company revealed it, and on the computer she used, was Sarah O'Connor. Harry wondered if this meant she was Irish. It was typical of Snip to name her after the nurse in M*A*S*H. They had all loved watching that on telly. He had already declared her 'sexy'. And when he added he wouldn't mind 'giving her one', perhaps sensibly Harry and Fergie let him get on with it.

Parker was still sat there.

Two men entered. A hood was put over his head and he was bundled out of her office. The CCTV outside revealed an unmarked van. Parker was bundled into it.

He was clearly still alive at that point. You would not give much for his chances.

Pyro had an idea but wanted to make sure Harry was happy with it first.

"You can do what?"

"I could send the police, probably the Met, a feed to this CCTV footage, which might produce an interesting response."

Harry allowed himself a moment to think and then expressed his thoughts aloud. "But it's out of control then isn't it? I suppose you can reassure me they cannot trace the feed back to you. It would be good to let the state deal with these people. I think there is advantage in delay here. Yes feed it but make sure we have cleaned up any trace of our involvement."

"The firewalls in place are probably sufficient. To make sure I will destroy this hard drive. You really can leave the clean-up to me."

Pyro added, "Look I have made sure there is no CCTV that picked up any of our movements."

"Including Fergie?"

"Including Fergie."

That was not to say, thought Harry, *that no one had observed any of their activities*. He simply chose to proceed optimistically. What choice did he have?

FIFTY-THREE

"We have film of what?"

"A direct feed into this building."

"Who is feeding this material?"

"We don't know."

"Well we had better find out."

"I have one interesting call that was made and registered which I can play back to you."

"On the roof, sir?"

"Yes, yes on the roof."

Then an address.

"Hold on, passing you through to the operations room, please hold on."

He rang off.

Here was Robbie. She was glad to see him. He had been so happy when she rang to say she needed him. The local force was offering little or no help.

Robbie said, "But I can take you there now."

Ruth found herself on the street looking up at the roof and across the road at the office building. The Met had already contacted the local force to raise the alarm concerning a possible kidnapping – a man being bundled into a van with a hood over his head. The van had false numberplates. It was the ubiquitous white van beloved of small builders and their like.

The local police had been all over the roof. They had found

nothing. Ruth's gut told her this was all connected. But how? And why were the security services interested?

There had been some activity and some expenditure, the police budget being what it was she was surprised in fact to see so much thrown at it. There were no obvious leads. Perhaps forensics would turn something up? She detected very little interest by the local force. Liverpool was a long way from London. The Met had handed it over to the local force. What were they going to do? She guessed little or nothing.

More surprising was that the serious crime squad had been stood down. Initially the events in Dinorwic had attracted considerable interest, and yet now they were no longer interested. Who had ordered this and why? And yet here was the continued interest by the security services. This nagged at her. What interest of the state was affected? Given this she was surprised she hadn't been stood down herself.

As usual the security services man was less than helpful. "Please just keep us informed," he said.

He had flashed his ID at her, Drakeford, but he was unknown to her. She would ask Tim later perhaps. He was quite young, but this did not indicate his seniority, but Ruth's instinct was he was there just to monitor what the local police did and any other interest including hers.

She asked, "Does it not surprise you there are no laptops or PCs in this office? All the cabling is there?"

He seemed to know that the local police had not taken it all for forensic examination. She tried asking a few more pertinent questions but she was rapidly forming the view that she was not going to get much actual help.

"Is there a server? It's gone too. Can we trace it back to some sort of cloud back up?" Ruth had no idea what she was talking about, but Robbie did, and he was surprised to hear the security services man say that it was unlikely there would be any trace left of any help, but that they could leave all that sort of thing to them. If they found anything interesting of course they would pass it on.

Robbie confirmed her suspicions.

"It makes no sense, ma'am. Of course there will be traces, digital footprints."

Ruth appreciated his input but did not want to listen to more of this, what to her, was gobbledegook. iCloud backup did it for her. "Enough, Robbie, I have no idea what you are talking about.

"Do you think Robbie you might allow me a little quiet to think?"

Robbie drove on in silence, which he accepted with good grace. After all Ruth had asked him politely to be quiet though he knew it was an instruction.

Then she asked him, "You believe we are being given the brush off?"

"Exactly, ma'am."

That evening they stayed in a Premier Inn. She asked Robbie to write out a summary of what they knew, and any lines of enquiry he thought they might take up. She felt she was going to lose him soon and wanted all she could have from him in the meantime. Further she wanted to give him a task so he might leave her to proceed in peace. She reckoned she was probably going to be told to quit her enquires. She wondered how it would be done.

Once settled in her room, she put a call through to Tim. Tim simply said, "I don't know him." For some reason known only to her she didn't believe him but had no evidence for this feeling. In a way it annoyed her that she was now, again, relying on intuition.

FIFTY-FOUR

"Thanks for coming to see me."

The DCC was not known personally to Ruth. His assistant offered coffee. There were the usual pleasantries,

Then he got down to it.

"You must leave the incident in Wales to the serious crime squad."

Ruth through Robbie already knew they were doing very little. It was almost as if they had already been stood down. Ruth decided to try another tack. She did not expect to make any progress.

"Why can I not interview Ms O'Connor?"

"I'm afraid I cannot give you any reason beyond telling you that you cannot."

"You do realise this is a murder investigation?"

Even as Ruth said it she felt like a character in a TV crime series. What was worse was the suspicion in her mind that she had sunk to some kind of parody of herself.

"Yes I know. But what in fact do you have linking this woman to any murders?" The DCC picked up the file that Robbie had prepared. She knew the connections were thin. She had not included material on the murders in Harrogate or Bradford. She did not know whom she could trust and really the connections were pretty tenuous, not least because she found little or no forensics had been conducted. She had ordered them, but nothing had emerged. It was support in her mind for how there was some kind of conspiracy emerging.

Ruth realised she was getting nowhere here, but she couldn't help herself. She was not going to let him off the hook that easily.

She crossed and uncrossed her legs. This had the desired effect as he could not help himself but be distracted. She caught him looking where he shouldn't.

"Is this your decision, sir?" She looked him directly in the eye.

She had enough experience to know that practised liars with real self-confidence saw the opportunity to tell an untruth as part of their daily bread, and such lies were not easily read. Still, she wanted to see what his response would be.

Interestingly there was just enough of a pause, enough to have her suspicions confirmed.

She was well aware this could just be irrational bias in favour of her own hypothesis. Not that she was sure she actually had one. Christ was she relying on intuition alone?

Ruth had a gut feeling and she trusted it. She was not about to admit to the DCC that this was the basis of her desire to interview the woman.

This woman was not merely working as a police informer, but was undercover.

Undercover for whom? The police or something deeper, murkier.

Was the connection Irish, or what?

This lack of trust, of clarity, also annoyed her, but she decided not to challenge further, at least openly. Better if the 'higher ups' thought she was cooperating.

"Well, it's your decision, sir," Ruth said dutifully but pointedly. She sailed close to the wind here, as her reputation had gone before her and no doubt the DCC had expected more hassle, indeed protest and argument, as he looked somewhat surprised. He stared at Ruth for a moment and then he breathed out again as he had been holding his breath. He could not hide a deep sigh. And then he said something which was undoubtedly a triumph of hope over expectation.

"I am glad we have an understanding."

FIFTY-FIVE

"But should we still be following her, ma'am?" asked Robbie.

"Of course not," said Ruth.

"But we are going to anyway?"

Even he knew that this did not need asking.

"We are going to take it in turns Robbie, and I am going to do the bulk of it, so you can still have a domestic life."

Robbie looked ready to argue, but then thought better of it. He had decided to just be generous and give her whatever support he could… as a matter of fact he was willing to do more or less anything she asked.

So the vigil began and went on for two nights and three days.

Robbie had just handed over. Ruth sat in her car with the engine idling, clearing her windscreen and keeping her warm. *What this investigation needs*, thought Ruth, *is a bit of luck.*

And then as if she had uttered a prayer, luck came her way.

Ms O'Connor did what she always did, and took another route, and never at the same time, varying her habits, being unpredictable, always keeping to where there were people, which again indicated she had had training by someone in how to keep those who might mean her harm, guessing. But at some point she had to head down the street where her posh apartment was situated. Sometimes she took a taxi which dropped her off outside or nearby. Sometimes she had a lift. Ruth decided to ignore these other vehicles but noted down the reg numbers. She had a car which she rarely used, which was kept in the dedicated underground car park. Ruth and Robbie worried that she might be attacked in the car park but entry was not easy without codes and it was used quite frequently which provided some kind of cover.

Someone had run out of patience, and as the small motorbike passed her car Ruth saw the gun held by the pillion passenger cradled next to the assassin's chest. She tracked its progress as if in slow motion as it swiftly reduced the distance between the gun and the target.

Ms O'Connor was going to be shot, Ruth was certain of it. She fortunately had her car idling, and she pressed hard on the accelerator and without hesitation drove hard at the motorbike, ramming it up the back wheel, just as the gun barrel was raised into a shooting position. The bullet went off. It spiralled into the wall a few inches from its target. A miss. The rider of the bike was sent sprawling down the road. Strangely the pillion passenger looked as if he were still in control of the bike as it splayed this way and that. Then the bike gave up the battle with gravity and slid to the ground and shed the pillion passenger.

Ruth was able to open her rear door and with courtesy invite Ms O'Connor to get in, almost as if she were her chauffeur.

The target who had after all had a near-death experience, did not argue and got in. Perhaps it helped that Ruth was a woman of a certain age.

Ruth took her back to her hotel. She was going to get her chance to interview her. She was not going to invite Robbie. This would have to be a private affair.

FIFTY-SIX

"Shall I call you Sarah? My name is Ruth. Ruth McIntyre."

The woman didn't answer. But there was no protest.

The hotel room on the top floor had a small table and two chairs which benefited from the natural lights from the large windows, and Sarah sat in one of them. This presented her with quite a wide vista of the old docks and marina. Ruth had planted a whisky glass in her hand with a decent slug of malt in it.

Sarah had hardly said a word, and her hand holding the whisky glass betrayed her, as it trembled slightly. The woman's self-control was admirable and Ruth who admired this quality in herself, was impressed. Ruth looked closer. This woman was used to this kind of attention for she remained quiet and unconcerned by the direct personal attention. She really was very striking-looking, clear complexion, and her hair was interesting. It had caught the shaft of sunlight from the late evening sun and seemed to shimmer as if it had a separate life of its own. But this was not what caught Ruth's eye. The hair was black but there was just a suspicion at the roots of the true colour, perhaps a deep red, or maybe a classic redhead. Sarah turned her eyes away from the sun, the effect of which was to accentuate the green glint of her eyes. Ruth noticed the essential modesty of the rest of her make up, no bright red lipstick or any other vulgar display. The clothing was expensive, designer, but not new. This woman wore her clothes as if they had been fitted for her, which perhaps they had been. Very expensive then, but still understated.

Ruth cast her eyes down, almost as if the direct gaze of this woman might be not quite so easy to outstare. Ruth was keen not to alarm her. She was determined not to provide any excuse for friction.

Very fine shoes, kid leather, dark blue. Comfortable but well-fitted. Bespoke then, like the rest of her wardrobe.

Also, the obvious fitness. Gym workouts or a personal trainer? Ruth thought not. Natural fitness and personal determination then.

Then the woman spoke.

"You are from the police I suppose?"

Ruth nodded.

"Do we know each other?"

Ruth was noncommittal. Ruth tried to place the accent. The voice was cultured, elocution or privately educated. Irish certainly. Northern.

"Do you mean me harm?"

"Sarah, the last thing I want to do is harm you. Who do you think does mean to harm you?"

Sarah looked unsure, or at any rate not keen to answer this question.

"Frankly," she said, "there might be quite a long list."

Then she said, "I don't think there is a safe place for me." This was said without self-pity or even regret. *Her matter-of-fact tone and manner was a testament to her self-control*, thought Ruth, *but she detected underneath this, an undertow of fear*. There were currents pulling at this woman that she could not completely hide.

Ruth was glad that Robbie was outside the room standing guard. He couldn't be expected to be there all night. They might need backup. But who could she trust?

It would be remarkable if simply walking into the hotel, leaving Sarah by the lift, which was in full sight of the reception desk, had gone completely unnoticed. She could not even be sure she had not been followed to the hotel. What if the assassins had had backup?

Perhaps they had been lucky. Ruth was not keen on relying on such a surmise especially if true.

She felt she had to some extent won this woman's trust, but if she was working undercover, why on earth would she reveal anything to someone she had never met before?

It was worth trying to win her over. After all someone had just tried to kill her.

As if reading her mind, "I think you may have saved my life."

Ruth came at the problem indirectly. "You must be tired."

"You have no idea," Sarah admitted.

Actually, I think I do, thought Ruth. Ruth made a suggestion. "What if I were to stay here in this room with you while you rested. You can even take a bath. You can have a sleep. I can send for food."

It was all a question of trust, more haste less speed.

FIFTY-SEVEN

It had occurred to Ruth that the diminutive figure now sleeping in the hotel bedroom might herself be dangerous. She had the opportunity to look through her bag. No gun. And not much else of any significance. Sarah had kept her phone with her. It was switched off. The phone was in a protective wallet of the kind that kept bank cards and perhaps a driving licence. There was interestingly a change of underwear, a spare pair of tights and a toothbrush. Ruth speculated, a lover perhaps. In the inside zip pocket was her passport. Ruth wondered if this meant she was prepared for swift flight, or was she always ready for whatever may come to pass?

Ruth made a quiet call to reception from her mobile phone. She did not reveal she was from the police but booked a room for Robbie in his name. She also booked a room in her own name and gave her police rank and made sure it was on another floor well away from where she and Robbie and Sarah were camped.

She went out into the hotel corridor. There was faithful Robbie, standing outside as if on guard, which was reasonable as he was in fact doing just that. She briefed him not to reveal he was police at all. That he was to sleep in the room opposite.

She told him she would be back in five.

She went down to the other room she had booked and asked for a tray of food to be left outside as 'she didn't want to be disturbed'. She could quietly retrieve it later, she hoped, and maybe even eat it or give it to Sarah. This plan was not without its flaws but unless Sarah was being followed by a whole team she thought it might provide some cover.

They would take it in turns to use the room and that way keep Sarah safe. She urged Robbie to take care, without wishing to alarm him. She had very grave misgivings about their going it alone. At least she knew she could trust him.

Ruth knew it was unfair to think this way about him, but it was as if Robbie wagged his tail enthusiastically when Ruth briefed him on what she had in mind. She sought to justify herself. She had said 'Well done' now and then hadn't she?

Ruth wanted to be there when Sarah woke up and did not think she should let Robbie into the room without first introducing him. She would have to do the first shift as Sarah was fast asleep. She pulled the seats closer to each other and settled into one of the not uncomfy armchairs.

She could not stop her mind from racing on. She thought about their situation.

Not ideal if Sarah woke up to find a man in her room, even the deceptively diminutive figure Robbie presented. He was in fact one of those very tough, lithe, skinny types of men, who made up for their lack of strength with speed and skill. Ruth had never seen him arrest anyone but he had a first-class reputation, and she would have to rely on that. What was it he did, jiu jitsu or some such? She wished she had read his file more carefully.

There was a gentle knock at the door. She sprang up fully alert and looked through the viewing hole, and saw Robbie armed with a tray. He had ordered from room service, and here he was making sure she was fed and watered. What a lovely thoughtful young man he is, and she realised he was one of the very few people she felt she could trust completely.

Sarah woke up. She sat up and stared about her, no doubt taking in her surroundings. Ruth asked if she was hungry. She nodded.

"Thirsty more than anything."

Ruth handed her a drink of water and sat on the edge of her bed.

"Who knows I'm here?"

"Only Robbie and me."

"Who's Robbie?"

"He is my sergeant, and I trust him implicitly."

Sarah was still impassive but Ruth picked up a degree of anxiety which she was convinced hid a greater anxiety than the young woman revealed on the surface.

"Anyone else?"

"Not as far as I know."

Ruth had no way of knowing for sure. They may have been lucky.

Robbie had checked for any report of the motorbike 'accident'. There was none. No ambulance had been called. There seemed to be no police interest.

Ruth shared this with Sarah.

"Maybe just luck," proffered Ruth.

"Maybe," agreed Sarah, but with no real conviction.

Then Ruth came out with it.

"I don't expect you to confirm or deny it, but my guess is that you are working undercover.

You must be a deep plant because there is no record of you on the police database. Your name exists but only with skeleton information, rather like someone who has never been in trouble with the police or broken any rules.

"I guess there is a Sarah O'Connor somewhere but it's not you. Or if it is it's a state-sanctioned new identity.

"You will be asking yourself, can you trust me, and probably you have been trained to trust no one except your handler, and even then by disposition you trust no one.

"I want to help you. I don't think the killers were big time hitters do you? Although I suppose if you wanted to hide that you had official sanction for the hit you might use what could pass for young thugs on a moped.

"I think there was a clean-up as no ambulance or police were or are on record."

Ruth carried on with her surmising as it was obvious Sarah was hanging onto every word. There was no interruption, no challenge, no contradiction. Just those green staring eyes.

"The thing is the people you have infiltrated cannot be trusted, the police cannot be trusted and whichever is your handler and who he or she works for, may not be trusted or entirely in the know. Perhaps it has been decided to simply take you out."

Sarah said nothing. Then she said, "Look it's not about drugs not really. It's about people."

After their talks she felt her eyes closing. Sarah had fallen asleep again, reassured by the presence of Ruth. Sarah slept on. Ruth could not help herself. What would it be like in bed with Sarah? She was undoubtedly beautiful. In her half sleep, she imagined herself beside her, perhaps just holding her. This would never do. Still there were worse thoughts to drift off into sleep with. No one need ever know.

FIFTY-EIGHT

Ruth woke to find Sarah already up, showered and dressed. She smiled at Ruth and said, "Do use the facilities, they're free now. I've ordered breakfast, for one," in the same matter of fact tones Ruth now realised were typical of this woman.

"Please read this only after I have left." She handed Ruth an envelope. It was the hotel stationary. Ruth was taken aback but appreciated the act of simple formality. She couldn't wait to rip the envelope open. She seemed in a hurry to go, so Ruth took her at her word. She wished she had been as prepared as Sarah. She would have to manage in yesterday's clothes.

Ruth admired this brave young woman as she was sure she intended to simply carry on as if nothing had happened. She knew not to trust anyone but what choice did she have but to report to her handler, assuming Ruth was right.

Who was running her? Ruth was pretty sure given what Sarah had told her that this was a young woman who had been identified long ago as a potential agent for internal security. But what exactly was the mission? Sarah had been less than discreet which must mean she did trust Ruth to some degree. What did she mean when she said 'it's not drugs. It's about people?'

She read the contents of the note in the envelope. It was short but informative, leaving nevertheless more questions unanswered.

Dear Ruth,
I trust you.
Thank you.

I have placed a small gift in your makeup bag.
I hope it helps.
I know you will have the common sense to destroy this note.
S.
P.S. The initials are my mother's.

She felt much better after her shower and called Robbie. In her hand was a SIM card she had found inside her makeup bag wrapped in a small lace hand-embroidered vintage handkerchief of indeterminate age, but Ruth thought really quite old.

The initials on the handkerchief were A C. Perhaps she had allowed sentimentality to dictate the choice of Christian name retained even as her identity was hidden.

Ruth's first task was to send Robbie out, discreetly, to buy a couple of new phones. She was not really up on contemporary surveillance and what could or could not be tracked. But she was taking no chances.

Ruth read the contents of the note to herself. 'My mother showed me my birth certificate. No father. She told me, and I recall her accent changing imperceptibly to a broader Northern Irish, that this was not the whole story. She then handed me a copy of my certificate in which she had written in her own hand under father, 'Henry Case'; and his profession 'Army Officer'. I kept wanting to track him down. What daughter wouldn't? I decided then and there I wanted to do something with my life though I wasn't at all sure what. I tried to track him down. Then this much older but very nice man contacted me. He said his name was Tim, and he told me he knew my father. I trusted him. My mother's name was Aoife by the way.'

FIFTY-NINE

"Harry these shipments are coming in from everywhere. It is hard to distinguish legitimate ones from illegitimate."

Harry said, "We need to identify who is making money from the drugs."

"I don't think it is just drugs Harry. I think this is a serious criminal network. The money men are just looking for returns."

"Drugs then but not limited to drugs. Maybe not even mainly drugs."

"But look here," said Pyro and showed Harry an entry for 'live cargo'.

"And again, 'live cargo'. Every few days."

"What exactly do they mean by 'live cargo'?"

"I don't see any animals or veterinary-type certificates, or involvement of the DEFRA. Nothing that would indicate animal transport."

"So, it must be people."

"Illegal immigrants."

"It's the scale of it all that is hard to identify. There are shipping containers coming in from all over the world."

"How else could you get people in. By truck and container. By smaller van."

"Who is funding this and how do they get paid?"

"That's it: follow the money."

"This woman seems important."

"Do we know her name?"

"Sarah O'Connor."

"Pyro can we check her out? She surely knows where the money comes from and where it goes. Can we concentrate on her.

"I'm already on it," said Pyro. "The thing is she seems legit, but I think not."

"What do you mean?"

"All too neat and tidy."

"I have her CV here from HR records for the company. It gives her secondary school as St Benedict's Grammar School, Belfast."

"But there is a Sarah O'Connor on the school records."

"How do you know that?"

"That bit was easy.

"The thing is looking through the photographs on the school website, there is a year group, and names of the sixth form. There is a Sarah O'Connor, but she is nothing like this woman. Photo of her as captain of the hockey team. Allowing even for the ravages of time it's not the same person.

It is so hard to be sure from photographs on the net, but though she went to this school I think her name has changed to Sarah O'Connor."

"So what happened to the original O'Connor?"

"A local newspaper carried this story, two young women in a car crash and one died."

"Does it give the name of the other passenger?"

"Yes. She has her university as Queens, Belfast. They do have a Sarah O'Connor. She studied modern languages. Gap year in Russia."

"Someone has worked hard to give her this identity, but not hard enough, unless she had some other reason for changing her name."

"I think we need to talk to 'Sarah O'Connor'."

Harry had a strange sense of déjà vu on staring at the photograph of the woman, and the photos on the web. She looked Irish for sure, though her hair was now black.

The deep red hair on the university photograph was a surprise, and reinforced his sense of having seen this woman somewhere before.

"OK," said Harry.

"What about this bloke, and he pointed to the photograph Pyro had blown up, of a tough-looking, very clean shaven bald, Slavic type. "Russian?" asked Harry.

"That's right Harry. Goes under the name 'Igor Ivanovitch'."

"What do we know about him?"

"That's the thing Harry. Nothing."

"Nothing?"

"Nothing at all. There is no trace of him. I have used all possible sources."

Harry did not enquire and never had what these sources might be.

"Seems very chummy with O'Connor."

"Let's see where he goes when not in the office."

"He doesn't use his mobile much, or a computer."

"So what?"

"It's harder to find out what his role is, what he is up to, to get useful intel."

"I think we should have a chat with Igor."

"Where's Fergie?"

"You know him. If not active best to sleep. "Shall I wake him?"

"Yes but take care."

"What do you mean?"

"If woken suddenly he thinks he is in danger and reacts accordingly.

"Do we have eyes on Igor, do we know how he gets about?"

"Actually, he uses an Uber. But here is the interesting bit: it's always the same Uber with one of two drivers, one of whom seems to be the usual, or more often."

"So, he has a preferred driver."

"No, I think it's more than that. It's probably to allow him to move about relatively unnoticed, especially by the police."

SIXTY

"Fergie. Fergie wake up."

The big man seemed fast asleep but then he suddenly reared up out of bed and placed Pyro in a headlock.

"No Fergie, it's me," Pyro struggled to communicate. "It's me Pyro," squeaked his voice from what was a very tight hold Fergie had on him constricting his windpipe.

Just as suddenly as he had put Pyro in difficulty, he released him.

Fergie could not have been more apologetic. "I'm sorry wee man. I wasna sure who ye were there for a moment."

"No harm done," Pyro said, rubbing his neck. "This is the target Fergie."

They briefed him which was literally 'brief' as they had little or nothing on him.

"Russian we think. He looks quite physically competent."

Fergie was unimpressed.

"Hey Harry, didna ye recall that Russian?"

"I don't think we have time for reminiscences right now, Fergie."

"Sure we do," said Fergie, and pressed he on, and Harry knew there was no stopping him.

"In the unmarked car in Germany. They spied on us, you remember Harry.

"So, we decided to spy on them. I loved the look on his face, when we tapped on his window waving a bottle of vodka.

"I can still remember that song he taught us, no I canna." Fergie's great brow was furrowed with the effort of recalling this important musical memory. "Oh yes I can," and Fergie broke into a sort of remembered Russian of the folksong of his memory, probably not quite a carbon copy of the original.

Harry was not stupid enough to seek to curtail Fergie's vocal efforts. He knew it had to run its course.

Eventually Fergie stopped. "Aye they were good times," he murmured. "Good times."

"And we are going to have good times again Fergie, and we might try and see if this Russian is similarly amenable, I suppose."

"Reet," said Fergie, "and if not, not." Fergie was still smiling, but it had ceased to be a friendly smile of shared memory and camaraderie.

"Fergie, your logic is as ever unimpeachable," remarked Harry.

"We also don't know if the driver is some kind of protection and a threat or merely a driver. We must assume he will be more than benign and armed and at least useful, maybe professional."

Pyro pointed out, "If you think about it neither of our vehicles are very understated for an urban environment, neither the Landy nor the BMW M. The latter is better as there are plenty of flash fuckers in Liverpool with similar cars." He grinned at Snip.

"So, pick up in BMW and transfer to Landy, and into lockup. That's basically the plan."

"What about the driver?"

"Not very interested in him, so just temporarily take him out of the game. And render his vehicle useless. Sand in the fuel tank job I think."

So, a plan emerged. Pyro to stay and monitor surveillance and to be the comms centre. Snip was to drive Fergie and apprehend the target. Harry to follow up with the Landy. Fergie would also deal with the driver and his vehicle, and Snip would collect him. Harry would take Igor to the lockup and begin his interrogation.

"Who was it who said, 'No plan survives first contact with the enemy'?" asked Snip.

"Napoleon," replied Pyro, "or was it Alexander the Great, or Rommel?"

"Where would be the fun in that?"

"What?"

"Things going according to plan."

SIXTY-ONE

Igor Ivanovitch was a big man. He liked gyms. He liked weapons. He was unhappy. He could remember when he was last happy – 1989. It was the end for him, though he was still useful to Russian secret service operatives who needed old style training in unarmed combat. Igor liked to call it, 'I'm armed and you're not' combat, because he would make sure he had a weapon and remove the target's weapon as a priority. Concealed weapons were important to him. The Russian combat knife is very similar to the commando knife, and equally as useful in the right hands.

The NPD had decided to dispense with his services. He had sustained damage, though more mental than physical, in Afghanistan. Here was an enemy that didn't care if they lived or died. Hard to combat. Igor learnt to destroy first, and only ask questions if the enemy were rendered truly harmless. This often meant no answers were possible. He was not given to patience and so his methods didn't always produce the best results. He recognised rather late in the day that if you kill a father, his sons might be inclined not to forgive.

Why in the end did the modern Russian Special Forces dispense with his services? Not so much because his methods were counterproductive. It was basically because he inflicted too much damage on those he was training. He did not know when to stop.

They told him it was age.

He was, it is true, nearing sixty-six.

A man had to earn a living.

These girls, what were they anyway?

They saw their chance as the driver dropped Igor near the fence surrounding the docks, where there was a staff entrance. The staff entrance looked unmanned, but someone arrived on cue and ushered Igor through. The driver sat in his car, as he was no doubt expected to wait.

The service road that ran the length of this side of the docks had no obvious purpose and was quiet. On the other side of the road was wasteland, perhaps zoned for some future expansion plan that never happened. There was the usual hopeful-looking commercial land agents signs which had seen themselves better days.

Harry hung back so his Landy was not obvious, in a handy bit of muddy layby, still with line of sight to the target but far enough away not to attract attention. Snip and Pyro drove right up behind the Uber. The driver got out which may or may not have been the right response, and started throwing his weight around. He was fat but clearly no pushover.

Fergie meanwhile had sauntered up the road from the Landy and was by now in earshot. The driver had an accent, eastern European maybe, or Albanian, hard to tell. He was partly unshaven, and his trousers were far too tight, which accentuated his belly flopping over in a display which a PR man might call 'tired muscle'. Not a good look.

"What is it you want?" he asked not unreasonably. He had his hand in the pocket of his jerkin, which barely fitted around his belly and fell short of the top of his trousers.

Snip turned to Pyro and said, "He needs a new wardrobe. He is not dressed for the occasion."

"What you say?"

"I said you are not dressed for the occasion."

"What? You fuck off."

"You are a very poor dresser."

"Look fuck off right," said the driver who was used to throwing his weight around.

"Now that's not very polite."

His patience was of course being tested, and he produced his weapon. A very poor decision.

Fergie who by now was right behind him, tapped him on the shoulder and then his fist which barely moved passed through the face of its target and beyond into thin air. Where the man's head had been, though still attached to its body, was now simply unoccupied. The body crumpling almost in slow motion was the immediate effect. Pyro stepped forward and said almost as a rhetorical question, "I'll take that," and neatly removed the small arm in one deft move that saw it briefly in his hand, made safe and then into his capacious coat pocket.

Snip checked him over. "Still breathing. Into his boot then."

"Yep."

How to disable the car. Pyro began pouring a 2lb bag of Tate and Lyle into the fuel tank. Works just as well as sand if not better.

"How far will it run?"

"Maybe ten miles."

"Right a convoy then. Back and park up next to the Landy."

"Yep, that should encourage Igor to come looking. He can see it from the entrance there, I reckon."

Igor emerged with his mobile in hand. The phone rang in the boot of the Uber.

"Ah perhaps we should have…"

"I think no answer is fine."

Igor looked up the street. Fergie took charge.

"Look it's no fun if ye all pile in. I want to teach this laddie a lesson."

No one argued. Harry looked a bit unsure, but the time for talking was already past.

Igor was striding towards the Uber.

Fergie presented himself at the rear of the taxi.

There was a small clearing not obvious from the road, which Fergie made a great show of heading for.

Quite how he knew Igor would not simply try and shoot him was simply a matter of knowing something about the Russian mentality. And Fergie knew more than he let on.

"You and me then, laddie."

"Odin na odin."

Harry translated for the audience: 'one on one' in Russian.

Effectively it was Fergie in the blue corner fighting for Scotland and Igor in the red corner for Russia.

Igor did not believe in missing a ceremonial opening and so he offered a handshake to Fergie. This rather took the Scot by surprise, who willingly grasped the proffered hand. A strange standoff took place as each man was determined not to be the first to loosen his grip. Each began to exert more force. And it was perhaps worrying to the supporters of the blue corner, that Fergie was not obviously emerging victorious in this early skirmish. What the careful observer might have noticed though was that Fergie was gradually drawing his man towards him, then the quick release, and Fergie moved to embrace his adversary. He had his great arms around him now and was obviously doing the simple thing and began squeezing the life out of the Russian.

There was an irony in placing Igor in what was after all a bear hug.

Igor looked beaten, or certainly gave that impression as he went limp, which must have distracted Fergie, or perhaps he thought it was already over. A slight relaxation of his grip and the Russian slipped sideways and in a move that would not have disgraced the Bolshoi, down and under and swept Fergie's legs from under him. The larger they are the harder the fall.

The Russian was gasping for air, and instead of going on for the kill, backed off bent over trying to get air in his lungs, with desperate rasping heavy sounds drawing in life-giving oxygen.

Of course, all that Igor had done, in effect, was enrage Fergie, who did not like being humiliated and was not used to being put on his back. Then the strange ballet that is all rules boxing. The Romany know it well. As does a certain kind of Russian, and so do those brought up in Glasgow back streets. It's a matter of taking time to seek an opening. Fergie did not have it all his own way, and only just moved enough to distort the impact of a straight punch to the face into more of a glancing blow. The next he parried with his great paws. Igor was not as strong as Fergie but he was still mighty strong, and quick. A flurry of punches to the body left the big Scot somewhat breathless so he went in close and did what all angry Glaswegians do in these situations. He launched a sandwich with his forehead and only Igor's speed saved him from what would undoubtedly have been the end for him. As it was he managed to move his head rapidly to one side taking some of the force out of the blow. He staggered back.

It would have been a draw but for two things. Igor produced a short stiletto style knife, which Harry spotted. Harry was not about to let Fergie suffer any further harm.

Harry had taken the precaution of revving up the Landy and burst through into the clearing. Igor was strong, but a Mark 1 Landy driven by a determined man, and Harry was very determined, was not going to be stopped by any Russian unless in a tank. Igor was not in a tank and was simply taken out by the British military vehicle.

The perhaps amazing thing is this collision did not kill him but rendered him unconscious and his leg fetched up at a very unhealthy-looking angle.

"Why did you do that, laddie? I had him. It was under control."

And looking at his adversary on the ground, he added, "And I was enjoying myself."

"Load him up" said Harry, "and let's get out of here."

SIXTY-TWO

Back at the lockup, Igor was lying in the recovery position, and had not recovered consciousness.

"Right his phone then."

"I can't get into his phone. It has some kind of super tech defence. Russian probably. It changes number at random I think. We need access to wherever the code is sent, and it's not obvious where that is."

"OK so we have to question him."

"Not much chance of that and I don't think he will tell you anything anyway."

Fergie expressed his view,

Finally, someone worth fighting. Why did you do it Harry, why? He was a worthy opponent."

"Oh, shut up Fergie," said Harry finally losing his patience with this silly honour-amongst-adversaries nonsense. "He was going to kill you with this," and produced the stiletto knife. Fergie was silent for a moment and then said,

"I would still have had him, laddie."

"Sure Fergie of course you would."

SIXTY-THREE

"How much longer are you going to let this go on? They are getting closer."

"Oh come on, you have nothing to fear from Dad's army. We have your back. Stop worrying."

"They are doing quite well for old men so far aren't they. And what about all the collateral damage. Is this not a worry?"

"No one who matters and some who we might have wanted to eradicate ourselves. Saved us the trouble and it cannot be traced back to us, so no I'm not worried."

"It draws attention to it."

"That is regrettable. However, we are confident that it will quieten down.

"And it's useful. We want access to the supply chain which is governed by the dark web, but there must be some phone activity. And we just haven't been able to tie it down."

"What about your asset, surely she can be the key? The Irish woman."

"She is working hard, but the Russian is no fool."

"Why not use a honeypot. Maybe use your asset in this way?"

"Wouldn't do any good. That is never going to work with Ivanovitch. One piece of relatively good news, we don't think he is state sponsored. He has fallen out with his masters. Of course, that could be part of the deception. He is not acting alone but the network is not clear. We must let this run as it may reveal what we need."

"And what is it we need?"

"Enough information to remove the threats."

SIXTY-FOUR

"Sir, I believe these events are all connected."

"I beg your pardon. Where is your evidence? It is frankly not your remit to go chasing all over the country on the tail of one man."

Ruth sat saying nothing. She could not show any direct evidence linking any of the incidents to the man she was hunting. She really could not suggest it was instinct. She knew she could trust her gut feeling, even if she had to put up with scoffing from her so-called superiors concerning her female intuition. Be this as it may, she heard an inner voice whisper, *Why is he so keen to shut down the investigation?*

He then said, "I asked you to leave it to serious crime. I do not want to shut down your investigation. But there are serious questions of usefulness and resources. To be fair to you I see it's only really Sergeant Robbie who you have wasted on this."

"Wasted, sir?"

"Wasted."

"I am transferring the case to the organised crimes squad. I am sure we can find you other cases to work on.

"However, my advice is to take some leave. This obsession with this Harry Case is not consistent with good policing and is not good for your mental welfare."

"Well thanks for your encouragement as ever," she said under her breath.

"What was that?"

"Thanks for your helpful advice and encouragement," she said out loud.

"Close the door behind you when you leave won't you Superintendent."

Ruth was tempted to slam it, but left it just a little ajar, just enough to irritate, and to leave it questionable whether she had done this as a protest.

She texted Robbie and invited him to meet her in the favoured greasy spoon they both liked, not least because it was not greasy at all but was run by a very amusing Greek Cypriot refugee. He had arrived over forty years ago, and served up all kinds of breakfast food, healthy and perhaps not so healthy but delicious. After all what could be better than, say, a fried slice, bacon, and tomatoes, especially after an interview with the DCC. She wanted to remove the bad taste in her mouth.

And here was Robbie, looking worried, and ready as ever to talk. Ruth briefed him on her instructions.

"Will you be going on leave?" Robbie asked this with the look of a spaniel who was being denied his favourite walk that day. She told herself off silently. Why must she think this kind of thing of him?

"In a manner of speaking," she said. "Of course, I may still need a bit of help now and then."

"I'll be standing by," said Robbie loyally. She couldn't help herself but see in her imagination his tail wagging a bit now.

Now that really won't do, thought Ruth, again giving herself a silent telling off. *He is intelligent and helpful. Tell him you appreciate him,* she heard the voice of her conscience quite loudly express itself.

"Thank you, Robbie," she said, and she meant it. 'That wasn't so hard was it' she told herself.

SIXTY-FIVE

Fergie had been left to mind the Russian. He cleared his airways and made him more comfortable. He gave him some water. A grateful look passed over the injured man's face. There was no substantial blood loss. There was a gash on his head, more of a graze where the Land Rover had knocked him to the ground and he had sought to break his own fall with his free arm. No bones were broken. Truly amazing, a worthy opponent indeed. Ivanovitch turned out to have fluency of a kind in English, and his brand of linguistics was not far from Fergie's own. The two men immediately got on. Of course, Ivanovitch was no fool. He was trying to win his man over.

The Russian indicated that he felt vodka might be very helpful.

"Vodka will make all easy. Enough vodka no pain," said Ivanovitch.

Fergie looked doubtful but thought, *Away man why not?*

He sent Snip out to fetch a couple of bottles.

"Harry, he has been in Kandahar, and many of the other places we know well."

"Doesn't mean we can trust him Fergie. Far from it."

"I ken that I do. But in a way he's one of us."

"What do you mean?" Harry asked, but he knew full well.

Harry had not shared with Fergie the full complexity of his own relationship with the Afghans.

Fergie volunteered a thought, which Harry did not instantly

dismiss.

"Do ye think we migh' harness the Russian?"

"We might be able to use him you mean?"

"Can ye put a tracker in his phone Pyro?"

"For sure."

"He is in a bit of a mess."

"He'll recover."

"He is a worthy opponent." Fergie said this under his breath, but they all heard.

"I think we need to get him some help."

"What about Doc Martin?" Snip said. "You know the commando guy, did all the Antarctic missions. He lives nearby."

"How do you know that?"

"Works on the Ocean Youth Trust boat, it's docked in Liverpool right now. Before all this more important stuff, I was going to meet up with him, have a bit of a sail you know."

"Worth a try."

"OK, Fergie we'll get him some help if we can."

Fergie looked like a man who always knew this would be the outcome.

Fergie had made this more likely by getting Snip and Pyro on side, in the absence of Harry. Quite why Fergie wanted to do this was never fully established, but it was undoubtedly the case that both men had faced the same enemy and the same trials of strength and resilience. They were built from the same DNA at least metaphorically speaking.

SIXTY-SIX

Ivanovitch was now up and about. He was drinking copious amounts of water. Fergie handed him a spare pair of plain combats, and a T-shirt.

"And a fleece."

"Fergie, you spoiling me."

"Reet laddie, off you go now to the latrines."

"Latrines?"

"For a wash and brush up."

Igor got the message.

While he was engaged in his toilet, Fergie asked Harry, who had become a brooding presence, to leave Ivanovitch to him. Against his better a judgement, a very tired Harry simply nodded and left for the main gaff to get some sleep.

When Igor emerged he looked almost human again, bruised but clean.

There were now two chairs sat opposite each other across the small table. Fergie asked him what his full name was.

"Igor Stavros Ivanovitch Stavoski."

"I like it," said Fergie. "Especially the son of a bitch."

"Not son of a bitch. Ivanovitch. My father, he was Ivan—"

"The Terrible?" asked Fergie.

"Why you ask that? He wonderful not terrible."

"What is that... is it Russian?"

"It's not Russian. It Polish," said Igor.

"Whoa," said Fergie. "Are you Russian or what?"

"Born under Soviets, moved to Moscow. My father was in Red army.

"My mother Russian from Moscow. Met father soldier as she work in military office.

"What you call it, diplomatist.

"And you Ferg, what is it, your whole name?"

Fergie looked a bit uncertain, almost as if he had not heard the question, and then admitted to 'Fergus Oscar Ferguson'.

"Oscar? That makes you F' Off Fergie."

"No one has ever tried that on with me, laddie. Not twice at any rate."

He smiled revealing another side to his character.

"My mother was Irish and loved the Irish writers, especially Oscar Wilde."

"Da da, he homo niet?"

"Who cares about that?"

Igor looked at him quizzically, and then turning his head to one side decided to drop it.

"I remember one story, in Russian, it called Little Prince. My mother read it to me."

"Mine too."

There was a pause as each man tried to sum the other up.

"I'll make you an offer," said Fergie. "You tell me the whole show, tie up a few loose ends and I'll let ye go."

"You won't though, will you Ferg?"

"For me to know, laddie."

Fergie offered him a fill up for his coffee. No more Vodka.

SIXTY-SEVEN

The doctor had arrived. He was not fazed at all by finding an injured Russian in a lockup. He was clearly a man who was used to the kind of operations Snip and his comrades had found routine. His real name was not of course Doc Martin, though the soubriquet owed nothing to the TV programme set in Cornwall, and everything to a sort of boot that the good doctor preferred to normal footwear. These were known as 'Doc Martins' to a certain generation. It implied a certain background as well, not usually well-heeled. There was an implication of the wrong side of the tracks.

"Doc."

"So this is Stavoski? Igor is it?"

Igor nodded.

"I think it would help if he were not trussed up like a turkey at Christmas."

"No funny business right?"

Doc Martin was an imposing figure. Admittedly, like the rest of them, not in the first blush of youth. But the beard was very imposing and still black and very bushy. He looked like the kind of man who might have been mistaken for say Doctor Livingstone in another epoch or Brian Blessed, in this.

Once Igor was seated he began to check him over. Blood pressure was good. "A bit high maybe but how old are you?"

"I'm sixty-six," said Igor proudly. He had every right to be, because although in some ways he looked much older, like a man who had battled the elements all his life, a sailor say or polar explorer which to some extent had been Igor's history, he did not carry fat and still had very good muscle mass, as Fergie had already discovered.

"Your eyes tell me drink may be a problem."

Igor looked a bit shamefaced. "I soory I drank it all."

"What?" said Doc Martin.

"I sorry I drank, it all gone."

He glanced over at Fergie and shook his head. He was not going to let on to the doctor that they had drunk the bottle together.

Doc Martin smiled.

"I meant you will find that the amount you drink may have done you some harm. Hard to tell without more tests."

"I am not big drinker," claimed Igor.

"Right," said Doc Martin.

He stood him up and gently moved his limbs this way and that. The man didn't even wince though there must have been serious pain. "No permanent damage there, bones not broken, ligaments intact.

"I see there is soft tissue damage. Some swelling and splendid, even magnificent bruising, which is a good sign. Your body is already trying to repair itself.

"I would prescribe rest, and ibuprofen.

"Your heart is strong and regular."

"Doctor?"

"Yep."

"Your boots."

"What?"

"I like very much. Where you buy?"

"Well-known brand."

"What one?"

"Clarks. Anyway, you will survive I think," and he got up to leave.

"I will survive. That good!"

SIXTY-EIGHT

"Harry will be back soon."

"Where has he gone?"

"He wants to see who else meets up with Sarah O'Connor. Actually, I think he has started minding her."

"How do you mean?"

"Well, he wants to know where she is at all times and keeps asking if we are making sure there are no threats, no repeat of the men with guns."

SIXTY-NINE

"She is your asset."

Sir Neil Barrinton Crawley adjusted his OE tie. His shirt cut into his neck, not because it was too small but rather that the minister's neck was so large and indistinct, looking like a bad case of goiter but in fact being just eating to excess.

"Why is she meeting up with that policewoman... what's her name again?"

"McIntyre, Ruth McIntyre."

"Yes, well she is proving to be a bloody nuisance.

"Takes no notice even when her very senior commander orders her to stop, the DCC."

"She's supposed to be on leave dammit."

"I really can't go into details, sir, but we have it under control."

The minister looked doubtful.

"I bloody well hope so."

Tim left the meeting less than happy. He was not at all sure he did have it under control. Where the hell was Stavoski for instance?

Ruth on the other hand was more than happy to receive a text from Sarah. She suggested a rendezvous but this involved quite a convoluted route, and seemed to propose meeting in a hospice, or the grounds at any rate. Ruth thought this might just mean a quiet place where they could meet unobserved.

Sarah had made some enquiries. Her handler gave her very little. She knew he had been in the British Army. Why nothing on his record for so very long? Where had he disappeared? Was he dead?

The gardens were indeed beautiful, and Ruth decided to take a walk through the grounds, conducting a kind of recce. There was only one joint exit and entrance for vehicles and pedestrians. It had a gatehouse, but this was unmanned. Not the most secure place but Ruth decided that such concerns were born of the street incident and general caution. She hoped, not the reality.

She walked down the access road along the path beside it which took her through trees, and she was struck by how quiet it was, and the emerging birdsong in the spring light which filtered through the newly greened trees, their leaves budding and shooting with new life. A squirrel darted across her path. Two magpies cawed raucously above her.

A paradox perhaps to find so much new life in this place which existed to manage the end of life. And there sitting on a bench with her back to Ruth was Sarah O'Connor.

Ruth approached her quietly and was rather impressed when without turning round Sarah simply voiced a mild greeting.

"Why don't we sit here together and have a chat? It's quite a view don't you think.

The bench looked out over a viaduct, an old railway bridge of the heavy impressive Victorian time, when Britain ruled, and all was well in the world.

A small two carriage train was crossing the bridge in the mid distance, and then disappeared into the trees in the far distance. The impression was of stasis reinforced by being seated on the bench, but the possibility of movement indicated by the passage of the small train.

"I want you to help me."

"If I can," said Ruth.

"My mother is dying you see."

Ruth said nothing but tried to look encouraging and sympathetic.

"In there," and Sarah indicated with a nod of her head in the direction of the hospice building.

"Cancer?"

"Bowel cancer." There was quite a long pause. Then Sarah answered the unasked question.

"Inoperable. Moved everywhere, unstoppable. They gave her four weeks at first, and she managed over a year. Announced on Valentine's Day and here we are nearly Easter.

"She has one wish, well two actually.

"One was to see me which was easy, though I wish I had been a better daughter."

Here she faltered.

"And the other?"

"To see the man she fell in love with all those years ago."

"And who was that?"

"He was called Henry Case.

"He was a soldier, an officer in the British Army.

"My father. Actually I knew this already, at least his name and that he had been in the army. She doesn't remember much about that time. But she does remember him. In fact, all she could say was, 'Harry is my darling. Not British, Welsh'."

"What?"

"Ysbyty Ifan."

"Where he was from? Maybe."

"It's not just the cancer you see. The end is coming, and there it is.

"She had dementia too you see.

"She always talked of him but never a name or any detail apart from this Ysbyty Ifan.

"I knew he was army. She never hid it. I hated the Troubles and the nonsense. I was drawn in by people who approached me."

"People?"

"You know, government men. They offered me a chance to do something."

Here she found no words.

"The thing is I've had it with them.

"I want out."

Ruth tried not to look worried. How was she supposed to help? After all she could not make this woman promises she couldn't keep.

"Did you tell anyone you wanted out?"

"Not yet. Apart from you." And here she looked at Ruth and she realised this woman had decided to simply place herself in her care.

She was not at all sure this was a good decision. After all what resources did Ruth have? What options could she offer her? Still, she would do what she could. She gave her the key and address of her little house. "Stay there," she said, "Try and lie low. I'll come for you in a few days. A police officer will keep an eye. He is totally trustworthy."

"His name?"

"Robbie."

SEVENTY

"Robbie, can you look up the record and anything else you can find on one Harry Case aka Nutter. He is ex-military, maybe sixty-six to seventy years old. Was in NI in the late seventies and early eighties.

"Be as quiet as you can be about it Robbie."

"Ma'am, are you not on leave then?"

"Of course, I am Robbie."

"Mum's the word, ma'am."

"Not funny Robbie."

How strange she thought to be hearing this phrase, poor joke though it was, as she was not a mother, and not old enough anyway to be Robbie's mother, but he did arouse maternal instincts. She felt protective, or perhaps, and this only just dawned on her, she just liked him.

He promised to do his best to mind the young woman. Ruth did not need to tell him just how dangerous a task this might be. What an intelligent and good-hearted young man he was she surmised and felt this made up for her silliness and intolerance on first meeting him.

She put Ysbyty Ifan in her satnav. Not without misgivings. After all it was very little to go on. Where would this lead? Probably nowhere, but she had no better ideas. And that curious thing intuition was operating, as it should, as her guide. Her gut feeling was that this was the right thing to do.

SEVENTY-ONE

Pyro looked upon his handiwork, ably assisted by conditions and perhaps not inconsiderable help from the Almighty.

Instead of blowing up the building which was his first thought, Pyro had worked out that the snow in the mountain behind the chalet, which was set on its own looking down the valley, with its own access road carved into the edge of the mountainside, was unstable.

He had enjoyed their drive up there. He had loved skiing which was a by-product of an enthusiasm for life and what the army offered. Free skiing, lessons, equipment and so on. He remembered time in the mountains with Harry, and they had taken time out of the serious mountain warfare training to simply ski, downhill, langlauf, some combination work, using seal skins and telemark skis to climb to remote places and skiing back to this or that village. The apres-ski in the mountains, which meant skiing, frankly very drunk, and injury thought unlikely as they were so relaxed. Miraculously these young men were not hurt, at least not badly and no lasting injuries.

Harry coming over a remote hut roof when skiing the deep powder, that magical winter, when they were all there. Herbie, the German guide who became their friend, Piers who was employed to train the SAS in mountain warfare, at over 10,000 ft. The Drei Laender langlauf. How far was it, a testing training run for the Zermatt to Verbier mountain trek.

"Kontrollieren," shouted Herbie as he looked back up the

mountain to see Harry coming through the deep powder and up onto the rooftop, his view of it totally obscured by the snow, which lay in massive folds over the building so that from the rear, the drop over the front was hidden. Over came Harry, then in the air like a massive ungainly flightless bird. Who knew he could fly?

Of course, he crash-landed but into deep powder which cushioned his fall. His skis came off and rose up in the air and came to rest a few yards from their guide, who had already begun to rush, as fast as you can on skis, up the mountain, to where Harry had disappeared into a hole of his own making. Tremendous anxiety turned to relief, as the top of his head emerged, and then more of him shaking off the snow, and asking, "Where am I?"

So much more fun than Norway, though that had its moments too. Harry ought not to have put the rat in the second in command's sleeping bag. Pyro began laughing out loud as he remembered the fat POM's reaction. He shrieked and ran out of the tent naked into the snow. Of course, no one was willing to tell him who had done it, but he knew it was Harry. Of course, it was Harry.

As Pyro set the charges. He asked himself, *What's the likely effect?*

Who knows for sure, he told himself. He was only joking as he knew as far as anyone could what the effect would be.

He had not wasted his opportunities when in the mountains to go up with the guides and work with them, as they showed him a little-known aspect of their work involving controlled avalanches. They showed how they set the charges to achieve the most efficient results, and under what conditions. Pyro noticed they enjoyed this aspect of their work, and they saw his interest was professional and not merely amateur. It was not long before he had a few suggestions of his own, which worked well. He earned their respect.

He moved to a safe position where there was a nice view. He had already checked that the chalet was empty.

Boom, and echo, boom and echo again. The charges set off a chain of echoes.

At first the recent snow seemed to stubbornly resist, but then a thin disturbance on the higher reaches just above the charges, became evident, a suspicion at first but then much more obvious as it turned into a large crack, and the snow slide began, small at first and then gathering force exponentially as the mass of snow hitherto held up by tenuous balance, gave way. It was a quite a rumble. Pyro was grinning now and hoped there was not overkill. He did not want collateral damage.

He didn't wait to see.

Right job done.

SEVENTY-TWO

Pyro had shown great skill in setting the charges so that the fall took out just the one building and then fell over the ridge below the chalet, harmlessly taking the remains of the building with the fall.

A little later, Pyro texted to the boys' WhatsApp group a 'before and after' photograph. It was entitled 'Avalanche'. He was tempted to write Timber, for old times' sake.

He was irritated that he couldn't build up his air miles. Each trip meant a new identity. He booked onto the Swiss Air flight to Antigua as Stephen Smith. While waiting for the flight he amused himself tracking his mates. He assumed they did not know he was doing this. He particularly kept an eye on Harry's movements. His justification for this quite intrusive approach was that he could alert the others if needed. He could even tap into CCTV where available and capture real-time events on camera.

He thought about Harry. So many adventures. Climbing with Harry. Skiing with Harry. Sailing with Harry. Classic race week in Antigua, how many years ago, at least twenty. In this very place. Beautiful old yacht.

He sat on the veranda of the bar. The Nelson Museum had provided some interest as he waited for the right moment. It was quiet, there being many more touristy bars nearer the harbour entrance. The snag was that the yacht seemed to have staff. It was moored in a quiet part of English Harbour.

Pyro felt OK, actually more than OK. He had a rum punch in his hand sitting in the comfy club chair, contemplating one of the finest maritime views in the world. He silently toasted his friends. He thought that Fergie would enjoy this spot very much, and particularly admire a stake out with a good drink in hand. He lifted his drink to absent friends.

He ordered another one and cursed his timing for the tender was being lowered from the yacht. Two figures, a man and a woman stepped down into it. They had two large kit bags with them. Pyro watched them carefully. He was pretty sure that the yacht was now empty.

The tender came ashore right below him and was left by the steps leading up to the museum.

How convenient.

He watched their backs as they disappeared along the path leading out of the harbour.

He left cash on the table and quietly untied the tender and set off for the yacht.

Once there he busied himself opening up the sea cocks. He slipped the yacht from its mooring. As sea water began to pour into the yacht he waited until he was able to step up into the tender, and away, without even getting his feet wet.

He made landfall near the entrance to the harbour and climbed the steep ground till he was in the old artillery battery from where he had a fine view. The yacht had now foundered in the entrance to the harbour and was gradually sinking. Eventually all that was left to view were the twin masts, the tips of which stood up above the waves.

As the sun began to set Pyro was rewarded by a spectacular sunset. He sent a photo to the WhatsApp group which showed the little that could still be seen of the yacht. It was a rather beautiful picture. He headed it, *What yacht?*

Pyro wandered back along the promontory and into the market. He bought a rather fine Caribbean shirt as a memento.

SEVENTY-THREE

"My yacht."

His wife could see that he was not taking the news well, whatever it was.

"Queen's Legend."

"What about it?"

"Her."

"Her, I mean."

"It's blocking English Harbour."

"What do you mean?"

The minister's wife had never really liked the yacht but did her best to be loyal. She never forgot her husband's drunken behaviour on board, his lack of skill. His bombastic pretentious use of nautical language. He loved the idea of being a latter-day Nelson. Poncing about on naval vessels. She had seen what the naval officers and competent sailors thought of him. It was obvious. His appalling idea of what he thought funny.

He once referred to the sea cocks as needing renaming to honour, as he put it, the feminist lobby and the 'wokeys'. He renamed them 'sea cxxts', and the cockpit became of course the cxxx pit.

She did not think this remotely funny. Who did?

"It's sunk, in the entrance to the harbour."

"Maybe it lost its ropes, its what's the word, mornings, no moorings."

The minister looked like he might be about to explode.

"All its sea cocks had been left open."

No misuse of language then. The man had obviously had a sense of humour failure.

His wife was not at all sure what this meant, but it was clearly not a good thing. Then of course in an attempt to show empathy, she supposed there was insurance.

"It won't bloody pay out, you stupid fucking twat," and he started picking things up and throwing them about. This peer of the realm, this government minister, albeit a junior minister, was now behaving like a child who had had a favourite toy denied him.

This is what happened quite often. She had ceased to care much but she did try to make the right noises.

"The insurers will think I did it on purpose."

Here she did ask the wrong question. It came into her mind and out before she could prevent it.

"Did you?"

She did not have a high opinion of him. She liked of course all the trappings and trimmings, the chauffeur-driven cars, the seemingly never-ending resources to spend as she liked. She especially liked the latest security and enjoyed flirting with him. If he had wanted more, she would not have refused him. She fantasised about this on the frequent occasions her husband was busy working, and whose excuse was always 'government business' as if that were a complete explanation for his nocturnal activities away from home. This excuse was always delivered in a pompous self-important dismissive voice. She had long ago given up caring.

They had been packing for Verbier. This was a property held in her name. She had a Swiss mother, so this eased the purchase in an area usually not permitted to foreigners. Her father had been the local postman. She remembered him with fondness, perhaps the only man to have loved her for herself and who was always pleased to see her. Her mother was now so grand and seemed not to miss the early death of her husband. The poor man suffered a heart attack, and though he lingered on, the Swiss health system tended not to encourage long drawn-out deaths. The decision was left to her, and she quite rapidly pulled the plug so to speak. The daughter was not even consulted.

She loved it that her daughter married the English lord, even though he was in fact the grandson of a former political operator who had been some kind of builder, and had given by various means quite a bit of money to the party and to the other party too, though by different routes. Not much principle. She turned a blind eye when he hit her daughter. A small price to pay. She felt that she had probably earned it. No point rocking the boat, especially as this ship was a luxury liner helping them to pass through life without the usual need to earn a living or trouble about money at all. She had found plenty of compensations in her marriage.

What had Eton taught him. Public service was the aim of life? He hadn't bought into that. Certainly not generosity towards others, and his pose, which certainly wasn't sincerity, was anyone's guess. No, Eton had taught him to bear any amount of cruelty and go on to win. She had tried to be a good wife and support him. She was undeniably well trained for the part and if you didn't look too closely had the right features, like a kind of poor man's Grace Kelly. Also, she had an almost Germanic willingness, at least in the early days, to actively seek his sexual satisfaction.

Her mobile rang. More bad news. What was the trope? Bad luck came in threes. The chalet was under a mass of snow, an avalanche apparently. No one hurt she was told. She had not asked. Frankly she didn't care.

SEVENTY-FOUR

The country house was picture-book Queen Anne, and to be fair not too large or obviously vulgar. It had been his father's and his grandfather's before him, who had been in cement.

It had its own drive and was not overlooked. Private planning had seen to that, owning enough land to protect views and ensure no encroachment by developers and the hoi polloi. Beyond this land was a Ministry of Defence training area which provided a further cushion to prevent undesirable development.

Sir Neil Barrinton, Crawley Bt had always voted for increases in housing but not of course anywhere near his home. He had personally made sure a new road did not go close enough to even provide a distant noise nuisance.

Igor knew this kind of feature, where the wall to the grassy grounds ended in a drop walled on the retaining side into a ditch, had a name. It gave the impression of a never-ending vista from the terrace. It provided very good cover for a man who didn't want to be seen.

It annoyed Igor that he couldn't remember the name for this bit of country house design. He liked to think he had a grasp of esoteric English and the vernacular.

Then it came to him.

Ha-ha-ha, no that's not it. Just two ha.
But why is it called that, he wondered. *It is not funny is it.*

Stavoski skirted along the wall of the ha-ha at a crouch,

which kept him hidden from the main grounds.

Suddenly he looped over the wall and in a trice rolled over and was in amongst the rhododendrons which provided perfect cover almost up to the stable block at the side of the house.

Stavoski was a little surprised how easy it had been. Where was his security? Ah there they were, one outside. Very casual. He could see another in the kitchen. His bino's picked out staff, a cook probably.

No CCTV. The minister's vanity perhaps. He wanted the house to be domestic and perfect in every way. Perhaps he prided himself on his own ability as a trained soldier. *Those days were long gone*, thought Stavoski.

How nice, a flask of coffee for the man outside.

There was only the one car pulled up on the driveway near the front entrance to the house, the Bentley. No sign of any chauffeur. Stavoski liked that model, waiting list, very expensive. Perhaps he would steal it. No, that would not work.

He was relying on his wits. He had an escape plan, the light aircraft sitting at the private airdrome at Black Bush, a short drive away, or at a push he could make it on foot.

And there was the man himself, sitting at his study desk. He was unmistakable not least because of his vast bulk, the enormous swelling belly, the great fat jowls. The picture of excess.

Stavoski decided to take a chance. He simply walked up to the Bentley, opened the door, and slammed it shut then crouched down behind it on the passenger side.

The security man, who it was clear was not alarmed and had not sensed danger, strolled over to the car perhaps expecting to see the chauffeur or even the boss. He was perhaps some kind of civilian drafted in to save money.

Stavoski simply rapped him smartly on the head and used a cord to asphyxiate him. He was not aiming to kill, and as soon as he was sure he was out of the game, he simply bundled his comatose body into the back of the capacious vehicle. Stavoski made a rapid recce of the house from the outside, taking care not to be visible from any windows. He was beginning to enjoy himself.

It was quite a house. He admired it.

He let himself in via the orangery which was open. It might as well have had a sign on the outside saying 'Hitman's entrance'.

The minister was sitting at his father's desk, the very desk where he had taken beating after beating for misdemeanours hardly worth a mention, now long forgotten. The beatings he had not forgotten. His father insisted he thank him after each beating was complete. "Thank you, sir."

He had hated school too. He had been humiliated on an almost daily basis.

"Crawley," the shout would go up.

"Crawley where are you, you worm."

The older boys, members of Pop, resplendent in their embroidered fancy waistcoats, were lounging in the senior common room.

"In Crawley."

"Crawl, Crawley."

"Kneel, Crawley."

Then he would receive a good kicking. He knew it was coming. There was nothing he could do.

"My God he's got a boner."

"Do you Crawley, do you have a boner?"

"He does."

"Kick him again."

The fact is that such memories created a stirring in Sir Neil's trousers even now.

He slipped his fat hand inside his flies.

He was interrupted as the phone rang.

He didn't like what he was hearing, not one bit. He began to shout down the phone. He was working himself up into a fury.

His shouting must have been a normal event for it attracted no attention. Stavoski was able to slip into the study unnoticed.

"What do you mean the yacht is not salvageable? Do you know who I am?" he shouted.

The minister was just trying to compute the bad news concerning the avalanche, now this. He turned round, perhaps some remedial part of his brain finally sensed danger, to find the Russian within touching distance.

"You!"

He managed to get this expletive out though his voice sounded quite strangulated, squeaky even. Certainly not very manly sounding, but then the threat must have been obvious even to him. Bravado was not going to help him now.

Stavoski was aiming to hit him hard. He ran it rapidly through his mind. A knock-out blow to silence him. Given more space he would have delivered his top move, a flying kick to the face. Indeed, he prepared to deliver the blow standing on one leg in the crane position. But before anything so balletic could take place the fat man simply keeled over.

Stavoski leaned over him, his target's eyes were wide open. *How disappointing*, he thought. It was of course a sudden massive heart attack. You couldn't blame the poor organ. Think what it had had to put up with. It is no joke pumping away through increasingly blocked arteries, the heavy lunches, the drunken excess. He had been warned about the atherosclerosis and the hypertension. He knew better than the doctors of course. He had been in the army after all. It should be noted that a couple of years in a cavalry regiment did not really qualify you as a trained killer or even imply much fitness. The drinking sessions and overeating started then and in a way set him up for both life and death. The mere sight of Igor probably gave him quite a fright. The poor organ simply gave up. But not before it had gripped him tightly and painfully, with the certainty that the end was coming inexorably. Such an easy despatch was not really justice but there it was.

The phone was still on, and a voice asking urgently,

"Hello, hello."

Stavoski leaned over and thought it only polite to speak before clicking it off.

"Dasvidaniya," he said.

Stavoski did not linger.

Once in the light aircraft over the North Sea, he put in his call.

Fergie's phone rang.

"Fat man is gone."

"Where has he gone?"

"To meet God," said Stavoski in his own brand of fluent English.

Pyro's pre-set explosives were triggered by the phone call, just as he had planned it. The small explosion brought the plane down.

The RNLI later found just the tail wing.

SEVENTY-FIVE

Lady Crawley was in London. She liked the house. Who wouldn't want to live in Kensington, though since she had brought no money or property into the marriage it was unclear how her husband was able to afford it. She simply didn't ask questions. It was all none of her business. She had not thought at first that she might make it her home.

She did not want to revert to her maiden name with all its German associations. Mrs or Ms Markel was not very distinguished-sounding to her ear at any rate.

The images sent to her, rather surprisingly, didn't upset her at all, but then she had already written him out of the picture. His predilection for sado-masochism had excited her at first, but there seemed no end to it. She had not understood till now the desire for her to dress as a schoolgirl. She was always worried that she was rather flat chested, which she thought might disappoint, but it all made much more sense now. She had been loyal and kept his secrets, but she did not know them all.

What really were her pleasures? She had written her mother out of the story. She realised she had no real friends. Shopping in Harrods? The school fees paid. She had bred a little aristocrat and he had no time for his mother. She was sad of course she had only the one child. The meeting royalty. Never quite comfortable with that but then who was? She wouldn't miss it.

In the end, she simply wanted to know what she might be able to keep from the spoils. The proceeds of crime acts, which she had vaguely read about in the newspaper, came anxiously to mind.

The phone call when it came was no surprise either. He had had a heart attack. That was all she was told. The nice young police liaison officer wanted to sit with her. Perhaps they suspected her. She was surprised the end came as natural causes. Hiring a hit man was something she had considered herself but had no idea how to go about it. She liked a good crime drama on telly and her reading matter was full of this kind of thing. But she did know the difference between a fantasy and reality. Too many of her fantasies had become realities and that was not on the whole, to her taste at all.

SEVENTY-SIX

The two men were quietly sat in their club. They were immaculately dressed. One wearing an OE tie the other an OH. If one were to criticise, it might be the slightly louche looking Gucci loafers one of them sported.

"It's a bit of a shambles," one said eventually.

"Saved us the trouble I suppose."

"Removing his security so rapidly was the right decision, you think?"

"Well, he was about to be found out wasn't he?"

"MI6 were on to him."

"He had to go."

"We will have to find someone else."

"Have we anyone in mind?"

"One or two candidates."

"They need to be able to ensure freedom of movement for our activities, or at least be able to warn us of any moves."

"Yes, yes, that's all taken as read."

"I don't like the interest being shown by the security services."

"They have to be seen to be taking an interest."

They were sitting in the anteroom to the private dining room in the exclusive gentlemen's club. It was one that had yet to allow women members. It was doubtful they ever would except perhaps, as one put it, 'over my dead body'. His wife was heard to say, "I wonder if that could be arranged."

These men had known each other all their lives, even going back to preparatory schools, and the gardens of shared heritage. Some of them met still in the House of Lords, but recent moves to limit hereditary aristocrats had reduced the convenience of that place.

They each had seats on the boards of large city firms, but none of them had come up the hard way. It had all been assumed. Their ability was never really questioned. They might have said there were only two kinds of people in the world, winners and wankers. They were living proof that this was not so, as they were in a way, winners.

They were used to not being disturbed in these meetings, and only by convention when their chairman rang the bell, now an electronic push-button affair discreetly found by the fireplace. They were joined by more of their type, two more winners. They seemed quite untroubled.

The private dining room had very imposing mahogany doors. It was said that the doors though not much else had survived the blitz. Pyro, who was dressed as a club waiter, entered without knocking. This predictably irritated the toff sitting at the end of the table.

"I told you. No interruptions."

"Well that's not up to you is it," said Pyro.

He then rolled the pineapple across the floor, till it came to rest under the table.

"What the fuck."

Pyro could just make out their last words as he rapidly closed the huge doors behind him.

"It's a Pi—"

No more words were heard, as they were interrupted by the

very loud explosion.

Pyro, who had taken a seat in the park opposite the club, sent a photo to the WhatsApp group of the fire engines and ambulances and police cars.

The windows had been blown out of the first floor dining room. The flames had been put out. The white stucco walls already blackened and charred.

SEVENTY-SEVEN

Harry called a meeting. It was a rather sad affair.

"I told you already that the party is over."

"The bloody yacht."

"Yachts sink."

"Not usually in the entrance to English Harbour."

"Come on Harry. He has been pretty discreet."

"An avalanche is not discreet."

"Happens all the time."

"It made international news."

"No one was hurt. No police investigation."

"You told us to do it."

"The problem is Pyro is a loose canon."

At that moment, the photograph of the club appeared in the WhatsApp chat. Harry sat quietly for a minute or two controlling his emotions. He decided to draw a line under it all. What else could he do?

"Any news of police action?"

"Actually, I have some good news, and some bad news.

"The bad news is, there is one policewoman involved and she will not leave it alone.

"The good news is any others were warned off by higher authority."

"MI6 maybe?"

"The explosion at the club is being treated as a terrorist incident."

"Pyro's contact there. He was asking about you Harry." Snip sounded anxious.

"For the first time?" asked Harry.

"Well no, but not for over ten years, maybe twelve or more."

"They must have given up, given you up for dead maybe?"

"They never give up."

"All for one and one for all Matey you know that."

"Not this time."

"We have done enough to honour our George."

"Not quite Harry. Not quite."

"Well, we must split up for a time anyway and lie low."

"Where will you go?"

"You know it's best for you not to know."

Snip simply listened and said nothing.

"What about your secret service chums Harry?"

"They are not my chums."

"Will they let it go?"

"I doubt it."

"Well then." Fergie leaned towards him and said, "You canna expect us to leave it there."

"It's my problem now." Harry wanted to be clear. "You must leave it to me now."

Fergie growled. "Leave it lads, just leave it."

SEVENTY-EIGHT

Harry took a train ride, to Wrexham. From there he took a taxi ride. Quite expensive. He still had quite a bit of cash but the roll of banknotes was appreciably smaller. To Pentrefoelas, an almost ignored village split by the A5, the old royal mail route, a stopping-off point on the way to Betwys-y-Coed.

The taxi driver attempted to engage him in conversation. "You lucky to get me, just dropped someone off, see. But it's no problem. I live in Pentre. Visiting are you? You can get a bus from Llanrwst you know, to Pentre I mean."

Harry merely nodded. The taxi driver tried again.

"Not really the weather for it. Visiting is it?"

Harry ignored him.

Mercifully he then resigned himself to his taciturn passenger's silence and kept quiet.

He dropped Harry by the post office. The very one that Harry used to buy an ice cream in all those years before. He walked down memory lane from Pentre to Ysbyty Ifan. The small village beloved of filmmakers for its unspoilt rural aspects, somehow timeless. The River Conwy flowed through the village, the picturesque bridge, Harry knew it so well from visits to the farm. He remembered his aunt had friends there. In his memory one ran a bed and breakfast.

He found no signage to help him. But then he was rewarded for here was Mrs Edwards, still alive and well, looking remarkably fit and well for a woman of over ninety. She recognised him. Her daughter Olwen now ran the little bed and breakfast. Harry knew her very well indeed. Harry hoped that he may find sanctuary and lay his head in this place.

The village was ancient and known to the knights of St John. Crusaders would try to reach the place notwithstanding the great distances to find the healing clean mountain water of the upper Conwy and the chance of recovery. Here the river passed by huge slabs of grey rock upon which wounded men could be laid out and the water could be used to cleanse their wounds by natural action. Thus, John's Hospital came into being, in Welsh, Ysbyty Ifan.

It was now as then a spiritual place. The medieval mind never separated the physical and the spiritual. Indeed, Harry doubted the historical orthodoxy that there had been a great schism, and reformation that had directed the contemporary mind. He thought back to his tutorials at Clare and the debates he had had then which seemed so important. He was so much more certain then of his ground, and his first class degree was due reward for intelligence, hard effort and the maintenance of an independence of mind.

In this place such historical events seemed mere ripples on the surface that is the great ocean of man's progress in the world.

Harry's wounds were not of the flesh but the mind. Nevertheless, he hoped to find, like many others before him, healing here.

If he was still being hunted he doubted he would be able to rest here for long.

He was pretty sure he was being pursued. He had an instinct for this, a kind of ancient intuition. Anyway, he did not want to bring trouble to these people who were after all his kith and kin.

He rested and the old lady had the common sense to know he needed peace and quiet. Olwen also needed no telling. She made sure he was comfortable. She showed him up to his room and encouraged him to take a bath.

"I should think a good long soak might suit you," she suggested.

Her gentle warm singsong Welsh voice was balm to his soul.

He was touched to find warm towels on the towel rail laid out ready for his use. He took advantage of the hot water and deep, old cast iron bathtub.

Harry slept well in this home from home. So many memories.

He woke to the sound of the early milkers. Another sound that he recalled from his childhood.

Olwen served him in the little parlour.

"You'll be wanting the works I expect?"

As she brought him his food and saw that he was content, she mentioned that her mother had asked if he might step through to the back for a little chat. Only when he had eaten. No rush.

After a full Welsh breakfast, he sought out the old lady who was in her kitchen, not hard to find, in a big comfy chair by the open fire. She indicated the seat for Harry to sit down on next to her. The quiet fell upon them, shrouding them both.

They each contemplated the fire in front of them, Harry recalling the old woman rather younger then, pointing out the dragons that played in the fire.

She said, "You're a sight for sore eyes. Not that I can see much these days."

She asked him no questions.

"Your mother would be very proud of you, you know. We

all are."

Harry felt he had done little or nothing to earn this but did not contradict her.

She then said something that he did not immediately understand.

"Lle I'r enaid ddodo hyd I heddwch."

"I'm sorry you'll have to give me that in the English."

"You'll be wanting a place for the soul to find peace."

He wandered out to the river and sat on one of the vast flat grey stones. He then lay back on the stone which had been warmed in the late morning sun, and contemplated the water which passed musically around him, diverted up small smooth stone pathways, and back on itself to meet with little disruptions to the surface which caught the light creating myriad miniature kaleidoscopes and melodies known only to nature. There was constancy and purity in this, yet with just enough flux to engage every man, if that person had his eyes open. Harry the crusader let his mind and body rest, minutely stimulated but almost as if there were nothing that could possibly now disturb his peace of mind.

Inevitably this mindfulness did not last. He became reflective.

Can't stop all drugs. Harry knew that if not from here then there, if not from his village in the Hindu Kush then another. It was a way of life. If not Afghanistan then another part of the world. It was no longer his problem.

Prostitution, people trafficking, even of very young people was inevitable. This he knew. George would not have expected all this nonsense to have been generated by his death. Where was it going to end?

They had tried.

He now felt tired, very tired. It was as if he had run from his life and kept running. Surely it was time to stop.

He had needed somewhere to rest, that much was obvious. He had to make a decision. In the end only two things are certain, birth and death. Even taxes are in the hands of the city money men and their accountants or the corrupt worshippers of Mamon. Who were the goodies and who the baddies, he no longer knew. What mattered? He became aware of his heart beating more and more noisily. It was almost as if this was a surprise. He could hear it. What mattered? Love? That was hard to find, and even harder to keep. Peace of mind perhaps then was the greater prize.

SEVENTY-NINE

In the rather insalubrious offices south of the river, the chief was holding his operatives to account.

"Do we have any idea who caused the explosion in the club?"

"Not really."

"We know how the explosive was delivered."

There was a pause.

"Go on."

They told him.

"A pineapple you say?"

A very unusual expression crossed his face. Almost a smile. Privately the chief thought this quite apt. Symbol of wealth, usually acquired corruptly.

"Did we have anything on the deceased?"

"One was senior in Ministry of Defence one in the Foreign Office."

"And the other two, city financiers. We have been interested in their activities for some time, never could pin anything on them. They won't be missed."

"I couldn't possibly confirm or deny that."

"Better get your operative out."

"Operative?"

"The O'Connor girl."

"She is unlikely to be a problem."

"She had better not turn into one."

"We know where she is, and she is safe enough. I think we should leave her for now, perhaps for ever. Don't want to stir up what might be quite a hornet's nest. Ruth McIntyre is not to be underestimated. It seems O'Connor has taken refuge in her house, and the local police are keeping an eye on her. Best left alone."

After they had all left, the chief walked to the window and peered into its griminess, preventing much of a view. There wasn't much of one anyway.

He spoke out loud to himself.

"Will someone rid me of Case?"

EIGHTY

Ruth found her satnav failed to take her right to the destination. No signal.

Pentrefoelas. She stopped. She went into the Voelas Arms and asked,

"Ysbyty Ifan?" She hoped she had pronounced it correctly.

"Yes it's nearby, not far," responded the girl behind the desk, and gave her directions.

The woman in reception was too young surely?

Ruth asked about Harry Case, did she know him? She racked her brains. If he was from Ysbyty Ifan then she could perhaps ask her mother, Mrs Edwards. Olwen. She explained she ran a B&B and tea house in the village. "My grandmother lives there. She knows everyone."

Ruth asked if she could connect to the Wi-Fi and make a call. "Robbie?"

"Yes, ma'am."

"Is all well? How is the babysitting going?"

"Nothing to worry about, ma'am, I saw one odd vehicle which stopped but they scarpered pretty quickly when I took an interest. I have reported the problem as needing regular patrol by a squad car."

Ruth was only partially reassured but felt there was little more she could do.

"Thank you, Robbie," she said, but he had gone.

Ruth was greeted by a woman of great age armed with two sticks. She stood on the doorway and looked Ruth up and down.

"Yei?" This was Welsh, her first language, which she used always when greeting strangers. It didn't do to be too welcoming you know, she might have said.

"English is it?"

Ruth smiled her best harmless-looking smile intending to convey 'I mean you no harm'. She explained who she had come to find. She did not say she was from the police.

"Romance is it?"

"Yes," Ruth lied.

She was pleased by the open response this received.

"You've just missed him. He was here, now let me think.

"Yes, the day before yesterday.

"Happy we were to see him too. He looked a bit tired.

"I think he has gone up to Capel Curig. His family had a shepherd's cottage up there. Not sure if he is still there though mind, or even if he went up there."

She sounded unsure.

"There is a track leads up there, but I doubt you would be able to go in that." She pointed to Ruth's car.

"How close do you think I could get?"

"Maybe half a mile or so." Mrs Edwards was not really able to measure distance in modern ways, that is by reference to miles much less kilometres.

"We used to walk there you know."

"From here?"

"Yes well different times wasn't it. Mostly on foot in those days. Nothing to do with clocks. All about the light available and the seasons."

Then she added, almost as an afterthought, "He loved it here as a boy you know."

"He often came back then?"

"Very welcome he was. Daisy's boy. Last of them. The whole family has gone, no work you see."

"Was he driving?"

"No, come to think of it he arrived by taxi. There is only one in the village."

Ruth went to talk to the taxi driver who turned out to be a small farmer, and taxi driver as a side-line, usually taking those about who, annoyingly for them, were not able to drive to the pub and back given the new drink-driving law.

"Opportunity for me you see."

"Yes, I see. Can you tell me where you dropped him?"

She got back in her car and made her way up to Capel Curig. Here the road to the shepherd's cottage became, as she had been warned more of a track, passable perhaps in a suitable vehicle or a tractor.

She parked her car and determined to set off on foot. She was glad she had packed her walking boots. A quick change into these, and she felt emboldened.

The track dipped down, and as it rose again the shepherd's hut appeared quite some way off, and well hidden from the road.

She clambered up trying to stay out of sight of the cottage, and made her way up and beyond the high ground behind the dwelling. From there she began the quite torturous scramble, arriving at last at the wall behind the hut. She was knackered truth be told and rested with her back to the wall under a weather-beaten tree. It began to rain, the tree offering little protection. Also, she had no plan.

EIGHTY-ONE

Harry put the gun down on the small kitchen table in front of him.

He fancied he could hear the sound of his mother, long dead, singing. She knew so many songs, and poems. The poems had all been learnt by heart mostly when she was still a young schoolgirl, and could still be recited even when the rest of her mind had gone. "Only the King's English, though he is descended from the Welsh kings you know Harry. Tudors were Welsh, Harry." She knew plenty of poems and songs in Welsh too. He did not contradict her.

Calon Lân. He hummed it to himself.

I ask for a happy heart, Truthful heart, pure heart.

He was no Sir Gawain, that was for sure.

He did not know his mother's mother tongue well. The real problem for Harry was that even the Welshness was a myth, as his birth mother was not from Wales at all. His adoption had been a happy accident.

He got up and wiped the condensation from the small rear window and peered out pressing his face against the glass. He remembered the children's home, all the hopeful faces.

They were always the younger children, not of course the babies, but once they could walk, they would peer out looking for the adults, a mother and father, who were coming hopefully to take them out, and maybe joy of joys away to a new life as part of a family. The children who had hope were rarely over five because by then, except for the most optimistic, they had realised they were never going to be chosen. And yet Harry at four had been chosen. A happy accident.

Had it all led to this? This small mountain where some happy days had passed. Was it all the same to him, this mountain range or that? The Hindu Kush? He had faced many dangers there and entered another world for over fifteen years. It had been a happy surprise to find himself accepted by the tribesmen. It all seemed to have happened to someone else.

If it had to end let it end here.

Ruth edged her way over the wall and peered into the small window at the back of the cottage. There was Harry seated and she saw his gun on the table in front of him.

She now did something reckless. She was never sure why she did it. She simply went to the back door and knocked gently on it. Harry answered, strangely without his gun in his hand.

"You'd better come in. I've been expecting you."

What could Ruth do but follow him in. She wiped her boots on the doormat. Harry nodded an appreciative gesture.

They sat at the table, Harry with his back to the front door, Ruth facing him.

"What now?"

"I imagine you would prefer to arrest me, and you might hope I shall come quietly?"

Then he said, "Shall we have a cup of tea first?"

Ruth, who had been holding her breath without realising it, let out a long breath.

Harry made the tea, and even found some rather nice biscuits, oddly Ruth's favourites, a kind of fruit Hobnob.

He had decided to talk if she would listen.

Ruth was willing.

He told her most of it, leaving out any reference to any comrades other than George.

The front door behind Harry opened, and a man armed with a pistol entered.

EIGHTY-TWO

The gunshot was so unexpected. Its effect shocked Ruth.

Tim was dead, cleanly shot through the back of the head, his face was a mess, as the bullet passed through his skull and out through the front taking quite a large part of his face with it.

She lay flat on the floor.

Harry was gone.

She wondered where, but was disinclined, for the moment at any rate, to find out.

The gunman might still be out there. She suspected a sniper of some ability, for the gunshot had been some way off, hardly heard at all.

She could hear the unmistakable sound of an old Land Rover being fired up and not too far off. Then she became aware of engine noise coming closer.

She decided she would try to leave via the back door, the way she had come in.

She opened the door and waited.

Then she edged out, as low as she could get to the ground. Not comfortable but she was still unsure that the threat was gone.

Why did I come alone? Why do I have to do these things without help?

Then she told herself off out loud, "Come on Ruth, just get on with it."

She was out now and made it to the wall at the back of the cottage, which she slithered over, and into the field beyond.

She climbed up the steep bank and then over the next drystone wall, which had looked at first glance as if it had partially fallen near a tree trunk but was probably by the hand of man as it allowed a shepherd or farmer through, onto high ground from where the valley opened up to view.

There, in the distance, was the old Land Rover, and though she couldn't be sure, there was a figure, surely Harry Case, moving towards it at a surprisingly fast pace. A sort of loping run. A huge figure emerged from the driver's side. From the woods on the opposite side of the valley running fast was a much smaller man, carrying a long shoulder bag. *Old soldiers never die, they simply fade away*, she thought as the Landy turned round and headed off down the valley and what remained of their destiny.

So many questions answered. So many left unanswered. A kind of summary of her own life right there.

She lay back looking up to the sky as clouds skitted across her eyeline. The soft bank she lay on, covered in moss, provided a kind of cushion. Maybe she could just lie like this for ever.